BETWEEN

BETWEEN

a novel by

Shelby Beckett

Options Unlimited Press

©2006 Shelby Beckett. Printed and bound in the United States of America. All rights reserved. No part of this book may be reproduced or transmitted in any form or by any means, electronic or mechanical, including photocopying, recording, or by an information storage and retrieval system—except by a reviewer who may quote brief passages in a review to be printed in a magazine, newspaper, or on the Web—without permission in writing from the publisher. For information, please contact Options Unlimited Press, 2304 S. Florence Place, Tulsa, OK, 74114.

If you purchased this book without a cover, be aware that it has likely been reported to the publisher as "unsold and destroyed," and neither the author nor the publisher has received any payment for this "stripped book."

This is a work of fiction. Names, characters, places and incidents are either imaginary or used fictitiously. Any resemblance to actual persons, living or dead, institution or business establishment, events or places is entirely coincidental.

ISBN 0-9767425-2-7

LCCN 2005902033

Cover design and title page art by Big Media Studios®
www.BigMediaStudios.com

Book manufactured by BookMasters, Inc.
www.bookmasters.com

Options Unlimited Press, LLC
2304 S. Florence Place
Tulsa, Oklahoma 74114

For Jared, who knows more about Between than anyone else.

ACKNOWLEDGMENTS

This book's multiple transformations have resulted from the assistance received from all those who have read it over the past seven years. Thank you from the depths of my soul!

I'm going to list your names in alphabetical order. It's a long list and I trust I haven't left out anyone. If so, please forgive my oversight. My deep appreciation and gratitude go to: Allyson Barrett, Kathy Bassett, Mary Blanchard, Star Bradbury, Charlotte Carlson, Carol Collins, Jocelyn Collins, Val Curley, Anne DaMitz, Maxine Downs, Iris Greenfield, Priscilla Greenwood, Wanda GreyEyes, Rev. Julie Keene, Marshall Koons, Mindy Kshywonis, Mimi LePage, Amber Madison, Mary Stewart Murray, Sherry Nuss, April O'Connell, Kathryn Oliver, Willibelle Parham, Charal Paterson, Marty Peters, Cherie Ritter, Melane Rose, Sandy Wythawai Songbird, Tom Sonsini, Bahira Sugarman, Susan Tiano, Frances Towle, Patrice Walker, Kevin Ward, Annie Welch, and Jacqueline Whitmore.

I also want to thank my first editor, Joe Shaw, for unsparing comments that kept me moving forward; my final editor, Marilyn Cox, for her critical eye and good ideas; author Timmothy McCann, for his advice and support; Bruce Peverley of the Oklahoma Extension Service, who provided me with information on hay harvesting; Matthew Marvin, of Tulsa New Holland, Inc., who explained the logistics of tractors and balers; Nicole Kemps of the National Weather Service, for helping me understand how Oklahoma storms behave; and Brenda McDonald, for information on horses and barns. And special thanks to my medical advisor, Dr. Ronald Holley.

Finally, my heartfelt gratitude to my husband, Pete Beckett, who is my first reader, my unfailing support, and my greatest fan; and to my daughter, Kit Holley, whose impeccable sense of what makes good reading (and what doesn't!) has saved me from numerous pitfalls in plot construction and pacing. I am grateful beyond words for your presence in my life.

BETWEEN

Prologue

A sliver of darkness darted purposefully through the sullen dusk, dodging between thorny, twisted arms of what once had been trees. Reaching the heart of this blighted landscape, it halted. Here the earth was glazed and crusted as if seared by incredible heat. Towering over the center of this devastation churned a massive, smoky column. Nightmarish apparitions whirled within it in a grotesque dance, accompanied by muted screams and moans.

A rumble like the earth splitting open issued from the center of the writhing column.

"Iblis?"

The sliver of darkness swelled, flickered briefly, then stabilized. A thin, whistling voice emerged from it. "Yes, my lord. It is Iblis."

"You have located the tool I sent you to find?"

"I have, Lord Serizzin. He is an opportunity waiting to be taken. It will be easy to make him believe that I am a part of his own mind."

"You have done well, thus far."

"Thank you, my lord."

"Continue to establish your connection with him. I do not yet know in what manner he shall serve me, but it is clear that he is essential to my success."

"Yes, my lord."

"I grow restless, Iblis. It is a sign that events are at last arranging themselves in my favor." The column of darkness twisted and whirled more rapidly, discharging tongues of sooty vapor that licked toward

❧ ❧ ❧ Between ❧ ❧ ❧

Iblis, who edged away. The voice rumbled again from the column's center. "Go, then. See to it that this tool is under your control when the time for his use arrives."

"Yes, Lord Serizzin."

Turning, Iblis fled.

Chapter 1

The child's body weighed lightly in Stacy Addison's arms. His hairless head gave him the appearance of a tiny, wizened old man, whose sunken eyes stared up at her with the weariness of one resigned to suffering.

His mother, a thin woman in her late twenties, stood nearby, watching anxiously. "The chemotherapy didn't work," she whispered into the microphone positioned at the center of the stage. "The doctors have given him a month at the most." Turning pleading eyes toward Stacy, she said, "He's only three years old! You're our last hope."

Stacy smiled briefly at the mother, then bent over the boy, the halo of her copper-penny hair glowing in the muted spotlight. The entire auditorium fell silent; not even a cough interrupted the collective sense of intense anticipation. Stacy looked into the child's face. His pale blue eyes were now gazing steadily into her dark ones.

"All right, then," she murmured. "This thing's not going to cheat you out of your future if I can help it!"

Bending over him, she opened herself to the energy pulsating insistently against her. It rushed in through the top of her head, filling her as if it would burst the boundaries of her skin, leaving her barely aware of herself and of the child in her arms. Only the power existed, flooding her, pouring through her hands and out her very pores, flowing from her into his fragile body.

Finally, she lifted her head, her upper lip dewed with perspiration. The child stirred and began to push against her, stretching his arms and legs. The audience watched as a pink flush crept across his pale cheeks, and even those seated at the back of the room could see the dark circles surrounding his eyes beginning to fade. Squirming out of Stacy's arms, he staggered toward his mother and clutched her knees.

"Ice cweam!" he demanded, tugging at her skirt.

The sound of breath being released rippled through the meeting hall; then pandemonium broke loose, as the crowd clapped, cheered, whistled, and wept. The child's tearful mother swept him into her arms and was assisted from the stage by volunteers waiting in the wings. Spreading her arms as if embracing every person in the room, Stacy pivoted toward each corner of the auditorium. Arms still raised, she smiled the smile that had already captivated crowds across four states.

The little boy had been last on this evening's schedule, but his response had been so rapid that a few minutes still remained of the time allotted to the meeting.

"One more." Stacy spoke into the microphone. "We have time for one more."

A stout woman in a blue dress stood up, her face creased with pain. Walking carefully, as if each movement hurt, she mounted the stairs leading to the stage. Stacy met her at the top of the steps, helped her to a chair near the microphone, and placed her hands on the woman's head.

She always savored the moment when a completed healing clicked into place. It seemed an actual physical sensation, as if something inside her brain rotated and locked itself into position. That impression had been so intense with the little boy, that she had actually taken a step backward. This time, to her surprise and dismay, the feeling didn't come.

Finally, she removed her hands and stepped to one side. The woman slowly stood up, tears streaming down her face, and squeezed Stacy's hands. Stacy tried to pull away. She wanted to explain that she wasn't sure, that this time the healing might not have completed itself, but the woman had already turned back toward the crowded auditorium.

Raising one of Stacy's arms into the air, as if announcing her the winner by a knockout, she sobbed, "It's gone; my migraine's gone. I could hardly see for the pain, and now it's gone!"

Applause again rolled across the hall like thunder. Turning back, the woman enveloped Stacy in a hug that lifted her off the floor of the stage. "You're an angel, Stacy Addison; you're an angel!"

Still disturbed by the absence of the indicator upon which she had come to depend, Stacy smiled automatically at the woman and turned her over to the backstage volunteers. Continuing to smile, she faced the crowd, once again raising her arms in her signature embrace.

This time, however, both smile and lifted arms felt mechanical. As she pivoted from side to side, smiling, most of her attention was focused on the fact that her validation, the signal that all was as it should be, had failed.

Again.

Two years earlier a woman suffering from epilepsy had attended a meeting in Liberal, Kansas. After a few minutes with Stacy's hands on her head, the woman had leaped to her feet, exultant, claiming that healing energy had filled her and made her whole. She had embraced Stacy, and, to the accompaniment of deafening applause, had been surrounded by a crowd of friends who swept her from the stage.

Stacy had stared after them, uncertain. It was the first time that the sense of completion she always experienced when a healing took place had not been present. She opened her mouth to call the woman back, to tell her she wasn't sure, then closed it again. If she broke momentum now, admitting this possible failure, it would throw off the whole rhythm of the meeting; worse, it might damage the faith her followers placed in her. Even though she knew that the energy flowing through her brought about genuine healing, she also understood that faith made people more receptive to that energy.

The epileptic woman was still speaking animatedly to the rapt group around her, so it was obvious that she had felt something. Surely, Stacy told herself, the energy must have worked on her the same way it always did on the multitude of others who came seeking healing. The audience continued to applaud and, looking across the stage, Stacy saw the next person in line limping toward her. She hesitated a moment longer, then moved forward, hands extended, to greet him.

The woman never attended another meeting. Stacy tried to convince herself that the healing must have taken place, or she would have returned. But she could never completely rid herself of an uncertainty that nibbled at the edges of her mind when she least expected it and sometimes kept her company in the dark of sleepless nights.

And now the strange glitch had happened again.

At least this time, she thought, it only concerned a migraine, not something life-threatening like epilepsy. Arms still raised, she forced her attention back into the present, to the wildly applauding audience.

They love what I do; they love me. Do you see them, Mother? Do you hear them, Father? Are you proud of me?

Tears sprang to her eyes and she brushed them away with the back of her hand.

§

The auditorium was almost empty. A few stragglers remained around the refreshment table at the back of the room, chatting or finishing the last crumbs of homemade peanut butter cookies. The woman in the blue dress had departed with her entourage soon after the close of the meeting, still caught up in excitement and wonder. Stacy had almost waylaid her, almost mentioned being unsure that the energy had worked as it appeared to, but what would be gained by sharing her doubts? The woman's headache was gone; that was all that concerned her and her friends.

So far, Stacy's impressive record had spoken for itself. Admitting even the possibility of failure would not only make her vulnerable to the skeptics, but would also definitely curb the momentum her work had been steadily gaining for the past year.

Pushing this dilemma to the back of her mind, she began gathering up used paper napkins and styrofoam cups. Despite the tremendous amount of energy she had expended over the past several hours, she felt strong and exhilarated. A few more meetings like this one, and she would be well on her way toward being nationally recognized as a genuine healer!

She had just dropped a handful of litter into the wastebasket when she noticed a well-groomed couple standing by the door. The woman looked about thirty-five, attractive, her fair hair stylishly windblown. The man was at least ten years older, but the shoulders under his form-fitting, expensively casual shirt spoke of frequent visits to the gym. A single streak of silver through his thick brown hair added a touch of rakishness to his otherwise glossy appearance. Seeing Stacy's glance, he broke off his conversation with the woman and moved back into the room toward her.

"Ms. Addison." He offered his hand. "I'm Evan Chastain." Turning to the woman, who had stepped up beside him, he continued, "This is my assistant, Laurie Tolliver. We'd like to talk to you for a few minutes."

Stacy shook his hand and nodded to his companion. "It's getting late, but I guess I can spare a few minutes." Picking up one of the several folding chairs stacked against the back wall, she opened it and sat down. Evan Chastain took two more chairs and arranged them opposite her. Seating himself with a quick, economical movement, he set his briefcase on the floor beside him. Laurie Tolliver took the chair next to his.

"Your work is very impressive, Ms. Addison, especially what happened tonight with that little boy." Chastain's smile displayed white, perfect teeth.

"Thank you." Stacy looked from Chastain to his assistant. "You chose an especially exciting evening to attend."

Laurie Tolliver smiled. "Actually, this is our fourth time. We sat in the back row the other times and left soon after you were finished."

Chastain briefly touched the wave of silver above his right ear in what looked like a habitual gesture. "We wanted to just observe, to be sure you were genuine, before we made up our minds."

Stacy wrinkled her forehead. "Made up your minds about what?"

"About you, Ms. Addison; you and your abilities." Chastain's gaze became serious. "As I said earlier, your work is very impressive. Not only have we observed your sessions, but we have also taken the liberty of interviewing a number of the people you've laid hands on, here in Tulsa and also in Missouri, Arkansas, and Kansas."

Laurie Tolliver nodded. "Those we spoke with were very enthusiastic about you, Ms. Addison." She leaned forward and smiled. "We felt it was the best way we could find out whether or not you were, as the saying goes, 'for real.' It seems that you are."

"That's right. According to all the evidence, you're a genuine healer." Chastain picked up his briefcase and laid it on his lap. Snapping open the locks, he reached inside and extracted a small stack of papers, which he offered Stacy.

"This is a contract. Take it home with you and read it through carefully. Talk it over with your family and give it sufficient thought before making your decision. However, we do need your answer before the end of next week."

"My answer to what?" Stacy peered at the printed form. "What is this contract, anyway?"

Evan Chastain and Laurie Tolliver looked at each other and smiled. Chastain turned to Stacy, white teeth dazzling.

"Ms. Addison, how would you like to host your own television show?"

Chapter 2

David Kinnard worked to keep a straight face as he watched his daughter pout. Even though she bore little outward resemblance to her mother, Katie's mannerisms sometimes mimicked Stacy's so exactly it never failed to amaze him.

Katie was propped against her pillows, holding a crayon drawing of a black-and-white cat whose long, ringed tail looked as if it might have a life of its own. Lower lip stuck out, she gazed soulfully up at David, who was sitting on the side of the bed.

"I made this just for Mommy. Can't I stay up and give it to her?" The lower lip protruded another fraction of an inch.

David allowed himself the hint of a smile. "It's late, kitten. Time to go to sleep."

"But Mommy said she'd tuck me in when she got home. I need to stay up until she gets here."

"Mommy must have been delayed." He made an effort to keep irritation out of his voice. "Anyhow, you have to be up early tomorrow, remember?"

Katie scrunched down until the covers touched her chin. "I don't want to go on a stupid field trip. Why can't I just stay home with Mommy, or 'Nerva?"

"Because you can't. You signed up to go, and you need to honor that commitment. Besides," David stood up, stretching, "I'm sure Mommy has things to do tomorrow. And just because Minerva lives next door and spends a lot of time with you doesn't mean she isn't busy, too."

"Oh, poop!" Katie grudgingly handed him the drawing. "Put this on my desk."

"Only if you say the magic word."

"Please."

David took the paper. "Thank you."

"Hmpf." She threw all but one of the pillows on the floor and flopped down with her face turned away from him.

Laying the drawing on the small table that served as a desk, David switched on the nightlight and turned off the bedside lamp. As he started out the door, Katie murmured sleepily, "Goodnight, Daddy. I forgive you."

"Goodnight, kitten. Sleep tight."

Smiling, he tiptoed out and closed the door behind him.

§

Stacy parked in the driveway of the big, old mid-town Tulsa house she had inherited from her parents. Leaving the motor running, she leaned her head against the seat back. She often did her best thinking here, in the 1956 Thunderbird that had legally belonged to her since she was eight years old.

The bright red T-Bird had been her father's prized possession. During those infrequent times when he and her mother had been in Tulsa, Randolph Addison had whisked his only child away for long drives in the little sports car, sharing with her details of their latest expeditions to the Peruvian Andes and his insights into the lives and, particularly, the deaths and burials of the ancient Incas.

The fact that she had been an infant when these excursions began made no difference to her father. She had always listened carefully, even when she was not yet old enough to understand what he was saying. By the time she was five she had delighted him by not only understanding most of his lectures, but by asking intelligent, if somewhat uncomplicated, questions.

He and her beautiful, remote mother had habitually appeared and disappeared without much advance notice, and Stacy had always tried to make the most of what little time they spent with her. Her drives with her father had allowed her glimpses into the world that he and her mother had created for themselves, but had never helped her comprehend their obsession with the past.

Her parents' passion for their work was obvious, but she found it impossible to know with certainty if that love extended to her. Sometimes, during their infrequent visits, she would be almost certain that they cared; but before she could hold onto that feeling long enough to absorb it and make it truly hers, Drs. Randolph and Margaret Addison would depart again into the wilds of Peru. When they finally disappeared into the rugged Andean heights a few days after Stacy's eighth birthday, the chance of ever learning whether or not they truly loved her vanished with them.

She leaned her head against the seat back, wondering how her parents might have been affected by the knowledge that their daughter was about to become a television personality. Would they have been proud of her? Would they have felt that what she was doing was worthy of their name?

She sighed. No use wasting time questioning the dead; her parents had spent their adult lives on just such a quest, and look where it had gotten them! She needed to focus on convincing David that this TV show was going to be a good thing. Never enthusiastic about the exciting things that took place at her healing meetings, he had become increasingly tied up in his work over the past few months. Lately it seemed that his focus was mostly on what was taking place at St. Mark's, as if his whole world revolved around his neurosurgery. She was beginning to feel that she and Katie hardly mattered any more.

Shifting her position against the back of the car's seat, she remembered how different things had been in the beginning, when David was still in medical school. Then their intense attraction to each other had made it possible for them to overlook a multitude of differences. Even though they had sometimes argued about what "real" healing was, he had seemed to respect what she did, and she had tried to do the same for his work. And despite the demands made on David's time by the hospital and his studies, he and Stacy had snatched every possible moment to be together.

She had done her best to keep up with the cooking and housework, but as increasing numbers of people discovered her abilities, everyday tasks began to suffer. She found herself on call as much as David, visiting clients in the hospitals, as well as those at home who were too ill to attend the meetings she held three times a week.

When she became pregnant two years after their marriage, she was dismayed. There was already far too much going on in her life; she wasn't certain she could also be a good mother. It was eight years, now, since Katie's birth and she still wasn't sure.

❧ ❧ ❧ Between ❧ ❧ ❧

She sighed again. Katie, at least, would be excited to learn that her mother was about to become a television star. Hitting the button that opened the garage door, Stacy drove the T-bird in and turned off the engine. She gathered up the tote bag of supplies for the refreshment table and the file folder containing Evan Chastain's contract and let herself into the kitchen.

An enticing aroma from the stainless steel oven made her mouth water; peanut butter cookies and coffee were definitely no substitute for one of David's cordon bleu concoctions. Flipping on the oven light, she peered through the glass-fronted door and was rewarded by the sight of a golden, green-flecked crust just beginning to rise above the rim of a white casserole. Asparagus souffle´—her favorite! The delicious smell rekindled her former excitement about the incredible opportunity she had been offered less than an hour ago.

"David!" Dropping her purse and tote bag on the gleaming counter, she pounded up the back stairs. "David, where are you?"

"Shhh! Katie's just gone to sleep." Tall and as lean as a long-distance runner, David Kinnard raised a warning hand.

Stopping just below the top landing, Stacy checked her watch and looked up at him. "It's past ten-thirty. She should have been in bed half an hour ago."

"She was waiting for you. She did an amazing drawing of Max and wanted to give it to you as soon as you came home, but she finally gave up. She's really good, you know. He looks like he could walk right off the paper."

Stacy frowned. "Damn! I promised her I'd be here to tuck her in, didn't I?" She shrugged. "Well, I'll have to see Max's portrait tomorrow." Running up the last two steps, she met her husband at the top of the narrow staircase and flung her arms around his neck, squeezing him hard. "Oh, David, wait till I tell you what happened! Then you'll understand why I'm late."

Hugging her back, David smiled down at her. "Whatever it is, it must be good. I haven't seen you this excited in a long time."

"It's an incredible opportunity! It's going to be the real beginning of my career—I just know it."

She could feel herself trembling with excitement. David took her hand and she followed him back down the stairs and into the kitchen, where he lowered himself onto a chrome-backed stool, while she dragged the one next to his away from the bar and sat down opposite him.

David smiled at her. "Now tell me what this is about."

Stacy reached over and closed her fingers around his wrist. "It's about reaching a lot more people than I've ever been able to! And," she squeezed his wrist, "it's about having the chance to become famous!"

David stared at her intently. "And just how is this going to happen?"

Eyes sparkling, she leaned toward him until her knees touched his. "David, I've been offered my own television show!" She sat back and shrugged. "Of course, it'll just be local and weekly to start with, but Evan–Mr. Chastain–told me that with my looks and talent, we should be able to go daily before too many months, and eventually expand nationwide." She smiled. "He said that, with any luck, I'll help them put KPSI on the broadcasting map."

David frowned. "What the hell is KPSI?"

Ignoring the edge in his voice, Stacy spread her hands. "It's a new channel, ready to debut in about a month right here in Tulsa. It's all about psi–related stuff; you know, psychic functioning—healing, mediumship, astrology, things like that. They want me to host the very first program!"

David stared at her, frowning; then he jumped to his feet. "God, Stace, I can't believe you'd even consider doing such a thing!"

"David, I know you don't think my work is very important, but I hoped you'd be happy for me."

He put his hands on her shoulders. "Sweetheart, under other circumstances, I'd be delighted for you to have an opportunity like this. But Stace, you know—you've known for months—that I'm finally in line for assistant chief of neurosurgery."

Stacy felt her excitement and anticipation drain away. "David, I'm sorry this is coming at a bad time for you, but I may never get another chance like this."

He dropped down on the stool opposite her again. "Stace, please try to understand. It's never bothered me that the other docs, even the nurses, tease me about having a witch for a wife. But if you go on TV with some psychic side show, I'm not sure Elmore, or the board, will overlook that. Some of those guys are pretty straight-laced." He scrubbed the top of his head with one hand. "If you do this, it could flush my whole career down the toilet."

She drew herself up stiffly. "Well, I certainly wouldn't want to stand in your way! I guess it doesn't matter that I set my career aside for years so that you could finish medical school and get started at St. Mark's."

"Whoa! Wait a minute, here." David held up his hand. "I wouldn't call your running off every few days for your tent meetings setting your career aside. How many times did you cook or do laundry while I was studying and making rounds?"

Stacy slid from the stool, eyes sparkling again, this time with anger. "I've cooked plenty of meals for you. And done your laundry."

"Oh, sure. Like once or twice a week."

"That's not fair. I'm busy, too. Anyhow, you know you're a better cook than I am."

"Damn right I am." Suddenly he raised his head, sniffing. "Oh, my God!" He sprinted across the floor and grabbed a pot holder lying on the counter beside the stove. Throwing open the oven door, he one-handedly extracted the casserole and slid it onto an unlit burner.

"Damn, damn, damn!" Flipping on the vent over the stove, he fanned at the plumes of smoke ascending from the ruined soufflé´. Then, turning away from their ravaged dinner, he slid his arms around her waist. "Hey," he whispered, "I'm sorry about the soufflé´. And I'm sorry I blew up about your news."

Stacy held her body rigid. Trying to wheedle her into seeing things his way wasn't going to work, not after what he had said!

He sighed "Come on, Stace. You sort of broadsided me. I wasn't expecting anything like that."

Refusing to look at him, she said in a tight voice, "Please let me go." When he didn't release her, she began to push against his chest. "I said, let me go!"

"Stace, please! We can work this out. Don't get so upset."

Freeing herself, she stepped back. Tiny lights flickered in her dark eyes, like the sparks flint makes when it strikes rock. "Upset? Why would I be upset, David? Because you called me a witch, or because you referred to my work as a side show? Or maybe because my career doesn't mean a thing to you, except as an obstacle to your success?" He began to speak, but she raised her hand. "Don't bother. I certainly wouldn't want to get in the way of your upward mobility."

David shook his head. "For God's sake, Stace, you know I've worked for years to get in position for this promotion. Why can't you understand?"

"Oh, I understand, all right. I understand that you think you're the only one in this family who has a right to be successful."

David flushed. "That's not fair. You've been gone whenever you wanted and run all over the place, and I haven't complained—or not much. First it was the bookstore with Glynis. Then it was the healing meetings. Now you're talking about a television show. I thought when Katie was born that you'd settle down, be more of a real wife and mother, but that hasn't happened"

Stacy's eyes narrowed. "I've done the best I could to be a 'real' mother, as you put it. And, poor deluded me, I thought I was a 'real' wife. Guess I've been fooling myself all along."

With quick, jerky movements she scooped up her purse from the counter and pushed past him. She opened the kitchen door, then looked back. David was still standing in the middle of the floor, staring at her. Somehow things had gotten completely out of hand, but she couldn't admit that now. It would be like saying he was right and she was wrong.

She hitched her purse over her shoulder. "I'm going to Glynis's. Katie's supposed to meet her at the store tomorrow after school and then spend the night. I'll already be there, so we can make it a threesome. Who knows—I might even have the chance to be a 'real' mother."

She started out the door, then turned back again. "And since neither Katie nor I will be here, you won't have to worry about leaving your precious hospital. In fact, why don't you go ahead and plan to stay there tomorrow night; it should be a 'real' experience!"

Biting her lip to hold back the tears, she slammed the door behind her.

Chapter 3

Katie Addison-Kinnnard examined the book in her hand and wrinkled her freckled nose.

"Yuck! Somebody spilled coffee on two of the pages, Aunt Glinda."

Glynis Steele looked up from the cash drawer whose contents she was counting. "This is a café, as well as bookstore, sweetie. I can't tell customers they're not allowed to look at the books while they're having coffee; they might not come back. Anyway, it's one of the used books, so it's not such a big deal."

Katie shoved the offending volume into its proper slot on the shelf. "I don't see why you don't put a spell on them, or something, when they do stuff like that. You know, like the real Glinda in the "Wizard of Oz."

Without looking up Glynis said, "The real Glinda didn't put nasty spells on people. She only did good magic."

Katie wandered over to the counter and perched on a chair next to Glynis. "You can do good magic, can't you, Aunt Glinda?"

Glynis raised her head and smiled. "I'm afraid not, sweetie. Your mommy just gave me that nickname because we used to pretend that we lived in Oz. She was Dorothy and I was Glinda, because that sounds like my real name."

"Was that when you and Mommy were as big as me?"

"Yep." Bending across the counter, Glynis reached for a penny that had rolled across it. "I absolutely despise this part of being in business!" she muttered. "It was so much easier when your mother still had time to help me close the store every day."

Katie kicked her heel against the chair leg. "Mommy doesn't have time for anything anymore. She's too busy healing people."

"I know, I know." Glynis retrieved the penny and stuck it into its proper compartment. "I just thought, when we opened this place, that your mother would be around to do her share of the donkey work. She pays her half of the bills, but that doesn't—" She broke off in mid-sentence and looked up at Katie. "Forget I said that, sweetie."

Katie eyed her with interest. "Are you mad at Mommy?" When Glynis didn't respond, she continued, "It's OK to be mad at her. Daddy says so. I think he's mad at her, too, because he told me this morning that it's OK if I am, and he understands." She studied the strand of sandy-colored hair she was twisting around one finger. "I don't think Mommy loves us any more. Daddy says she mostly loves making other people feel better."

Pushing her reading glasses up onto the top of her short, brown hair, Glynis took Katie's chin in her hand. "Your mother loves you very much, Katie. You mustn't ever doubt that."

Katie pulled her head away. "No, she doesn't. She doesn't care about me or Daddy. She wouldn't be going away all the time, if she did."

"She goes away because people need her, sweetie."

"But I need her, too. I need her more than those strangers do." Katie stuck out her lower lip.

Glynis sighed. "I know you do. I think your mommy doesn't realize how much you miss her. I'm sure that if she understood, she'd stay home with you more often. She's just—well, she's a very special person, with special talents." She stroked Katie's hair. "I'd like for her to spend more time with me, too, but I guess we have to be willing to share her." She gave Katie a hug. "Come on, help me finish up, so we can get out of here."

Together, they made a sweep of the room, picking up the last few empty coffee cups and wiping off the cleared tables. Glynis set the cups in the little sink back of the counter and ran hot water over them.

"I'll wash those in the morning; I'm too tired to do it tonight. Let me put the leftovers away, and we're out of here."

She covered the cookie plates with plastic wrap and stored the milk and cream in the refrigerator. Digging her purse out of a drawer under the counter, she squeezed Katie's shoulder. "Come on, sweet potato, get your stuff together and let's go home. You say your mommy doesn't want to be with you, but she's already at my place, waiting for us."

Katie scooped up her school books and homework papers. "She is?

Really?"

"Really. The three of us are going to have a big girls' slumber party. And," she extracted her keys from her purse, "if we don't get there pretty soon, your mommy will think some wicked scoundrel has carried you off to his dark dungeon and is holding you hostage until you reveal the location of your secret cache of bubble gum."

Katie giggled. "You're so silly! What would a wicked scoundrel want with a whole bunch of bubble gum?"

"Use it to stick up a bank, I guess."

"Oh, Aunt Glinda!"

Laughing, they quick-stepped out the door sideways, arm-in-arm, and Glynis locked it behind them.

§

"Gin! I win again!" Clapping her hands, Katie bounced up and down on her chair at the dining room table.

It had been her evening. Glynis and Stacy had prepared a supper of hot dogs, potato salad and strawberry ice cream, then the three of them had watched Katie's favorite video, *Willy Wonka and the Chocolate Factory*. Later, they had played two games of gin rummy, both of which Katie had won.

Yawning, Stacy stretched and began to gather up the cards. "Time for bed, honeybunch."

"Not yet!" Katie fixed her mother with pleading eyes. "Just one more game?"

Stacy shook her head. "It's a quarter of ten. You have school tomorrow, remember?"

Katie stuck out her lower lip. "Oh, poop on school! Why can't I stay home for one day?"

"Because school is important. It may not always be fun, but it gives you knowledge and knowledge—"

"I know, I know," Katie sighed. "Knowledge is power."

"You got it!" Stacy tugged her daughter's sandy hair teasingly.

"Poop, anyway!" Moving as slowly as possible, Katie pushed her chair back from the table, kissed her mother and Glynis, and reluctantly dragged herself down the hall toward the bedroom.

"Better watch that poop," Stacy called after her. "I'll start making you scoop it up and spread it on 'Nerva's garden."

Picking up the empty popcorn bowl, Glynis carried it into the kitchen. She could see Stacy still sitting in the dining room, her lips now thinned and tight, the fingers of her right hand rhythmically tapping the table.

Stacy had appeared without warning the previous evening and spent the night in the room they had both considered hers since Glynis had purchased the little house five years ago. Glynis had not questioned her, knowing from long experience that when Stacy was ready, the information would pour out. The tight lips and tapping fingers signaled that the moment of revelation had arrived.

Glynis poured two cups of coffee, gave Stacy one, and set the other at her own place across the dining room table. Stacy took a sip and looked over at her. "OK, I know you've been waiting to hear what happened, so here it is. I've been offered my own television show."

Glynis drew in her breath. "Wow! That's fantastic! How did it happen? When do you start?"

"Maybe next month. And it happened almost like you'd see in a movie. This man and woman came up after last night's meeting and handed me a contract. I'll be hosting my own show, healing people in the audience. Maybe I'll even work out a long-distance segment, where people in the viewing audience can tune into the energy and get some healing at home."

Stacy took a sip of the hot coffee. "It's a new channel, just local, but it's a start. And," she looked across the table, "if the show's a success, it will eventually go national."

Glynis stared at her, puzzled. "That sounds great! So why are you upset? I mean, you are upset, aren't you?"

Stacy made a face. "Oh, it's David; he doesn't want me to do it. In fact, he was downright insulting about it."

"Really? That doesn't sound like David."

"Well, it sounded like him last night." Stacy glared at the coffee cup in her hand. "He thinks that if people from the hospital see me holding meetings on television, they'll believe he's a kook, like me, and he won't get his advancement." Her frown deepened. "Damn it, Glinda, he knows how much this means to me. Or if he doesn't, he ought to!"

"Stacy, don't you think . . ."

Setting the cup down with a clatter, Stacy looked across the table at Glynis with narrowed eyes. "Don't I think what?"

Glynis took a deep breath. "Well, that David has a lot on his mind right now. He's been working toward becoming assistant chief of neurology for a long time. I'm sure he didn't intend to belittle your opportunity."

Stacy's dark eyes grew darker. "Whose side are you on, anyway?"

"Yours, of course, if I have to take sides. I just meant that—"

"Glinda, he insulted me. He called me names and totally demeaned my work." Her fingers began tapping the table again. "It seems like everything is about him lately—him and his work. If he wasn't so wrapped up in himself, he'd realize how important this show could be for me."

Reaching across the table, Glynis put her hand over Stacy's. "Are you sure you're not misinterpreting what he said? Maybe it wasn't as bad as you thought."

Stacy pulled her hand away. " I am not misinterpreting anything! He called my work a side show. Those were his exact words!"

Glynis frowned. "I've got to admit that's pretty strong. I guess I'd feel hurt, too."

"Thank you."

Stacy stared into what was left of her coffee as if she were trying to locate something in it. The silence lengthened. Finally, she lifted her eyes.

Glynis was disturbed by the look in them. "What is it? What's the matter?"

Stacy sighed. "Oh, I don't know. I just—" She shook her head slightly. "I just don't know if I did the right thing."

"You mean about walking out on David last night?"

Anger flickered in Stacy's eyes, then was replaced by something Glynis thought might be sadness. "No," she said. "I don't feel I had any choice about that." She ran a finger around the rim of her coffee cup. "But I did have a choice about what happened at last night's meeting."

Glynis wrinkled her forehead as Stacy told her about the woman with the migraine and how the usual sense of completion had been lacking.

"So is that a big deal?" she asked. "It was just a headache, wasn't it?"

Stacy shrugged. "As far as I know. But the headache might have been a symptom of something more serious. It probably wasn't, but it could have been." She chewed her lower lip. "And there's more. I've never told anyone this, not even you, but the same thing happened once before, almost two years ago. Only that woman had epilepsy."

She looked directly into Glynis's eyes. "I didn't know what to do, Glinda. I didn't know last night and I didn't know two years ago. Both times I was scared to say I might not have connected properly, that maybe the healing hadn't worked. I was afraid it would make me look like a fake. You know how skeptical people can be."

Glynis nodded. "Sure, but not your people, the ones who come all the time. They know you're for real."

"But will they keep knowing it if the healing doesn't always work?"

Glynis shrugged. "I don't know. Maybe some of them would doubt, but you know what Minerva always says—to be human and to be perfect is a contradiction in terms. Nobody can do it."

"I know, but they expect me to be perfect. They expect me to perform, to deliver. If I let them down, they may not come back." She leaned her elbows on the table, head in her hands.

"Would that be so awful?" Glynis asked softly.

"Yes!" Stacy's head jerked up. "It would be worse than awful." She jumped to her feet and clutched the chair back, hands trembling, as if her intensity was trying to push itself out through her fingers. "I can't let them think something's gone wrong, that I can't give them what they've come for." Her voice dropped. "I don't know. Maybe it's already happening. I mean, if my own husband thinks I'm a fake . . ."

Glynis leaned forward. "I don't believe that David thinks you're a fake. He shouldn't have said what he did, but I don't think he really meant it."

Stacy stared at her for a long minute, then sighed. "Oh, I suppose you're right." She chewed her lower lip. "He's never said anything mean like that before. And he did apologize."

"Yes, he did."

"And those people wouldn't be wanting me to sign a TV contract if the folks they talked to thought I was a fake, would they?"

Glynis shook her head. "Of course not."

Frowning down at the floor, Stacy tapped her right index finger on the chair back. Glynis waited, knowing from long experience that she was working things through, retracing her mental steps to the moment of last night's verbal explosion, reviewing that scene through Glynis's eyes, as well as through her own.

After a time Stacy looked up. "David said I wasn't trying to see his side of it," she said slowly. "Maybe he was right. I was so mad, I didn't pay any attention to what he was telling me. And I do know he's been working a long time to get this promotion." She sighed again. "What he said was cruel, but I guess I said some pretty mean things too." Sinking back down into the chair, she dropped her head onto her hands again.

"I don't understand what's happening to us. We never used to pick at each other like this. We've always argued about stuff, but they were sort of good-natured arguments." She shook her head. "I don't know when things started turning nasty; but last night was the worst, ever." She looked up at Glynis. "I don't want to give up this TV show, but I don't want to lose David, either."

Glynis reached across the table and touched her hand. "Why don't you talk to him about it? Really talk to him. I'm sure he'll be reasonable."

Stacy jumped to her feet. "You're right!" Scooping up her purse from the table, she headed for the kitchen. "Could you take Katie to school in the morning? I need to go home."

Glynis pushed back her chair and stood up. "Sure, I'll take her, but it's almost midnight." She glanced out the dining room window. "And it's raining. Why don't you wait until morning?"

Stacy shook her head. "I need to get back and straighten things out."

Glynis put a hand on Stacy's arm. "At least, wait until this downpour lets up a bit."

Stacy shook her head. "I'm perfectly capable of driving across town in a little rain."

"Why don't you call first; be sure he's there."

Stacy shook her head again. "Nope. If he's not home, I'll track him down at the hospital."

Glynis sighed. Ever since they were children together, Stacy had made impulsive decisions, neither stopping to ask directions nor slowing for traffic until she reached her goal. Why should tonight be any different?

"Well, at least let me know you've reached home safely," Glynis

🐾 🐾 🐾 Between 🐾 🐾 🐾

called, following her onto the back porch.

Swinging herself into the Thunderbird, Stacy waved briefly, then backed out of the drive with a scream of tires. Wincing slightly, Glynis watched as at the red car skidded around the corner, lights gleaming on the wet pavement.

Chapter 4

A flat, gray landscape stretched toward a gray horizon, its sameness interrupted by a few stunted trees. Completely alone, a man sat upon a small mound of dirt, the only raised ground in this unrelenting monotony. Fair hair and light blue eyes, startling against his tanned skin, might have made his narrow face handsome, except for thin lips that hinted at discontent, perhaps even cruelty.

Sunk in thought, Arthur Craddock might have been a statue by Rodin. He played his frustrations over and over in his mind, straining to see how he could carry out the sole purpose that gave meaning to his existence. The answer continued to elude him.

He struck the ground with his fist, causing a small cloud of dust to spume up. Leaping to his feet, he kicked at the fine ash blanketing the little slope, then finally sank to his knees. The muscles in his temples knotted as he threw back his head and screamed.

Arthur Craddock's cry sped across the gray plain, like a hunter tracking quarry, until it reached the boundary of his spacious prison. Here it struck an invisible barrier and splintered into a chaos of echoes, all shrieking a single name: S T A C Y   A D D I S O N !

Chapter 5

The train released a long, drawn-out moan as it approached the crossing. Stacy hated the sound. It reminded her of her eight-year-old self, crying in the shower after learning that her parents were never coming back. Their final trip to the Peruvian Andes, tracking rumors of a mysterious lost village, had metamorphosed into a personal mystery that had never been solved. Randolph and Margaret Addison had disappeared as completely as if they had stepped into another dimension, or had never lived at all.

The train moaned again, this time nearer. Stacy noticed with a start that she was almost up to the long arm of the barrier, which was slowly lowering itself across the rain-glazed street. Gritting her teeth, she hit the brakes. The Thunderbird fish-tailed on the slippery pavement, rear end slewing to the left, then smashed through the railroad crossing arm, slinging the driver's side of the car against the moving engine.

Her seat collapsed backwards. Gasping, Stacy clutched the steering wheel and dragged herself into an upright position, struggling to free the car from the train, which slid screeching along the track, dragging the captive Thunderbird with it. Stacy frantically twisted the wheel in an effort to loosen the engine's grip.

Suddenly she felt the car lurch to the right. Relief shot through her as she realized it was no longer attached to the metal juggernaut. Then relief shifted into terror as the Thunderbird tipped slowly over the edge of a ravine hidden by the night. The drop seemed to go on forever; then the car struck bottom, exploding her terror into a million shards of pain. The darkness outside rolled in, filling her, and she lost the night, the train, the car, and herself.

David Kinnard woke suddenly. The piercing tone that had interrupted his sleep sounded again. Not the alarm. The telephone. His groping hand almost knocked the receiver from its cradle, as he fumbled it to his ear.

"Kinnard here." His voice was husky with sleep.

"Oh, doctor, I'm so glad I reached you!"

Yawning, David rubbed his eyes. "Who is this?"

"Rose Carradine. I was charge nurse on your ER rotation several years ago." She paused. "I'm also the one who, ah, danced the shimmy at your wedding."

The image of a pleasant, motherly woman balancing a champagne glass on one hand while she undulated her plump hips surfaced in his mind. He smiled slightly. "Oh, yeah. I remember." Stifling another yawn, he looked at the clock on the bedside table. Two a.m. "What can I do for you, Rose?"

"Your wife is here, Dr. Kinnard. The EMTs brought her in a little while ago."

David sat up on the side of the bed. "My wife? She's across town, sound asleep at her best friend's house."

There was a pause. Then Rose Carradine said, "Red hair, name Stacy Addison, drives a red '59 Thunderbird."

"Oh, my God!" David leaped to his feet, groping in the dimness for the shirt and slacks he had dropped earlier on the cedar chest at the foot of the bed. "What happened? How is she?"

"Unconscious. The EMTs said her car went into a ravine and she hit the windshield. Apparently, a train was involved."

"Ravine? Train? What the hell's going on?" Phone tucked under his ear, David struggled into his khakis and shoved his bare feet into loafers. "Who's on tonight?"

"Dr. Elmore's just arrived."

"Good. Stay with her, will you, Rose?"

"Of course."

"I'll be there in ten minutes." Grabbing his shirt, David tossed the receiver onto the bed and sprinted for the garage.

Between

§

"We're not sure yet how extensive the damage is; they're finishing the CT scan right now." Colin Elmore looked at David over a steaming paper cup of stale coffee as they sat in the doctors' lounge. "Of course, cranial trauma is obvious, even without a scan, and I'm almost certain she's hemorrhaging internally."

David winced. "Liver? Kidneys? Spleen?"

"We'll know before long." Elmore massaged his eyes. "Severe facial lacerations and cranial bruising, blood pressure ninety over fifty on arrival, so she's on fluids and vasopressers, but still unconscious." He looked at David. "I'm sorry, really sorry. Things like this are never easy, but it's especially bad when it's someone close."

David rubbed the top of his head. "I just can't understand how it happened; Stace has always been such a careful driver. And she shouldn't have been on the road. She's supposed to be spending the night with a friend."

Elmore shrugged. "Too bad she didn't do that. Apparently a train dragged her car into a ravine. She's lucky the impact didn't break her neck."

The door opened and Rose Carridine bustled in. "Here's the scan, Dr. Elmore. She looked at David. "I'm so sorry, Dr. Kinnard. We're all doing our very best for her."

David tried to smile. "I know you are, Rose. Thanks."

Colin Elmore examined the scan and frowned. "Liver," he said, without looking up. "Stage three. Means we'll have to watch her carefully." He handed the printout to David. "Brain shows considerable swelling. If she doesn't respond shortly, we'll have to go ahead with the works—craniotomy, ICM, intubation—you know the drill."

David nodded again, feeling sick. "Do what you have to do."

Elmore pushed his chair back from the table. "Want to come along?"

David hesitated. Ethics denied him participation in the care of a family member, and he wasn't sure he could stand by and watch Stacy's treatment, with no right to suggest or intervene.

"I'll take a quick look-in, then check on her later, after she's stabilized," he said finally. It was going to be hard enough to see her broken and damaged; doing so with an audience felt almost impossible.

He stood up and sighed. "Then I guess the next thing will be telling Katie that her mother is badly injured, and letting Stace's best friend and, oh, God, the aunt who helped raise her, know what's happened." He rubbed the top of his head again. "This isn't going to be easy."

Elmore nodded. "It never is."

§

Katie lay curled under the green-and-cream quilt that matched the cream curtains and green carpet in her room at the top of the stairs. It was almost morning and she was home in her own bed. Her father had come to Aunt Glinda's in the middle of the night, gently telling her that her mother had been hurt in an accident and was in the hospital, unconscious. He had tried to give the impression that things were not as bad as they seemed, but Katie could tell from his gray, unshaven face and from Aunt Glinda's horrified gaze that he was pretending.

Pulling the quilt close around her ears, she tried to find some comfort in its warmth. Her right hand clutched the little woven Guatemalan worry doll given to her mother many years ago by the grandparents Katie had never met, a souvenir of one of their many trips to South America. Years of rubbing by two sets of anxious young fingers had worn the once colorful figure threadbare. Tonight, however, even the doll's familiar smoothness failed to comfort Katie's fears.

Her mother had been eight years old when *her* parents had disappeared without a trace. Katie had heard the story many times from her mother, from Aunt Jenn, and from Minerva. She had just celebrated her own eighth birthday less than a month ago. Maybe she was going to be orphaned at the same age her mother had been.

Of course, she would still have her father. He was the one who, even though he had to spend a lot of time at the hospital, was mostly around to attend her school events and tried to be there when she felt sad or scraped her knee. Katie loved her father, but despite the fact that he spent more time with her than her mother did, he was more like a familiar and trusted friend than the center of her world. Her father was the earth, solid and reliable; her mother the fiery sun that illuminated both their lives. If her mother died, that radiance would be quenched, leaving the world cold and lonely.

Her fist tightened around the worry doll. It wasn't fair, she thought.

🐾 🐾 🐾 Between 🐾 🐾 🐾

She had overheard her father tell Aunt Glinda that the doctors thought there was nothing more that could be done right now, nothing but to wait and see what happened. Unconsciously copying her mother, Katie chewed her lower lip. There had to be something someone could do! She squeezed the worry doll harder.

Maybe there was something *she* could do, something grown-ups couldn't. She would ask 'Nerva tomorrow; 'Nerva would know. Her hand gradually relaxed. The faded doll slipped down beside her pillow and at last Katie slept.

Chapter 6

Minerva Potts straightened up, pressing a hand to the small of her back. Every year her joints seemed a little stiffer and tending her herb garden became a little more difficult. *I need to get more exercise*, she thought. But despite a touch of pain, she enjoyed being out in the sunshine and the warm spring breeze, working in the yard like a normal human being.

She pushed an unruly strand of faded brown hair back into the bun at her neck. It wasn't often that she had time available during the day to be outdoors. She had lived in this house all her life, having inherited it, along with a substantial annuity, from her parents when she was twenty-five, and had worked out of it since she was fourteen. Her neighbors were under the impression that she had never worked at all, except as a sometime nanny to Stacy Addison, whose parents had owned the house next door and spent the majority of their time traipsing off to foreign lands.

It amused Minerva that the entire neighborhood thought her peculiar, a reclusive old maid who worked in her garden and probably sat around the house knitting scarves for the poor.

"I think it's just as well they don't know what I really do," she had remarked more than once to Max, the black and white cat who was her constant companion.

Adjusting her lavender gardening gloves, she hitched up her long, purple skirt and stepped back, surveying her efforts.

"Well, Max, what do you think?"

Max, who was sunning himself on the back porch, raised his head. "It seems all right, as far as I can tell. Of course, you understand that I don't take a great deal of interest in plants, with the exception of catnip." He yawned. "You might want to straighten up that section of basil; it seems to be out of alignment with the rest."

"Minerva, are you there?" David Kinnard appeared around the corner of the house.

"I'm in the herb garden. Come give me your opinion. Does the basil patch seem out of line to you?"

David glanced at the herbs. "Looks fine to me." He climbed the back steps and dropped down beside Max. "Hello, there, old fellow." He stroked the furry black and white head, then scratched behind the cat's ears; Max pushed against his hand, purring loudly. Minerva smiled, knowing that even though David thought Max just an ordinary cat, Max had a high opinion of David, considering him one of the few humans who treated him with proper deference.

David looked up at Minerva. "I'm afraid I have bad news."

Minerva's smiled faded. "Concerning. . . ?"

"Stacy. She's at St. Mark's, in a coma. She was supposed to spend last night with Glynis and Katie, but she left to come home just before midnight. Glynis tried to get her to stay, but she insisted on leaving." David's face was bleak. "The police say she ran into the side of a train."

Pulling off her gardening gloves, Minerva joined him and Max on the back porch and sat down on the top step. "How sad, especially for Katie." She began stroking Max's back.

David's expression became bleaker. "You might as well know that she spent the night before last at Glynis's, too. We were having a fight and she just grabbed her purse and left." He paused for a moment. "It's the last time I saw her."

Minerva put her small hand over David's large one. "I hope you aren't trying to take responsibility for this accident."

David gave her hand a little squeeze. "I guess not, but I can't help believing that some of the things I said played a part."

"They may have played a part in Stacy leaving the house, but you can't reasonably blame yourself for something she did a day later. She could have let go of her anger, had she chosen to do so."

David rubbed the top of his head. "I don't know how you can sound so calm. She could die! And if she doesn't, there's a lot of damage; the whole right side of her face was smashed. You know how important her looks are to her."

Minerva straightened her lavender gloves and laid them down beside her. "Certainly I would prefer that none of this had happened, but since it *has* happened, I must accept it. And while I can't do anything about Stacy's medical treatment, I can try to see that you don't blame yourself for her accident."

David frowned. "But if I'd done something different, it might not have happened at all."

Minerva looked directly into David's eyes. "The only thing you can be certain of is that, if you had done something different, the results would have been different. Not even necessarily better—just different. For all you know, they might have been worse."

"How could it possibly be worse?"

"Stacy could be dead right now. But she isn't."

David stared at her, then shrugged. "I guess you're right."

Minerva smiled. "Now I suggest that, if it's possible, you go home and take a nap. You look like you haven't slept much."

David sighed. "I have to tell Jenn first." He shook his head. "I'm not looking forward to that!"

Minerva patted his hand again. "Don't worry. Jenn is not going to blame you for what happened. She certainly didn't spend all those years raising Stacy without learning how stubborn she can be."

"I know; but if I hadn't upset Stace, she wouldn't have left mad, and maybe . . ."

Minerva shook her head. "All you're doing is making a bad situation worse. Your wallowing in undeserved guilt is sending negative energy toward Stacy, just when she needs all the positive energy she can get."

David frowned again. "You know I don't believe in that mumbo-jumbo."

Minerva smiled slightly. "I haven't forgotten. But do keep in mind that it can't hurt to be as positive as possible in a difficult situation."

David stared at her for a moment, then stood up. "I guess I can go with that." Bending, he gave Max's head a parting scratch. "I'd better get over to Jenn's before she finds out about the accident from somebody else."

"Nice fellow," Max remarked, as David disappeared around the corner of the house. "It's always a pleasure to find a human who knows the proper way to treat a cat."

Minerva looked thoughtful. "You know, Max, I think we should go inside and lie down for awhile."

"We're going to nap, too?"

🐾 🐾 🐾 Between 🐾 🐾 🐾

"Actually, I'm thinking more in terms of a little trip." Minerva took off her sun hat and carried it across the porch. Holding the back door open, she nodded to Max. "I think we need to see if we are permitted to pay Stacy a visit."

Chapter 7

Stacy lay with her eyes closed. Something was wrong—very wrong. She wasn't sure what it was, but she had the feeling that it was important. She could faintly recall driving away from Glynis's house, skidding around the corner in the rain. Her only other memory was an incomprehensible jumble of grinding metal and shattering glass, mixed with excruciating pain in her face and neck. Then darkness.

It was still dark, but that, she told herself, was because she had not yet tried to open her eyes. It felt safer, at least for now, to keep them closed. She was almost certain that she was no longer in the car. For one thing, she was horizontal, arms and legs stretched out at full length; there was also a solid softness beneath her that must be a bed. She wondered for a moment why the terrible pain was no longer present, but decided she would think about that later. For now, it was a delicious relief to just lie there, comfortable and apparently safe. She sighed. Maybe it had all been a dream and she was at home in her own bed with David asleep beside her.

"She's genuine," a voice spoke from somewhere over to her right. "I told you that a long time ago."

"Could be," a second voice replied. "Can't prove it yet, of course."

The first voice seemed familiar, although she couldn't place it at the moment. The second was completely unfamiliar. It sounded like a child's voice, although it definitely was not Katie's.

A tremor of alarm vibrated through Stacy. What was going on? Cautiously, she opened her right eye. She was lying on a narrow bed with pale blue sheets and a darker blue spread. The wall opposite was also blue, with fluffy white clouds painted on the upper edge, near the ceiling.

Not her bedroom.

🐾 🐾 🐾 Between 🐾 🐾 🐾

Opening her other eye, she slid her gaze toward the location of the voices, which seemed to be near the room's only window. Suddenly she jerked herself into a sitting position. Clearing her throat, she croaked, "Max?"

The pair by the window turned, apparently startled by her sudden entry into their conversation.

"Good. You're awake." Minerva's black-and-white cat leaped lightly from the windowsill and transferred himself to the foot of her bed, wrapping his tail around his feet. His companion followed, a handsome boy a little older than Katie, with dark eyes and darker hair curling almost to his shoulders.

The handsome boy grinned at her. "We've been waiting for you to wake up."

Stacy looked at him more closely. His long hair was not in style, nor was the odd white garment he was wearing. It was cut from a single piece of cloth, belted at the waist, and fell just above his knees. Why would a ten-year-old boy be wearing a dress?

"Tunic," he said.

"What?"

"It's a tunic, not a dress. Besides," he continued, "I wouldn't refer to what you have on as high fashion."

Looking down, Stacy saw that her arms and upper body were encased in soft, yellow cloth. Pushing back the blue cover, she realized that this material extended all the way to her ankles, separating into blousy leggings to form a loose-fitting jumpsuit. Her alarm was no longer quivering; it was full-blown, with panic bells ringing non-stop. She flung an arm up in protest, and the gauzy material of her yellow sleeve expanded, as if her movement had pumped it full of air.

"It's all right, Stacy." Max's voice sounded comforting. "Things are a bit different here, but you'll get used to them."

She sank back against the pillow and shut her eyes. Maybe if she kept them closed for awhile, this nutty kid, who answered questions she hadn't asked aloud, would be gone when she opened them again. Max, too. Even though Max was special, hospitals did not allow cats.

"It isn't exactly a hospital, Stacy." She opened her eyes again. Max was now standing beside her on the bed, staring down into her face.

She frowned. "Why are you talking to a stranger? You never do that. And how did you get here, anyway?"

Max's furry mouth quirked up at the corners in his feline version of a smile, reminding her of the Cheshire cat, except all of him was here. He turned to the boy. "She's usually quite perceptive, for a human, but she isn't demonstrating that right now because she lacks key information."

The boy nodded. "Makes sense to me."

"She doesn't understand that you aren't a stranger—at least, not to me—and of course she doesn't realize where she is. I believe that excuses her confusion."

"That's enough!" Stacy said sharply. "Stop discussing me as if I'm not here!" She sat up again, almost flipping Max onto the floor.

"Temper, too," the dark-haired boy murmured.

She glared at him. "Yes, I've got a temper. What business is it of yours?"

The boy vaulted onto the foot of the bed, where he settled himself cross-legged. "No offense intended. I admire tempers. Got one myself, though I rarely get a chance to use it."

Pushing the pillows behind her back, Stacy propped herself against the head of the bed. This was the craziest dream she had ever had! At least, it had better be a dream. Otherwise . . . . Panic brushed her throat with cold, jittery fingers. What if the jumble of noise and the horrible pain had been real? Had there been an accident? Was it possible she was injured and hallucinating? She crossed her arms to keep herself from shivering and returned the boy's stare.

"If you're going to talk about me," she said, "you can at least tell me who you are."

He flashed a brilliant smile. "You may call me Herm."

Stacy blinked. "Your name is Herman?"

"I didn't say that. I said you could call me Herm."

Before Stacy could reply, the door in the opposite wall burst open to admit a young woman in a bright pink jumpsuit. The girl bustled in, pushing a metal cart loaded with empty glasses and several rows of what looked like plastic carafes.

"Hello, Stacy. How are you feeling?" Without waiting for a reply, she shooed Herm and Max off the foot of the bed. Smiling cheerfully, she pulled out the pillows Stacy had piled behind her back, plumped and replaced them, then began smoothing the rumpled covers. "Now, let's get you ready."

"Ready for what?" Stacy grabbed the bedspread and pulled it up to her chin. "Who are you, anyway—a nurse?

The young woman smiled. "There are no nurses here. I'm a temporary technician. *Your* temporary technician."

"I never heard of a hospital hiring a temporary technician."

The young woman laughed. "Oh, this isn't a hospital."

"It isn't?"

"No."

"What is it?"

"It's a temporary facility." Selecting a carafe from the cart, the young woman poured what looked like water into a glass that she set on the table near the head of Stacy's bed. Placing the carafe next to it, she said, "Actually, the facility isn't temporary—you are."

Before Stacy could speak again, she continued, "We're getting you ready for a special visitor." She smiled again. "Enjoy your time with her." Twitching a last wrinkle out of the sheet, the attendant rolled the carafe-laden cart out of the room, leaving the door open.

To Stacy's amazement, Minerva Potts appeared in the doorway, tucking an edge of her lavender blouse into the waistband of her long purple skirt.

Minerva smiled. "May I come in, my dear?" When Stacy simply stared at her without replying, she stepped into the room and closed the door behind her.

Chapter 8

Arthur Craddock was as close to despair as he had ever come. The gloom stretching endlessly in every direction pressed down on him, threatening to grind him into the dust beneath his feet. Time seemed suspended; no sun rose or set, no moon glimmered in the lowering sky. Nothing moved throughout this breathless landscape, except himself.

He had discovered no evidence that escape from this gray desolation was possible, but he refused to relinquish hope. He understood that as long as he was trapped here, he could not accomplish the unswerving goal that gave meaning to his existence—the location and destruction of someone named Stacy Addison.

As he constantly sent forth searching cries, and these were just as constantly turned back by the invisible barrier, a seed of fear began to germinate within him. Perhaps there was no escape. Perhaps he was doomed to remain here, forever isolated, with only his rage to sustain him, a rage that repeatedly built him up, tore him down, and again restructured him.

Once more he sent forth his hounds of sound, more out of habit than of hope. This time, however, he sensed a difference: a trembling of anticipation, followed by the wild fierceness of fulfillment. He could actually see the vibrations of his voice shimmering back to him, twining, as they reached him, into a single, triumphant howl: "HERE!"

Chapter 9

Glynis Steele stared at the roasted chicken leg in front of her. She had forced herself to eat some brown rice and steamed broccoli, but the chicken was more than she could manage. Sighing, she stored the untouched leg in the refrigerator, scraped the remains of rice and broccoli into the garbage, and set her plate in the sink. Pouring herself a glass of wine, she wandered into the living room, kicked off her shoes, and curled up on the sofa. She studied her glass for several minutes, then set it on the coffee table and tried to sort out her scattered thoughts.

David had awakened her about five o'clock this morning with a call from his cell phone, telling her that he was outside the back door, waiting for her to let him in. She had hurried down the stairs, quivering with dread, and when she opened the door, the look on his face had made her feel that she'd been given an intravenous injection of ice water.

Ever since she had watched him carry a groggy Katie down the stairs to his car, she'd been trying to accept what he had told her: Stacy was in the hospital, hanging between life and death. Stacy—her hero, her best friend, the most important person in her world.

They had known each other since childhood. From the time she was an infant, Stacy stayed with her mother's sister, Jenn Sinclair, while her parents continued their anthropological work in Peru. Glynis's grandparents, Helen and John Steele, lived next door to Jenn. They and their older son, Rudy, made every effort to see that Stacy felt welcome, even allowing her to stay with them on the days she did not have school, while Jenn tended to her massage practice in Tulsa.

Shortly after Stacy's eighth birthday and her parents' disappearance, six-year-old Glynis's family moved back to Tulsa from Missouri.

Glynis began spending every weekend she could with her grandparents, finding with them and her Uncle Rudy the attention and warmth she lacked at home. Stacy's frequent presence was a constant irritation. "Grandma Helen and Grandpa John like her better than me," she complained to her mother. "Even Uncle Rudy thinks she's special."

Mrs. Steele smoothed her youngest daughter's straight, brown hair. "She's just lost her mother and father, Glynis. Your grandparents feel sorry for her and are trying to be nice."

Glynis scowled. "Well, they don't have to be that nice. When she's around, nobody even notices that I'm there!"

These feelings lasted for almost a year. There were no other children in the area, so she and Stacy often played together, but Glynis refused to consider her more than an available convenience. But on Glynis's seventh birthday, Stacy gave her a gift-wrapped copy of *The Wizard of Oz*. The discovery that this beloved story was also the newcomer's favorite sparked an ongoing fantasy play with Stacy in the role of Dorothy and Glynis as her protector and supporter, Glinda, the Good Witch of the North.

It also laid the foundation for a friendship that was solidly cemented two months after Glynis's birthday party. Stacy's twelve-year-old cousin, Keith Addison, came out from Tulsa to spend the weekend with Jenn, while his parents went to Kansas City on business. Wheedled into playing cops and robbers with the two older children, Glynis found herself cast as an outlaw. She went along with this arrangement, running and hiding on command, until Sheriff Keith knocked her down, because she refused to die after he shot her with his cap gun.

Responding to her cry of protest, Stacy sprinted across the yard shouting, "Don't you dare hit my best friend!"

"Oh, who cares about her?" Making a face, Keith prodded the tearful Glynis with his foot. "She's a crybaby."

"I care, you big bully!" Three inches shorter and ten pounds lighter than her cousin, Stacy glared up into his face, her hands balled into fists. When Keith laughed and tried to push her away, Stacy decked him. It was a feat that instantly transformed her, in Glynis's eyes, into a hero of the first rank.

This incident set the tone for their relationship. Stacy originated exciting games and daring plans, and Glynis steadfastly carried out her assigned roles, regardless of discomfort and sometimes even danger. Only once did Stacy venture where Glynis could not follow. The experience created a small, unbridgeable gap between the two friends, but even that did not weaken the tie that bound them.

It happened when Keith, then twelve, again visited Jenn for a weekend. Stacy and Glynis were playing in the Steele front yard, when they noticed that the sky was darkening and a vigorous wind was beginning to turn the tree leaves upside down. As they were gathering up their toys, Keith wandered into the yard.

"Here," he grabbed Glynis's Barbie doll out of her hand. "I'll carry this for you."

Waving his prize above his head, he let out a whoop and raced around the side of the house, pursued by Glynis and Stacy. He stopped at the foot of the huge maple tree shading almost half of the Steele back yard and, just as the two girls reached him, flung the doll up into the branches. She hung there, twisting wildly in the strong breeze now whipping through the yard, her long hair snagged on a limb halfway up.

Running to the maple, Glynis began to climb, but her foot slipped and she cried out as the rough bark scraped her legs. She started up the tree again, but Stacy pushed her aside, shouting "I'll do it. Just wait till I get my hands on that stupid Keith!"

Glynis watched as Stacy crept upward, carefully searching out crevices for fingers and toes. Billows of dirty clouds pressed the growing dusk against the earth and the maple leaves danced wildly to recurring drum rolls of thunder. Finally, she reached the branch that held the doll captive and inched along the limb, a dozen feet above the ground.

The sky abruptly opened in a drenching downpour, and a dazzling crack of brilliance silhouetted Stacy, arm outstretched, reaching toward the doll. She lurched sideways, her cry almost drowned out by a gigantic crash that sounded like a thousand dishes shattering. Glynis, transfixed by fear, waited for her to fall, but she dangled limply from the tree, her right forearm welded to the maple limb by the lightning that, after splitting the side of the tree where it entered, had chosen that branch as one of its exits.

Breaking out of her trance, Glynis ran screaming toward the house. Her grandfather, who was reading the newspaper in the living room, quickly followed her down the back steps into the cloudburst.

Although Grandpa John scaled the maple as quickly as a man thirty years younger, he was unable to free Stacy's arm. Anchoring himself to the tree trunk with one hand, he stretched himself along the branch, carefully easing her limp body across the limb with his other hand, while he shouted to Glynis to run to the barn and find her Uncle Rudy. Glynis turned, almost bumping into Keith, who by this time had returned to the back yard. She gave him an angry shove, ignoring his startled look as she raced for the barn.

"Keith," she could hear Grandpa John yelling over the roar of the storm, "go to the shed and bring me the ladder and hand saw!"

By the time she returned with Rudy, Keith was dragging the equipment to the foot of the tree. Rudy grabbed the hand saw and, with Keith bracing the ladder against the part of the branch nearest the trunk, climbed up to hold Stacy's unconscious body steady. Reaching past her, Grandpa John sawed off the small end of the branch imprisoning her arm, then cut carefully through the part nearer the trunk. Cradling her against his chest as best he could, Rudy carried her down the ladder. It was not an easy job, given the good-sized chunk of maple limb still attached to her forearm.

Keith, in the meantime, ran next door to tell Stacy's Aunt Jenn what had happened. They all accompanied Stacy to the emergency room at St. Mark's, where Rudy filled out the necessary paperwork, and she was rushed into the first available operating room. It took the rest of the night to free her arm from the branch, then clean and sew up the terrible tear that the combination of the lightning's heat and the fused wood had caused.

Stacy's arm slowly healed and the scar eventually faded to a pale crimson, but something deep within her had shifted. After her return from the hospital, she would not wear anything with short sleeves. She also refused to discuss her experience with anyone, even Glynis, and never again played with Barbie dolls, or devised adventures or risky games. While Glynis did not understand the change, she eventually realized that it was permanent. And although she missed the old games, the laughing and the make-believe, she staunchly remained Stacy's ally and confidante.

As the two girls entered their teen years, Stacy continued to grow more serious, focusing her energies even more intensely on what she referred to as her work. By this she meant the ability to heal others that had begun to manifest itself a couple of months after the Barbie doll incident. Word of the beautiful, copper-haired girl whose touch could stop bleeding and eliminate pain eventually spread beyond the family circle, drawing increasing numbers of people to her. By the time she was twenty, she had begun to hold the healing meetings for which she was gradually becoming famous.

Looking back, Glynis realized that Keith, once again, had been the catalyst for that shift, as he had for other major changes in her relationship with Stacy. The three of them had been running barefoot in Minerva's back yard about a month after Stacy's release from the hospital. Suddenly Keith yelped and sat down hard, holding his right foot. Both girls watched as he carefully stood up and limped across the yard to them, obviously struggling to hold back tears.

"What happened?" Glynis helped him sit on the small, stone bench near the back door.

"Dunno." He squeezed his eyes together hard. "Stepped on something."

Kneeling in front of him, Stacy picked up his bare foot and, closing her eyes, cradled it in her hands.

Keith's eyes popped open in surprise. "Your hands are hot!" Glynis thought he was going to pull away, but instead he clenched his teeth and squinted his eyes shut again. After what seemed like a long time, his face relaxed.

Reaching under the sole of his foot, Stacy made a sudden movement.

"Ow!" Keith's eyes flew open again.

Stacy silently offered him a long, blood-covered nail. She and Keith stared at each other, then she turned without a word and walked away into the house.

Looking down, Glynis's eyes widened. The angry-looking puncture in the sole of Keith's foot was rapidly changing. As she watched, it shrank to a tiny indentation, then disappeared completely, leaving a spot of pale, fresh-looking skin, cleaner than the rest of the sole surrounding it.

Keith, mouth open, stared at his foot. Finally, he put it on the ground and leaned his weight on it.

Glynis stared, fascinated. "Does it hurt?"

He shook his head without looking at her. Still limping slightly, he crossed to the back porch and began pulling on his socks and shoes. When his parents arrived to pick him up, he went immediately to the car and climbed into the backseat. His mother followed, looking worried, and when neither of them emerged from the car, his father shrugged and told Jenn they would see her later.

It was the last time Keith played with them; three months later, he and his family moved to Kansas City. Glynis secretly believed that he had talked his parents into leaving, but had never shared this unlikely notion with anyone, not even Stacy. She held Keith responsible for most of the events that had caused such tremendous changes in Stacy, and was pleased to think that he might have been frightened enough to have fled the state.

Picking up her wine glass, Glynis tilted it and stared into the ruby liquid. Good old Keith. She made a face. Too bad Stacy had wasted her talents on such a chucklehead! It seemed so unfair that she was unconscious and couldn't do for herself what she had done for him and so many others.

Shaking her head, Glynis set the glass down again and tried to find a comfortable position on the sofa. Leaning against its cushioned arm, she hugged her knees to her chin. The thought of going on without Stacy made her feel that she was teetering on the edge of a terrifying void.

Life, which had always seemed stable and relatively predictable, had overnight mutated into one of those movies in which a shocking twist shatters all preconceived assumptions, leaving the ending precarious and uncertain. She didn't know what to do about it, but she didn't like it. She didn't like it at all.

Chapter 10

The massive column of darkness that was Serizzin churned and swelled, the screams and moans within it muted to something resembling a purr, as he savored the knowledge that events were, indeed, arranging themselves in his favor.

His servant, Iblis, had just informed him that the tool known in its human life as Arthur Craddock was almost entirely under his influence. When that process was complete, Craddock would be ready to serve as a liaison between Serizzin and the special soul for whom he had long been waiting. A soul that had at last arrived Between.

This soul fulfilled every necessary condition. First, though presently detained Between, she was determined to return to her physical body, which was in a comatose state on Earth. This dual situation was essential, if Serizzin was to have access to both the physical and nonphysical realms. Second, her healing abilities and connections offered him the power he needed to finally liberate himself from bondage to the human beings whose negative emotions had created him millennia ago. Third, a crucial detail as yet unknown to this soul almost guaranteed his success in binding her to him.

He had also discovered that a powerful bond already existed between Craddock and this special soul, even though she was presently unaware of it. The human mind might explain such a convergence as coincidence, but Serizzin knew that coincidence did not exist; such intertwining occurred only when a deep-level orchestration of events was in progress.

His time was approaching; everything was falling into place. The shrieks and growls within him swelled with anticipation.

His patience was about to be rewarded.

Chapter 11

Stacy stared in amazement as Minerva Potts smiled at her, then stepped all the way into the room. Closing the door behind her, Minerva glanced over at the pair by the window.

"Hello, Herm," she said. "It's been awhile, hasn't it?"

The boy in the tunic grinned and, jumping to his feet, bowed from the waist. "A pleasure at any time, Minerva."

Minerva nodded graciously, then looked at Max. "I see that you arrived ahead of me."

"Quite some time ahead of you, as a matter of fact. What took you so long?"

Minerva absent-mindedly shoved her rebel strand of hair back into place. "I had to stop in the Entry Processing Center and help them organize a large group of new arrivals from China."

Sitting up in bed, Stacy arranged herself in a cross-legged position. "Excuse me. I hate to interrupt, but could someone tell me what's going on?"

Minerva turned toward her and smiled again. "I'm sorry, my dear. I'm afraid we're being rude." Crossing the room, she opened her arms; Stacy slid her legs over the side of the bed and leaned into them. Enveloped in Minerva's hug, she was horrified to feel the pressure of tears behind her eyes.

Quickly straightening up, she sat back on the bed. "I'm awfully glad to see you, 'Nerva, but what are you doing here, in my dream?" Glancing toward the window she frowned. "And why is Max here with a kid wearing a dress?"

"Tunic," Herm said.

Sitting down beside her, Minerva took one of Stacy's hands in hers. "We'll discuss the dream issue in a moment, but first I'll answer your other questions. To begin with, the person you refer to as a "kid" is not a child at all. In fact, he's far older than you are."

"You've got to be joking!" Stacy raised an eyebrow. "He can't be more than twelve, tops."

Minerva smiled again. "Twelve hundred would be a closer guess, but even that almost certainly falls short of his true age. Of course, I don't know exactly how old he is." She raised an eyebrow at Herm, who shrugged. "I'm not even sure that he does."

Stacy wrinkled her forehead. "That's ridiculous! How can he not know his own age? And what's this 'twelve hundred' business? Nobody can be that old and still be alive."

"Aha!" Herm leaped to his feet again. "The lady is astute. She thinks. She reasons. However," he wagged a finger in Stacy's direction, "she is still locked into misguided beliefs. She needs to expand her thinking."

Laughing, he raised his arms and seemed to melt. Stacy blinked. The boy was gone; in his place, smiling down at her, stood a handsome young man. A larger version of the boy's tunic did little to hide his tanned, muscular arms and legs, and on his dark curls rested a small, rounded cap with what looked like a bird's wing fastened on either side. An instant later, the young man disappeared, followed briefly by a rough-coated coyote, its teeth gleaming in a grin; then the tunic-clad boy was back.

Laughing again, he looked from Stacy to Minerva. "How was that for a mind-opener?"

Minerva eyed him sternly. "That was far more than enough."

Stacy, eyes wide, found her throat too dry to swallow. She reached for the glass of water the technician had left on the bedside table, her hand shaking so hard that she slopped most of the liquid on the floor. Gently taking the glass from her, Minerva refilled it and placed it in her trembling hand.

Stacy accepted the glass, her eyes still fixed on Herm. "Who—who in the world are you?"

The boy chuckled. "Not in the world—at least, not the world you're familiar with. Although I do occasionally visit your sector of reality."

Still sitting on the side of the bed, Stacy sipped the water. She could not stop shaking, and some of the liquid spilled down the front of the blousy, yellow jumpsuit in which she had found herself when she awakened. She had grown up accepting the fact that Max could talk, even though he never did it in front of anyone but herself and Minerva. But what she had just witnessed couldn't happen, except in a dream, yet Minerva seemed to be acting like all this was real. Clutching the water glass firmly, she forced herself to take another sip.

She looked at Minerva. "Please tell me this is a dream! I am dreaming, right? I mean, whatever that was that just happened, that can't be real—can it?"

Minerva took the empty glass that Stacy was still clutching and set it on the bedside table. "I know this isn't what you want to hear, my dear, but all of this is, indeed, very real." She gave Stacy's hand a squeeze. "That's the main reason I'm here—to help you understand what has happened to you."

"Good!" Stacy's voice trembled slightly. "Somebody had better explain something pretty soon!"

Minerva sat down on the bed beside her. "The short of it, my dear, is that you were in a bad accident and your body is now in a coma."

Stacy stared at her, uncomprehending. "How can I be in a coma? I'm here, talking to you."

Max leaped off the window ledge and onto the bed. "She didn't say that *you* were in a coma; she said your body was."

Minerva nodded. "I know this is a very stressful time for you, but you haven't forgotten what we discussed when you were younger, have you?"

Stacy stared at her blankly.

"I'm talking about the conversations we had when your parents disappeared, and later, with Glynis, when her Grandpa John and Grandma Helen died."

"Oh." Memories began to trickle around the wall that seem to have raised itself in her mind. "You mean about it just being their bodies that had died, not their true selves."

Minerva smiled. "That's right. That's what Max is talking about. Your body is, indeed, in a coma, but not your true self. Your true self is here in this room with me, and Max and Herm."

"But where is 'here'? I don't understand."

Minerva's face became serious. "This area is known as Between, because it lies between our physical world and what is often referred to as the next world. It is a temporary stopping place for many types of souls and other beings. People like yourself, whose physical bodies are in a comatose state, usually come here. So do those who have permanently lost their bodies. Those whose bodies are in comas stay here until it is decided whether or not they will return to their Earth lives. Those whose bodies have already died come here to be checked in and have their information processed, before they move on into whatever areas fit their needs."

Stacy thought about this for a moment. "So, where is my body?"

"It's back on Earth, in an intensive care room at St. Mark's. David's chief of staff, Dr. Elmore, is in charge of your case. He and David are doing their best to help your physical body recover, but as long as it's in a coma, you'll remain here, Between."

Stacy could feel panic filling her chest again. "But I can't stay here! I have to get back right away. It's really important!"

Minerva put an arm around her shoulders. "It's all right, my dear. We all know this isn't easy for you."

Stacy shook her head. "No, it's not all right! I know you said I was in a bad accident, and I remember some of what happened—at least, I think I do—but that Pollyanna in the baggy suit said this isn't a hospital, and I seem to be just fine, so I need to get out of here. I need to get back into my body. Now!"

Max leaped from the window sill and onto Minerva's lap, where he settled himself so that he could look into Stacy's eyes. "*You* may be fine," he told her, "but right now your body isn't. Even if you could get back into it, you almost certainly wouldn't be able to make it stand up and walk out of the hospital."

Stacy felt the panic tighten. "But I have to get back! I had a terrible fight with David and I need to tell him I'm sorry." Slipping off the bed, she knelt in front of Minerva and took her hands. "And I didn't have a chance to tell you yet, 'Nerva, but I've been offered my own television show! Things are finally starting to open up for me."

When the older woman did not reply, Stacy continued, "It's going to start in about a month. I just have to be ready for that!" Gripping Minerva's hands tightly, she looked up, her eyes wide and pleading. "All my life you've helped make things right. Please help me now; tell me how I can get back, how I can make all this go away!"

Minerva shook her head sadly. "I'm afraid I'm not able to do that, my dear." She freed one of her hands and stroked the copper cloud of Stacy's hair. "You know I would help if I could. It's very painful for me to have to tell you that what you ask is impossible."

Stacy's chest felt ready to explode. "But why? Why is it impossible? I just don't understand! Isn't there anything you can do?"

Minerva shook her head. "What has happened is far beyond my ability to change."

Jumping to her feet, Stacy flung herself onto the bed, collapsed against the pillows, and closed her eyes. No matter which way she turned, she seemed to be trapped. Gritting her teeth again, she forced the panic out to the edges of her mind. Then slowly and deliberately, she opened her eyes and slid out of the bed. Willing her hand to be steady, she poured herself half a glass of water and slowly drank without spilling any. *Focus on the water. Quit thinking about what she said.* Holding the glass up to the light, she looked at Minerva.

"How come, if I don't have a body, I can drink this? That doesn't seem to make any sense."

Minerva took the empty glass from her and set it back on the table. "You do have a body. It's just constructed of a more subtle energy than your physical body, which is far too dense to exist here, between worlds. When you return to your physical body, this spirit body will go with you and once again become a part of who you are at the physical level."

She tapped the water pitcher with her fingertip. "As for this, it's something you're familiar with; it helps you feel more at home here. Your spirit body doesn't really need the water, but it enjoys the comfort that the concept of water gives."

Stacy mulled this over. "OK, I suppose that makes sense." She thought for a moment. "I don't even know what time it is. How long have I been here?"

Max, still lying on the bed, yawned. "A couple of days, according to earth time."

Stacy looked down at him, shocked. "A couple of days! I thought—" She stopped and sighed. "I guess it could be worse. At least, you didn't say a couple of weeks."

"Days, weeks—it doesn't really matter; time here is not the same as on the Earth level. Here there is only *now* time."

"What does that mean?"

Max yawned again and stretched into an elongated version of himself. "It means that everything is constantly happening *now*."

She frowned. "I don't understand. How can everything be happening at the same time?"

"Ask Herm to explain it to you. He's better at that than I am."

The tunic-clad boy perched on the window sill nodded. "Happy to oblige whenever you're ready."

Smiling at them, Minerva lowered herself into a blue upholstered chair next to the bedside table and crossed her hands in her lap. "I understand your confusion, my dear. Let me see if I can help you better understand what has happened."

"Please!" Stacy settled herself cross-legged on the bed, next to Max.

Minerva looked at her intently. "Tell me the last thing you recall before awakening here."

Stacy frowned with concentration. "I think it was starting up the Thunderbird and peeling out of Glynis's driveway." Her eyes unfocused for a moment. "No, there was something else; I remembered when I first woke up. Something big and noisy and—oh, my God!" She looked back at Minerva. "There was a train. I slid, because of the wet pavement, and—" She closed her eyes for a moment. "I got hit by a train, didn't I?"

Minerva shook her head. "Not exactly. As a matter of fact, it was you who did the hitting. The train dragged your car into a little ravine, about ten feet deep. Since there was no air bag, the seat belt wasn't enough to prevent you from being thrown into the windshield. You hit your head hard enough to cause your brain to swell, producing a comatose state." She leaned forward in the chair and reached over to touch Stacy's arm. "But please keep in mind that David and Dr. Elmore's team are working hard to find out exactly what needs to be done to heal your physical body and bring it back to consciousness."

As Stacy listened, she could sense panic circling the edges of her awareness, ready to strike the moment she let down her guard. It wouldn't take much to make that happen! The thought of her head smashing into the Thunderbird's windshield hard enough to make her brain swell was extremely disquieting. *And what about my face? Was my face damaged, too?*

She could imagine herself, scarred and ugly, standing onstage as the audience pointed and whispered in pity and disgust. *What will I do if my face is smashed? I couldn't bear it!*

The panic dug icy talons into her chest, and she began to twist her head from side to side like a trapped animal. Suddenly she became aware of two strong hands grasping her own and warmth flowed into her, driving out the panic and the cold. She looked up to see Herm, now a handsome young man again, watching her with understanding eyes.

"Don't try to live in the future, Stacy." His deep voice was soft. "You can't do it; you can only project and assume. The future isn't even real; when it finally arrives, it's nothing but another present moment, another *now*." His warmth was circulating through her entire body. "The only *now* you can live in is the one you are experiencing right this very moment, and the next moment, and the next moment after that. Just take each *now* as it presents itself. Nothing more is required of you, and that much you certainly can do."

Stacy nodded shakily. The panic had withdrawn again to the outer edges of her awareness and, even though she was uncertain that she understood everything he had said, she felt comforted. Herm gently squeezed her hands and released them.

Leaping lightly off the bed, Max sauntered toward Minerva, tail swaying. "Why don't we take Stacy on a tour? She'll probably understand better what we've been talking about, when she sees more of Between for herself."

Minerva smiled at him. "That's an excellent idea."

Determined to focus away from her fears, Stacy examined her voluminous yellow uniform with distaste. "I can't go traipsing around in this thing. I look like a banana with a balloon complex!"

"What would you like to wear?" Minerva walked toward a door opposite the window. "Just decide what you want and you'll find it in this closet."

"You're kidding!" Stacy crossed to where Minerva was standing. "Anything I want?"

Minerva smiled. "Anything you want. The creative power of thought works at the Earth level, but the results often take awhile to manifest there. Here, they are instantaneous. Just focus on the closet and think about what you'd like to wear. Be as specific as possible."

Stacy looked at her skeptically. "OK." She squinted her eyes shut. "I'd like a medium size, long-sleeved, green knit shirt; a size eight pair of jeans; medium bikini panties; a thirty-six 'B' bra; and some sandals, size eight."

Minerva nodded. "Now, open the door."

Following her direction, Stacy found part of the wardrobe she had ordered arranged on hangers; the rest was neatly folded on a small shelf. She blinked. "Wow! What I could do with this closet at home!"

Taking the clothes, she slipped through a door Minerva indicated in the far wall and found herself in a small dressing room. Every item fit perfectly and she was delighted to find that being dressed in something familiar made her feel more normal.

She emerged, tucking the shirt into the jeans. Turning from side to side in front of a mirror mounted on the inside of the closet door, she said, "OK, I guess I'm ready for your tour. At least I feel more like myself." Aware again that the panic was still hovering, she glanced anxiously at her three companions. "You *are* all coming with me, aren't you?"

"Wouldn't miss it!" Herm, who had been staring admiringly at her, turned to Minerva and assisted her out of the blue chair.

Shaking himself, Max joined them. "I doubt that you'd get very far without us."

Feeling their support surrounding her like a comforting cloak, Stacy crossed to the door through which Minerva had entered and put her hand on the knob.

"Well, here goes!"

Throwing open the door with a flourish, she stepped through it into the unknown.

Chapter 12

Jenn Sinclair stood just inside the door of the hospital room, staring at her niece's immobile figure in the bed. The sight brought back vividly the moment when twelve-year-old Keith Addison had pounded on her back door, shouting that Stacy had been struck by lightning.

Despite the difficult surgery required to release Stacy's arm from the fragment of maple branch the lightning had seared into it, and the anxious days that followed, Jenn had always known that the chances for her recovery were good. It was unnerving to realize that now, unlike that other time, the prognosis was not so positive, that Stacy in this present moment had moved somewhere far beyond the reach of any help that Jenn, or perhaps any human being, might offer.

Before her knees could betray her, she sank onto the orange Naugahyde-covered recliner near the bed. Leaning her head against the cool, firm chair back, she closed her eyes and let herself slip backward through time.

Thirty-five years ago her older sister, Margaret, had married Randolph Addison, a fellow anthropology student who shared her enthusiasm for the ancient Incan civilization. After receiving their Ph.D. degrees, the Drs. Addison had spent the majority of each year excavating in the Andes, building, within a relatively short time, a reputation that positioned them among the best known anthropologists of the twentieth century. The arrival of a baby, five years after their marriage, was an unplanned and unwelcome interruption of the established rhythm of their lives.

The little girl inherited her mother's flawless features, as well as her dark eyes and copper curls; but there the resemblance ended. Where Margaret was by nature cool and contained, her daughter's passionate nature and magnetic smile drew others to her wherever she went.

🐾 🐾 🐾 Between 🐾 🐾 🐾

Christened Anastasia, she soon began calling herself Stacy, and Stacy she became to everyone but her parents. And although Randolph and Margaret appreciated their child's delicate beauty and took pride in her obvious intelligence, they had no idea of what to do with her.

Jenn, who had been cheated of motherhood by her husband's early death, found their attitude impossible to understand. "You treat her like she's some rare animal you brought home from an expedition!" she once burst out. She and Margaret were having tea in the gracious dining room of the Addison house, while Stacy napped in a bassinet upstairs.

Margaret stared blankly at her. "I have no idea what you are talking about."

Jenn shook her head. "You really don't get it, do you?"

"Get what?" A faint line appeared across Margaret's smooth forehead. "We keep a close eye on Anastasia when we're home, and when we're gone, you and Miss Potts take excellent care of her. What more could a child want?"

What, indeed? Jenn thought. Once again she marveled that she and Margaret had been raised by the same parents.

Jenn had gladly accepted responsibility for Stacy during her parents' frequent absences. Sometimes the two of them stayed in the big, mid-town Tulsa house Randolph Addison had inherited on the death of his parents, but mostly Jenn took the little girl to her own home in the country. There Stacy played in the big back yard and acquired what quickly became an extended family.

John and Helen Steele, owners of the small farm adjoining Jenn's property, were delighted to act as surrogate grandparents, willingly opening their home and hearts to the lonely little girl. Their son, Rudy, who lived with his parents, soon considered Stacy an unofficial niece.

At times, Stacy stayed in town with Minerva Potts, the older woman who lived in the house next door to the Addisons and had been a close friend of Randolph's late parents. Stacy always enjoyed these visits, although Jenn was never certain whom she adored more—Minerva, or Minerva's black-and-white cat, Max.

As Stacy grew older, she divided her time more or less equally between her three homes. The Steeles provided a warm, family interaction; Jenn loved her like a mother; and Minerva told her stories and baked brownies for her, with Max supervising from his perch on the cushioned window seat. They all worked together to give her the most caring childhood they could manage, understanding that it would never be enough to fill the empty space left in Stacy's heart by the constant absence of the parents she tried so hard to please.

The day after Stacy's eighth birthday, Margaret and Randolph Addison set out for the Peruvian Andes on what would be their last expedition. After several weeks of silence, their sponsor sent out a team to locate the now-famous anthropological team; but the Doctors Addison had disappeared as completely as the lost civilizations they had devoted their lives to unearthing.

Jenn found solace for her grief in the gift of a permanent, if unofficial daughter. After considerable internal debate, she decided against formally adopting Stacy, because she did not want to diminish her niece's heritage. When she informed Stacy of this decision, the little girl's response shocked her.

"It doesn't matter," Stacy said. "They didn't want me, anyway."

Jenn, horrified, began to stammer a disclaimer, but the eight year old's clear gaze dried the words up in her throat. Stacy, who had been reading at ninth grade level by the time she was eight years old, was not only drawing on her personal experience with her parents. She had seen Time Magazine's tribute to the missing Addisons and was very much aware that there had been no mention of a bereaved daughter. Her parents' negligence where she was concerned had not only diminished her importance in her own eyes; it had made her invisible to the eyes of the world. In that moment, Jenn understood that nothing she could ever do would erase that knowledge from Stacy's heart and mind.

Sighing deeply, Jenn opened her eyes. She leaned forward in the hospital chair and stretched out her hand toward the undamaged side of Stacy's still face, then pulled it back. *I don't really know how badly you're hurt. I don't want to make things worse.* "Oh, sweetheart," she murmured aloud, "why did this have to happen?"

Taking a tissue from her capacious purse, Jenn blotted her eyes, then closed them again. "Please," she whispered, "please let her come through this all right." Opening her eyes, she got to her feet, blew a kiss toward the still figure in the bed, then turned and left the room. As she closed the door behind her, David and Katie stepped out of the elevator.

"Nana Jenn!" Katie ran to her, throwing her arms around Jenn's waist. Jenn stroked her hair.

"How are you, lovey?"

"I'm OK. It's Mommy who isn't so good."

Jenn looked up at David. "Have you seen Stacy today?"

"I have, but this is Katie's first visit."

"Does she know what to expect?" Jenn asked in a low voice. David nodded.

"Well," Jenn smiled at Katie, "when you've finished your visit, why don't you meet me in the coffee shop? We'll get some ice cream. My treat."

For a moment, Katie's face brightened; then the brightness faded. The sudden shift sent a pain through Jenn's chest that was almost physical. Giving Katie a quick hug, she walked away toward the elevators before the little girl could see her tears.

§

Katie's father knelt and tucked a loose strand of sandy hair behind her ear. "You remember what I told you, don't you, kitten? Mommy isn't going to look the way we're used to seeing her."

Katie nodded, her right hand clenched around the worry doll, safe in her jeans pocket. "I remember." She took a deep breath. "Her head and her face have bandages," she recited, "and she's very pale and bruised and looks like she's asleep, but she can't wake up right now, because she's in a coma. And she has a tube in her mouth that helps her breathe."

"That's right." Giving her a hug, her father got to his feet and took her free hand. "You're sure you want to do this now?"

Lifting her chin, Katie nodded again. If she didn't go to see her mother today, she might give in to the nightmarish fears that had plagued her since the accident. Surely the truth could not be more frightening than the images her mind kept churning out. She held her breath as her father opened the door.

The hospital bed was surrounded by a lot of metal poles with boxes on them, most with what looked like little computer screens on their fronts. Wires coming out of the boxes were attached to different places on her mother's body, and the tube going into her mouth made a whishing noise, like something being pumped. The whole top of her head and the right side of her face were wrapped in white bandages. *At least,* Katie thought with relief, *there isn't any blood.* Blood had featured largely in both her sleeping and waking dreams.

Taking a step nearer, she noticed that the left side of her mother's face was bruised and swollen. The skin surrounding her closed eye was a sickly purplish yellow, and her nose, now an unfamiliar dark red, seemed twice as large as Katie remembered it. Clutching the doll in her pocket tightly, she moved closer to her father. He put his arm around her and she leaned against him.

"You O.K., kitten?"

Katie nodded, blinking away tears. After a moment, she looked up at him. "Can I touch her?"

Her father hesitated, then squeezed her shoulders. "Sure. Just don't shake her, or anything like that. It's important not to disturb her." Taking her hand, he led her toward the bed.

How, Katie wondered, could she disturb someone who was so deeply asleep that she couldn't wake up? She waited while her father reached under the covers and, gently lifting one of her mother's arms out of its spotless cocoon, arranged it carefully on top of the bedspread. Then he stepped back, allowing Katie to take his place.

Not sure of what to expect, Katie tentatively slipped her hand into her mother's. The skin felt cool and dry—completely unfamiliar. Cautiously, Katie squeezed. The muscles of this strange hand did not contract in response. A faint medicinal odor crept into her nose, making her feel sick and a little dizzy. After a moment she pulled her hand away and stumbled back from the bed, suddenly terrified of this unresisting limpness, this alien person who looked and felt and smelled nothing like the mother she had known for the past eight years. For a wild moment, she wondered if her mother was really dead and her father was showing her some strange woman, pretending that it was her mother, until Katie had grown used to the idea of losing her.

Her father stepped to the bedside and, gently lifting the woman's arm, placed it back under the covers. He stood for a long moment, looking at the still face on the pillow. Then, putting his arm around Katie's shoulders, he led her from the room.

Chapter 13

Everything had changed. Without warning, a gentle wind had sprung up, wafting the gray dust away in eddies. Showers softened the arid soil, reorganizing its solid composition into a honeycomb of earthworm-crowded corridors, and turning the dreary landscape into a flower-spangled meadowland. Tortured trees transformed themselves, swelling with buds and blossoms, and on a branch near the now verdant mound where Arthur Craddock sat, a bright-colored bird piped a tentative song.

Arthur realized that something momentous had taken place. This astounding metamorphosis had begun the exact moment he had learned of Stacy Addison's presence and seemed to reproduce itself exponentially, like cells endlessly dividing. He had no idea, as yet, why this was so. Two things, however, he did fully comprehend, even though he did not understand how he knew them. The first was that his altered surroundings no longer confined him. The second was that Stacy Addison—whom he had never met, but who was, nevertheless, the focus of his fury—was finally "here."

He also knew with absolute conviction that wherever "here" was, and wherever Stacy Addison might be hiding in it, he would find her. *The rest will follow*, whispered a voice in that part of his mind still able to think and reason. He knew it spoke the truth and he was satisfied.

Chapter 14

"Uncle Rudy. Uncle Rudy!" Glynis knocked on the back door of the farmhouse.

She knew he was home; his pickup was parked under the big cottonwood in the back yard. Even though the truck was approaching its twentieth anniversary, Rudy kept it in excellent repair, vowing that a later model would be only half as well made. Glynis, who periodically helped him tune up or repair the vehicle, suspected that this was really an excuse to hide his emotional attachment to it.

She wished he didn't do the same sort of thing with his attachment to Jenn. She had known since her teen years that Rudy was hopelessly in love with Stacy's aunt, but his intense privacy about personal matters had always made her hesitate to mention the subject. Certain that Jenn felt the same way about him, she had once tried talking to her about it, but Jenn had instantly changed the subject and Glynis had not felt brave enough to bring it up again.

Frowning, she knocked louder.

"C'mon in; it's unlocked."

Pushing open the door, she saw that the kitchen was littered with wood scraps. Rudy Steele was sitting at the enamel-topped table, his attention on two delicate ears emerging from the rough piece of cherry wood in his hands. Glynis could not count the times that she had sat beside her uncle, watching him coax incredibly lifelike animals out of formless blocks of wood with only his clever fingers and a small knife. Forest dwellers were his specialty; deer, his favorites. This piece would likely be the mother of the dainty fawn presently grazing on wood shavings in the center of the table.

"How's Stacy?" Rudy turned the carving so he could work on it from a different angle.

🐾 🐾 🐾 **Between** 🐾 🐾 🐾

Setting her purse on the counter, Glynis dropped into a chair opposite him. "The same as she has been. I wasn't sure you'd heard; I know you've been gone for several days."

Rudy nodded. "Had to deliver some critters to Little Rock, bring back some orders." He finally looked up from his work. "Jenn told me almost before I could get out of the truck." He carefully laid the wood and his knife on the white enamel surface of the table. "Been real hard for me to take in what's happened, and I'm sorrier than I can say. Stacy's real special."

Glynis nodded. "She's the most special friend I've ever had." She ran shaky fingers through her short, brown hair. "Oh, Uncle Rudy, I don't know what I'll do, if she dies!"

Pushing back his chair, Rudy came around the table and pulled her to her feet. "Come on, Little Bit, let's take a few minutes and relax on the couch."

She followed him into the living room, where they sank into the cushiony old sofa that had held a place of honor in front of the fireplace ever since she could remember. Glynis could not begin to count the hours spent cradled in its comforting squashiness, crying, daydreaming, or sharing secrets with Stacy.

"One of these days," she told him, "this thing's going to swallow you alive."

Rudy's blue eyes crinkled at the corners. "There are worse ways to go."

They sat side by side without speaking. After a few minutes, Rudy reached over and began to massage Glynis's shoulders.

She closed her eyes. "That feels wonderful! I guess I'm tenser than I thought." She sighed. "You know, sometimes I wish that Stacy had never met David."

"Thought you liked David."

"Oh, I like him. It's just that, if she hadn't gotten involved with him, she'd probably be just fine right now."

Rudy stopped massaging her shoulders and turned her so that he could look into her eyes. "You got no idea what would've happened, honey, if Stacy and David hadn't met. For all you know, she could've run off with some no-good and had ten kids by now."

Glynis made a face. "I hope she'd have had better sense than that. But I can't help thinking that if David had been more interested, more sensitive to Stacy's needs, maybe the accident wouldn't have happened."

Rudy resumed his massage. "If 'ifs' and 'buts' were bells and nuts, it'd be Christmas every day, wouldn't it? Besides, I'd be willin' to bet you only heard Stacy's side of the story."

Glynis considered his statement, then sighed. "You're right. But it just seems so unfair. Stacy has a husband and a child, and a career that helps people and is getting ready to really take off. And there she is, hanging between life and death. And here I am with nobody, and a business that doesn't do much of anything except make a living for me, and I'm just fine."

Rudy gave her shoulders a pinch. "So now I'm nobody, eh? Does that include your parents and sisters, too?"

Glynis twisted around so she could see his face. "You know I didn't mean it that way!"

"Maybe not, but you need to realize that everybody counts—not just husbands and kids. And you do make a difference to all of us—to me and your family, and to those folks who come to enjoy their coffee and have a chance to visit or just lose themselves in books for a little while."

Glynis shrugged. "Maybe. But it still seems terribly unfair."

"Ahhh, you should know better'n that. How many times've I heard Minerva tell you fairness is not a ground rule of this old world of ours?"

Glynis raised her hands in a gesture of surrender. "OK, OK! I give up. Although it really isn't fair to bring Minerva into it." Leaning back against his kneading hands again, she frowned slightly. "Actually, I sometimes have the feeling that there's a reason this is happening. I usually leave the intuitive stuff to Stacy, but I keep getting this odd idea that there's more to her accident than we can see on the surface."

"That's interestin.'"

"You don't think I'm nuts?"

Rudy chuckled. "I know you're nuts—you're a Steele, aren't you? However, that doesn't mean you aren't right about what you just said. Why don't you just keep payin' attention to that feelin', an' keep me posted on it?"

He gave her shoulders a final squeeze, then stood up, stretching, and looked at the hand-carved clock on the mantle. "Don't want to seem insensitive myself, honey, but I gotta get back to work. Have a new order to finish by next weekend."

Glynis dug herself out of the couch and followed him back into the kitchen. Picking up her purse, she kissed Rudy's cheek.

"Thanks, Uncle Rudy. Thanks for being you and for always being here when I need you."

"You just keep your spirits up," he told her, as she opened the back door, "that's your job right now. Our Stacy's a fighter and she's not goin' to give up easy. You watch; might take awhile, but she'll likely surprise the doctors yet."

Chapter 15

"Watch it! Coming through!"

Stacy quickly stepped aside as two blue-suited attendants carrying a stretcher hurried past and disappeared through the door she had just exited.

"New arrival." Max told her. "Probably someone in a condition similar to yours." He looked at the door, which had been left ajar. "Excuse me. I need to check what's going on." He trotted back in the direction from which they had come.

Stacy looked anxiously after him.

"Don't worry." Minerva took her arm. "Max will be back soon. In the meantime, let's go this way." She guided Stacy toward the center of an enormous, vaulted room filled with row upon row of desks separated by wide aisles. Looking up, Stacy saw that the entire ceiling was a skylight through which light was pouring, filling the vast space with airy luminosity.

The section of the room toward which they were moving was crowded with people. Most of them were standing in lines that moved slowly past a row of desks set about three-quarters of the way toward the back of the room. Behind the desks sat men and women in green jump suits, busy at what appeared to be computers. One by one, each person in line took a seat in a chair beside one of the desks, where the official in charge engaged him or her in a brief dialogue, typing busily throughout the conversation. At the end of the discussion, an attendant in a blue jumpsuit stationed near the rear of the room stepped forward and led the interviewed person toward a large set of double doors set in the back wall.

These doors were unlike any Stacy had seen since awakening in the temporary unit. All the doors in her room, as well as the one opening into the space where they were now standing, had appeared ordinary, like those with which she was familiar. This massive double portal, however, arched half way toward the distant ceiling, each side wider than her outstretched arms. The doors themselves were huge slabs of a material that glowed like highly polished mahogany, yet exuded a vibrant, welcoming warmth, as if they were alive.

Every inch of their glossy surfaces was intricately embossed with landscapes and figures. Stacy was unable to decide what these carvings depicted, because each time she looked, they seemed to have changed. She began to wonder if the images were somehow moving, shifting positions, as if they, too, were alive. To her surprise, this did not make her feel uneasy; rather, it tapped into a wellspring of wonder she had almost forgotten she possessed and flooded her with an almost overwhelming longing to press herself against the warm, living wood, to push open the doors and pass through them into what lay beyond.

A sudden explosion of noise interrupted. Turning toward the opposite wall, she saw a set of what looked like standard issue double doors burst open, and a large, disorganized mass of brown-skinned people in brightly colored clothing poured into the room. Some were crying, some moaning and holding onto various parts of their bodies or to each other; many were silent and appeared dazed. A small girl with dark braids and a tear-stained face wove her way through the confusion, pulling at each woman she passed, sobbing, "Mama? Mama?"

Several attendants in blue jump suits were attempting to form the group into lines, while a cheerful-looking man in a similar outfit moved through the crowd, patting shoulders and speaking to each one, obviously comforting and reassuring them.

Stacy turned toward Minerva. "Who are all these people? And what is this place?"

"This is the Entry Processing Center and these are new arrivals. To judge from their clothing, I'd say they're from India. They have just lost their physical bodies, probably in a train wreck, and they have come here to be processed."

"Processed! What does that mean?"

"It means that all their information must be taken by a Greeter, who then assigns them to an appropriate recuperation unit. Those whose bodies were badly injured," she indicated an old man clutching a bloody stump where his arm had been, "and who need to recover from the tremendous shock this has caused, will go to what you would consider a hospital recovery unit. Those who are emotionally traumatized will be sent to a unit that specializes in psychological care."

Stacy stared at the old man with the missing arm, who was moaning and rocking from one foot to the other. "You said that everyone here is in his or her spirit body, right?"

Minerva nodded. "That's right."

"Then why does he," she pointed in the man's direction, "look like that? I thought you said the spirit body was perfect."

"It is. But his death was probably so sudden that he doesn't even realize his physical body is gone. He still believes his arm is missing; therefore his spirit body responds with evidence of that injury. It's an ideal illustration of the universal law that what you believe, you receive."

Stacy gazed around the immense space. "Is this where you come when you work here?"

Minerva smiled. "I'm in this room more often than not." Turning away for a moment, she gently pointed the little girl with the braids toward an anxious-looking woman whose dirt-smudged face lit up with relief at the sight of the child.

Stacy frowned. "I still don't understand how you can come and go here without being dead, or in a coma, like I'm supposed to be."

"I'm called when the regular processors find their caseloads excessive. Whenever there's some sort of disaster that results in large numbers of souls arriving Between, it's necessary for them to draw upon the goodwill of people like me, who have the ability to function in both worlds. At those times my physical body is asleep, but the most real, aware part of me is here, working."

Minerva led her to the nearest desk, where the green-suited woman sitting behind it glanced up and smiled, then went back to typing. Seated in a chair beside her was a dazed-looking man with a deep gash across his forehead. After asking his name three times, the woman lifted a small, flat object from the desktop and pressed it briefly against the undamaged part of his forehead. Immediately his picture and name appeared on the screen.

"What is that?" Stacy whispered to Minerva.

The woman at the computer looked up again. "This? It's a mnemometer. It instantly extracts all the data necessary to complete an individual's file. Watch." She pressed a button on the front of the device and instantly the man's life history scrolled across the screen.

"It not only gives us information about the person from birth until the moment of death, but also provides a biography of the True Self and a complete cross-referencing of every lifetime lived."

Stacy was intrigued. "Do you use it for everybody?"

"No, only with those whose stress levels or injuries prevent them from communicating verbally with us."

"But wouldn't it be easier just to get what you need from this little gizmo all the time? Why bother to listen to all that stuff and type it in?"

The woman smiled. "Most people need to talk about what has happened to them. In fact, many of them have to go back over their experiences several times, before they can even begin to let go of the trauma. The sooner they do that, the faster they heal."

She pointed toward a desk closer to the massive double doors at the back, where a young man was quickly waving what looked like a long, slender wand back and forth in front of an older woman's face. The woman sat, unmoving, steadily blinking her eyes. Stacy could faintly hear her describing the train wreck, sobbing over and over, like a litany, "There was a big boom and we all turned upside down. Something heavy fell on me. It was terrible! It was terrible!"

Minerva put her hand on Stacy's arm. "That's Jeremy. On the Earth level, he's a Rapid Eye Technician; he's using the wand to help the woman discharge her terror by blinking it out. He's here the way I am; his physical body is at home, sound asleep."

"This place is amazing!" Stacy gazed around the enormous room. "And the craziest thing is, I understand what everyone is saying. How can I do that? I don't know the Indian language." She looked at Minerva. "I didn't know you did, either."

Minerva shook her head. "As a matter of fact, I don't. But here it doesn't matter. We aren't really speaking with our voices; it just seems that we are. It's actually mind-to-mind communication."

"Oh!" Stacy thought of Max, whose mental conversations she had always taken for granted.

Minerva smiled. "Exactly."

Stacy watched as the last of the train wreck line exited through the huge, carved double doors in the back wall. "What's behind those? Everyone I've seen checked in here is always taken through them. Where do they go?"

Minerva shook her head. "I can answer that in a general way, but until you're ready to leave your body behind permanently, you can't find out for yourself. In fact," her expression seemed a little wistful to Stacy, "I'm not allowed through those doors yet, either."

"So it's a big secret?"

"Not really. They are part of the boundary that divides Between from Home. Only those who have permanently lost their bodies, what you think of as died, are allowed to cross that line."

"Oh." Stacy moved a little away from the back wall. "Maybe I'll hold off awhile on finding out more about that."

Movement near the front of the room caught her attention. An elderly woman in a hospital gown was hovering just inside the entrance. As Stacy watched, she peered out through the large window mounted in the door, took a few steps toward the rows of desks, then, almost as if she were being pulled, moved back toward the door again. After a brief pause, she repeated the same actions.

"What's the matter with her?" Stacy frowned. "Why doesn't she come through with the rest of the people?"

Minerva shook her head. "It may be awhile before she is able to be processed."

"Is she afraid? She looks like she wants to come, but then she changes her mind."

"It's a difficult situation. She's what is referred to as a hold-on."

"What's a hold-on?"

"A person whose physical body is more or less maintaining itself, but whose brain has stopped performing any but the most basic tasks, such as breathing and sleeping. In this woman's case, which is typical, her family can't bring themselves to let go of her, because they love her. They think that her physical self is who she really is and, that when that is gone, she'll be gone forever. They don't realize that they will see her again, when the time is right, and they certainly don't understand that they are keeping her tied to a body whose usefulness has ended. I'm sure they would be distressed if they knew that they are making it impossible for her to move forward into a new life here, even though her old life there is completed."

Stacy watched as the woman again repeated her unsuccessful attempts to move away from the entrance. "The poor thing looks exhausted."

"She is, at least mentally and emotionally." Minerva sighed. "It will take considerable effort on her part to break loose, and she may not be able to bring herself to do that. Because she loves them, freeing herself from their desires would make her feel she was betraying them."

Stacy watched the woman's repeated movements. "What happens if she can't move on?"

"Oh, eventually she will. If nothing else, her body will finally just wear out and let her go. Despite the frustration she is presently experiencing, being stuck like this is not a permanent condition or a disaster."

Minerva gazed around the room filled with lines of souls being checked in. "You soon learn here that there are no permanent conditions, because everything is always in a state of change. No disasters, either. In fact, even events that appear disastrous at the Earth level are actually viewed as simply experience here. And every experience is useful for learning and growth."

"What? Even the really awful stuff?"

"Even that."

Before Stacy could sort out the questions churning in her mind, Minerva turned briskly back toward the desk of the green-suited Greeter with whom they had spoken earlier. "Thank you for letting us observe, Margery."

Looking up, the woman smiled. "You're very welcome, Minerva. Come help us out next time."

"I'll do my best."

Smiling, Minerva took Stacy's arm again. "Well, my dear, you have been allowed to share something very special here, something most people who still have their physical bodies don't often see."

"It certainly has been . . . unusual." Stacy gazed around the vast space. "This place is so huge! It looks like an overgrown version of Grand Central Station."

Minerva nodded. "It looks the way we are seeing it because we are familiar with this appearance and it makes sense to us. Some of the other souls you've watched being processed have a different impression of it. Each one sees what will be most comforting to them at a time when they need all the solace they can find."

Stacy wrinkled her forehead. "So, you're saying that to some people, this place would look different?"

"That's right. For those from small, third-world villages, for example, this room seems much smaller, because there are fewer people in their experience and very few, if any, really large buildings. And they don't see computers. As far as they are concerned, the information is spoken, or taken down by hand. However, it all feeds directly into a communication repository concealed within the desk which, by the way, looks to them like a simple wooden table."

"What about really primitive peoples?"

Minerva smiled. "Ah, for them, this place would seem like a great open desert, a sea shore, a forested area—whatever would make them feel most at home. The Greeters would also appear in forms familiar to them, since they change their appearance to what is appropriate, so that each soul may go through processing as comfortably as possible. Coming here is difficult enough, without the surroundings causing further trauma." She gazed around the room. "As you can see, life here is considerably more versatile than at the physical level."

"That's got to be an understatement!"

"What you might call mind-blowing, isn't it?" Max's voice dropped into her mind.

Stacy jumped, startled by his unexpected reappearance. Beside him stood Herm, still in his handsome young man form.

"Mind-blowing is another understatement!" she told him. "I'm totally confused. I want to believe that this is all just a fantastic dream, but it seems so real!"

Minerva looked at her thoughtfully. "You know, I think we can show you something that will help you understand what has happened. After that, we'll discuss what the next step needs to be."

Stacy shrugged. "Whatever you think will help is OK with me."

Suddenly Minerva held up her hand. Her eyes unfocused as if she were listening to something, then she nodded slightly and sighed. "I'm sorry, my dear, but I won't be able to go with you after all. Max and Herm will accompany you on this trip; I'm afraid I'm needed elsewhere." She seemed to flow backward. At the same time, Max and Herm stepped forward and positioned themselves on either side of Stacy.

🐾 🐾 🐾 Between 🐾 🐾 🐾

"Wait!" Stacy put out her hand, but Minerva and the Entry Processing Center were already shimmering, as if she were seeing them through heat waves on a summer day. She opened her mouth to protest further, but the room tilted and disappeared in a flash of light.

Chapter 16

Arthur Craddock stood, hesitating, where the invisible wall had always turned him back. Like the rest of his formerly desolate prison, the area surrounding this unseen boundary had altered almost beyond recognition; only the large pile of stones marking the perimeter was still familiar. This rocky formation had been barren, except for a small, muddy puddle caused by moisture oozing down the face of the middle boulder. Now a spring gushing from between the two largest outcrops fed a deep, sparkling pool, and velvety moss covered the sloping shoulders of the rocks.

Arthur had no interest in admiring the scenery. His focus was, as it had always been, single and unswerving—find Stacy Addison. What he would do when he located her had not yet entered the equation; that would reveal itself when the time was right. All that mattered now was the next step, the one that would take him past the barrier that had previously blocked him. He was torn between eagerness to get on with his pursuit and fear that, despite the changes everywhere else, the wall might still be there.

He extended his foot a little, then a little more. The invisible block was gone! There was nothing to prevent him from leaving. Unconsciously clenching his jaw, he took a long step forward, and a tension he had not realized was constricting him melted away. Stretching with amazement and relief, he looked around. His former prison had disappeared. He was now standing at the edge of a plain blanketed with knee-high grass that stretched to the horizon in every direction, an ocean of green, undulating in a ceaseless breeze.

His attention was distracted by a movement on his left. A short distance away, a woman was walking toward him along a narrow path through the waving grass. Feeling certain that neither she nor the path had been there a moment ago, he shaded his eyes in an attempt to see her better, but the brightness emanating from her face and clothing made this difficult. She moved closer to him.

"Hello, Arthur." Her voice sounded familiar.

Squinting, he tried to see through the brilliance that surrounded her.

"Don't you know me?" As she stepped nearer, her features stabilized and became clear.

"Charlotte!" For an instant, the sight of her familiar face and form comforted and warmed him. He took a step toward her, but even as her name left his lips, everything came flooding back—who she was, who he had been, what had happened. He saw her again as he had last seen her, body contorted in a grand mal seizure, arms and legs thrashing in the closeness of the town car's passenger seat. He could almost taste the shock of fear that had shot through him as he struggled, at eighty miles an hour, to keep the car on the expressway.

He remembered the sick drop of his stomach as he felt the wheels leave the road, skidding across the shoulder and sliding toward the dip between it and the open land beyond. For an instant he had regained control; then her outflung arm caught him across the face and the car veered sharply. Almost as if in slow motion, the earth rose up to meet them and they slid into the dip and began to roll.

Fragments of memory flashed through his mind: the offer from St. Olaf's—a position worthy of his education and talents, finally within his reach; Charlotte, babbling that she had been healed, that she no longer needed her medication; his anger at her gullible willingness to let some quack's fakery take precedence over the legitimate medicine to which he had devoted the last twenty years of his life; her nervous reassurance that the bottle of Dilantin was full because it had just been refilled, that she had taken the last dose of the old prescription the previous day.

With the irrefutable finality of a gun fired point-blank, a final, horrifying realization exploded in his mind: he was dead. He and Charlotte had not survived the accident. Not only was his life gone, but also his chance to at last receive the respect and salary he deserved, all because of a goddamned charlatan named Stacy Addison! And here Charlotte stood, clothed in light, her vapid face soft and ethereal, sweetly smiling at him. It made him want to puke.

"Come Home with me, Arthur." She stretched out her arms. "Now that you've set yourself free, you can come Home."

Rage roared through him again and, face twisting, he raised his fist. "Get away from me, Charlotte! Take your goddamned sanctimonious pap and get out of here."

Her sweet expression shifted toward anxiety. "You can't mean that."

He took a step toward her. "Oh, I mean it," he said softly. He moved another step closer. "I don't know if I can hurt you the way you are now, but I'm more than willing to try, you traitorous bitch." The last words slid out of his mouth in a hiss.

She lowered her arms, shock and disappointment flowing across her open countenance. For a moment, she turned her head as if listening to something he could not hear. Then she looked back at him with an expression of regret.

"I'm sorry, Arthur. I'm sorry I lied to you, I'm sorry about the accident. Most of all, I'm sorry that you refuse to let go of your anger." Her eyes pleaded with him. "You mustn't blame Stacy Addison for what happened; she didn't tell me to stop taking my medicine—that was my decision. It was my fault that I had the seizure, not hers." She held out her arms to him again. "Let your anger go, Arthur, let it go before it destroys you. Come Home with me; you can't imagine how beautiful it is there."

Bending down, Arthur Craddock scooped up a fistful of loose rocks from the side of the path. With a snarl more animal than human, he hurled them at his wife. She flung up her arms protectively, and although he saw the missiles pass through her, she doubled up, as if in pain.

"Get out!" he screamed. "Leave me alone!" Falling to his knees, he scrabbled in the dirt, frantically flinging every bit of solid matter he could lay his hands on. Flecks of foam spilled from the corners of his mouth and he began to sob, choking, until he sank face down onto the path, struggling to recover control. Finally he dragged himself to his knees again and looked at the place where Charlotte had been standing.

She was gone.

Wiping his mouth with the back of his hand, he staggered to his feet. Before him stretched the seemingly endless expanse of knee-high grass, still swaying to the rhythm of the shifting breeze. As he stared at the spot where she had stood, he was suddenly assailed by a sense of relationship between her disappearance and his recent escape from his former prison. The voice within him whispered, *Find out. Find out what that is.* The intensity of the words caused him to immediately drop down in the grass, close his eyes, and apply the discipline trained into him in medical school.

First he examined, then rejected, the idea that the link he sought could be found in his act of throwing rocks and debris at Charlotte. Nothing of that nature had taken place in the desolate area from which he had recently found release; in fact, he had indulged in very little physical activity there. Yet he knew with a certainty he could not explain, that there was a point where his sudden release from that place intersected with whatever had caused Charlotte's disappearance. He also understood that discovering this connection was vitally important to any further success in reaching his goal of finding Stacy Addison.

There was something that Charlotte had said, something . . . his eyes popped open. "Now that you've set yourself free, you can come home." That was it! Not, "now that you're free", but "now that you've set yourself free." That statement indicated that the change that had taken place in his former prison was the result of something he had done. Closing his eyes again, Arthur began to probe deeper in his memory for what he was missing.

He recalled the certainty of his feeling that the moment of his release had been somehow connected to the instant when he learned that Stacy Addison was finally where he could reach her. But what had he done that would connect that revelation with him setting himself free? And how could he link that to Charlotte's disappearance? What action had he taken both times that tied these two events together?

And all at once, he knew. He could not find connecting physical actions, but both times he had experienced intense mental reactions. The first time, his response had been exultation because he could now carry out his determination to make Stacy Addison pay for her sins; the second time, it had been resentment and rage because of Charlotte's duplicity, resulting in his intense desire to make her go away. Two extremes, each producing the same result: the carrying through of his deeply felt intention.

A statement from a long-forgotten medical school lecture surfaced in his mind. Something about the healer's intent being as important as the medicine or therapy prescribed. Then he had barely given the concept lip service; not until this moment had he realized the stunning depth of power it implied. *He* had been responsible for the seemingly incomprehensible transformation of his surroundings from wasteland to Eden. It was *his* focus on Charlotte's departure that had brought about the desired result.

Raising his arms above his head, he shook his fists and shouted, "Yes! Yes! Yes!" He leaped and cavorted, laughing almost hysterically. Finally, letting his arms drop, he stood perfectly still. Even though he had made the connection, he had not yet located Stacy Addison. He did not even know what she looked like.

The voice spoke again inside his head: *That doesn't matter.* A burst of understanding and confidence surged through him and he reached out with his mind, seeking and instantly finding Charlotte. Swiftly dipping into her memory, he located the moment of her supposed healing. Next to Charlotte, hands on her head, stood a young woman with the face of a Botticelli angel and a blazing halo of coppery curls. She took her hands away from Charlotte's head and her dark, luminous eyes seemed to look directly into his. Arthur's lips stretched back in the smile of a hunter who had just sighted his prey. He had her!

Focusing intensely on Stacy Addison's flawless face, he locked in his intention to be where she was. A moment later, the wind ruffled an empty prairie, still whispering to the long grass as it passed.

Arthur Craddock was gone, as if he had never been there.

Chapter 17

Afternoon shadows were stretching across the back yard as Jenn closed the kitchen door behind David and Katie. Sunday dinners at the Sinclair house had been a tradition since before Stacy's birth, but this afternoon's gathering had been solemn and short. Glynis left soon after the meal to catch up on bookkeeping at the store, and Minerva only stayed long enough to help Jenn clear the table. David and Katie remained behind, playing a half-hearted game of Uno, but then agreed that they, too, needed to get home. Everyone seemed caught up in his or her own individual space, overlapping long enough to share the meal Jenn had prepared, then shifting back again into their own separate worlds of anxiety and concern.

Jenn started a fresh pot of coffee for herself and Rudy, who was on his back halfway under the kitchen sink, tinkering with her increasingly cranky disposal. Rudy had helped her with household problems ever since her husband, James, had died only two years after their wedding. Although Jenn rarely asked for his help, Rudy seemed to know when she needed him, showing up with his tool box at the back door to assist her when the plumbing backed up, gutters clogged, or heavy work needed to be done.

Many years ago he had cut a passageway through the hedge between the Sinclair and Steele properties, so that Stacy and Glynis could run back and forth to play. He continued to keep that corridor open, although he used it only when prompted by Jenn's necessity. Always self-effacing, Rudy had withdrawn even more deeply into himself after the death of his parents. He still attended family dinners at Jenn's when invited, especially if Glynis would be there, but he never stayed long and never came just to visit. And he always behaved as if he considered Jenn simply a friend and neighbor.

🐾 🐾 🐾 Between 🐾 🐾 🐾

Her heart ached for his loneliness—and for her own. It would be thirty-one years next month since James's death; she was fifty-five years old and still alone. About six months ago, she had finally realized why she couldn't bring herself to make a commitment to any of the men she occasionally dated—she was in love with Rudy Steele.

She heard him swearing under his breath as he struggled with the disposal. If only she had some idea of his true feelings! Sometimes she caught him watching her with a look in his eyes she found difficult to read, a look she thought—she hoped—was more than just neighborly, but she could not be sure. She wanted to hold him close, to stroke his graying blond curls, to make him understand what a wonderful person he was. She yearned for him to hold her and comfort her; but could not bring herself to intrude on his privacy. If he did not reciprocate her feelings, the wonderful friendship they had shared for so long might be destroyed, and she could not bear the thought of that.

Sighing, she poured two mugs of steaming coffee, opened a tin of Rudy's favorite pecan cookies, and called to him that it was time to take a break.

§

The disposal was working smoothly and dusk had settled itself like a blanket over the back yard, as Rudy strode toward the opening in the hedge. He pushed through it, then turned back, stepping to one side so he could see, but not be seen. Jenn was still on the back porch, standing in the same place she had stood when she told him goodbye.

It was not the first time he had found himself here, at the edge of the cut. The idea of spying didn't set well with him, but once in awhile, when he would hear Jenn moving about on the porch or in the yard, he could not resist soaking up her presence and beauty in the only way he had ever felt was possible.

He had loved Jennifer Sinclair from the moment he'd laid eyes on her, over thirty years ago. From the beginning, she had been beyond his reach—first, as the bride of his best friend, James; and after James's death, as his grieving widow. Since then she had become a neighbor and a friend. And always, she was the only woman he had ever cared about, except for his mother. At times he felt seized by an urge to open his heart to her, to tell her what she meant to him. But if he did and she laughed, or worse, pitied him, he would not be able to stand it.

Closing his eyes, he bowed his head. He wasn't sure whether or not there was a God; if there was, He didn't, as far as Rudy could see, care much about humankind. Nevertheless, just in case, he whispered a prayer.

"Please bring someone good to love her like she deserves."

He longed, as he always had, to be that someone, but he knew she was out of his reach. Might as well hanker after the moon.

Chapter 18

The brilliance surrounding Stacy swelled to supernova proportions, then began to wane into a cool, muted glow. As her eyes adjusted, she saw that she was in a small room with pale green walls and a tile floor of darker green. Most of the space was occupied by a bed flanked by an assortment of IV poles and monitors of various kinds. Except for a faint whishing sound, the room was wrapped in silence.

The bed itself was like a pristine snowfield; the only spot of color was the face on the white pillow. Stacy felt certain the features were female, despite the red, misshapen nose and the single bruised eye that was visible. Gauze hid the right side of the woman's face, and her head was so wrapped in bandages that she looked like a nun sleeping in her wimple. What could be seen of her chin had a wide abrasion all the way across it. Extending from her mouth was a long, ribbed tube that was connected to the machine from which the whishing sound emanated. A ventilator. Whoever this was must really be in bad shape.

Stacy was startled to feel movement beside her. Max chirruped softly and leaned against her right knee and, an instant later, the air shimmered and Herm materialized on her other side. Feeling a little less vulnerable, Stacy allowed her curiosity to surface. "What is this place—the hospital wing of the temporary facility?"

Herm looked around the room. "Not exactly."

"What does that mean?"

"It means this is, indeed, a hospital room, but not the hospital you assume it is."

Max, who had been sniffing around the corners of the room, looked over at them. "Hang on a minute, you two." He padded back to where they were standing. "There's something funny about this place. I think we need to finish what we came to do and get out of here."

🐾 🐾 🐾 Between 🐾 🐾 🐾

Stacy was barely listening to him. There was something about the bed and its occupant that intrigued her. Picking her way over cords and around poles, she cautiously approached the still figure under the covers.

Max followed her. "Don't worry, you can't disturb her—or anything else." He walked toward the ventilator. "Watch this!" Leaping toward the machine, he disappeared into it—first his head, followed by his abdomen, hind quarters, and long, ringed tail. A moment later he emerged in the same order on the other side. "See? No problem."

Stacy stared at him, her eyes wide. "How did you do that?"

"It's easy." Sauntering back, he looked up at her. "You can do it, too, if you want to." When she continued to stare at him, he butted her legs gently. "Go on. It's an interesting experience."

"I thought you said we needed to hurry."

"We do, but it's a perfect opportunity to learn for yourself what's possible."

Herm, who had been examining the room's various mechanisms, looked up. "He's right; any of us can walk through anything in this room. Our atoms don't vibrate at the same rate as those of objects on this level of existence, so we can slip through the empty spaces with no trouble at all."

When Stacy still did not respond, he shrugged. "Maybe," he said to Max, "she's what the people of this planet refer to as a chicken."

Stacy frowned at him. "I am not chicken! I just have to get used to being different from the way I've always thought of myself." Slowly extending her right arm, she took a hesitant step toward the ventilator. She looked over at Herm, who grinned and made 'go ahead' motions with his hands. Clenching her teeth, she turned back and walked straight toward the machine.

Bracing herself for the cold solidity of metal, she was amazed to find her hand slipping into something dense and slightly warm. Her fingers disappeared completely into the box, but she could feel them tingling, as if caught in an electrical field. Yanking her hand back out, she was relieved to see it still attached to her arm. After a moment, she inserted it into the ventilator again and finally pushed her arm in all the way up to her shoulder, watching with fascination as her fingers appeared on the other side.

"That is so weird!" Pulling her arm back out, she examined it carefully, shaking her hand a little to rid it of the tingling feeling. "I can't believe I just did that!"

Herm smiled approvingly. "Definitely not a chicken."

Max was glancing around the room again. "Something about this place bothers me. We really do need to take care of business and leave."

Stacy looked again at the figure on the bed. "Who is that, anyway? She seems vaguely familiar."

"Don't you recognize her?"

Moving closer, she scrutinized what she could see of the woman's face. A cold feeling began to settle in her stomach, as if she had swallowed a cup of ice cubes. "Max," she whispered, "please tell me this isn't who I think it is."

"I'm not able to do that, Stacy." Max's voice had a sympathetic tinge. "Sorry."

"Oh, my God!" Stacy stared at the bruised and swollen face. "That can't be me; please tell me that's not me!" She raised her eyes toward the ceiling. "Please, please, somebody wake me up!" Sinking to her knees, she wrapped her arms over her midriff and rocked back and forth, her stomach churning at the thought of what might lie hidden under the snowy gauze covering the right side of the woman's face.

A click sounded behind her. The door was being opened! The realization yanked her back into the present and, jumping to her feet, she scanned the room frantically for a place to hide.

"Not necessary!" Max's voice dropped into her mind. "No one can see you. Just stay where you are."

Trembling, Stacy watched as David stepped into the room. At the sight of him, the most intense longing she had ever experienced flooded her. She had always known that she loved him, but until this moment that knowledge had never so completely permeated her awareness. She wanted to touch him, to hold him. She wanted to tell him she was sorry she'd said things that hurt him. Had she been promised that she could be with him again if she traded the beauty she had trusted for thirty years for whatever her bandages concealed, she would have paid that price without hesitation.

She was, however, presented no such offer, and the moment passed. She watched as David checked the IV bags and examined the ventilator, then carefully lifted the limp arm of the woman in the bed from under the covers. Pulling a chair over, he sat down and began massaging her fingers.

Moving closer, Stacy put a tentative hand on his shoulder, watching with horror as it disappeared inside his body. Jerking it back out, she shot Max an anguished look.

"I've got to let him know I'm here!" Balling both her hands into fists, she began to chew her lower lip. "I don't know what to do!"

Max's voice was calm. "Simply do what you just did."

"What? Stick my hand in his shoulder again?"

"Of course not. Use that same principal to get back inside your body."

"Just push myself in? Can I really do that?" She moved closer to the bed, then stepped back as David reached out and gently touched the woman's unbandaged cheek.

"Oh, Stace," he said softly, "I'm sorry I was such a horse's ass. I never should have said what I did." He lifted the unresponsive hand to his cheek. "Please come back. I miss you; I need you. Katie needs you."

He was actually apologizing! Tears pricked her eyes. She had to get back into her body, had to let him know she was here!

"Go on, then!" Max butted the backs of her legs and she stumbled forward.

Stepping carefully around David, Stacy fixed her eyes on the white-swathed figure under the covers. "How do I do this?"

"You use thought energy." Max moved up to stand beside her. "That's how we got here from the Entry Processing Center."

"We did? I didn't think about coming here."

"No, but Herm and I did. And we focused on bringing you with us."

Stacy looked from him to Herm, who was now standing on the other side of the bed. "I'm not sure I'm wild about the idea of you two thinking me places, but right now I don't care. Just help me get in!"

The corners of Max's mouth twitched. "All right. Focus on your body. Concentrate on feeling yourself back inside it."

"That's it?"

"That's it. Focus. Imagine that you are in your body again; remember how it feels to be there."

With all the intensity she could muster, Stacy willed herself to move into the motionless form on the bed. Nothing happened.

"Ease up." Max's voice sounded in her head. "Don't want it so much; you're blocking yourself."

Stacy frowned. "How can I not want it? I've got to get into my body before David leaves!"

"Well, actually, you don't. If you can't get in now, there will be another opportunity. Besides," Max fixed his yellow eyes on her, "the more intensely you crave something, the more you push it away from you."

"What kind of double talk is that?"

"No double talk—just fact. The intensity of your craving acts like a propelling force, always pushing what you want just out of reach. It's sort of like the old carrot-on-the-stick-in-front-of-the-donkey thing."

"That's ridiculous! Everyone knows you have to really want something to get it. And I—oh, Max!" She broke off as David shifted in the chair. "He's getting up; he's going to leave! Help me, please help me get in!"

Max glanced across the bed at Herm, who nodded. "All right. Just remember what it feels like to be in your body, focus on how it would feel to be there right now. Concentrate. Herm and I will help think you in."

Clenching her fists, Stacy stared at the white-clad figure on the bed, then forced herself to relax. She remembered how it felt to have a mattress under her, how it must feel to be swathed in blankets and bandages, how wonderful it would be to have David holding her hand.

Without warning, the room went dark. Startled, she started to reach down, to see if Max was still sitting beside her knee, and was even more surprised to find that she could not move. A gigantic mass seemed to be weighing her down, holding her prisoner. She struggled with every ounce of energy she could summon, but could not even open her eyes. *What is this? What's happening?*

She became aware of a warm hand holding hers. David! She must have made it back into her body. She struggled to open her mouth, to tell him that she was here, but her muscles refused to obey. The whishing of the ventilator filled her head and she could feel her chest rising and falling automatically, as the machine forced air into her lungs. The sensation brought home to her with a rush how completely helpless she was.

Hands gently gripped her right arm and lifted it. Stacy made an intense effort to move her fingers, but the muscles would not respond.

🐾 🐾 🐾 **Between** 🐾 🐾 🐾

The hands holding her arm carefully bent it at the elbow, laid it down, and straightened it out. She could feel the coolness of a sheet against her skin, then a slight pressure on her hand, as if someone were squeezing her fingers.

"I'll be back before long, sweetheart," David's voice sounded tender. She could feel the top sheet, weighted by the blanket, being pulled up to her shoulders.

He was leaving! She was back in her body and he didn't know! She tried frantically to open her eyes, but everything remained black. In a moment, he would be gone, leaving her trapped, frozen in darkness, unable to move, unable to see or speak, at the mercy of whatever came along. Terror rushed through her. Perhaps she was not in a coma, after all; perhaps she was dead, and this was hell!

Panic flooded her. She couldn't do this; she had to get out! Screaming soundlessly for Max and Herm to help, she strained to lift her head, to move her fingers—anything—but it was hopeless. The darkness swelled against her from every side, threatening to engulf and obliterate her.

"Stacy!" Max's voice dropped into her mind. She could barely hear him over the pounding of her heart. "Stacy! Calm yourself. We're going to get you out, but we can't do it if you don't calm down."

She thrust the panic away with iron determination. Just be calm, she told herself. Just be calm, and you'll be able to get out. Just do what Max said—be calm. Calm. As she repeated the word over and over, the internal noise gradually lessened. Relief washed over her as she sensed Max's comforting presence in the darkness, joined a moment later by Herm's vibrant energy.

"Just imagine your atoms and molecules temporarily attaching themselves to ours." Max's voice was soothing. "Concentrate. That's good. Now, give permission for us to lift you out. Good. Now, think about yourself moving out of this body, back into the room, to the place you were standing before we thought you in."

Stacy found herself trembling beside the bed. She was aware of the comforting softness of Max's fur, as he rubbed his head against her legs, then a pair of strong arms picked her up. Leaning her head against the muscular chest to which the arms were attached, she gratefully filled her awareness with the glow of the lamp above the hospital bed. Gazing up at the face above her, she saw that it belonged to Herm.

🐾 🐾 🐾 Between 🐾 🐾 🐾

She was vaguely aware of Max saying, "There's definitely a negative presence in this room. We need to get Stacy out of here, now!"

Then the brightness of the light intensified into a swirling brilliance, and the room tilted and disappeared.

Chapter 19

Arthur Craddock's pursuit of Stacy Addison had taken an unexpected turn. Exhilarated by the understanding that his thoughts could control his environment, he had located her image in Charlotte's memory and confidently homed in on her energy pattern. She should now be, if not in front of him, at least within easy reach. Yet he found himself alone in what appeared to be an intensive care cubicle of a hospital.

He examined his surroundings closely. The room was a duplicate of numerous similar units he had visited in the course of his medical duties. The machines, the IV poles, the body in the bed—all were routinely familiar. The only mystery was Stacy Addison's absence.

The door opened to admit a dark-haired young nurse carrying a fresh bag of intravenous solution. She moved toward the bed, ignoring him, and he stepped deliberately into her path, bracing himself as she approached. She walked right through him, creating a not unpleasant prickling sensation, and he watched her unhook the empty bag of saline and fasten the full one in its place.

Satisfied that she was unaware of his presence, he lost interest in her and approached the bed. What little was visible of its occupant certainly bore no resemblance to the angelic countenance he had encountered in Charlotte's memory. Arthur felt confused.

His focus was distracted by a shimmering, like heat waves, near the bed. *Hide yourself!* the voice in his mind commanded, and he instantly scanned the room for a place that would allow him to see without being seen.

In here! ordered the voice. A strong impulse backed him toward the wall behind him. A moment later he found himself inside its structure. There was a peculiar sensation of disorientation as his atoms streamed into the spaces between the atoms that composed the wall. Then his new molecular configuration stabilized and his sense of identity returned, allowing him to focus on the phenomenon that had driven him into this unexpected refuge.

As he watched, the rippling energy resolved itself into two separate figures. One was, surprisingly, a black-and-white cat; the other was Stacy Addison. Triumph surged through Arthur Craddock. His guidance had not failed him; it had, instead, delivered him to the very place he wanted to be and had seen to it that he arrived early enough to be able to observe the object of his search without being noticed.

A moment later a muscular young man in a short, belted garment materialized next to Stacy. Although Arthur was becoming accustomed to the fact that people and objects now often appeared, disappeared or changed with unaccountable suddenness, he was surprised to find such unlikely companions accompanying his quarry. He had no idea of the extent of their willingness or ability to protect her, but their presence indicated that any action against her on his part might well have to take them into account.

This knowledge did not discourage him. Instead, it heightened his excitement, adding a delicious dimension of danger to the accomplishment of his goal. He watched as the cat, then Stacy, played hide and seek with the ventilator, an exercise which greatly interested him.

Before Arthur could decide what he should do, the door to the hall opened. A tall, dark-haired man entered the room and pulled a chair over beside the bed, oblivious of the fact that he was being watched by four pairs of eyes. Lifting the arm of the person in the bed from under the covers, he took the limp hand in his.

"Oh, Stace," he said softly, "I'm sorry I was such a horse's ass." When there was no response, he murmured something else, lifted the hand to his cheek and continued, "Please come back. I miss you; I need you. Katie needs you."

"Stace." The man had called the person in the bed "Stace." The information slid into a slot in Arthur Craddock's mind, producing an explanation for behaviors he had so far failed to understand: Stacy Addison and her entourage were here because it was her body in that bed! She must have been in some kind of accident.

Her body was obviously still alive, but she had suffered a serious head trauma, given the amount of bandages and the way they were

❦ ❦ ❦ Between ❦ ❦ ❦

wrapped. She, herself, was not in her body—that was why he had finally been able to locate her. He frowned. If she found a way to get back into her body, she might escape him; there was no certainty, at least not yet, that his mental influence extended to control over physical objects.

He gritted his teeth; he couldn't lose her now, not when he had finally found her! Yet without further information, he was unable to act without creating repercussions that might well destroy any chance of revenge. Certainly he did not dare reveal his presence.

The man sitting in the chair leaned forward and gently touched Stacy's pale cheek. As he did so, a gold band on the third finger of his left hand glinted in the light shining over the head of the bed. This must be her husband! Arthur had not thought of his enemy as a person, especially one with a family. He clenched his jaw. He couldn't afford to let such considerations weaken his resolve. The possibility of Charlotte possessing a family had certainly not influenced Stacy Addison's decision to practice her quackery!

The enormity of Stacy's offense, combined with the sight of her husband's wedding band, brought forcibly to Arthur's mind the memory of another gold ring. This one had adorned the finger of a fellow student waving a small stack of prescriptions he had intercepted on their way to a source outside the medical school. The signature on each of them was just legible enough for Arthur Craddock's name to be decipherable. No amount of persuasion had been able to compel the sanctimonious little twit to relinquish his incriminating prize. He had, in fact, presented it to the medical school's administrator that very day, two months before graduation.

The administrator, well aware that writing illegal prescriptions to be sold on the street was punishable by expulsion from school, was forced into a difficult position. The seriousness of the situation demanded punitive action, but he also knew on which side his fund-raising bread was buttered—the money with which Arthur Craddock's father and grandfather supported their alma mater could not be jeopardized. He had taken the dilemma directly to the university president, who had presented it to the ethics committee.

After a short discussion, the committee had decided that, although Arthur had been allowed to escape the fires of several minor offenses with only minimal scorch marks, they could not permit this violation of the rules to be glossed over. He had received a harsh and humiliating rebuke, and the incident had been entered into his permanent records.

It had taken fifteen years to overcome that stigma; fifteen years of boot-licking, of following the orders of inferior supervisors and administrators, before he had been offered a position worthy of his abilities.

And Stacy Addison's interference had snatched it out of his grasp! Even the loss of his life paled beside the incredible affront of being cheated out of what was rightfully his. His rage flared and expanded into a red fog that clouded his vision.

The voice in his mind spoke sharply. *Stop! It is now time for you to control your anger. Clear your mind. See the possibilities.*

Arthur Craddock made an intense effort to reclaim himself. The voice was right. He had allowed the rage free rein for an unmeasured time; now he must relegate it to the status of servant, and take his place as master. *Pay attention!* he told himself. *The guidance would not have brought you here, just to be disappointed. There must be something you're supposed to see or hear, something you can learn only as an observer.*

He watched Stacy try to attract the attention of her husband, who was obviously unaware of her presence. Finally, she turned to the cat and actually appeared to be communicating with the animal; then she closed her eyes and disappeared.

Startled, Arthur continued to watch the cat and the muscular young man. They fixed their attention on the blanket-covered body in the bed and seemed to barely notice when Stacy's husband left the room. Soon after his departure, Stacy reappeared in a state of near collapse.

The young man scooped Stacy up in his arms before she could fall. He nodded to the cat, who carefully scrutinized the room again, his gaze resting briefly on the wall concealing Arthur before moving on. A moment later the trio disappeared in a flash of light.

Arthur Craddock blinked. Now what? *First things first*, his inner voice responded. *First, take charge of your emotions; then take the next step.*

Aware that he could do nothing more where he was, Arthur focused on divorcing his atoms from those of the wall. He struggled briefly with the temptation to see if he could further damage Stacy's untenanted body, but almost instantly rejected that as unworthy of his ingenuity. She had destroyed his life, both figuratively and literally, and he was going to see that she paid for that. But there were too many creative ways to make her suffer for him to waste his abilities on crassness.

The fact that she had disappeared did not disturb him. He had found her once; he would find her again. As he savored this prospect, a slow smile snaked across his face. He would return to the empty, windblown prairie where he had met Charlotte. There, in undisturbed consultation with his guiding voice, he would work out the perfect revenge. Still smiling, he, too, disappeared.

Chapter 20

"'Nerva?" Katie looked up from the math problem with which she had been struggling.

"What is it, Katie?" Minerva stood at the kitchen counter, stirring eggs and milk into the dry ingredients for a spice cake, a mauve flowered apron shielding her purple blouse and skirt from any errant splashes of batter.

Katie liked the fact that Minerva never called her "sweetie," or "pumpkin," or some other pet name, the way everyone else did. She knew that, with Minerva, the use of her name was a sign of respect, of acknowledgment of her as a person, not just as a child. She also liked knowing that Minerva always answered her questions as completely as possible, instead of filtering information to make her feel better.

"Where's Mommy?"

Minerva stopped stirring. Removing the wooden spoon from the bowl, she offered it to Katie, who ran her tongue slowly across its surface, making a wavy track through the cinnamony coating. Next she poured the batter into an oiled pan, slid it into the hot oven, and set the timer for twenty minutes.

"I suppose I could tell you she's in the hospital, but I don't think that's what you're asking me, is it?"

Katie shook her head.

Minerva pulled out the chair next to Katie's from under the small, round table. "Excuse me," she said to Max, who had been dozing there. Picking him up, she sat down and resettled him on her lap. "If I tell you the truth, will you promise not to share it with anyone just yet?"

Katie nodded. "I promise." She made an 'X' on her chest with the second finger of her right hand. "Cross my heart!"

Minerva looked at Katie and sighed. "I'll explain the best I can."

She took the little girl's hand in hers. "You know that your mother's body is in a coma."

Katie nodded again. "She just lies there and can't do anything." The memory of the strange, silent woman in the bed made the cinnamon taste in her mouth seem a little bitter.

Minerva gently squeezed Katie's hand. "Being in a coma means that her body and her spirit, her true self, are not working together the way they usually do. Sometimes, when there has been an accident, the spirit can be inside the body, but it can't use the brain to control the muscles that open the eyes, or allow the body to talk, or eat, or move. Part of the reason for that is because the doctors often give the person's body drugs that paralyze it, make it so it can't move around, so that it can rest better and heal more quickly."

Katie frowned anxiously. "Is Mommy stuck in her body like that?" She shivered. That would be awfully scary! I hope she isn't stuck like that."

Minerva shook her head. "Don't worry. She was given the drugs, but she isn't stuck inside her body."

Katie released a breath she hadn't realized she had been holding. "That's good!" Her forehead wrinkled more deeply. "But where is she, then?"

"She's in a place where people go when they are temporarily out of their physical bodies. It's called 'Between,' because it is in between this world and the next one."

"Is she there all by herself?"

"No, she's not alone. Max is often with her; he goes when his physical body is asleep. Sometimes, I'm able to be there, too. And there are other people who are helping her and looking after her."

Katie regarded her with interest. "Do you leave your body here asleep, like Max, when you visit Mommy?"

Minerva nodded. "Yes, I do."

A tingle of excitement buzzed through Katie. "Can I do that, too? Can I go be with Mommy when I'm asleep?" She looked hopefully at Minerva. "Can I, 'Nerva?"

"Perhaps, but we'll have to check to see if that's permitted."

Max stretched and leaped lightly to the floor. Looking from Katie to Minerva, he said, "I'll take care of that. I have to tend to some other business first, but I'll let you know what I find out as soon as I can."

Padding off toward the living room, he jumped up on the sofa, circled three times, then curled up, tail over his nose, and promptly went to sleep.

Katie watched, fascinated. "Is he going Between now?"

Minerva nodded. "He is."

"Why do people—and cats—have to be asleep to go there?"

"No one can go Between while they are awake here, because their physical bodies are too dense to function there." Minerva rubbed the side of her nose. "Do you understand what dense means?"

Katie shook her head.

"It means that the bodies we have here, in this world, are sort of," she closed her eyes for a moment, "well, I guess you could say thick. Thick and heavy. And because of that, they aren't able to interact with people and objects that are not so dense, so thick and heavy."

"Sort of like if I sat on a ping pong ball, I would squash it?"

Minerva rubbed her nose again. "Not exactly. It's more like . . . well, like a balloon, maybe. A balloon is a bag made out of rubber, isn't it?"

"I guess so." Katie thought for a moment. "Yeah, that's what it is—a rubber bag."

"All right." Minerva smiled at her. "If I want that rubber bag to be able to float up on the ceiling, I have to fill it with something that will allow it to do that, don't I?"

Katie nodded.

"If I fill it with water, will it float?"

Katie chuckled. "That's silly. Of course not!"

"What if I fill it with helium?"

"That's easy. Helium's the stuff that came in those big bottles at Jamie's birthday party. Her daddy was squirting it into balloons and giving them to all the kids. It made the balloons so light that you had to hold them really tight, so they didn't float off."

"That's right. Being in your physical body is very much like being a balloon filled with water. You're so heavy, so dense, you can't float around here, or go Between. But if you are in your spirit body, you're like a balloon filled with helium. You can go Between, you can float around and go places and do things you can't possibly do when you're tied to your physical body."

Katie frowned. "So, why do we have physical bodies? Wouldn't everyone be happier without them?"

🐾 🐾 🐾 **Between** 🐾 🐾 🐾

Reaching over, Minerva gently tugged one of Katie's sandy braids. "I suppose we would, but we couldn't be here, on Earth, without them. And if we weren't here, we wouldn't be able to learn the lessons we've come to learn." A bell on the stove dinged and she pushed back her chair and stood up. "And there are nice things here, too. For example, if you didn't have your physical body, you wouldn't be able to eat the spice cake I'm going to take out of the oven right now."

Katie uncrossed her legs and jumped to her feet. "Can I test it? Let me test it!"

Smiling, Minerva crossed to the cupboard, took out a long bamboo skewer and handed it to the little girl. Opening the oven door, she pulled the cake out far enough for Katie to stick the sharp end of the skewer into its center. When the tester came out clean, Minerva lifted the pan out of the oven and set it on a cooling rack.

Sniffing the delicious scents of cinnamon and nutmeg, Katie gazed expectantly up at Minerva. "Max always says cake is at its very best when it's hot."

Smiling, Minerva opened the top drawer and pulled out a wedge-shaped cutter. "I'm sure that Max, being an authority on cakes, must be right." Carefully removing a steaming slice from the pan, she laid it on a waiting plate and handed it to Katie with a small fork. "Just don't blame me, if you scorch your tongue."

Katie slid the plate onto the table and sat down again. Stabbing a small piece of hot cake with her fork, she waved it under her nose, savoring the delectable aroma, then looked up at Minerva. "I bet nobody in that Between place can bake like you!"

"Thank you." Minerva smiled. "When you finish eating, I think we should follow Max's example and take a short nap. That will make the time pass faster, until he returns with his news."

"OK." Katie examined the bit of cake on her fork again. "I do want to go see Mommy, but for now I like being in my physical body." Smiling happily, she popped the morsel into her mouth.

Chapter 21

Stacy found it difficult to lose the sense of whirling through a darkness punctuated by bursts of light so brilliant that she had to squeeze her eyes tightly shut for fear of being blinded. She could no longer feel Herm's strong arms holding her safe, and the chilling memory of being trapped in the midnight prison of her body began to creep into her mind.

What if something had gone wrong? What if she had somehow gone back into her body and was caught there? Her chest constricted with terror, as suffocating darkness pressed in from all sides. *Stop it!* she told herself. *Your eyes are closed, that's why it's dark. Remember what Max said. Be calm, just be calm.*

As the panic gradually receded, she realized that she was lying against something solid, something much firmer than a bed. Cautiously putting out her hand, she discovered that it was not only firm, but smooth and slightly warm. It extended a distance on either side, then curved gently downward. Slowly she opened her eyes.

She was sitting on what appeared to be an exceptionally broad tree branch. Its brown surface was glossy, as if polished by loving hands, and it was wide enough for her to place both hands beside her and still have plenty of room. Forcing herself to look down, she was relieved to see that it was not a branch, after all, but a root extending from the base of a huge tree. She relaxed further as she realized that the view in front of her was as far removed as possible from either the whirling brilliance or the sterile, machine-filled hospital room where she had last seen her physical body.

Like an emerald tapestry embroidered with brilliant clusters of multi-colored threads, a flower-studded meadow spread itself a good half mile in front of and to both sides of where she was sitting. Massive, ancient trees embraced the entire area with leafy arms, and a warm breeze softly brushed her cheeks. It was a scene from a fairy tale, or a dream.

"Neither of those." Max's words dropped into her mind. "Actually, we're in the Children's Garden."

Relieved to hear his voice, she let her gaze drop to where he lay curled between two of the lower roots of the huge tree, then frowned. "Children's Garden? I don't see any children."

"They're hiding. You really don't belong here yet, but Herm and I felt you needed someplace to recuperate from your experience that would not remind you of a hospital room."

Stacy's gaze ranged over the peaceful scene. "Why don't I belong here?"

"Because you still have a physical body, even though you're not inhabiting it at the moment."

She brought her attention back to him. "You sound like you think *you* belong here. But you still have a physical body."

Max's face looked smug. "Cats belong anywhere. We come and go as we please."

"In that case," Stacy informed him, "I think I'll be a cat in my next life."

"Sorry." Max stretched elaborately. "I might come back as a human, if I choose—I've been offered that option—but you can't go the other direction."

Stepping out from between the tree roots, he rolled over twice, shook himself, and curled into a comfortable position in the lush, ankle-deep grass.

Stacy stared at him. "I didn't know that. I thought—"

A quivering in the large stand of ferns under a nearby tree distracted her. Certain she could hear a faint giggle, she jumped to her feet; but by the time she reached the ferns, no one was there. She peered beyond the greenery into a pleasant, sun-flecked forest. The trailing branches of a bush swayed, and once again she felt certain she heard childish laughter.

"Someone's there, Max. They're watching us!"

Max checked his right paw. "I wouldn't worry about it. Children are notoriously curious."

"I'd like to see these kids who have a whole little realm of their own."

Max looked up. "Be my guest." He returned his attention to his paw, then called after her, "Just be careful not to go too far."

Stacy pushed her way past the ferns and, finding the thread of a trail, followed the laughter into the forest. The sun-dappled floor grew dimmer with each step she took, as the entwined arms of the massive trees shut out the sunlight. She looked back, wondering if she should return to the meadow, but the laughter sounded again and she continued on. Shadows, glimpsed from the corners of her eyes, darted away as she turned her head, and the undergrowth became increasingly dense, gradually closing in until its sharp thorns began to catch at her jeans and snag her hair.

A large bush just ahead quivered, but she discovered that she no longer had any desire to find out who—or what—was causing the movement. She turned, hoping to find that Max had followed her, and saw that the narrow path had vanished; in its place was a thick, twisted mass of spiky branches. Standing on tiptoe, she strained to see if she could catch a glimpse of him; but Max, like the path, was nowhere in sight.

She was reminded of the hideous dreams from which she used to awaken, terrified and sweating, after her parents' disappearance, dreams of ominous landscapes peopled by shriveled mummies tottering on stumps of legs that crumbled into dust with each step, reaching for her with clawed hands.

As she stood hemmed in by thorns, the tall bush ahead of her quivered again, then shook violently. Its branches parted, revealing the most horrible monster she had ever encountered outside of her childhood nightmares. It towered over her, red eyes glaring, rotting flesh hanging from its face and limbs. As it leaned nearer, she could see fangs dripping with what she felt sure must be poison. Her knees refused to support her and she collapsed, putting her hands over her head in a useless attempt to protect herself.

"Napping so early in the day? The familiar voice jolted her and she looked up between her arms into Max's furry face.

"Be careful!" she whispered.

He seemed unaware of the danger looming only a few feet away. Her chest felt ready to burst, as the hideous monstrosity stretched a twisted arm toward him.

Suddenly she was furious. Whatever this thing was, it was spoiling what was supposed to be a lovely, peaceful forest. It had committed the unforgivable sin of reducing her to a coward and now it was threatening her only friend in this strange place, someone at least ten times smaller than itself.

Gritting her teeth, she struggled to her feet, her hand closing over a broken tree branch. Standing erect, she brandished this at the creature, screaming, "Get back, you! Go away and leave us alone!"

To her amazement, the monster wavered and began to dissolve, melting and shrinking into a small, red-haired boy, who pointed at her, giggling. She recognized the sound.

"You have such a funny look on your face!" He laughed again.

Max wove around the child's legs, purring, and the boy gazed up at her with a sheepish expression.

"I didn't mean to scare you." His voice was high and clear. "I just wanted to play, 'cause you're pretty and your hair's the same color as mine. But then you got scared and thought I was a monster and I couldn't help myself." His expression became pleading. "Please don't be mad at me."

Stacy made an effort to smile. "I guess you're forgiven." Her voice sounded breathless, like she'd been running.

"Thanks!" The child darted across the clearing and hugged her, then skipped away through the forest, which had now returned to its former park-like appearance. Swinging the branch loosely in her right hand, Stacy looked at Max.

"I suppose that was good timing, although I'm not sure whether I should put this stick back where I found it, or give you a whack with it instead."

Max raised a furry eyebrow. "That seems a bit unjust." Unfurling his tail, he let the breeze ruffle it. "After all, you're the one who rushed heedlessly off in such a hurry." Without another look in her direction, he trotted back toward the meadow.

Stacy followed, running a little to keep up. "You don't have to look so pleased with yourself."

"Why not?" He didn't bother to turn around. "Because of my timing, as you put it, you had the opportunity to learn an important lesson."

She stared at his back, frowning. "What lesson?"

"That what you allow yourself to believe, is what you receive."

"Now wait a minute!"

Max turned around. "You have a problem with that?"

"You're telling me it's my fault that kid turned into something out of a horror story?"

"In a manner of speaking." He sat down in the shade of one of the ancient trees and began grooming his leg, ignoring her until she lowered herself onto the grass beside him. Giving his fur one last stroke, he looked up at her.

"Are you familiar, Stacy, with the medical discovery that fear causes the human nervous system to react as if there were a physical threat to the body, whether or not there actually is such a threat?"

She stared at him for a moment, then muttered, "The 'fight or flight' syndrome."

"Exactly. If you are frightened, your body will produce a rapid heartbeat, clammy skin, limited thinking ability, and other unpleasant symptoms. This response will take place even if you only imagine that something frightening is happening."

"So?"

Curling his tail around his feet, Max returned her stare. "So here, Between, all principles are intensified and made concrete. Your fear that those bushes concealed a monster practically obligated that child to see to it that one emerged from them. You really didn't give him much choice."

Stacy shook her head. "That's ridiculous!"

"No, it's simply the carrying through of the universal principle that what you believe is what you receive."

She narrowed her eyes. "If there had actually been a monster in that bush, would it have become a little boy, if I'd believed it was a little boy?"

Max's gaze was solemn. "Possibly. Certainly, your theoretical monster would have lost a great deal of its power over you, simply because you did not believe in it. I say 'theoretical', not only because there was no real monster, but also because monsters of that type can only exist if someone believes that they do."

The tip of his tail twitched. "When you picked up that stick and threatened your apparent monster, you more or less uncreated it." His eyes held hers. "By the way, what you did on my behalf required courage. Even though your actions weren't necessary, I appreciate them."

Stacy gazed out over the meadow, noticing that its center was now filled with laughing children engaged in a variety of games. Looking beyond them, she was surprised to see two figures making their way toward the place where she and Max were sitting. She immediately recognized the first, because of his muscular shoulders and snowy tunic. The other was dressed in a lavender blouse and long purple skirt.

"Max, that's Herm, and he's got Minerva with him! What's she doing here? I thought you said that people who still had physical bodies weren't supposed to be in the Children's Garden. She's not dead, is she?"

Max turned to follow her pointing finger. "I assume not," he told her, but we'll find out when they get here."

"Hello!" Minerva waved as they approached. Reaching the shelter of the tree, she sank down on the grass, fanning herself. "That certainly was a brisk walk!" Her brown eyes sparkled. "Much more invigorating and less tiring than it would have been back in Tulsa."

She looked closely at Stacy. "I talked Herm into letting me come with him, because I'm quite concerned about you," she said. "I'm afraid you haven't been having a very good time of it lately."

Stacy simply nodded; if she opened her mouth, she would burst into tears of relief.

Minerva moved closer to her, and Stacy laid her head on the older woman's shoulder. They sat together without speaking for a few moments; then Minerva said, "I also came to take you back with me."

Stacy sat up with a look of hopeful surprise, but Minerva shook her head. "I'm sorry, my dear. I didn't mean I could help you reintegrate with your body. I can, however, help you accomplish something else that I hope will cheer you up a bit."

Stacy struggled to contain her disappointment. "What is it?"

"Katie wants to see you."

"What?"

"Katie has asked to spend some time with you."

"But, 'Nerva, that's not possible—is it?"

Minerva smiled. "I've been discussing ways and means with Herm, and I think we've worked out a method to accomplish it."

Herm, who had been leaning against the huge trunk one of the trees, nodded. "If everything goes as it should, you will be able to spend time with your daughter after she falls asleep tonight."

A wave of homesickness swept over Stacy. "Can David be there, too?"

Herm shook his head. "Not this time. We're already bending several rules."

Stacy was amazed at the mixture of anticipation and anxiety racing through her. The thought of being able to spend time with Katie excited her, but the prospect of making the connection also increased her sense of urgency about returning to her body.

Herm smiled. "Max and I will take care of the mechanics of the operation. All you need to do is enjoy your time with your daughter." Turning to Minerva, he continued, "Why don't you take Stacy back to the Entry Processing Center? She can browse around until time to leave, while you return to the Earth level and prepare Katie for her visit. Max and I will check out some technicalities here and join you as soon as we can."

Minerva stood up and held out her hand to Stacy. Stepping behind them, Herm placed his hands on their shoulders, and the Children's Garden began to waver. The whirling sensation and flashes of brilliance that followed now seemed to Stacy more familiar than frightening, and this time they carried with them a promise of hope.

Chapter 22

The prairie was not exactly as Arthur Craddock remembered it. Although a constant breeze still murmured through the tall, waving grass, he now noticed that there were trees, some solitary, some in clusters, randomly scattered across the broad expanse of open space. After a moment's consideration, he set off toward a small grove of four, all of them twisted and stunted by the relentless assault of the wind. Though not much taller than oversized bushes, they would provide sufficient shelter from both sun and wind while he turned his formidable mental powers toward designing the perfect revenge on Stacy Addison.

He had almost reached the tiny copse when a high-pitched screech brought him up short. A second, slightly lower screech followed, as if in reply. Arthur dropped into a crouch and cautiously pushed his way through the tall grass. Reaching the cluster of trees, he positioned himself behind the largest and peered around it. He had undergone many strange experiences since becoming aware of himself in the area of gray desolation, but none of them had prepared him for the bizarre occupants of this little grove.

Under the tree opposite him huddled two immense, vulture-like birds, their feathers dull and tattered, as if they were molting. The smell they gave off was indescribably foul, like the stench of rotting garbage. Arthur covered his nose with his hand. Backs turned toward him, these monstrous figures were hunched over something in the grass. The larger of the two lurched suddenly, as if trying to shove the smaller one aside.

"Stop that!"

Arthur recognized in these words the shrill screech he had heard earlier. The lower-pitched one followed immediately.

"I thought it here; it belongs to me!"

"Does not! I thought it here, too, so I get half. Share and share alike." The screech rose more shrilly. "Share and share alike!" The smaller one hopped up and down in obvious fury, then began to circle its companion, still shrieking.

As it turned in his direction, Arthur gasped. The creature whipped its head toward him, red-rimmed eyes glowing with interest. Arthur felt frozen, unable to look away. The eyes holding his did not belong to a bird, neither did the face in which they were set. Whatever this thing was, it possessed what might be described as a woman's features, but so perversely formed as to be a cruel caricature. The narrow forehead was creased with wrinkles, as were the cheeks. A sharp, beak-like nose balanced the pointed chin protruding below thick, bulbous lips. This nightmare face contorted in what might be a smile, displaying two rows of sharp, yellow teeth.

"Look, sister!" it screeched.

Lifting its head, the larger monstrosity slowly turned toward Arthur. Its features were similar to, but even more grotesque than those of the smaller one, and behind it he could see what appeared to be a heap of rotting meat lying under the tree.

"Look, indeed!" The larger one lurched a step toward him. Arthur stepped backward.

"You didn't think him here, too, did you?" The smaller one's shriek was so high-pitched that he was tempted to place his fingers in his ears, but decided it might be construed as an insult.

The larger one shook its head. "He must have come on his own." Lurching another step closer, it crooned, "Came here of your own will, did you?"

The stench emanating from its body made Arthur want to gag. A memory was playing hide and seek in his brain. Something his mother had read to him long ago from a book about mythology, something… "Harpies!" he exclaimed. "You must be Harpies!"

The larger creature stopped its advance. Spreading its lips in the same expression he had seen earlier on the face of the smaller one, it began to hop up and down, first on one clawed foot, then on the other.

"He knows us, sister, knows us, knows us!"

The smaller one joined her, hopping in rhythm, as if to a beat beyond Arthur's hearing.

"Through our belief, we do exist. Through his belief we will grow strong!"

Suddenly, both Harpies halted their fantastic two-step and turned toward him.

"We welcome you, human," screeched the larger one.

"Welcome, welcome!" the smaller echoed.

Arthur attempted a smile. As he did so, he inadvertently inhaled, causing a bout of choking and coughing. It was obvious that if he planned to make friends of these creatures, he would have to remind himself to stay downwind or breathe through his mouth. He cleared his throat.

"Thank you, ah, ladies." He bowed slightly toward each of them in turn, noting their obvious delight. "Happy if I can be of service."

Bobbing their heads, the Harpies displayed their razor-sharp smiles. "You have, indeed, served us," the smaller one told him. "Your recognition has strengthened us better than a meal."

Arthur smiled and nodded, remembering the pile of rotting meat and hoping they would forbear to share any gastronomic details with him.

"Now we must return some benefit to you." The larger spoke again. "Balance is essential."

Arthur nodded. "Balance is essential," he repeated. Whatever that meant, it sounded like something he should be able to use to his advantage.

The Harpy nodded in return. "Tell us how we may now serve you."

Arthur considered. Although the voice that so often advised him seemed to be absent, he felt strongly that these two bizarre creatures could somehow be put to good use.

"I thank you for your offer," he told them. "I do not yet know what that service should be, but if you are willing, I will tell you when the time comes." That should give him an opportunity to come up with something. "My name, by the way, is Arthur Craddock."

"We shall be honored to wait until the appropriate time, Arthur-craddock." The larger Harpy bobbed its head again. "You have shared your name, so I will tell you that I am Klio, and this," it nodded toward the smaller one, "is my sister, Urania."

Urania sidled up to him, stink rolling off her feathers with every hop. "We gave ourselves those names," she confided. "They originally belonged to two of the Muses, but they rarely use them any more, because there is no one left who believes in them." Her red-rimmed eyes looked sad. "When no one believes in you, bit by bit you fade away, until nothing is left but the shadow of what you were."

Arthur breathed through his mouth. "Well, here you both are, so someone must still believe in Harpies." He made another effort to smile.

Urania's eyes looked even sadder. "Not exactly. All of our other sisters have become helpless, twittering shades, unable to even remember who they once were."

"Then how—?"

Klio fluttered her wings, shedding loose feathers and sending another wave of foulness in his direction. "We have survived all these centuries, because we found the secret." Her shriek dropped a decibel to what Arthur assumed must be a Harpy whisper. "You see, it doesn't matter who believes, just that someone does believe. And so," she spread bloated lips in her sharp, yellow smile, "we survive because Urania believes in me and I believe in her." She nudged her sister, and both Harpies cackled with laughter until the cloud of fetid breath made Arthur fear he would faint. Their laughter finally tapered off into clucking chuckles.

Making an effort to overcome his bout of nausea, Arthur smiled. "I must credit you both with great ingenuity."

Klio actually blushed. "We would wish we had thought of it while our sisters were still with us. However," she sighed deeply, "we do what we can."

Nodding, Arthur took a step backward. It was time to extricate himself from this grotesque get-together. "I fear that I must ask you ladies to excuse me. I have a previous and unavoidable engagement." He smiled again. "If I may, I will return at another time, when I can take up your very generous offer of service."

Both Harpies bobbed their heads again. "It will be our pleasure, Arthurcraddock," Klio told him.

"Our pleasure, our pleasure," echoed Urania.

Continuing to back away until he was a good distance from the tiny grove of trees, Arthur Craddock allowed himself several deep breaths of clean, wind-scented air. He gazed around the prairie thoughtfully.

Certainly his time here had not produced what he had intended, but the visit had not been wasted. Even though close association with the Harpies posed some problems, he sensed that staying in their good graces might provide definite advantages.

He considered his next step. Probably his best choice would be to continue his reconnaissance of Stacy. The more he knew about her behavior and her movements, the sooner he could bring about her destruction. Enjoying another deep breath, he focused on her once more.

A moment later, the prairie was again empty of everything but wind-blown grass, scattered trees, and the Harpies in their grove, still discussing in excited squawks the first human visitor they had entertained in centuries.

Chapter 23

Katie curled herself under the green-and-cream quilt, the worry doll clutched in her hand. She had gone to bed early, to be ready for her meeting with her mother, but a lineup of worries insisted on parading itself across her mind. What if she did things wrong? What if she couldn't fall asleep? What if she fell asleep too soon and went into the dream world before her mother got there? Worst of all, what if her mother didn't come?

Squinting her eyes shut, she tried to relax, but her whole body felt tight, like it would break into pieces, if she fell down. She had always taken her world for granted, but since her mother's accident, she had begun to realize it might not be as safe as she had thought it was.

A tiny popping sound, like a bubble bursting, cut through the silence of the room. Cautiously Katie opened her eyes. When she had pulled the quilt up around her chin, the room had been bathed in its usual comforting, bedtime glow; now it was as dark as a bogeyman's cellar. A long, terrifying minute passed before she realized that the sound she had heard must have been the nightlight burning out. With a squeak of relief, she reached over and switched on the bedside lamp, then fell back against the pillow, clenching the worry doll so tightly her hand hurt. Tiny beads of perspiration spangled her upper lip and her chest felt like it had shrunk until it was too small to hold the air she tried to suck in.

Gasping, she recalled something Minerva had told her to say when she felt frightened. "Wherever I am, God is, and all is well." She whispered the words under her breath several times, still holding the worry doll tight, until her breathing steadied and she didn't feel she would jump out of her skin at the next tick of the wall clock. A faint sound of whistling floated up the stairwell; her father must be puttering in the kitchen. If she needed help, she could call out and he would come racing up the stairs in a minute.

Looking over at the clock, she saw that the time was almost ten. She gritted her teeth. It was getting later and later, and she still didn't feel the least bit sleepy. At this rate, her mother would come and go before she could settle down enough to drop off. She sighed.

Leaving the lamp on, she closed her eyes again. She could hear faint sounds of her father putting away the supper dishes and getting things ready for tomorrow's breakfast. Just knowing he was there made her feel better. Sighing, she took a breath, then a deeper one, then another. Her tense muscles relaxed and her grip slackened, until the worry doll rested on the pillow next to her freckled cheek. She slept.

Suddenly she heard someone calling her name. To her surprise, she found she was standing beside the bed. Minerva, in a lavender sweater and her old purple skirt, was also there, smiling down at her.

"'Nerva!" Katie hugged her. "I didn't hear you come in."

Minerva's smile broadened. "I didn't come through the door, my dear. Here," she turned Katie toward the center of the room, "I've brought someone to see you."

Katie's eyes widened with wonder and delight. "Mommy!" Lunging toward her mother, she threw her arms around her waist.

"Oh, Katie, Katie!" Holding her tight, her mother kissed the top of her head, then her face. "I'm so glad to see you!"

Katie clung to her wordlessly, face wet with tears of joy. She could sense love pouring into her and gratefully soaked it up, like parched earth drinking in long-awaited rain. Finally her mother stopped hugging her and tenderly smoothed back her sandy hair. Katie gazed up into her face.

"I miss you so much, Mommy. When are you coming home?"

Looking sad, her mother shook her head. "I don't know, honeybunch. My body won't work right yet, and I'm stuck where I am until it does."

"Is it nice there?"

Her mother touched her cheek. "It's OK."

"'Nerva says it's a place where people go when they're not in their bodies. I'm not in my body right now. Can I go there?"

Her mother put an arm around Katie's shoulders. "I honestly don't know." Turning to Minerva, who had been standing off to one side, she asked, "Is Katie allowed to visit Between?"

Minerva looked thoughtful. "That's a question for Max. He and Herm should be here in a jiffy."

Katie brightened. "Max is coming? When will he get here?"

Sparkles of light began to flash and the air seemed to ripple. A moment later, Max appeared. Katie ran to him and, reaching down, scooped him up in her arms. She hugged him hard, his furry warmth familiar and comforting.

"Oh, Max, I'm so glad to see you!"

"Put me down, please, Katie. I am not a sack of groceries."

Katie set him at her feet, then hunkered down beside him. "Mommy isn't sure if I can go with her to Between, but Minerva says I can ask you."

Max gave himself a little shake. "As a matter of fact, I have come to tell you that Herm has received permission for you to do that very thing."

"Oh, wow!" She turned wide eyes toward her mother. "I can go with you, Mommy! Herm got permission for me to go Between!" Turning back to Max, she wrinkled her forehead. "Who's Herm?"

"You'll meet him shortly." Suddenly Max's head went up. He looked around the room, a puzzled expression on his face.

"Is anything wrong?" Minerva's voice was quiet.

"I'm not sure. There's something . . . something not quite right. Whatever it is reminds me of what I sensed in Stacy's hospital room." He gazed around the bedroom again. "I can't pin it down, but I think we would be wise to leave immediately."

He looked up at Katie's mother. "Pick me up and hold me under your arm," he told her, "then take Minerva's right hand. Katie, you take her left hand."

Katie quickly thrust her hand into Minerva's.

"Everybody hold tight!" Max instructed.

Sparkling lights began to dance around them.

"Oooh!" Katie giggled, shivering. "That tickles!"

An instant later they were gone.

§

Arthur Craddock was disconcerted to find himself in the bedroom of a child. Trusting, however, that his internal homing device had brought him a little early to the location where Stacy Addison would shortly arrive, he set about finding a spot from which he could observe undetected.

The room offered several possibilities for concealment. Most promising was the wall opposite the bed, where he would have full view of whatever might take place in the room. Using the technique he had learned during his visit to Stacy's intensive care room, Arthur allowed his atoms to flow into the empty spaces in the wall's molecular structure.

A sharp popping noise startled him, momentarily freezing him half in, half out of his destination. Turning his awareness toward the source of the sound, he realized that his own electrical field must have interfered with that of the nightlight plugged into the baseboard. With a sigh of relief, he continued the process of meshing his atoms with those of the wall.

He had barely stabilized himself there before two figures materialized beside the bed. An old woman in purple accompanied Stacy this time, instead of the nosy cat who had seemed to detect his presence in the hospital room. Running to Stacy, the little girl hugged her tightly. Arthur smiled. His inner guidance had proven its value again—he could tell from the way Stacy returned the embrace that this was her daughter! Fate was making up to him for its earlier cruelty. What better way to hurt a mother, than by injuring or destroying her child!

The air beside the bed began to shimmer, and the cat suddenly appeared. There was a dangerous moment when he could feel the animal searching for him, but after a brief interchange with the child and the two adults, it allowed Stacy to pick it up and all four of them disappeared. Arthur waited a few minutes, to be sure that none of them would return, then carefully extricated himself from the bedroom wall.

He knew, now, what his next move should be. He would return to the Harpies and cash in his rain check for the service they owed him. The bird-women would probably be willing to help him take the little girl hostage; they might even know of a location where he could hide her. Once that was accomplished, he could devise the best method of causing her mother the greatest possible distress.

So many exciting prospects!

🐾 🐾 🐾 Between 🐾 🐾 🐾

Exhilarated, he focused on the grove of trees and his future accomplices. A moment later, the only occupant of the bedroom was Katie's body, peacefully slumbering under the green-and-cream quilt.

Chapter 24

Katie, eyes squinted shut, felt like a tornado was whirling her around and around. *Just like going to Oz!* she thought. The spinning sensation gradually faded and her feet touched something solid. Opening her eyes, she gazed around with interest and surprise.

She was standing with her mother and Minerva at the top of a grassy hill. Max was sitting beside them. Below, on a wide stretch of the greenest grass she had ever seen, girls and boys in brightly colored clothing were running and laughing.

The children suddenly broke off the game they had been playing and raced, squealing with delight, toward a tall man who had just stepped out of the circle of huge trees that bordered the meadow. They surrounded him, jumping up and down with excitement. Some caught at the edges of the short, white dress he was wearing, and one child grabbed his hand. The joyful energy of the group swept him along, as he climbed the little rise toward Katie and her companions.

"Play with us!" commanded the little boy who was tugging at his hand.

The man smiled and ruffled the boy's fair hair. "Not right now, little one. I have some business to tend to. Run on now, all of you, and finish your game."

Sighing, the children hugged the man and blew him kisses, then dragged their feet back toward the center of the meadow, looking over their shoulders at Katie. She stared back at them with equal interest.

"Hello, Katie." The man was smiling now at her.

Katie smiled back at him. "Hello." She looked him over, frowning slightly. "Why are you wearing a dress?"

The man threw back his head and laughed. "You sound like your mother." He knelt in front of her. "Have you ever heard of the Greeks and Romans?"

"A Greek family lives down the street from us."

The man chuckled. "The Greeks I'm asking about lived a long time ago, at least as far as you're concerned."

Katie nodded. "Oh, I know who you mean! Our teacher read us some stories about them, and I saw a movie once with gods and goddesses, and a man who fought with a mean lady who had snakes on her head."

The man nodded. "Those are the ones. Do you remember what their clothing was like?"

Katie thought for a moment. "Yes! They all wore dresses, even the men."

He smiled. "Those dresses are called 'tunics.' That's what I'm wearing—a tunic."

"But why are you wearing one?"

The man grinned at her. "Because it's comfortable."

Minerva looked at him. "I think it's time for some straight answers," she said. "I appreciate the fact that you are restraining yourself enough to stay in one form, which I assume is to prevent Katie from becoming overly confused. However, it's only fair that Stacy and Katie know your real identity."

The man made his face look solemn. "You know perfectly well, my wise friend, that fairness is not a ground rule, either of Earth reality or true reality."

Minerva looked stern. "Let's not play word games. Are you going to share who you really are, or shall I have Max tell them?"

The man spread his hands, palms up. "In the interest of modesty, I shall let Max have the honor."

Max, who was lazily batting an acorn around in the grass, looked up at them.

"He's a god." He yawned. "Hermes, to be exact, messenger god of the ancient Greeks, with whom he still spends time. Mercury, if you want to give him his Roman name."

Katie looked at the man. "Is that true? Are you really a god?"

The man smiled. "Guilty as charged, I'm afraid. And you may call me 'Herm,' if you like."

Katie looked at her mother. "Mommy, I like him. He's nice and his laugh makes me feel tickly inside. Besides, I never met a god before."

Her mother smiled, then turned to the man. "I'm glad to finally know who you really are," she said, "but you're going to have to do some explaining if you expect us to understand how you can spend time with the ancient Greeks and Romans, and also be here with us."

Herm leaned against the broad, smooth trunk of the nearest tree. "The key lies in the true nature of time," he told her. "You must understand that here, Between, we are governed by true time, which is not the same as the time you experience on Earth. Here the only time is *now*. I can be here with all of you in this particular *now*, and I can also be with my Greeks and Romans in their *now*, even though, as far as you are concerned, their *now* is what you consider the past."

Katie frowned. "I don't understand. How can what happened a long time ago be happening now?"

Herm knelt in front of her. "The Greeks and Romans don't think of themselves as living in the past, any more than you think of yourself that way. Yet, even though you don't realize it, you are part of someone else's past, someone who is living right now in what you think of as the future."

His eyes crinkled in a smile. "Think of it this way, little one. Imagine that time is a river with lots of curves and bends." Picking up a twig, he drew in the dirt at the foot of the tree. "See?"

Katie nodded. "It looks sort of like a slithery snake."

"Now, pretend you are in a boat, sailing down one of the straight legs of the river," he began to move the twig down one of the lines, "and there's a bend up ahead of you. Can you see around that bend from here, where you are now?"

Katie shook her head. "No, of course I can't."

"When will you be able to see around it?"

"When I get there."

"Very good, Katie."

Dropping the twig, Herm picked up a stone, and held it high above the lines he had drawn. "Now, suppose you are sitting up here in a helicopter, hovering over the river. How much can you see?"

Katie clapped her hands. "Everything! I can see the whole river!"

"Exactly." Herm set the stone on the ground and stood up. "That's how time really is. When you're limited to what you can observe on Earth, you're like a traveler sailing on the river. The past has disappeared around the bend behind you, while the future waits around the bend ahead. And when you go around that bend, what you've been thinking of as the present becomes a part of the past, and what was the future is now the present. But, if you're in a helicopter, everything is available at the same time. It's all *now*."

He smiled at Katie. "That's how I can be with my Greeks and Romans in 200 B.C. and also be here with you, or in your mother's hospital room back on Earth. I simply choose which part of the river I want to land my helicopter on. In other words, I choose which *now* I want to experience."

Max cleared his throat. "I hate to interrupt this dissertation," he told Herm, "but you'd better set your 'copter's controls for Katie's bedroom. Night is over back there and she's due at school in about two hours."

Katie looked at him, distressed. "Oh, Max, do I have to go back? Can't I stay here?"

Max rubbed his head against her leg. "Sorry. That isn't possible."

Katie made a face. "Rats! They don't teach us neat stuff like *now* time in school."

Running to her mother, she threw her arms around her waist. "Mommy, please come back to your body; I miss you something awful!"

"I will as soon as I possibly can, Katie. I promise." Her mother squeezed her so tightly that she almost squeaked, but Katie didn't mind. It was a hug to treasure, her mother's way of telling her that she did love her and would soon return, making life brighter and happier than it had ever been.

"Time to leave." Max gently pushed himself between them. "Pick me up," he told Katie, "and I'll take you back."

With a sigh, Katie gathered him up in her arms. Her eyes were so blurred by tears that she could hardly distinguish between the sunlight of the meadow and the sparks of light now dancing around her.

"I love you, Mommy!" she called; then the strange whirling sensation forced her to close her eyes.

When she opened them, sunlight was streaming through her bedroom window in a pale imitation of the rich brilliance of Between, and her father was whistling on his way up the stairs to wake her for school. Sensing that Max had already departed, she felt abandoned and sad; then she recalled her mother's hug and promise. Excitement

Between

surged through her.

Her father bent over the bed and she threw her arms around his neck. "Oh, Daddy! Wait till I tell you where I've been!"

Chapter 25

Glynis's vintage VW Beetle bumped down the long, graveled drive leading to the Steele farmhouse. Rounding the last curve, she put the car in neutral and let it idle. The rambling old house, with its wide, grassy lawn and huge maple trees, had always seemed to provide at least a temporary cure for whatever stresses ailed her. But today even its magic could not erase the fact that Stacy, dearer to her than her own sisters, was lying in St. Mark's, on the brink of a realm far beyond Glynis's reach.

Shifting the car into first gear, she crept on down the driveway and parked behind the house. She cranked down her window and waved at Rudy, who was unloading boxes from the back of his pickup.

"Hey, Little Bit!" Rudy took off his hat and wiped his forehead. "Thought I heard you headin' down the drive." Crossing the yard, he leaned his arms on the car door. "Any news about Stacy?"

Glynis shook her head. "Not that I know of. I just came by to find out when you'll need me to help with the hay."

Rudy rubbed his right ear. "Baler's ready to go, but the tractor may need a little touch-up." He glanced across the hedge toward the Sinclair back door. "Could start on Monday, but since Jenn feels we still need to have our Memorial Day picnic for Katie's sake, it'll be Tuesday before I mow. So that means I'll need you Wednesday to help me bale."

"OK, I'll plan to drive for you then. Minerva says she'll take care of the store."

Rudy nodded. "Last time I checked the barometer, pressure was startin' to drop a bit. Might be wet weather by Thursday, but we'll surely have it in before then."

"I'll tell Minerva to plan on Wednesday, unless you let me know otherwise."

Blowing him a kiss, Glynis turned the car and let out the clutch. As she started back up the driveway, she sighed. Leaving the farm behind was easy; the memories associated with it, most of them involving Stacy, were another matter.

§

Arthur Craddock's sudden reappearance in the little copse of trees triggered an explosion of excitement in the two Harpies. Hopping up and down, they lurched toward him, shedding a storm of ragged feathers.

"Sister, sister, our friend has returned!" Klio spread her lips in her sharp-toothed smile.

"Our friend, our friend," Urania crooned, her grotesque head bobbing on its skinny neck.

Resisting the urge to take a step back, Arthur held his ground and breathed through his mouth. "Ladies," he bowed slightly in their direction, "I have come to accept your kind offer of service."

"We are honored, sir." Klio fluttered her wings, releasing a stench that made Arthur work hard not to gag.

"Honored, honored," echoed Urania.

Arthur smiled. "The honor is mine, dear friends."

Klio tilted her head. "Have you decided how we may complete the balance?"

Forcing himself to step toward them, he dropped his voice a little. "I wish you to help me capture a hostage."

The bird-women began to hop up and down again, fluttering their wings and murmuring to each other. "A hostage, sister, a hostage! So long, so long since we have had the opportunity . . . ."

Breathing determinedly through his mouth, Arthur held his ground. When the two had recovered from their excitement, he continued. "The hostage I'm talking about is a little girl. She—"

"A little girl! A child!" Klio interrupted him.

"A child! A child!" Urania shrieked.

They swivelled toward Arthur, eyes gleaming. His stomach turned. God, they were disgusting! Disgusting, yet fascinating and, he hoped, very useful.

"We have not carried off a child in centuries." Klio's screech was tinged with wistfulness.

Urania's head bobbed in agreement. "Centuries." She sidled closer to Arthur Craddock. "Children are our specialty," she confided.

Arthur smiled. "I'm delighted to know that my request pleases you."

"It pleases us, it does, it does." They began to hop rhythmically in time to their chanting.

Before they could set another celebratory dance in motion, Arthur held up his hand. "Let me tell you what I want you to do," he said. "Then you can advise me how you will do it and where we can hide our hostage."

The Harpies murmured to each other, then nodded. "Your words are wise. We will discuss your plan, then find the perfect place to keep the child."

Anticipation surged through Arthur Craddock. Everything was working out just as he had hoped. "Here's my idea," he said. Seating himself cross-legged a short distance from his monstrous confidantes, he began to outline his plan. He made sure he remembered to breathe through his mouth.

Chapter 26

"Dr. Kinnard?"

David felt a hand on his shoulder. Looking up, he saw Colin Elmore standing over him. He half rose to his feet, but Elmore gently pressed him back into his chair.

"Don't get up." Sinking into the seat opposite, his chief of staff gave him a tired smile. "I just came in for some coffee."

David rubbed the top of his head. "Guess I was wool-gathering." He stretched and picked up his empty cup. "One more shot of this sludge, and I should be ready to go. Want me to bring you a cup?"

Elmore nodded.

When they were settled with their coffee, Elmore studied him. "Getting any rest these days?"

David shrugged. "Some."

"Being wiped out doesn't help Stacy."

"I know." David paused. "I need an 'off' switch for my brain; it seems to be on full speed all the time." He tapped the table with his hand. "OK if I ask you something?"

"Sure, but you already know as much as I do about Stacy's condition."

"It's not about Stace." He rubbed the top of his head again. "Ah, hell, you'll think I'm nuts!"

Elmore straightened in his chair. "Go ahead; it sounds intriguing. And by the way, if you don't stop scrubbing your skull, you're going to induce early baldness."

Jerking his hand away from his head, David frowned. "My daughter told me something this morning that really has me going." He paused a moment, his jaw working. "She said she'd spent last night with Stace.

It was so real to her! She described in detail how it happened, where they went, who was there, everything. She told me how Stace looked, how her hug felt, what she said . . . ."

Elmore smiled. "So? Kids have vivid dreams. My son once insisted that he'd flown over our house. Without an airplane."

"I don't know. It's just that, while she was telling me about it, I could see everything she was describing; it felt real to me, too." He looked at Elmore with bloodshot eyes. "Crazy, huh? But I can't get it out of my mind."

Elmore pushed back his chair, then leaned across the table and squeezed David's shoulder. "It's called exhaustion, my young friend; exhaustion and anxiety. Right now, you're ready to believe anything that will make you feel better."

David watched as Elmore's swinging stride carried him out of the doctors' break room. Of course, it was what Colin had said—anxiety and exhaustion. Katie couldn't really have spent the night with her mother, doing the things she'd described. Tossing down the last of his coffee, he stood up. Katie's dream was just that—a dream, born of the need to feel that her mother wasn't lost to her. Something impossible. Something to comfort her.

He headed out the door, determinedly turning his focus toward the real world of problems and patients. But before his mind could turn the corner back into full reality, it had to swerve around a thought that firmly resisted his common sense's attempt to sweep it aside:

God, I wish it had been me!

§

Stacy leaned against the pillows on her bed in the temporary wing of the Entry Processing Center.

"A proverbial penny for your thoughts."

She looked up to see Max padding across the floor toward her and frowned. "Don't you ever come through a door the normal way? Or knock?"

He leaped onto the foot of the bed. "Explain how you think I'm going to open a door like a human being. Even if I could reach the knob, my paws don't work the way your hands do. The same for knocking. Besides," he stretched, curling his tail over his back, "it's so much simpler to just allow my atoms to move through those of whatever solid objects I encounter."

"Must be nice. I wouldn't know."

"Yes, you do. Don't you remember sticking your arm into the ventilator?"

"That was different. You and Herm were there, helping me."

"Not true. All we did was suggest that you could do it. You managed the rest completely on your own."

Stacy frowned. "Oh, maybe you're right. But at the moment, I'm thinking about something much more important."

"Which is?"

"Spending tonight with David."

Max eyed her with interest. "You do have an ambitious turn of mind, don't you?"

She shrugged. "I watched Minerva catch Katie's spirit body before it could go off into the dream state. The process didn't seem very complicated."

Max cocked his head to one side. "You're right; it's not complicated. It does, however, demand some awareness of when to act. If you try to touch the spirit body before it has completely exited the physical one, it will be shocked back in, and the person will wake up. If you wait too long, the spirit body will move so far toward the dream world that you can no longer influence it."

"So is there any problem with me trying to catch David after he comes out of his body tonight?"

Max briefly closed his eyes, then opened them. "I just checked with Herm. He says there is no objection, as far as he knows."

"Great!" Stacy projected her imagination forward to the coming night. "David doesn't believe in anything he can't prove in a laboratory. Is he going to be surprised!"

The corners of Max's mouth crooked up into a smile. "I think we can safely consider that an understatement."

§

Serizzin contemplated Iblis.

"I understand that the tool known as Craddock has freed himself from his prison and already established a connection with the special soul, Stacy Addison."

"'That is so, my lord. Under my tutelage, he is mastering the art of manipulating his surroundings. He learns quickly and still assumes my voice is a part of himself."

Serizzin leaned toward him. "You have done well. See that he continues to remain under your influence and that the connection is enhanced."

Iblis flickered briefly into the form he sometimes assumed in Serizzin's presence, that of a small, spindle-legged human male. He bowed low. "Rest assured, my lord, it shall be so."

Wavering back into a sliver of darkness, he hesitated, wondering if he should reveal Craddock's obsession with the Addison woman. He considered carefully. Failure was not an option, its consequences too devastating to consider. Success, on the other hand, promised his master's approval and a position of higher esteem.

Surely, he thought, Serizzin would not have given him this assignment, without the belief that he possessed the ability to do whatever was necessary to produce the desired results. The realization filled him with confidence and, deciding that he could handle Craddock's obsession by himself, Iblis sped away into the murk surrounding the clearing.

Chapter 27

Stacy sat on the bed that she and David had shared for the past twelve years and listened to him whistling in the bathroom. He had already tucked Katie in for the night. Only a few minutes earlier, Stacy had watched the little girl snuggle down under the covers; she would soon be asleep and on her way into the dream state.

Her time with Katie the previous night had increased her determination to get back into her body. She not only wanted to apologize to David and meet Evan Chastain's deadline, but she now understood that her daughter needed her. She compressed her lips. Why couldn't her parents have understood how much she needed them? Why had they always chosen their work and each other, instead of her? Maybe she just hadn't been good enough. Maybe—

She jerked her attention back into the present, as David emerged from the bathroom and sat down on the bed. Reaching under the pillow on her side of the bed, he pulled out a piece of tattered yellow cloth, the last remnant of what had once been her baby blanket. Her use of it as a sleep mask not only kept the light of the street lamp out of her eyes, but also provided her with an excuse for holding onto one of the few relics of her childhood. Pressing the strip of cloth against his face, David breathed in her scent, then wound it around his neck like a scarf.

Blinking back tears, Stacy saw that he looked exhausted. His dark hair was standing on end, which meant he'd been rubbing his head the way he did when he was upset; she longed to smooth it down and kiss away his fatigue. As she watched, he turned back the covers and stretched out on the bed. Pulling up the sheet, he closed his eyes. At first, he tossed restlessly, but eventually he relaxed and his breathing became deeper and more regular.

Remembering how she and Minerva had waylaid Katie's spirit body on its way into the dream state the previous night, Stacy watched him closely. A moment later, a whitish cloud began to rise from his body, taking on his form as it floated slowly upward toward the ceiling. A silvery thread, about the thickness of her index finger, connected the two Davids, elongating as his spirit form continued to move away from his physical body. He seemed completely unaware of her presence.

Despite the fact that she had observed a similar process with Katie the previous night, she was mesmerized by this temporary separation of spirit and body. David's head and shoulders had already disappeared through the bedroom ceiling before she realized that she was about to lose her opportunity. Propelling herself into the air, she grabbed one of his ankles and yanked him back into the room.

The unexpected action broke his spirit body's trance-like focus on wherever it was headed. Twisting in mid-air, he looked down at her in surprise. Joy illuminated his face.

"Stacy? Oh, my God, Stace, is it really you?"

Tears filled her eyes. "It is, David—it's really me!"

They stared at each other, then he opened his arms and she moved into his embrace. The feeling of happiness that swept through her was incredible.

"Oh, Stace," he murmured into her hair, "I must be asleep and dreaming."

She squeezed him tightly. "You're not dreaming, David. I caught you before you could get that far."

"How can that be?" Looking down into her face, he frowned; then he shook his head. "I don't know; maybe you're right. This doesn't feel like a dream."

"It's not a dream. We're really together!" Smiling, she touched his cheek. "I watched you fall asleep and grabbed you as you came out of your body."

They both looked back at the bed, where David's body lay curled, faintly snoring.

"That's me!" He sounded incredulous. Pulling away from her, he bent over the bed and studied the form under the sheet. "That's me! How can I be here, talking to you, and there at the same time?"

She pulled him around to face her. "Do you remember me reading you that section from one of Glynis's books about out-of-body experiences? You know, where the person is either asleep or unconscious, but his spirit has left his body and is able to see and hear what's going on."

"I don't know." He twisted his head back toward the bed, most of his awareness still focused on his sleeping self.

"Well, that's basically what you're doing—having an out-of-body experience."

He frowned. "Does that mean I'm just dreaming, that this isn't real?"

"No, out-of-body experiences truly happen." She looked up at him. "This is really happening." She hugged him tightly. "Doesn't it feel real to you?"

"I have to admit it does."

She shook her head. "It's taken me awhile to come to terms with how real it actually is. It wasn't until I spent time with Katie last night that I completely accepted the fact that my physical body is here, on Earth, in the hospital, and I'm stuck in a place somewhere between our world and the next one." Her forehead wrinkled. " Now I have to figure out how to get myself back into my body. I tried once, but it didn't work." She shivered. "It was totally dark in there and I couldn't even move a finger. You were there, holding my hand, but I couldn't let you know. It was really scary!"

David threaded his finger through a strand of copper hair curling in front of her ear. "I'm sorry, Stace. That must have been because of the barbiturate; Elmore's been keeping you in a coma, so you can recover more quickly."

She pulled her head away. "So that's why I couldn't make my body work! I don't know whether to be upset, or glad to find out there's a reason." She thought about what he had just told her. "So there's no use in my trying again?"

He shook his head. "Not until Elmore takes you off the phenobarbitol."

"Wonderful! It makes me feel so in charge of things!"

"You know that's not what it's about. Elmore only wants what's best for you."

"What's best for me is to get back in my body and get ready for that TV pilot." She struggled with the sense of urgency that filled her each time she thought about the opportunity Evan Chastain had offered her. "I wish I could make you understand how important this is to me!"

"I do understand, Stace, I really do. If I could change things, you know I'd do it in a heartbeat."

She put her hand on his arm. "I know. And I didn't even apologize to you yet, for saying all those mean things to you."

The look in his eyes was tender. "No need for that. I'm the one who ought to be apologizing to you."

She sighed. "I guess we both said things we shouldn't have." Taking his hand, she cradled it against her cheek. "Oh, David, I've missed you so much!"

"I've missed you, too." His voice was husky. He slid his hand down to cup her chin. "Maybe I'm dreaming, maybe I'm not; one thing I do know is that I'm not going to waste any more time trying to figure it out."

Pulling her to him, he lowered his mouth to hers. Their lips touched, and a sparkling sensation rushed through her, as if her whole body had exploded into a million splinters of stars. She could feel the same thing happening to David, and for a moment she was overwhelmed by wonder. Then she fell into him, their very molecules blending and whirling in ecstasy.

Everything external disappeared. There was no longer any sleeping body on the bed—no floor, no ceiling, no awareness of anything but each other. Time ceased; nothing existed but this shimmering, radiant union of desire and delight, blending and merging, again and again.

Suddenly, a harsh jangling jolted them, ripping their atoms apart. Traumatized, Stacy watched as the silvery cord attached to David's navel contracted, yanking his spirit back into his physical body. Groggy and disoriented, he struggled with the covers for a moment, then levered himself up on one elbow and groped for the clock on the bedside table. The din continued. Dropping the clock, he reached for the phone, almost knocking its base onto the floor.

"Kinnard here." His voice was raspy. He listened for a moment, then sighed. "OK, I'll be there within the hour."

Struggling to a sitting position, he looked around the room. Stacy, still trying to recover from the shock of their violent separation, hurried to his side, but it was hopeless; his awareness of her presence was gone. Finally David dragged himself out of the bed and into the bathroom. Watching him, she was flooded with longing, barely able to think of anything except repeating the incredible experience they had just shared. Last night was gone, but there would be tonight, and perhaps the night after that. If she couldn't get back into her body, surely the Universe owed her this time with David!

An image of Max's face suddenly intruded on her intensity, accompanied by the strong impression that she needed to return Between. She tried to recapture her earlier focus, but the sense of urgency prodded her again. With a frustrated look toward the bathroom, where she could now hear the shower running, she reluctantly closed her eyes and forced herself to focus on Max.

As the flashes of light and the now familiar spinning sensation began, she allowed herself to relive the intense pleasure she had just shared with David. Then her mind floated free, reveling in anticipated delights of the coming night.

Chapter 28

Katie sighed and rubbed her eyes. They felt tired and scratchy, as if there really was a Sandman who made evening rounds, blowing tiny clouds of grit into the faces of children who would much prefer to stay awake.

Only she didn't really want to stay awake. In fact, she had planned to go to sleep early tonight, just on the off chance that her mother might once again pay her a visit; but for some reason she felt reluctant to turn off the light and go to sleep. She told herself to stop being silly. This was her very own room, in her very own house. Her father was just down the hall, probably asleep by now, but easily awakened if she should call out to him. There was no reason for her to feel afraid.

"Oh, pooh!" Sticking out her tongue at any invisible monsters who might be lurking, she reached over and snapped off the bedside lamp. The nightlight, its burned-out bulb replaced, softly illuminated the room. But instead of providing its usual comfort, the dim glow threw sinister shadows she had never noticed before onto the walls and ceiling. Even the tightly closed closet door seemed poised on the verge of creaking open.

"Oh, stop it!" she said aloud. Her voice sounded peculiar, as if a stranger had spoken.

She considered running down the hall to cuddle up against her father, who would hold her warm and safe, but a stubbornness inherited from her mother kept her trembling between her own sheets. She gritted her teeth. She would not be driven out of her room by something that probably wasn't even there!

But that did not mean she had to lie here in creepy half darkness. Reaching over, she switched on the lamp again. The shadows retreated and the room resumed its everyday appearance. Nothing creaked or moaned; the closet door stayed shut; the nightlight did not burn out again. After several vigilant minutes, Katie lay back against the pillow and resolutely closed her eyes. When everything continued to remain quiet, she began to relax, gradually drifting into sleep.

A sharp pain, like needles sticking in her upper right arm, made her scream. She tried to pull the needles out with her left hand, but something hard and feather-covered seemed to be attached to them. An instant later, her left arm felt other, smaller needles pricking it, and the most dreadful smell washed over her, as if she had been dunked in dog poop. It made her want to throw up.

Forcing her eyes open, she screamed again. Two huge birds were dragging her out of the bed. Their claws were the needles she had felt and the awful stink was coming from their ratty-looking feathers. Katie twisted, trying to pull herself free, but she could not break their grip.

"Daddy! Daddy!" Her voice sounded thin and far away and she knew her father would never hear it. The birds were pulling her upward, toward the ceiling. Looking down, she could see herself, eyes closed, still curled under the green and cream quilt. She must be out of her body again, like she had been last night!

But last night had been exciting and wonderful, not scary and painful. What were these awful creatures who were carrying her off between them? Her mother would never send someone to frighten and hurt her like this.

She twisted again, trying to escape the pricking sharpness of their claws.

"Stop struggling!" She could barely pick the words out of the huge bird's harsh shriek.

She looked up. The glowing eyes of her captors were filled with a terrible, wild glee. Beaked noses, deeply lined cheeks, and bulgy lips made them seem like cartoons of birds pretending to be women.

"Daddy! Daddy, help me!"

Her voice was no more than a wisp of sound, and the tightly closed bedroom door grew dimmer and farther away. The ceiling, which had become thin and misty, disappeared altogether as the creatures lifted her higher and higher. Craning her neck, she looked down. The roof of their house was now below her, growing rapidly smaller. With each heavy flap, the wings of these nightmare monsters were carrying her farther and farther from any source of help.

The stink of their feathers filled her nose, almost suffocating her. Try as she would, she could not keep tears from seeping out of her eyes and trickling down her cheeks. The creature on her left turned its horrible face toward her and stretched its thick lips, showing sharp, yellow teeth. Katie screamed again. She gasped for air, sucking in the dreadful smell, and fell into a fit of coughing that made her head feel like it was bursting. Her next scream trailed away into a weak gagging sound. She coughed again. Her tear-stained eyes drooped and her head fell forward.

Screeching triumphantly, the Harpies rose with their burden into a starless night.

§

Squinting against the early morning light, David staggered into the bathroom. He was still shaking from the telephone's strident assault on his nervous system, as well as his wrenching separation from Stacy. Leaning against the tiles of the shower wall, he closed his eyes and let the water pour over him. Steam filled the stall, then gradually diminished as he turned the hot spray down lower and lower. When the water grew too cold to be comfortable, he cranked off the faucets and stood shivering for a moment, before stepping out into the air-cooled chill of the bathroom. Quickly toweling off, he shrugged on his underwear and scrubs.

He felt like he hadn't slept at all. Reaching the kitchen just as the timer-controlled coffee maker finished its brew cycle, he poured himself a generous dose of espresso. Holding the mug in one hand, he grabbed the wall phone and dropped into a chair at the glass-topped table. He punched in Minerva's number, sipping the scalding coffee as he waited for her to pick up on the other end.

"Come on, come on!" he muttered after the fourth ring. He was about to hang up when Minerva's sleepy voice answered.

"This is David," he told her. "Could you come over in about ten minutes and stay with Katie? I've been called in on an emergency." He listened with relief to her reply. "Thanks. Thanks a lot. Don't forget your key; I may have to leave before you get here."

Leaning over, he replaced the handset in its cradle, grateful that Minerva lived next door and that she was always willing to help out. She was a bit odd, but she never failed to be there when she was needed.

Setting his coffee on the table, he allowed himself to savor the past night's experience. He rarely remembered his dreams, but this one had been incredibly vivid, carrying sight, sound, touch, scent, even taste, to indescribable heights. Not only was the overall content still fresh in his mind, but he could also recall every detail—the yielding softness of Stacy in his arms; her familiar scent; the sweetness of her mouth on his. Then they had both exploded, the heat of their passion whirling them into and through each other, melting them together until they were fused into a single, incredible distillation of desire and love.

He could feel the craving for that fusion rising in him. God, how he loved her! He could no longer recall his grievances, only the happy times before the arguments started, the familiar warmth of her slender body wrapped around his, the smiling perfection of her face.

Her face! He sucked in an involuntary breath. How was he going to tell her about her face? How could he possibly tell her?

Wait a minute, he thought. *You're talking like last night really happened, like you'll be seeing her again the way you did in the dream.*

But they had discussed that; he remembered the conversation clearly. She had assured him that he was not dreaming, that they really were together. And it had felt real—incredibly, wonderfully real. Yet, how could that be? His pragmatic, medically trained left brain assured him that such a meeting could not have happened, that it had been nothing more than a figment born of his exhaustion, loneliness, and longing. Yet every synapse of his right brain flashed the conviction that last night's encounter had been more vivid, more real, than anything he had so far experienced in his thirty-six years of so-called daily reality.

Shaking his head, he pushed back the chair and stood up. His eye caught the wall clock over the sink, and with an exclamation, he grabbed his keys off the counter, snatched up his briefcase and laptop, and raced for the door. He paused, listening for sounds from upstairs, but Katie seemed to still be asleep. Minerva would arrive momentarily, almost certainly before she awakened.

As he peeled out of the driveway, he promised himself he wouldn't try to puzzle out anything more about last night. He had a full day's surgery on his plate, and he needed to keep his mind clear. He would give full attention to his work today—but tonight was another matter.

Last night might have been just a dream; but maybe, just maybe, it hadn't. With any luck at all, he would go to sleep tonight and find Stacy waiting for him. Smiling, he accelerated into traffic and headed for St. Mark's and his emergency patient.

Chapter 29

Katie opened her eyes to total darkness. Her arms ached and stung, and her head throbbed. Her bed seemed to be full of little stones, which didn't make any sense, because she had just helped her father change the sheets yesterday.

Pulling herself into a sitting position, she groped for the bedside lamp. A fiery pain shot through her index finger, as her hand struck something hard and rough. Sticking the finger in her mouth, she tasted blood. A memory thrust itself into her mind: huge, ugly birds and a sickening smell; sharp claws on her arms and the sensation of being lifted up and up. From a place deep inside her, fear uncoiled itself like a snake charmer's cobra.

"Mommy, Daddy, help!" The blackness seemed to absorb her words as they left her lips.

Jumping to her feet, she ran, sobbing, in what she thought was the opposite direction from the object that had cut her finger, but she almost immediately slammed into something solid. The impact threw her backward onto the floor, where she lay, stunned, her breath coming in ragged gasps.

Gradually her breathing quieted. Struggling against an almost overwhelming urge to run screaming into the darkness again, she dug her fingernails into the palms of her hands, biting her lower lip until she once again tasted blood.

"It's OK," she whispered, trembling. "It's OK. Wherever I am, God is. Wherever I am, God is." She continued to lie on her back, repeating this over and over, until her breathing became more regular. The panic gradually withdrew, leaving her soaked with perspiration. Drawing a shuddering breath, she sat up and carefully felt around her.

The floor was hard and cool and there was gravelly stuff every place she touched. Scooping some up, she sniffed it. Dirt! Dirt and stones! And something else, something nasty that she couldn't identify. This was not a floor; she must be outside. That's why it was so dark; she was outside in the night. But where? And how had she gotten here?

An image of the horrible bird-women carrying her flashed into her memory again. She shivered. Maybe they were real, not just a nightmare. Or maybe this *was* a nightmare, although it was much more detailed and nasty than any she had ever had. Whatever was going on, she could certainly feel pain, as if it was really happening.

Suddenly she remembered looking down and seeing herself lying in the bed. Maybe this was the same sort of thing that had taken place last night, when she came out of her body and spent time with her mother. If that was true, the body she was in now wasn't the one she wore in the daytime; but somehow it could still get hurt. She wondered if her physical body would show the cuts and scratches she was getting in this one when she got back into it. If she got back into it.

"Stop that!" she told herself again firmly. Of course, she would get back into her physical body—she couldn't stay here forever. Or could she? Maybe her body was in a coma, like Mommy's. What would Daddy do, when he came to call her for school and couldn't get her to wake up? Would he put her in the hospital with Mommy? What would he think if her body looked all scraped and bleeding, lying there in bed?

Suddenly she noticed that she was able to see a little; morning must be coming. As the light grew steadily stronger, she stretched out her right hand and saw that a deep scratch now ran from the base of her index finger up to the nail. Raising her head, she looked around. She was sitting at one side of a small clearing surrounded by four large, rough-barked trees. It must have been one of those she had bumped into.

Climbing to her feet, she leaned against the nearest tree. She had just worked up her courage to find out what lay beyond, when she heard screeching sounds approaching. A moment later, the two huge bird-women from her nightmare burst into the clearing, shrieking loudly. It sounded like they were arguing. Katie listened hard, but could catch only a few words here and there.

"... said to ... for him here."

"... do what we ... No! ... we promised."

Trying to ignore her throbbing finger and the pain in her arms and head, Katie carefully backed up against the nearest tree. When the bird-faced women continued to bicker, she began to inch her way around the trunk.

The head of the larger one shot up, bobbing on its long, skinny neck. With a croaking sound, it flapped toward her, its wings releasing the awful dog poop smell she remembered from her bedroom. She quickly edged back into the clearing. The bird-woman stopped moving in her direction and started screeching again at the smaller one, but this time its eyes kept darting toward Katie, who crouched down at the foot of the tree and tried to make herself as small as possible. Squinting her eyes tightly shut, she thought frantically, *Somebody get me out of here!*

A sudden image of Max flowed into her mind. He was gazing earnestly at her and his voice sounded clearly in her head. "Katie, I can hear you. Just keep the connection open and we'll find you."

He disappeared, but the message remained, strong and comforting: Max knew she was here! He was looking for her. He and Mommy would find her, if she helped them know where she was.

Taking a deep breath, she closed her eyes and pictured her mother standing in the beautiful place where she had seen her last night. Directing every ounce of energy she could muster, she sent out a mental cry.

"Mommy! Mommy, I need you! I'm in a place with trees all around and two nasty bird-ladies. Please, Mommy, come find me! Come find me as soon as you can!"

§

David stood at the foot of the hospital bed, Stacy's chart in his hand. It was difficult to think of the figure under the blankets as the vibrant woman with whom he had just spent the night. The swollen, discolored face on the pillow looked not only unfamiliar, but as different from the one he had recently kissed as Helen of Troy's fabled beauty would be from the cobbled-together features of the Bride of Frankenstein.

Here, surrounded by the cold sterility of medicines and machines, he was once again tempted to believe that last night's encounter had been nothing more than an incredibly vivid dream. But what a dream!

Recalling the warmth of Stacy's lips on his, he could feel his body, dissolved into its component atoms, intermingling with hers. He drew in his breath sharply. *God! What an experience!*

He jumped as a hand touched his shoulder.

"Sorry." Colin Elmore had entered the room and was standing just behind him. "Thought this might be a good time to discuss Stacy's condition."

David nodded. Hanging the chart back on the foot of the bed, he followed Elmore to the chief of staff's office. They sat down, one on either side of the desk, and Elmore leaned toward David.

"It's been a week, now."

David nodded.

"The craniotomy did well, her vital signs are stable—liver, too, although I was hoping it would be improved by now. I think we can begin to withdraw the barbiturates, see what her brain is doing." He leaned back in his leather chair. "Sound OK?"

David nodded again. "Sounds good."

Elmore smiled. "I'll put the order through for this afternoon and we'll do the scan in a couple of days. If her brain responds, we'll go from there." He raised a bushy eyebrow. "Even if everything progresses well, she'll need extensive plastic work to repair that right cheek. No guarantee of the outcome, either, except she probably won't ever look the way she did before."

"I know." Pushing back his chair, David stood up. "Anything else?"

"Not that I can think of." Elmore looked at him closely. "You OK?"

"I guess, given the circumstances." David smiled faintly, remembering his dream—if it was a dream. A moment of intense anticipation flashed through him. Tonight. If she came again tonight, he'd know it was real.

"David?" Elmore was watching him.

David forced himself back into the moment. "I'm fine. Just thinking." He smiled again. "Guess I'd better check recovery and see how our emergency's doing."

With a wave of his hand, he left the room, softly closing the door behind him.

Chapter 30

The whirling movement stopped and, her thoughts still immersed in the exciting prospect of spending another night with David, Stacy reluctantly opened her eyes. She was back in her room at the Entry Processing Center, with Max solemnly watching her from the windowsill, tail curled around his feet.

With an effort, she turned her attention toward him. "Max, is something wrong?"

"Very wrong."

A tingle of apprehension rippled through her. "What's happened?"

He gazed at her solemnly. "It's Katie—she's been taken by the Harpies."

"The what? What are you talking about?"

"Harpies—as in unpleasant mythological creatures, repulsive big birds with female faces. Two of them have been holed up in a grove of trees in the grassland area. For some unknown reason, they re-entered the Earth realm last night and went after Katie. They must have carried her off as she was coming out of her body, before she could reach the dream state. It's the only way they could bring her here."

Stacy's chest felt like a giant hand was constricting it. "My God! Where is she? Do you know?"

"Yes, I know; I've already been in mental contact with her." Standing up, he gave himself a spine-rippling shake. "She's in the little grove of trees where the Harpies have taken up residence. So far she's relatively unhurt, but we need to get her out of there as soon as we can."

"Relatively unhurt?"

"She's a bit scratched up and, of course, frightened. Other than that, she's fine."

"Fine? How can she be fine?" Stacy controlled an impulse to pick him up and give him a good shake. "How do we find her? Can we go right now?"

"I can only answer one question at a time, Stacy." Max looked at her with what she remembered Katie calling his patient face. "The first thing we need to do is let Herm and Minerva know what has happened."

"Do we have to take time for that? Can't we just go get her ourselves?" She gritted her teeth in exasperation. "Max, my daughter is being held hostage by what you've referred to as repulsive creatures who have already hurt her. How do we know they aren't getting ready to do her some real harm—or," the giant hand squeezed her chest harder, "have already done some?"

"Calm yourself, Stacy. We would both feel it if that had happened." His patient look shifted to a thoughtful one, and the tip of his ringed tail twitched. "All right," he told her, "we'll go. I've just sent a mental message to Minerva, and she will notify Herm. They should join us shortly after we arrive." He leaped lightly into her arms. "We need to arrive unnoticed, so do your best not to think about Katie. Just concentrate on the area a little distance from the grove of trees where the Harpies are holding her."

"Thanks, Max." Clutching him to her chest, she resolutely pushed the image of Katie, alone and threatened by monsters, out of her mind. She focused, instead, on seeing herself and Max outside a grove of trees concealing ugly, bird-faced women.

Lights flashed and sparkled again and she impatiently gave herself over to the now familiar whirling sensation. When she opened her eyes, she was standing in grass up to her thighs. Setting Max down beside her, she saw a small stand of trees punctuating the waving green expanse a short distance away.

"Is that where she is?" she hissed.

"You probably don't need to whisper; we're far enough away that it's unlikely they can hear us. However," he nudged her leg, "you might pick me up again. The view down here is rather limited."

"Sorry!" She bent down and gathered him into her arms. "I remember seeing pictures of Harpies in a mythology book, and they looked fairly small. Certainly not big enough to carry off an eight-year-old child."

"A picture may be worth ten thousand words, but it doesn't always

🐾 🐾 🐾 **Between** 🐾 🐾 🐾

tell the complete truth." Max squirmed around in her arms until he could look into her eyes. "Listen to me, Stacy. The Harpies are not to be taken lightly. They are not little twittery sparrows flapping helplessly around. They stand taller than you do and they have sharp talons, because they're modeled after birds of prey. They also have teeth. And," he added, "by their very nature, they are not well disposed toward human beings."

Stacy shivered, despite the warm breeze rippling the grass. "So, what do we do?"

"Minerva hasn't responded to my mental message, so I'll have to go look for her. Then we'll find Herm and join you here."

Stacy glanced at the grove of trees. "All right," she sighed, "if you think that's best. But please hurry!" She set Max on the ground again, where he was swallowed up by the sea of green.

"Just stay put." His voice floated up to her. "Do not, under any circumstances, try to get Katie out by yourself. I'll be back with the others as quickly as possible."

A few sparkles of light drifted up from the spot where she had set him down and she could feel his energy pattern disappear.

She was on her own in the vast emptiness of the wind-swept prairie.

§

"Iblis!"

Serizzin's voice rang like iron against stone.

"My lord?"

"Do you value my friendship?"

"My lord," Iblis quavered, "I do not understand the question. I exist only to serve you. My lord must be aware of that."

"Must I?" The voice scraped and grated. "I have learned that the human, Arthur Craddock, has ventured back into the physical world a second time without your counsel. What have you to say to this?"

Iblis trembled. His last visit to Serizzin had resulted in an unavoidable lack of vigilance on his part. During that short interval, Craddock had once again initiated certain actions of his own accord. After a brief internal debate, Iblis decided that pretending ignorance of the motivation for Craddock's behavior would only serve to further inflame

Serizzin's anger. "It is true, my lord." He tried to keep his voice from shaking. "Craddock desires revenge on the soul known as Stacy Addison."

A smoky appendage billowed out from the column and briefly touched him. Iblis recoiled in pain.

"I care nothing about Craddock's desires. Your task is to make his agenda my agenda. Fail, and you may find yourself becoming one with those who have already joined me as my constant companions." The moans and wails inside the churning column swelled, then subsided to their former muted roar. "He is your responsibility; see that you do not lose control of him again."

Iblis flickered. Even as they spoke, Craddock was unsupervised. He steadied himself with an effort.

"Yes, my lord."

The column of darkness churned and expanded. "I have also learned that he has roused the Harpies and set them upon Stacy Addison's child."

"It—it is so, my lord. He thinks to punish the mother through the child."

The whirling column was silent, except for the muted howls and groans within; then Serizzin leaned toward Iblis.

"Make certain that this does not happen. Influence Craddock to help Stacy Addison recover her daughter undamaged. Plant in his mind the conviction that doing so will place her in his debt and increase his opportunity for revenge at a later date. See to it that he continues to construe your words as his inner guidance."

"Yes, my lord. Do you suggest anything further?"

"Suggest? I suggest nothing, my expendable friend. Suggestions, like obedience, are your department."

For a moment, the column slowed its incessant spinning and the mewling groans within it sank to a hideous whisper. It inclined itself toward Iblis. A hissing, like steam escaping a great pressure, issued from its center.

"Listen to me, servant of Serizzin. The time approaches when my reality will no longer depend on the vagaries of humankind. Craddock must not escape you again. He is the necessary tool, the connection that will bring the soul known as Stacy Addison under my control."

The whirling motion began to gather speed again. "And I will have her, Iblis, do you hear me? With her in my power, I will take my place as master, not only of my own existence, but also of the human world to which she yearns to return."

The discordant chorus of screams and moans soared again, and the column began to churn faster and faster. A rumble emerged from its center, swelling in depth and volume until the blackened earth shook and the blighted trees surrounding the massive vortex began to split and shatter.

Serzizin's exultant laughter continued to swell and throb. Cautiously retreating into the curtains of dusk that swirled around the clearing, Iblis hurtled back through the blasted landscape toward his assignment and his burden—Arthur Craddock.

§

"Sssst!"

Minerva looked up from her coffee, startled, to see Max standing in the kitchen doorway.

"What are you doing here?" A frown creased her forehead. "I thought you were Between."

"I am Between, or I was. You need to be there, too."

Minerva shook her head. "Katie is still upstairs asleep. I'm going to wake her for school in about fifteen minutes, though. Once she's gone—"

"She's not going. You won't be able to wake her up, either. Those two mangy Harpies that have been hanging around the prairie carried her off last night and are holding her prisoner."

"Good Lord!" Minerva jumped to her feet. "We'd better find her right away!"

Max shook his head. "Stacy's there, keeping an eye on the grove. You and I need to locate Herm. It may take his authority to get Katie out."

"I understand. Just let me lie down beside Katie's body, and we'll be on our way."

She glanced back over her shoulder. "Check the doors, would you, to be sure they're all locked, and pray that nothing brings David home before we get back!"

Hiking up her long, purple skirt, she took the stairs two at a time.

Chapter 31

Stacy sat in the tall, waving grass, where Max had left her. He had ordered her to stay put, but what did that mean? Was she supposed to sit here until he returned with Minerva and Herm? Who knew how long that would be! And although the grass kept her hidden from sight, it also prevented her from seeing what might be approaching, a prospect she found extremely unappealing. Besides, knowing that Katie was a prisoner somewhere in that nearby grove of trees made it almost impossible for her to stay where she was, doing nothing.

She finally decided to compromise: she would stay down, out of sight, but she would also crawl toward the trees, hoping they would keep the grove's inhabitants from noticing her. She might even find a way of getting Katie safely away, despite Max's admonition!

Maneuvering herself onto her hands and knees, she crept slowly forward. What seemed like a long time later, the green stalks thinned and she could see ahead of her a space dotted with ragged scrub. Beyond this were the trees, the spaces between them bristling with thorny bushes. She carefully raised her head above the top of the waving grass, then ducked quickly back down.

A figure was moving near one of the trees! Heart pounding, she tried to decide what to do. The endless expanse of grass had seemed empty of any activity when she and Max arrived; surely he would have warned her if he'd been aware that they had company. Chewing her lower lip, she made an effort to be calm. Finally, she carefully raised herself into a modified crouch and peered out again.

The figure was still there, flattened against the trunk of the tree where she had first caught sight of it. Narrowing her eyes against the brightness of the day, she saw that it was a man. She dropped back down and crept closer, then cautiously lifted her head again so that it barely topped the grass. She could see now that he was shorter and heavier than David. Light brown hair reached almost to his shoulders and his tanned face was long and narrow. She watched, fascinated, as his eyes ranged over the expanse of grass in front of him, swept across her hiding place, then returned.

She stiffened with shock. He had seen her!

Max is not going to like this! Her first impulse was to crouch back down, see if she could back away and keep hidden. However, the thought of crawling blindly through the tall grass, not knowing where she was going, or where her pursuer—assuming he would pursue her—might be, seemed too cowardly to be entertained.

Clenching her jaw, she slowly stood up. To her surprise, the man immediately motioned her down again. Dropping back to her knees, she waited, wondering why he had given such a signal. Who was he? Why was he here? Was he a friend, or could he be working with the Harpies?

"Where are you?" His voice was only slightly louder than the whisper of the grass.

After a moment's indecision, she replied softly, "Here. To your left."

"Good. Be sure you stay low." He was beside her almost as he spoke.

He stared at her, an odd expression in his cool, blue eyes, until she felt a tinge of discomfort. Then he looked away, toward the grove of trees.

"Those things in there have a prisoner," he said. "A little girl."

Her heart leaped. "Have you seen her?"

The man cautiously raised his head above the grass, then lowered it again. "I have. I was passing by the trees and heard noises. When I looked through the bushes, I saw two huge birds hopping around. The child was sitting under a the tree opposite the one I was near. She looked really scared."

Stacy made an effort to control her anxiety. "Did she seem OK?"

"Scratched up some, maybe. She wasn't moving, so I couldn't tell anything else."

"She's my daughter. Those things carried her off earlier tonight."

The man gave a low whistle. "No wonder you're watching the grove."

He seated himself on the ground beside her. "What are you going to do?"

"I'm waiting for some friends, so we can go in and get her." She watched another expression she could not interpret flicker across his face.

"Will they be here soon?"

"I don't know." Her anxiety returned full force. "Do you think they need to be?"

The man shook his head. "I don't know. Those bird things seemed all worked up, like they were getting ready to do something."

Stacy gnawed her lower lip. "Damn! Maybe I shouldn't wait."

Faint sounds drifted to them from the direction of the trees. The man raised his head above the grass again, then dropped back beside her. "Seems to be some sort of commotion going on in there."

Stacy clenched her fists. "I've got to go in after her!"

She started to stand up, but the man grabbed her arm and pulled her back down beside him. "You can't go in there alone! It would be two against one." His voice sounded earnest. "At least let me go with you. That'll balance the odds."

Gratitude and relief surged through her. "You'd do that? You don't even know me!"

"I know that you're in trouble and need help." He rose to a crouching position, his head just enough above the grass to be able to see. Stacy joined him.

"I'll work my way around to the far side," he told her. "You move up to that larger tree over here. If we go in from opposite sides, we may be able to confuse and separate them. Just be sure you let me make the first move."

Stacy nodded and watched the man move, crab-like, around the perimeter of the grove, until he finally disappeared behind the trees. She herself crept forward until she reached the tree where her new companion had originally been standing. Carefully parting the thorny branches of the bush next to it, she peered through them and choked back a gasp.

Katie was sitting opposite her, leaning against the rough bark of the largest tree. Her eyes were closed, but Stacy could tell from the tension in her body that she was not sleeping. She bit back tears at the sight of a long cut on her daughter's finger and the bruises and scratches on her bare arms and legs.

The breeze shifted, wafting an incredible stench in her direction. Fighting down an urge to vomit, she became aware of movement near the tree on her right. Two monstrous, vulture-like figures detached themselves from the shadows and started toward Katie. Wings half raised, they hopped along, huge heads bobbing on skinny necks, nightmare faces grimacing in what Stacy interpreted as smiles of anticipation.

Suddenly the man sprang out from behind one of the bushes, shouting and waving his arms. The monsters stopped their advance, looking from him to Katie. The little girl's closed eyes had popped open and she was now shrinking back against the tree trunk.

"Grab her and get out of here!" the man yelled to Stacy. Electrified into action, she shot out from behind her bush toward Katie, who with a cry, ran into her arms.

"Come on, baby!" Grabbing her daughter's hand, Stacy half dragged her around the tree, trying to shield her from the thorny branches that seemed to snatch at them as they passed. Sobbing, the two of them raced into the tall grass, running until Katie could no longer stay on her feet. Sinking to the ground beside her, Stacy held the shaking child close, hoping the waving stalks would conceal them.

"It's all right, honeybunch, it's all right." Stacy smoothed Katie's tangled hair. "Mommy's here, Mommy's here." She rocked the little girl in her arms, kissing the top of her head. Katie clung to her wordlessly, as if she would never let go.

Stacy's muscles clenched as a whish sounded near them. A moment later, Max's furry face pushed through the grass. Stacy sat up, Katie still shivering in her arms. "Thank God you finally got here!"

He eyed her, one furry eyebrow lifted. "I see you take orders as well as you always have."

Before Stacy could explain what happened, Minerva crawled into the little clearing created by Stacy's body and enfolded her and Katie in a silent hug. A moment later Herm appeared and, gently detaching the little girl from her mother, gathered her up in his arms. Nodding to Max, he disappeared, taking Katie with him.

"Shall we go, too?" Minerva held out her hand to Stacy.

"I'm not sure. That man is still in there with those horrible monsters. We should check to see that he's OK, shouldn't we?"

"Man? What man?" Breaking off his examination of their surroundings, Max looked sharply at her.

"The man who helped me rescue Katie. He was over there, by that tree," she pointed, "and he distracted those things, so I could grab her and make a run for it."

"He did, did he?" Max looked thoughtful. "Nice of him, I must say."

"Yes, it was. Don't you think we should be sure he's OK before we leave? I mean, it's the least we can do."

"You're right. He needs to be checked on, but not by you." Max's tail twitched. "I'll go have a look and let him know that you and Katie are safe."

"OK." Stacy suddenly realized that she was shivering, too. "I guess I'll go with Minerva and see how Katie's doing."

Minerva again held out her hand, and this time Stacy took it. The last thing she saw before the familiar flashes of light obscured her view was Max weaving a purposeful trail through the long grass toward the Harpies' grove.

Chapter 32

Minerva straightened the bed covers around Katie, relieved that none of the scratches or bruises received during her experience with the Harpies had returned with her into the physical realm. Herm had taken the little girl to the Children's Garden, where the boys and girls had abandoned their games, listening open-mouthed as she related her adventure. One little boy had called her a hero, a title that seemed to immediately make worthwhile all the pain and fear she had undergone.

Minerva and Stacy had brought her home. After giving her mother a hug, the exhausted child had gone back into her body and Minerva had followed suit, slipping easily into her own body, which lay dozing next to Katie's. Waking almost immediately, she got up and watched as the little girl slowly opened her eyes and looked around the room, smiling when she reached Minerva's face.

Minerva returned the smile. "You had quite a night, didn't you?"

Katie nodded. "It was scary." She paused, looking thoughtful. "But parts of it were exciting, too."

Minerva nodded. "Life can be like that."

Katie craned her neck so that she could see her upper arms. "Nothing shows any more." Holding out her right hand, she examined the index finger. "No blood, either." She looked up at Minerva. "It doesn't even hurt now. How can that be?"

"It's because you're back in your physical body, Katie. What happened last night happened to your spirit body."

"Doesn't my physical body know what's going on with my spirit body?"

"In a way it does, but the marks on your spirit body don't often show outwardly on your physical one. They show in other ways, like being afraid of doing things that you think might make you hurt again."

"Oh." Katie wrinkled her forehead. "I'm not sure I know what that means."

Minerva looked at her thoughtfully. "Do you want me to demonstrate?"

Katie nodded.

"All right. Keep in mind that what I'm going to do now is simply in order to help you understand how this works." She reached down and gripped Katie's upper arm, squeezing it firmly and allowing her fingernails to press into the skin.

"Ow!" Katie sat up and pulled away. "Don't do that!"

Minerva immediately released her. "How did that make you feel?"

Rubbing her arm, Katie scowled at her. "It hurt!"

"And was it scary?"

"Oh." A thoughtful look replaced the scowl. "It *was* scary. It was what those nasty bird ladies did. All of a sudden I was afraid something bad was going to happen again."

Minerva helped her settle back on the pillow. "That's right. You felt that way because what I did reminded you of the bad things that happened when you were in your spirit body. Even though you know that I would never try to hurt you, the part of you that was hurt last night stepped in and made you feel afraid, anyway."

She watched Katie's face as the little girl, frowning, processed that information. When the frown cleared, she added, "Would you like to let go of those fears right now, before they get stuck in your physical body?"

"How, 'Nerva?"

"Close your eyes a minute. Good. Now, imagine what all that scary stuff would look like if it had a size, and a shape, and a color."

Katie squeezed her eyes together in concentration. "It would be big and black." She paused. "And it would look like a nasty, smelly bird."

Minerva smiled slightly. "All right. Now see a big bubble made of beautifully colored light in your mind. Can you imagine that?"

Katie nodded.

"Now put the big, black, nasty, smelly bird in the bubble, and let the bubble float away into a beautiful light that's waiting to carry it off."

Katie smiled. "OK." After a moment, her eyes popped open. "I did it, 'Nerva. I sent the nasty bird away! I like that."

Minerva smiled again. "Good. You can do that any time something scares you."

Katie nodded. "OK." She looked up at Minerva. "Do I have to get up for school now?"

"Not today. I'll call and tell the office that you are having some difficulties and will be staying home, at least until tomorrow."

Katie yawned. "That's good. Gives me another day to finish my math." She snuggled down against the pillow.

Minerva reached over and gently pulled her left arm from under the covers. The hand was curled into a tight fist. "Wouldn't you like to share what you have in there before you close your eyes? I think you'll sleep better."

Katie sighed. "I thought you'd ask before this."

"I thought you'd tell before I asked."

She watched the little girl slowly uncurl her fingers. In her pressure-reddened palm nestled two crushed feathers. The smell that rose from these made both of them wince. Katie closed her fist again.

Minerva eyed her in amazement. The ability to transfer objects from one realm of existence to another was a rare gift, one that appeared only once or twice a century, and then only in those whose talents had been trained.

But she should have known. Katie had been able to converse with Max since her infancy, and had been delighted to visit her mother Between. In addition, she had accepted all the events of the past several hours without any negative reaction other than the perfectly understandable fear engendered by a frightening experience. Katie was a natural. Minerva—and Max—definitely needed to keep an even closer watch over her development than they had realized.

She smiled at the little girl's expectant look. "So, what do you plan to do with those?" She nodded toward the feathers.

Katie slowly shook her head. "I don't know. I just needed to bring them back with me."

It was Minerva's turn to nod. "I expect you'll figure out how to use them when the time is right." She looked again at the clenched fist. "In the meantime, would you like to put them somewhere safe?"

Katie considered. "I have a penny jar in my bottom dresser drawer. We could dump the pennies out and put them in there."

🐾 🐾 🐾 Between 🐾 🐾 🐾

Minerva went to the dresser, poured the pennies into a pile, and carried the emptied jar back to the bed. Katie opened her fist and let the feathers float into the glass container. Minerva screwed the lid on tightly.

"Yuck! My hands smell just like those nasty bird things!"

Minerva turned back the covers and Katie trotted into the bathroom, returning a few minutes later with both hands scrubbed and smelling of lemon soap. She climbed back into bed and pulled the covers up around her chin.

"Will Mommy be back soon?"

Minerva smiled down into her drowsy eyes. "She's waiting for you now," she said. "She hasn't gone back Between yet, because she wants to see you safely into your dreams. And one of us will be here from now on, every time you fall asleep, to be sure you're always protected."

Katie smiled sleepily. "That's good. But when is Mommy really coming back—into her body, I mean?"

Tenderly tucking a strand of hair behind the little girl's ear, Minerva murmured, " As soon as she can. She'll be back as soon as she can. Go on, now; spend a little time with her before you dream."

She stood up, pressing a hand against her low back. Katie's mattress was definitely lacking in the firmness department! Closing the blinds against the day, she went downstairs and dialed the school; then she called St. Mark's, informing David that his daughter would be staying home to catch up on her sleep, after a restless night. She made a fresh pot of strong coffee and sat down on the sofa with a steaming cup, extracting a half-finished afghan and a skein of lavender yarn from the bag she always carried in her role as Katie's nanny.

This particular afghan closely resembled the virtually endless number of those she had turned out during the years that she had looked after Stacy. Frowning, she examined the row she had ended with last time; as usual, it needed to be unraveled; it almost always needed to be unraveled. Sighing, she began pulling out stitches. She had knitted since she was fifteen, and had always considered it an annoying occupation.

This aggravation factor was the sole reason she continued; by keeping her frustrated, knitting kept her awake. She had realized early on that it would never do for her to inadvertently fall asleep while someone was in her care. Sleeping was an activity she usually engaged in only at home, where time spent out of her body could not cause a potential problem to anyone else, child or adult.

Today she needed to stay awake until David came home. He had told her, when she called about Katie, that his emergency patient had developed a problem, which meant he might have to stay at the hospital as late as six o'clock. Glancing at the VCR, she saw that the digital readout registered eleven forty-five a.m. She had a lot of knitting and unraveling to go!

Sighing, Minerva unwound a length of yarn and stabbed her needle into the half-completed afghan.

Chapter 33

The phone shrilled. Wolfing down the last of the meat loaf and mashed potatoes that Minerva had left for him, David answered on the fifth ring.

"Dr. Addison?" The man's deep, pleasant voice was unfamiliar.

"Actually, I'm Dr. Kinnard. Addison is my wife's name."

"My apologies, Dr. Kinnard." The voice lost none of its resonance. "My name is Evan Chastain. I met your wife about a week ago, when we discussed her hosting the pilot show for our new television channel, KPSI. Perhaps she mentioned it to you."

David nodded, even though the man on the other end of the line could not see him. He had almost forgotten about the television show. The memory of his argument with Stacy rushed into his mind, followed by a stab of guilt. If he hadn't acted like such a total ass, she'd be getting ready for her debut right now. He could see her, exquisitely ethereal, in front of a battery of television cameras. This vision was immediately overlaid by the present reality of her battered body in the bed at St. Mark's. The contrast nauseated him.

"Dr. Kinnard?"

David swallowed. "I'm here."

"I'm sorry to be calling you at home in the evening, but we haven't heard back from Ms. Addison. Would it be possible for me to speak with her?"

Damn! He had no choice but to tell this man the truth. There was no way on God's green earth that Stace would be able to appear in front of a camera in the next few weeks, if ever. Even if her body healed enough to tolerate that stress, her appearance might well cause her to shrink from the thought of going before the public again. Damn! Damn! Damn!

🐾 🐾 🐾 Between 🐾 🐾 🐾

He cleared his throat. "I'm sorry, Mr. Chastain. My wife had an accident the night after she talked with you. She's in the hospital in a coma. At this time, we're not sure what the outcome will be."

"I'm very sorry!" Evan Chastain's voice sounded genuinely distressed. David had no idea whether it was on Stacy's behalf, or because he was going to have to find a new host for his show.

"I'm sorry, too," he said. *You have no idea how sorry*, he added mentally. "Perhaps when she recovers, she can give you a call?"

Evan Chastain paused a beat before replying. "Certainly, Dr. Kinnard. Have her do that. In the meantime, is there any way I can be of service?"

David shook his head again. "Can't think of a thing, but thanks for asking."

"You're most welcome. Please convey my regrets to Ms. Addison when she—" the deep voice paused again, "when she's herself again."

"I'll do that." David hung up the receiver.

If she's ever herself again. He squinted, feeling his eyes burn. Must be tireder than I realized, he told himself. He squinted again, then focused on Stacy as she had appeared to him last evening, incredibly lovely and desirable.

Maybe she would come again tonight! He quickly rinsed the dirty dishes and loaded them into the dishwasher. Then, whistling, he took the stairs two at a time.

Katie was standing in the hall, her rumpled hair and footed pajamas making her look like she was five years old. David smiled down at her.

"I thought you were already asleep. Minerva said you were all worn out."

She shook her head solemnly. "I slept a whole bunch today. Besides, I was waiting up for you."

"OK, here I am." He crossed his eyes and stuck out his tongue. Katie smiled wanly.

"Where's my giggle girl?" Picking her up, David tickled her tummy. Instead of squirming with laughter as she usually did, she reached up and fastened her arms around his neck.

"Hey," he said softly. They hugged for a long minute, then he carried her into her room and set her down on the bed. Kneeling in front of her, he touched her cheek. "What is it, kitten? What's the matter?"

She slid off the quilt and went to her dresser. Opening the bottom drawer, she pulled out an empty-looking Mason jar.

"What happened to the pennies?"

Mutely, she pointed to a pile of copper coins on the top of the dresser. David looked more closely at the jar and frowned. "What have you got in there?"

"Feathers."

He unscrewed the lid. "Phew!" Holding the jar away from him, he wrinkled his nose. "What the heck is that?"

"It's nasty bird-lady feathers," Katie informed him. "They stink."

David started to put his hand into the jar, but Katie pulled it away.

"They're mine. I have to keep them." She screwed the lid back on.

David rubbed the top of his head. "Okay, kitten, you've got me going on this one. I assume that, since you've showed me this much, you're also going to tell me what it's about."

Katie stared at him. She actually seemed to be considering whether or not she would go further with her revelation. David half smiled at her. "Well? Do I rate the rest of the story, or not?"

After a long moment, she carefully set the jar on her bedside table and turned back to him. Taking his face in her hands, she looked into his eyes.

"Promise me you won't laugh or say it's just my imagination."

David put his broad hands over her small ones. "I promise."

"Cross your heart and hope to die, stick a needle in your eye?"

He winced. "That is so gross!"

She started to pull her hands away, but he held them tightly.

"I agree, I agree!" Dropping one hand, he made an "X" over his heart.

"OK, then; I'll tell you." Reaching over, she picked up the jar again. "These are feathers from the stinky bird ladies who came into my room last night and flew away with me."

David opened his mouth to speak, but she laid her finger across his lips. "Don't say anything, Daddy. Just listen, OK?"

He nodded.

"Remember, I told you about being with Mommy night before last? Well, this was sort of like that, only it wasn't nice or fun."

Watching the changing expressions on her mobile little face, he listened as she related her most recent adventure. She had to set the jar down again, in order to use her hands to illustrate what she was describing, and once she slid off the bed and began to hop around the room, flapping her arms and bobbing her head up and down in what looked like a grotesque dance.

At first, he felt amused. What a great little storyteller she was! But as the tale progressed, a sense of uneasiness began to crawl up his spine. How could she just make all this up on the spur of the moment? And where had those rancid-smelling feathers come from? She hadn't been out of the house since he tucked her in last night, and he'd dropped a handful of pennies into that already half-filled jar on his way out of the room.

A memory of Stacy catching him by the heel and pulling him back into the bedroom as he was floating through the ceiling, flashed into his mind, and what felt like a cold finger touched the back of his neck. Could this improbable story actually be true? If it were, then Katie wasn't safe, even when she was asleep! Maybe nobody was! Maybe …

"Daddy! You aren't listening to me!"

David forced his attention back into the room. "Sorry, kitten. What you were saying made me think of something."

Katie was watching him intently. "What, Daddy? What did it make you think of?"

David picked her up and held her on his lap. "For one thing, it made me realize just how dear you are to me." He nuzzled her neck. This time she did giggle a little; then she threw her arms around him in a fierce hug, whispering, "You're very dear to me too, Daddy."

Tears stung his eyes. Whether Katie's story was true, or not, it had brought home something important to both of them.

Sitting back, she touched a single tear that had squeezed itself out onto his cheek. "Don't cry, Daddy." She leaned over and kissed him. "Mommy or 'Nerva or Max will always be there from now on when I come out of my body to go dreaming. They'll keep me safe." She looked at him earnestly. "I'm going to ask them to keep you safe, too."

Holding her tightly, David stood up and whirled in a circle. "God, I love you, Katie Addison-Kinnard! You'd better be safe; I don't know what I would do without you!"

"Me neither," Katie whispered, arms tight around his neck. "Me neither, Daddy."

🐾 🐾 🐾 Between 🐾 🐾 🐾

§

Dusk was gathering over the prairie like a gray mist, seeping down between the restless stalks of grass and drifting, wraith-like, between the branches of the trees. Herm, his tunic fresh and snowy white, stood at the edge of the Harpies' grove. A flat, winged cap covered most of his dark curls and he held a short, gold staff, around which two serpents twined, holding their heraldic positions despite a tendency to periodically hiss and strike at one another.

It wasn't often that he felt called upon to present himself in full divine regalia; however, this visit was official. A serious rebuke was in order, demanding proper presentation. Squaring his shoulders, he entered the grove.

The stench that rolled out to meet him was one he had not encountered in more centuries than he cared to remember. Only the fact that a god could not under any circumstances relinquish his dignity kept him from retreating into the fresher air of the open grassland beyond the trees. The small clearing was littered with piles of droppings, and scraggy feathers were strewn everywhere, infusing the entire area with the blended aroma of excrement and rotting refuse.

The Harpies were huddled together under the largest tree, apparently sleeping, although Herm doubted that such a normal animal act was possible for them. Taking care where he stepped, he picked his way to the center of the glade. The smaller Harpy raised her head and caught sight of him. Hopping excitedly up and down, she began to screech.

"Sister, sister, we have company again! Company again!"

The larger one turned bold eyes toward him. "Who are you, intruder? Why do you disturb us?"

Herm stared at them. "Do you not recognize me? I once intervened on your behalf, when the sons of the North Wind would have torn you to shreds."

The monstrous bird-women bent their heads together, whispering shrilly. The larger looked at him again.

"You are Hermes, messenger of the Olympians?"

"I am."

"Accept our apologies for not recognizing you sooner, Lord Hermes.

Between

What news do you bring us?"

"What news, what news?" echoed the smaller one, hopping from one foot to the other.

Herm's handsome face grew stern. "I come to inform you that you have overstepped your bounds."

The Harpies nervously fluttered their wings, creating a storm of noxious-smelling feathers.

Herm held his ground. "You no longer possess a rightful place in the human world, yet you have, without permission, left this grove and re-entered that world. You have stolen a human child and held her captive, with intent to harm her." His eyes held theirs. "Is this not true?"

Both Harpies seemed to shrink in on themselves. "It is true," the larger screeched, "that we stole the child and brought her here. But we did so only to balance our debt to the human, Arthurcraddock, who had rendered us a signal service. It was solely at his request that we carried off the child, and it was not our intent to harm her."

"Not our intent," echoed the smaller one. "And after we had carried out his wish, he confused us. He came here with a woman and helped her free the child." Her head bobbed furiously on her scrawny neck.

The larger Harpy fluttered her wings. "He did not even do us the courtesy of informing us that he would behave in such a manner." Her harsh voice took on a wheedling note. "We meant the child no harm, Lord Hermes. We only fulfilled Arthurcraddock's wishes, in order to repay his kindness to us."

Herm continued to regard them sternly. "Even if what you tell me is true, you have nevertheless overstepped your bounds. When you were given this grove, you were commanded to keep yourselves to it; you have undeniably broken that command. For that you should be punished."

The monstrous creatures began to hop up and down, feathers spraying in every direction. Doing his best to ignore the stench, Herm raised his staff again. "Stop!" The bird-women became still.

"I said '*should* be punished.' Since your motive was good, I shall overlook your behavior this time. But," he continued, seeing the gleam of hope in their eyes, "there is to be no more activity of this nature. If there is, you will be banished to the gray land, and there you will stay until you fade from existence."

🐾 🐾 🐾 Between 🐾 🐾 🐾

Both Harpies surged toward him, shrilling expressions of gratitude. Once again, Herm held up his golden staff, halting them before they could completely cross the clearing.

"One more thing." He pointed the rod toward the Harpies, who backed away as the serpent's heads hissed at them. "To assure me of your good will, I expect you to come to my assistance, should I call you, no matter when, or what the reason. In addition, you will refuse any further help to this human, Arthurcraddock, should he ask you for it."

The larger Harpy bobbed her head vigorously, followed by the smaller one. "Yes, Lord Hermes," they chorused.

"We will come whenever you wish our services," the larger shrilly assured him.

"And we will never again help Arthurcraddock, even should he request it," the smaller one agreed.

"I shall hold you to your word," Herm lowered the staff. "Know with certainty that I will be aware if you should break it."

Leaving them squawking excitedly behind him, he turned and strode toward the trees where he had entered the grove. Passing between them, he quickened his pace, taking a deep breath of clean air as he reached the open prairie. For a painful moment he missed the companionship of his fellow gods. This encounter with the two surviving Harpies would have made a good tale to tell around a table loaded with a smoking haunch of beef. But that was no longer possible, at least not here, in the *now* most closely interactive with the ongoing linear time of Earth.

His father, Zeus, had long since retired with the other gods to the gardens reserved for those once great divinities whose followers had transferred their loyalties elsewhere. In one sense, they still ruled the always-*now* realm of what Stacy and Katie considered ancient times. Nevertheless, according to the linear time-line of Earth, they had become simply a part of the past.

Because they represented forces of nature, rather than simply being thought forms, they could never completely cease to exist. Yet, as Earth's linear time-line advanced, the powers they had wielded gradually faded into mere echoes of the great strengths that once had guided and controlled the human world.

Herm, alone of the old gods, moved freely through all the *nows*

🐾 🐾 🐾 **Between** 🐾 🐾 🐾

with his energy intact, always open and adaptable to every change. Drawing on different aspects of his nature to accommodate new cultures and beliefs, he assumed the role of messenger, guide, prankster, or shape-shifter—whatever human need or desire dictated. Always curious and willing to learn, he offered himself as guide and mentor to those who interested him, and derived constant amusement and stimulation from humankind's inconsistencies.

Striding through the tall grass, he felt relieved to be free of the fetid stronghold of the Harpies. The encounter had left him with strong desire to cleanse himself of the scent, the vibrations, the very idea of the monstrous bird-women. A smile flickered across his face as he recalled a time when he had laughed and splashed in a little lake with forest nymphs and water sprites. One, in particular . . . .

Chuckling to himself, he shook his head. "I think," he told the darkening air, "that I definitely am in need of a bath!"

Chapter 34

Rudy dried the last plate. "That does it. Who'd think six people could make so many dirty dishes!"

"Six people's a lot." Jenn searched the dishwater for stray silverware, then pushed a strand of auburn hair off her forehead with the back of her wet hand. "In case you didn't notice, even a Memorial Day picnic takes on major proportions in this family!"

He chuckled. "I noticed, all right."

"Did you also notice how pale Katie looked? I wonder if she's getting enough rest."

Rudy accepted the single fork she rinsed and offered him. "I'm sure David and Minerva are taking good care of her."

"Of course they are. I'm just being a worrywart." She glanced out the window. "Will you be able to get the hay cut tomorrow?"

"Hope so. Weatherman's still saying no rain likely till Wednesday night. I'll get the mowing and raking done tomorrow, and Glynis is coming out Wednesday to help me bale. We'd better finish before it storms, or I'll end up having to buy feed for those fifteen oatburners in the barn." He folded the towel and laid it on the counter. "That'd about wipe me out."

Jenn pulled the stopper out of the sink and smiled. "Stacy's always after me to use the dishwasher, but I—" She stopped, a stricken expression on her face.

Resisting a strong urge to put his arms around her, Rudy cleared his throat. "David said Dr. Elmore's going to take her off the medicine. That'll give her a chance to wake up."

Jenn nodded. "I know." She squeezed the sponge dry and set it on the back of the sink. "But what if she doesn't wake up?"

He could feel her distress radiating toward him. She was so close!

Without taking time to think, he gently touched her shoulder. She glanced up in surprise and he quickly pulled his hand away. "She'll wake up," he mumbled.

"She has to, Rudy! She just has to!"

She put out her hand. She was going to touch him; he could feel it. If she did, there'd be no way he could hold himself back any longer.

A musical ring from the wall phone next to the back door made Jenn hesitate; then she turned and crossed the room.

"Hello." She listened for a minute. "I don't know, Eric. Let me check." Holding her hand over the receiver, she turned back to Rudy. "Is there anything else you want to tell me or something you want to do this evening?"

Rudy stared at her. *Yes, I want to tell you how beautiful you are, with your cheeks all pink and your hair mussed up. I want to touch your sweet face and kiss your lips. I want to make love to you tonight and every night from now on.*

He shook his head. "Nope, can't think of a thing."

Jenn stared at him for a moment, then slowly took her hand away from the mouthpiece. "All right Eric, I guess I can go to a movie with you," she said. "I'll be ready in an hour."

§

Rudy sat at his worktable in the tack room. He stared at the shelf of carvings on the opposite wall without seeing them.

"You goddamn stupid, backwoods idiot!" he said aloud. "Stupid, stupid, stupid!"

He looked at his carving knife. The shiny blade was sharp enough to slice his thumb right off. Maybe that pain would hurt so bad it would make him forget the suffocating one that was filling him all the way to the top of his head.

No! he told himself, pushing the knife away. *We're not gettin' into that! One kind of sickness is enough.* He felt like crying, but his eyes were too dry to squeeze out even a single tear. Anyway, crying was for goddamn sissies. Now, bourbon—that was for men.

Pushing back the chair, he went to a rickety cupboard nailed high on the wall, opened the door and lifted a half full bottle of Ancient Age from the shelf. Ignoring the shot glass next to it, he picked up a

🐾 🐾 🐾 Between 🐾 🐾 🐾

tumbler from the table and dumped the water in the bottom of it into the little corner sink. Filling the glass to the brim, he sat down again and set it in front of him.

"Goddamn stupid idiot!" he repeated. Lifting the glass, he toasted the wall and drank.

Chapter 35

David sat next to Katie's bed, watching her breathe. She had fallen asleep almost as soon as she laid her head on the pillow, secure in the belief that her mother would be waiting to see her safely out of her body. David wished that he felt as certain that all was well. He checked her pulse rate for the third time and noted the continued regularity of her breathing. Everything seemed perfectly normal, although he wasn't certain what would be different if, by some unthinkable chance, last night's events should repeat themselves.

You're getting paranoid, he told himself. Sitting up straighter, he noticed that her eyes were finally moving under her closed eyelids, an indicator that she was dreaming. With a sigh of relief, he relaxed in the chair.

He was surprised at how easily he had accepted her wild story of rapacious bird-women. *I guess I'm more convinced of the reality of this crazy stuff than I realized*, he thought. It was his time with Stacy that had done it; there was no getting around the fact that every facet of that experience remained vividly real to him. There was also no point in denying that he ached to be with her again.

But how could he go off into a different realm and leave Katie here alone? No matter how desperately he wanted to be with Stacy, he could not leave their daughter unmonitored and undefended. Getting carefully to his feet, he set the chair back against the wall and tiptoed from the room, leaving the door ajar.

Downstairs, he paced around the kitchen, frustrated. Feeling like a lovesick fool, he lifted the wall phone from its hook and dialed Minerva's number. She, more than anyone, would understand his predicament. A momentary pang for taking advantage again of the older woman's good nature touched his conscience and he contemplated hanging up after the second ring, but he pushed the feeling away.

"Yes, David?" Minerva's voice sounded brisk and alert, despite the fact that the evening was well advanced. His relief was so great that he didn't bother to ask how she knew he was calling, despite the fact that she didn't subscribe to Caller ID.

"Would it be too much to ask you to come back and stay here tonight?" He paused. "I– I have an opportunity to be with Stacy, but I don't like to leave Katie alone, after what she said happened to her last night."

"I can do that." Minerva sounded unperturbed. She made no comment on his unprecedented acceptance of situations he would previously have scoffed at as flights of imagination. "When would you like me to come?"

"Would now be OK?"

"I'll be right there."

His shoulders slumped in relief. With Minerva as watchdog, he would feel safe in spending as much time he could with Stacy. He paced the kitchen impatiently, listening for her key in the front door. Fifteen minutes later, she had arrived and been installed in Katie's bedroom, and he was free to wait until Stacy came for him—if she came. He realized he was almost afraid to believe it could happen; if it didn't, his disappointment might be more than he could handle.

He lay down on the bed. After a minute or so, he closed his eyes and tried to relax, but his muscles seemed to grow more tense. OK, he told himself, pretend you're back in med school, studying for a chemistry exam. Memories of complex formulas began to crowd his mind, gradually jumbling together, until they faded into darkness.

The next thing he knew, Stacy was holding him tightly; her soft curls tickling his chin. A mixture of excitement and relief surged through him and, slipping his hands under her arms, he lifted her into the air, laughing with delight.

She kissed the top of his head; then, arms outstretched, leaned back in his embrace. "We did it, David! We did it again!" Straightening up, she slid down until her cheek rested against his chest.

He hugged her hard, looking over her head at the bed, where his body was lying under the covers. He shivered a little. "That is so weird!"

She nodded. "At least you know you can get back into your body without any trouble."

"God, Stace, I didn't mean to remind you of that!"

"It's OK." After a moment, she took his hand and a mischievous smiled curved her mouth. "Let's try something special tonight!"

He raised an eyebrow. "You're saying that what we did last night was a commonplace sort of thing?"

She chuckled, then reached up and ran her finger down his cheek, making him shiver. "No, my love, it definitely was not commonplace. I just meant that, since there seems to be a universal law that says what we believe is what we receive, we might see if we can believe into existence a special place just for us."

David smiled down at her. "Sounds interesting, but I think you're going to have to do most of the believing, since I'm not sure I understand what you're talking about."

"That's OK. You just close your eyes and concentrate on backing up my thoughts. I'm going to believe in a beautiful place that exists just for us."

David had barely begun to concentrate when he heard her exclaim, "Oh, wow—it works! Open your eyes, David. Look what we just did!"

He saw, to his amazement, that they were now standing side by side on a small wooden bridge. The water below mirrored the colorful foliage of trees lining the rocky banks, and opposite them a huge willow dipped slender fingers into the stream. Banks of white and magenta azaleas blazed against the lush greenness of the grass, and birds called in the branches overhead. Although the sun was warm, a cool breeze eddied tiny drifts of orange and yellow leaves around their feet.

David whistled. "What a place! But how can it be spring and autumn at the same time?"

Stacy looked pleased. "Because I believed it was. How about that?" Taking his hand, she began to pull him across the bridge. "Come on, let's go!" He could hear excitement in her voice. "I know we don't need any stage props, but the one waiting for us ought to be really good."

They ducked under a natural arbor of climbing roses and found themselves in a small clearing. At its center stood a white gazebo, the upper part of its sides open to the air, the lower section encircled with a wall woven from flexible wooden strips. David followed Stacy up three broad, shallow steps and saw a heart-shaped bed, spread with pink coverlets. Plump pillows lay piled against the headboard, and the air was warmed by a fragrance he couldn't identify.

Stacy squeezed his hand. "Do you like it?"

He looked around the room, shaking his head. "It's absolutely amazing!"

Standing on tiptoe, she kissed him with a sweetness that made him dizzy. David scooped her up in his arms, carried her to the bed, and gently laid her against the pillows. For a moment they smiled at each other; then they surrendered themselves to indescribable delight.

§

They lay side by side on the pink coverlets, their bodies touching. Stacy smiled as David reached over and lazily wound one of her long, copper curls around his finger. Raising herself on her elbow, she gazed down into his face.

"It's almost unbelievable, isn't it?"

"What?"

"That coming together without our physical bodies should be so incredibly satisfying."

He smiled. Letting her curl spring back in place, he traced her full, soft lips with his finger. "I don't know. Seems to me it was always pretty incredible with our physical bodies, too."

"Mmhmm." Sighing, she nestled her head in the hollow of his shoulder. "I wish you didn't have to leave. I wish you could stay with me until my body lets me back in."

"Me, too. But what would happen to Katie?"

She sighed. "You're right. Katie needs you."

Suddenly she tensed. Someone else was in the gazebo with them; she could feel it!

"Excuse me," said a familiar voice. "I dislike interrupting you, especially as the bearer of unpleasant news, but I have no choice."

Max, tail wrapped around his feet, had materialized on the foot of the bed. When neither of them responded, he gazed around the space. "Very nice. Very nice, indeed. Is this your doing?" He looked at Stacy, who nodded, pulling one of the pink sheets around her.

Max cocked his head to one side. "I'm tempted to ask if the cat has your tongue, but I think I'd know if that were the case."

"My God!" David stared at him. "I must be going crazy." He looked at Stacy. "I could swear that cat is talking." Peering at Max, he shook his head. "In fact, I could swear that this is Minerva's cat, and he's talking."

Forgetting for the moment that Max had described himself as a purveyor of bad news, Stacy chuckled. "Max *is* Minerva's cat, and he *is* talking."

"But, how can that be? His lips don't even move."

She smiled wryly. "Don't try to figure it out. He can talk, and that's as good an answer as you're probably ever going to get."

David stared at Max, then shrugged. "Ah, what the hell; after these last two nights, why should I let a talking cat bother me?"

Stacy, recalling what Max had said about bad news, eyed him anxiously. "Is Katie all right?"

"This has nothing to do with Katie." Max stretched and began to pick his way daintily across the bed. When he was about a foot away from them, he sat down again.

"You might say I'm here in an official capacity." The tip of his tail twitched. "Much as I dislike being the bearer of unpleasant information, and much as I know you two need time together, I am nevertheless obligated to tell you that this is not the way to go about it."

A sudden chill seemed to touch the air. Pulling the sheet up farther, Stacy wrapped it around her shoulders like a cape. "What do you mean?"

Max actually looked apologetic. "I'm afraid that this has to be the last time you come together like this," he said.

Stacy felt like a child whose most cherished possession has just been snatched away. "But why, Max, why?"

"There are two reasons. First, David does not really belong here—not yet."

"But I don't belong here, either."

"In a sense you do. Your physical body is not dead, but it is presently non-functional and unable to respond to any effort on your part to reanimate it. Therefore, for whatever length of time it takes until you can reinhabit your body, you belong here."

He turned to David. "On the other hand, *your* physical body is quite responsive at the Earth level and reentry is not a problem for you at this time. Which brings us to the second part of this issue."

He looked sternly from David to Stacy. "Now, I am not going to tell either of you that what you have done is wrong. But it's important for you both to understand that if David continues to come here each night, instead of moving into the dream state as he should, he will deprive his body of the deep sleep it needs in order to repair itself from the wear and tear of daily living."

David frowned. "You mean I'll get sick if I keep spending the night here with Stacy?"

Max nodded. "Exactly. As a doctor, you should already be aware of this."

David nodded reluctantly, then muttered, "I can't believe I'm having this conversation with a cat!"

Stacy's face crumpled. "It isn't fair! If I can't get back into my body, I should at least be able to spend the nights with my husband!"

Max twitched his tail. "I think you know that fairness is not a ground rule of this reality, Stacy. You can spend the rest of forever beating your head against that particular wall, if you choose, but the only thing it will do is give you a headache."

"Oh, crap on ground rules and universal laws!" Stacy glared at him.

Max shook his head. "What would your clients think if they could hear you now?"

She pulled the sheet over her head. "I don't care what they'd think." Her voice was muffled. "Anyhow," she stuck her head back out from under the cover, "I probably won't have any clients, if I don't get back in my body in time for that TV pilot!"

A flicker of uneasiness crossed David's face.

Stacy put her hand on his arm. "What? Something's wrong, isn't it? I mean, more wrong than it already is."

He looked uncomfortable. "That Chastain fellow called last night."

"And . . . ?"

"And I had to tell him that you wouldn't be able to do the pilot for him."

"You what?" She stared at him. "How could you do that? You know what that show means to me!" Tears of anger and frustration stung her eyes.

"I couldn't do anything else! Colin's taking you off the medication that's kept your body sedated, but even when you wake up, you'll still need a lot of recuperation time. There's no way you'll even be out of the hospital by the time the show is taped. Please, Stace," his voice was pleading, "I couldn't lie to him. There was nothing else I could do."

"You could have told him I might be able to do the show later on."

"I said you'd call him when you got home from the hospital."

Stacy blinked back tears. "He'll already have somebody else to take my place by then!" Throwing herself flat on the bed, she stared at the gazebo ceiling. "I might as well just forget the whole thing."

Max turned his yellow gaze in her direction. "If you want your work to be successful, you must be willing to stop resisting events that don't please you." He paused to tease a snarl out of his tail with his claw. "Resistance to what is happening blocks success more quickly than anything else. I believe Minerva has shared that universal law with you."

David frowned. "What the hell does that mean?"

"It means, my human friend, that every time you get upset about something you've decided you don't like, you cause that situation to lock itself in place. In other words, resisting what you don't want guarantees that you'll be stuck with it."

Pulling herself back into a sitting position, Stacy glared at him. "Of course, Minerva's told me that. And I try to do it. But if you think I'm going to say it's just fine that I can't make the TV pilot, you're full of beans!"

Max raised a furry eyebrow. "I don't recall hearing myself say that."

Stacy paused. "No," she reluctantly conceded, "I guess you didn't."

"You can't fight what is, and win, Stacy. No one can." He raised a paw as she began to protest. "Stop wasting your energies on being upset about what you can't change, and pay attention to taking care of the next thing that needs to be done. You may open the door to events that can bring you greater happiness than what you've lost could ever do."

Stacy rolled her eyes toward the ceiling "Maybe you should hang out a shingle saying the guru is in."

"No, Stace, it kind of makes sense." David was staring at Max. "You're saying that if something I don't like has already happened, I can't change it by being upset. I need to let go of it and focus on something else, which actually might end up being better than the original thing."

The corners of Max's mouth quirked up in his version of a smile.

"Bingo! You are a very astute young man."

David looked pleased.

Wrapping the sheet around her, Stacy slid off the bed. "Well, you two just go ahead and indulge in your philosophical mutual admiration society! I'm going to believe myself some place where I don't have to listen to how I should think that losing my chance at national TV is an event to celebrate!"

She focused on being back in the Entry Processing Center. As the sparkle of lights began to rotate around her, David reached toward her, calling, "Stace, wait! Don't go!"

She put out her hand, but the lights were already flashing, and she could barely see him through the sparkling mist. Already regretting her angry words, she closed her eyes and gave herself up to the spinning sensation that carried her away.

§

David looked at Minerva's black and white cat. "What do we do now?"

"Offhand, I'd say that the best thing is for you to go back to your body. I will find Stacy and see if I can smooth her ruffled fur, so to speak." The cat's yellow eyes held his gaze. "You need to know, however, that there seems to be some sort of negative energy stalking her, something I can't yet identify. I'm telling you about it, so that you can protect her physical body, when you get back to the Earth level. I'll be watching over her here, Between."

"What negative energy? What are you talking about?"

The cat glanced around him. "I think we'll have to save that discussion for a later time. In case you haven't noticed, Stacy seems to have stopped believing in this place. If we're wise, we'll leave before it completely disappears."

Following his gaze, David saw that the walls were melting, dissolving into the rose-covered bed, which was itself already breaking down into clusters of sparkling luminescence.

"Close your eyes." The cat's voice cut through the vertigo that was sweeping over him. "I'll help you return."

There was a sensation of displacement; then the dizziness gradually diminished and he felt something solid, yet soft, beneath him.

Opening his eyes, he found himself on his bed at home. He lay for a moment recalling the events of the evening, ending with Stacy's angry departure. Sadness, like a heavy blanket, wrapped around him until he felt he would choke.

Glancing over at the lighted dial of the bedside clock, he saw that it was two a.m. He should get up and tell Minerva that he was back—she might want to spend the rest of the night at her own house—but the weight of his unhappiness was too great to shift.

Finally he rolled himself up in the covers. Turning on his side, he lay staring at the patterns of light and dark the street lamp made on the window shade, until exhaustion finally overcame him and he slept.

Chapter 36

Rudy shaded his eyes with his hand. So far, so good. All ten acres had been cut and raked, and the line of storms now slowly moving toward Tulsa were stalled over central Texas. If they held off until after dark tomorrow, he'd have the hay safely baled and in the barn, insuring his fifteen boarded horses plenty of feed for the winter. He patted the scratched fender of his aging New Holland 750. If the tractor's touchy starter switch would hold out just one more day, he'd make it through tomorrow.

Taking off his well-worn Stetson, he mopped his forehead with the blue handkerchief that had been his father's. Time to feed the horses. He refused to wonder if Jenn had enjoyed her movie date the previous evening. Not your business, he told himself sternly. Nothing she does is your business. Nothing.

Slapping the hat against his thigh, he repositioned it on his head and set off toward the barn.

§

"Aunt Glinda, are there any books here with pictures of monsters in them?"

Glynis looked up from her evening money count. "Probably, sweetie. What kind of monsters?"

"Oh, big birds with ladies' faces."

Glynis wrinkled her forehead. "Where on earth did you come up with something like that?"

Katie shrugged. "So are there any books with a picture of them?"

Glynis thought for a moment. "Actually, I think I know what you're looking for." Closing the cash drawer, she crossed the floor to an aisle on the back wall, Katie trotting at her heels. She ran her fingers along several shelves of tightly packed books, then stopped. "Here it is!" She extracted a volume with a worn brown cover and handed it to the little girl.

"Myths and Legends of the Greeks and Romans," Katie read. "Are they in here, Aunt Glinda?"

"I think so. Look under 'Harpies.' Sounds to me that's what you're describing."

Carrying the book to the nearest table, Katie leafed through the Index until she came to 'H', then flipped back through the volume until she reached the page indicated. A reproduction of an ancient Greek vase showed a ship with men on it being attacked by a group of small-ish birds with the faces of beautiful women.

"Oh, that's not right!"

Glynis, who had returned to her counting, looked up. "What's not right?"

"Harpies don't look like that. They're big and ugly and they stink something awful."

Locking the cash box away, Glynis crossed the room to Katie's table. "What are you talking about, sweetie?"

Katie pointed to the picture. "That's just wrong, Aunt Glinda."

"What makes you say that?"

The little girl gave her sandy hair a toss. "I saw them myself, and they don't look a thing like that picture."

"Is that so?" Glynis pulled out the chair next to Katie's and sat down. "When did this happen?"

"Night before last. They grabbed me when I left my body to go dreaming, and took me to a place that was all stinky with bird poop and their yucky-smelling feathers." She closed the book with a snap. "It was really scary. But some man helped Mommy get me away from them, and she and 'Nerva say they won't let that happen ever again."

Glynis smiled. "Well, I'm certainly glad to know that Minerva and your Mommy are taking good care of you." She picked up the book and replaced it on the shelf, smiling to herself at the magnitude of Katie's imagination.

"Let's go, sweet potato; we'll pick up a pizza on the way home. Want to spend the night with me tonight?"

Katie considered the invitation, then shook her head. "Thanks,

Aunt Glinda; I'd love some pizza, but I think I'd better sleep at home. I'm not sure Mommy would know where to find me, if I wasn't there."

Glynis smiled. "Your choice, Katie. When your mommy gets home from the hospital, we'll have another pajama party. How does that sound?"

"Great!" Katie looked up at Glynis, who was locking the door behind them. "Aunt Glinda, what do you s'pose Harpies eat?"

Glynis pulled the door shut behind them and locked it. "I have no idea, Katie, but I'll bet it isn't half as good as pepperoni and sausage pizza."

§

Stacy slouched over an empty desk in the Entry Processing Center, unable to decide whether she was more angry or hurt at David's betrayal. Max's, too. Instead of being on her side, all he could do was babble about resisting and not resisting. It was totally irritating!

"Not really." Max leaped lightly onto the corner of the desk. "It's actually just—"

"I know," she interrupted without looking up, "a universal law. Just go away and leave me alone."

"I could do that; but then you'd be left here wasting your time feeling sorry for yourself."

Drawing herself up, she crossed her arms. "I am not feeling sorry for myself!"

Max regarded her solemnly. "Of course you aren't."

They stared at each other until Max's eyes crossed. Despite her determination to nurse her grievances, Stacy giggled.

"Stop that! You won't even let me stay mad at you. It isn't fair!"

He blinked. "Actually, fairness—"

"Is not a ground rule," she finished for him, with a grudging smile. "But it really isn't fair. I had a perfectly good mad going, and now you've ruined it."

"Doesn't laughing feel better?"

She nodded. It did feel better, but David's behavior still rankled. Even though she had a niggling suspicion that he had only done what he had to do, she didn't feel ready to admit that, not even to herself. The incredible closeness they had shared the past two nights tried to reinstate itself in the forefront of her mind, but she resolutely refused it entrance. Pushing back her chair, she stood up.

"So, what do you suggest I do to keep from wasting my time in this place where there is no time?"

Max stood up, too, elongating his body in a stretch that culminated in a shake and a little jump to one side. He looked up at her. "I think a short trip would do you good, if you're willing to undertake that."

Stacy shrugged. "I guess I have nothing better to do."

The words had hardly left her lips before she found herself sitting next to Max in the balcony of a well-lit auditorium. No whirling sensation or sparking lights; just one minute there, in the Entry Processing Center; the next minute here, wherever 'here' was.

Gazing around the spacious room, she saw that it was filled with colorfully dressed people. Some were talking quietly; others sat in silence, their eyes fixed on the stage, which was empty except for two chairs facing each other.

Leaning over the balcony rail, she realized that what she had taken for colorful clothing was, in fact, a glimmering, multi-hued emanation surrounding each individual. Straining to see through this variegated haze, she was startled to realize that not only was every person completely without clothing, but each was also missing his or her skin.

"Max!" she whispered urgently. "They're– they're made of glass, or something! I can see right inside them!"

"You can speak in a normal tone, Stacy. No one will be offended by your comments, or your surprise."

"But how can they be like that and sit there, talking to each other?"

"Because this is a Zero Point Field classroom. This segment of their education concerns the interconnectedness of all things, and the best way to absorb that understanding is for everyone to see what is going on. That's why the students allow their personal energy fields, as well as the inner workings of their bodies, to be visible."

His gaze ranged around the auditorium. "All of the individuals you see here no longer have their physical bodies, but they are interested in assisting those still in the physical world. Once they have learned the true nature of existence through study and direct experience, they will make themselves available as guides to those in their physical bodies who wish to help others with healing.

Stacy opened her mouth to comment, then closed it again as a young man and an older woman walked onto the stage and stood facing each other. The woman moved slowly around the man, examining him carefully; then the young man sat down in one of the chairs and closed his eyes. The woman positioned herself in front of him and a sparkling stream of evanescent material began to flow out of her midriff, entering his body just above the waistline.

Stacy noticed that the sparkling stuff seemed drawn to a dark spot on his liver, which was clearly visible through the transparent structure of his body. The dark area began to lighten, finally dissolving in a tiny burst of light, and when the glow faded, the spot had disappeared; his liver looked normal.

"Max!" Stacy's voice was hoarse with excitement. "She healed his liver. I saw it!"

"That isn't quite accurate, even though it may appear that way." The instructor was looking up into the balcony directly at Stacy, and the other students turned in their seats, following her gaze. "No one can heal anyone else; the best we can do is act as conduits or catalysts for each other." Her voice carried as easily as if she were wearing a microphone. "All I did was concentrate on my desire to help him through our connection in the Zero Point Field. He and the Field did all the real work."

Startled and a little embarrassed by this attention, Stacy shook her head. "I don't understand. I saw you send out healing energy to him and saw his liver take it in. You healed his liver!"

Turning in his chair, the young man looked up at Stacy. "It looked like she healed me, but what you actually saw was her desire to help, interacting with the Field that connects us. My own willingness to be well, combined with her intent to help, shifted the vibrational rate of my atomic structure and allowed my liver to heal." He smiled. "It's really quite simple, once you understand how things work." He looked back at the instructor. "Did I explain that correctly?"

She nodded. "A little oversimplified, but, on the whole, an excellent job."

Stacy turned to Max, eyes shining. "That's it! That's how it works! I never really understood before." Looking back at the couple on the stage, she called, "Thank you!" They smiled and waved.

Jumping to her feet, she raced down the stairs to the ground level and danced out onto the porch. "They're right," she told Max, who had followed her. "I've been trying to make it complicated, and it's so simple!" Sinking down on the steps, she leaned back against the balustrade. "Oh, Max, this is incredibly exciting!"

"Things that really matter always are." She could see approval in his eyes. "Would you like to experience a fuller understanding of the Field?"

She sat up straight. "Of course!"

"Then follow me." He set off briskly around the corner of the building, Stacy almost running to keep up with him. As they hurried down the walkway, she saw a long, low building ahead, its red brick walls almost completely covered with ivy.

She was admiring the glossy runners climbing up one side of the building, when suddenly she found herself acutely conscious of their presence, of the life force animating them. An unexpected surge of gratitude for the elegant perfection of each leaf filled her. She was entranced by the fine, cream-colored veins reaching delicate fingers toward each tip and could sense the life-sustaining fluid flowing through them, nourishing each cell of every leaf.

Suddenly she felt herself merging with the ivy, her arms metamorphosing into slender branches, her fingertips adhering joyfully to the bricks and mortar of the wall. She could sense welcome all around her, delight in her presence, unconditional support for her very being.

Slipping deeper into this connection, she allowed the tapestry of existence to draw her in. She was a living thread woven through the fabric of all life, with no beginning and no end, a part of the whole, yet completely herself. Through this understanding flowed a love so pure, so absolute, that she surrendered herself to it. She possessed everything, was everything, that she could ever want or need.

"Stacy." Max's voice dropped into her mind. "Stacy."

She tried to ignore the sound and the tiny fissures it created in this ecstasy of oneness.

"Stacy! It's time to return."

The fissures widened into cracks. Her sense of connection shattered, and she was thrust back into her own limited awareness. The pain of separation seemed unbearable, even worse than when she and David had been wrenched apart. Desolate, she sank down on the grass beside the path.

🐾 🐾 🐾 Between 🐾 🐾 🐾

She started slightly as Max leaped onto her lap, where he curled up, pressing the solid warmth of his body against her. Out of habit, she stroked his silky fur and he gently kneaded her thigh with his front paws. She began to relax, soothed by the low, soft rumbling in his throat and the warmth of his energy enfolding her. Gradually, the intensity of her anguish receded.

They sat together in the timeless *now*, silent except for the comforting thrum of Max's purring.

Chapter 37

Rudy gazed across the field toward the horizon. Although the early morning air was hot and muggy, there was no sign of clouds yet; but the line of thunderstorms that the weather channel was tracking had begun to move during the night and was now rumbling slowly through southwestern Oklahoma, on a direct route toward Tulsa. Spitting on his finger, he tested the breeze and nodded; if the wind stayed low, the storms should hold off until late afternoon. At least he hoped they would.

Opening the barn doors, he hauled himself up onto the tractor and turned the starter key. The engine coughed and died. He tried again, and then again, until it shivered into life. Relieved, he gave the dashboard an encouraging pat. *OK, then, let's make it through today. Just through today!*

§

"Thanks for coming." Glynis held out the cash drawer key. Minerva slipped it into her pocket and set the basket in which Max was napping behind the counter.

"Uncle Rudy isn't expecting me for another hour, but the forecast says storms are moving this way and I think I need to get there earlier." She looked over in surprise as Katie, backpack slung over one shoulder, marched into the room.

"What are you doing here? I thought you were in school!"

Katie's smile was smug. "Didn't 'Nerva tell you? I'm recuperating."

"From what?"

"From the cold I got when those nasty bird-ladies carried me off."

Glynis looked at Minerva, who smiled.

"She did have a difficult time a couple of nights ago, and she does seem to have caught a cold. I thought another day's rest wouldn't do her any harm."

Glynis eyed the little girl sternly. "Well, you'd better do your homework while you're recuperating." She glanced at her watch. "Good grief! I've got to get out of here!"

Katie dumped her backpack on one of the tables. "Wait, Aunt Glinda! Where are you going?"

"To help Uncle Rudy bale the hay."

"Can I go, too? Please? I've done almost all of my homework." Katie looked from Glynis to Minerva. "The sunshine will do me good, 'Nerva. You always say that sunshine's good for what ails you."

Minerva felt a moment of uncertainty; then she shrugged. "If Glynis wants to take you, I suppose it's all right with me. Just don't pester her; she has work to do."

Glynis looked at Katie's pleading eyes. "Oh, well, come on, then. Just be sure you take it easy and do what I tell you." Picking up her purse, she put her arms around the little girl's shoulders. "Tractors are not toys, you know."

"I know. I've been on the tractor before. Uncle Rudy even let me drive once."

"Well, you aren't driving today, sweetie, so don't even ask."

"I won't. I'll be good."

As they reached the door, they turned and waved. Smiling, Minerva waved back. "Be careful," she called, but the door had already closed behind them.

She stared after them for a moment, wondering if she should have allowed Katie to accompany Glynis, then she busied herself getting ready for the store's first customers. As she waited for the coffee to brew, she frowned. Life had been quieter since Katie's return from the Harpies' grove, but she could not rid herself of the feeling that something was about to happen. She shook her head. Her perception of impending events was usually strong and almost always accurate. This time, however, she could not pin down any specifics. There was only a sense of uneasiness she found impossible to banish.

She sincerely hoped that, for once, her internal alarm system was mistaken.

🐾 🐾 🐾 Between 🐾 🐾 🐾

§

The late morning sun beat down. Rudy wiped his forehead, then turned the key for the third time, listening to the engine grind. *Please*, he mentally begged the little tractor, *please don't do this!* After the fourth try, he gave up and climbed down in disgust. He should have thought before he turned the damn thing off to take a bathroom break! He could restart it by hot-wiring, but he knew from experience that, given the tractor's age and the long, hot afternoon yet ahead, the results could be unreliable. The best solution would be a trip into town for a new starter switch, which meant at least an hour he might not be able to spare.

Squinting into the distance, he could see a faint haze building on the southwestern horizon. He did some rapid mental calculations. Half the hay was in. Glynis would be here before long, which would double his speed in getting the hay baled and under cover. If the storms continued their leisurely approach, he ought to be able to finish before they hit.

But if they picked up speed, the hour required to get to town and back could mean losing the rest of the crop. He frowned. The new switch would almost certainly guarantee the tractor's reliable performance, and he could probably get it installed by the time Glynis arrived. With any luck, they'd manage, maybe with time to spare.

Swearing under his breath, he started back toward the barn for his screwdriver and pliers.

§

Arthur Craddock was pleased by Stacy Addison's gratitude for his help in rescuing her daughter. Her view of him as a benefactor and friend offered exciting new possibilities, even though the Harpies had, at first, been upset and offended by his apparent reversal of their balancing act. It had taken considerable effort, but he thought he had finally convinced them that his behavior in freeing the child had been necessary.

Shifting his position in the long grass where he had been relaxing, he considered the phenomenon of what he thought of as his inner voice. He had lately realized that, instead of being a constant presence, it seemed to disappear from time to time. This inconsistency made him wonder if it truly was a part of his own mind, as he had thought, or something outside himself. Despite the fact that the voice had been consistently helpful, the idea that it might not be what it seemed disturbed him, as did the fact that it now seemed to carry an undertone of anxiety. Something had changed, and not for the better.

Pushing his disquiet aside, he turned his attention toward finding a means of revenging himself on Stacy Addison. Even though he agreed with his inner voice—or whatever it was—that his pretense of rescuing her daughter had been an intelligent move, he felt cheated. By now the little girl should have been in a condition that would be causing her mother intense emotional pain. Instead, she was safely back home in her physical body, probably protected at every turn.

Or at least he assumed she was. Excitement surged through him at the thought that perhaps she might not be inaccessible to him, after all. The voice he now questioned instantly reacted. *Leave the child alone*, it told him. *She is not to be tampered with.*

Pretending not to hear, Arthur closed his eyes and focused his attention on the little girl. A moment later, he sensed a shift in his atomic structure and opened his eyes to find himself in the cramped backseat of a Volkswagen Beetle. A young woman he had never seen before was driving. Next to her, on the passenger's side, sat Stacy Addison's daughter. Arthur felt pleased. The woman didn't look like much of a guardian. If he stayed with them, perhaps he would find another opportunity to make use of the little girl.

This is not the way to succeed, the voice informed him. *You must strengthen your friendship with Stacy Addison, not act in a manner that will damage the progress you have achieved. Go back where you can think clearly and plan a useful next step.*

Resolutely ignoring the intensity of his mental guide's insistence, Arthur settled back and prepared to enjoy the ride.

Chapter 38

Glynis shaded her eyes with one hand, gazing across the partially baled field to where the tractor sat, silent and abandoned. Uncle Rudy was nowhere in sight; neither was his truck. Something must be wrong.

She gave Katie's shoulder a squeeze. "Wait here."

Turning, she ran to the back porch and pounded on the door, knowing as she did so, that Rudy would not be in the house. To be absolutely positive he wasn't somewhere on the premises, she jogged across the yard to the barn. Several of the horses thrust inquisitive heads over their stall doors, but, except for them, the barn was empty.

She walked back to Katie. "He must have gone into town for some reason."

The distant clouds looked like a pile of gray marshmallows. She tested the wind, trying to gauge the speed at which they were advancing. As far as she could tell, they might be here, ready to drop their load of rain within three hours, four at the most.

Grabbing Katie's arm, she pulled her toward the car.

"Come on, sweetie, let's get out there. That storm'll be here before the hay is in, if we don't get moving."

Piling into the VW, they bounced along a strip of field that had already been harvested. As soon as they neared the tractor, Glynis was out of the car, running. Climbing into the driver's seat, she reached for the key, then stopped. The whole switch was missing; that was why Rudy had disappeared!

"The key switch is gone," she called down to Katie. "Uncle Rudy must have gone into town for a new one."

"Will we have to wait till he gets back?"

"No." Glynis shook her head. "If we did, we might not be able to finish before the storm gets here, and he can't afford to lose the rest of this field." She frowned. "I'll have to try to hot-wire it. I've helped him hot-wire the truck a couple of times; the tractor shouldn't be too different."

Kneeling on the platform, she peered under the dash. In the hole left by the tractor switch was a tangle of wires. "Look on floor of the Beetle's backseat and bring me my little tool chest and that old pair of leather gloves."

Katie scurried off, while Glynis tried to locate a comfortable position under the dashboard.

"Here they are," Katie called.

Reaching down, Glynis took the tool chest and set it next to her on the platform; then she maneuvered herself into the cramped space. She was slipping on her gloves when she realized that Katie was climbing up beside her.

"You'd better get down, sweetie. This thing might give a jolt, when the wires connect."

"But Aunt Glinda, I want to help!" Katie opened the tool box and handed her a pair of pliers. "See, I know what to do. I've helped Uncle Rudy work on his truck when it makes funny noises."

Glynis frowned. "I'm supposed to be taking care of you, not letting you get hurt."

"I won't get hurt, Aunt Glinda. I'm not a baby; I'll be careful and hold tight to the steering wheel."

Glynis sighed. Every passing minute was bringing the rain closer. "OK. Be sure you do." Reaching under the dash, she used the pliers to create a loop at the end of each of the two wires needed for the connection.

"Hang on now, Katie," she called. "We're about to be in business!"

§

Arthur Craddock watched with interest. He had certainly not expected to visit a farm, when he joined the young woman and Stacy Addison's child, but the hot-wiring of this out-of-commission tractor might offer just the opportunity he was hoping for. He recalled the nightlight he had inadvertently burned out in the child's room, as he merged his atoms with those of the wall. If he could insert his energy into the wires the young woman was getting ready to join, he should be able to amplify the electrical shock from the connection. The results might be very interesting.

Focusing intently, he willed himself into the junction of the wires as they touched.

§

Glynis dropped the curve of the hot wire over the loop of the second wire. Like a bolt of lightning, a crackling shock exploded up her arm and she felt the tractor jolt forward. Her legs, flung hard to the side, hit Katie, knocking her away from the steering wheel. As the little girl fought to regain her balance, Glynis reached out frantically and caught her by the bottom of one jeans leg, but the tractor continued to bump slowly ahead over the uneven field, making it impossible for her to keep her grip. With a scream, Katie toppled backward off the edge of the tractor platform.

Oh, my God! Hauling herself to her feet, Glynis looked down, horrified, to see Katie lying limply on the ground, the steel-toothed cylinder of the baler rotating slowly toward her.

"Katie!" she shouted. The child didn't move. In another minute, the baler would roll over her. Glynis launched herself from the tractor platform, striking the ground with her knees. She gasped as pain shot through her ribs, but thrust her hands under Katie's back and pushed as hard as she could. The child was dead weight. Frantic, Glynis shoved harder. Sobbing with pain and exertion, she pushed again and Katie's body rolled aside.

The effort threw her off balance and she fell heavily on her left shoulder, gasping again as the rough stubble of the newly mown hay slashed her skin. Looking over, she saw that the baler was almost on top of her. She tried to roll away, but its sharp metal teeth bit into her arm. She screamed, then screamed again as the baler, its forward movement barely slowed, sent a shock of unbearable agony through her chest and abdomen. In the instant before its next rotation, her gaze flashed up toward the tractor platform. Someone was standing on it, looking down at her. His narrow, tanned face was framed by light brown hair, and his light blue eyes seemed to be gleaming with anticipation. It was the face of a stranger.

🐾 🐾 🐾 Between 🐾 🐾 🐾

Then metal touched her cheek and there was a pain too great for screaming, followed by silence and darkness.

§

Steepling his fingertips, Colin Elmore looked across the desk at David. "I think we can begin withdrawing the phenobarbitol."

David nodded.

"Nervous?"

"A little."

Elmore leaned back in his leather chair. "She's young and healthy. There's a good chance she'll come out of it with her brain cells functioning as they should."

David nodded again.

Elmore sat forward and scribbled a few lines on a prescription pad. Tearing off the sheet, he said, "Take this down to the floor. Whoever's on meds this afternoon will be able to start weaning her off the phenobarbitol on today's rounds." He placed the script in David's hand. "Try not to worry. We're doing the best for her we can."

"I know." David tried to smile. "I appreciate it."

He stifled an urge to whistle, as he strode toward the Intensive Care Unit. Elmore had just given him the key that would unlock Stacy's ability to return! Once he had delivered the prescription, the nurses would begin weaning her off the phenobarbital that was keeping her body paralyzed and comatose. As the medication cleared itself out of her system, she would be able to return to consciousness and gradually recover. Recalling the two nights he had just spent with her, he felt a shiver of expectation.

Yet, despite his desire to believe in this outcome, his training forced him to grudgingly acknowledge the possibility that she might sink deeper into the coma and never return at all. Worst of all, she might regain her awareness, but never fully recover, physically or mentally. The thought of her damaged liver and shredded cheek rose in his mind, and he suddenly wondered if his shiver had been one of apprehension. *No*, he told himself, *I refuse to believe that*. He smiled a little, remembering Max's words. *And what I believe, is what I'll receive*.

Clutching the prescription, he took a deep breath and pushed open the double doors to Intensive Care.

🐾 🐾 🐾 **Between** 🐾 🐾 🐾

§

Max awakened in his basket under the bookstore's checkout counter. He had accompanied Stacy back to the Entry Processing Center and settled her in her room, so that she could finish assimilating her experience with the ivy. Expecting to find himself on the sofa where he had fallen asleep, he was surprised to discover that Minerva had carried his napping body to Glynis's store. Stretching lazily in his traveling basket, he listened as she waited on customers.

The telephone rang. Minerva answered and Max almost immediately felt a shift in the energy surrounding her. She hung up the receiver, more distressed than Max had seen her in a long time, and knelt beside him.

"That was Jenn; she sounded almost hysterical. We have to get out to Rudy's right away. Katie fell and had the breath knocked out of her. Even worse, Glynis is dead!"

After informing the customers that an emergency had arisen, Minerva put away the cash drawer and hurried Max out of the store, locking the door behind them. A short time later, they were in her little sedan, heading into traffic.

Max, never fond of car travel, flattened his ears against his head as Minerva guided them through traffic, darting back and forth between lanes as opportunities opened up. They reached the farm in record time, passing Rudy's truck on the road, and whipping into the driveway ahead of him. The two vehicles bounced down the long drive, Minerva tearing over the bumps at a speed that Max felt sure would spell the demise of the sedan's shocks.

Minerva stopped in front of the barn. Climbing out, she ran toward the end of the yard. Max bounded after her. He could see Glynis's VW parked in the field, some distance away. Next to it was an emergency vehicle, red light slowly revolving, and two figures lifting a gurney into the back. Rudy sprinted past them and they followed in his wake.

By the time they reached the ambulance, Rudy was talking to the EMTs. Max and Minerva stopped a little distance away, watching him peer through the open back doors, then step away, his shoulders sagging. The EMTs closed the doors and climbed into the front seat, and the vehicle, red light no longer revolving, slowly began to bump its way across the field toward the driveway. Rudy stood looking after it for a moment, then turned toward them, his face bleak. As they reached him, he fell to his knees, wrapped his arms around his stomach, and began to rock back and forth, moaning.

Looking beyond him, Max could see Katie, eyes closed, lying on her back on the rough ground. Jenn, tears streaming down her cheeks, was kneeling beside her, stroking her hair. Minerva paused beside Rudy. When he did not look up, she gently squeezed his shoulder.

Stay with him, Max, she ordered silently.

Max watched her pick her way across the intervening feet of stubble to Jenn and Katie, where she placed a hand on the little girl's forehead and lifted one of her eyelids. After a short conversation, Minerva hugged Jenn and returned to Max and Rudy, who was still doubled over, moaning.

Kneeling in front of Rudy, Minerva put her hands on his shoulders. "Stop, now," she told him. When he continued to rock and moan, she shook him. "Listen to me, Rudy!"

He slowly raised his head and stared as if he had never seen her before.

Minerva's face was stern. "You must stop this right now!"

Shaking his head, he tried to pull away from her. "You don't understand," he mumbled. "It's my fault. If I hadn't gone for that damn switch, she'd still be alive!"

"That's nonsense! You are not responsible for what happened. You were only doing what needed to be done." She shook him again, even more forcefully. "Listen to me. We're all shocked and saddened, but it's important that you save your grief for a later time." She turned him toward Jenn, who was trying to gather Katie into her arms.

"Jenn needs you. The EMTs checked Katie and said that she's all right, but the breath was knocked out of her and she's had a terrifying experience. She needs to be taken to her father. Jenn has been traumatized, too, and she can't carry Katie to the car by herself. They both need you, and they need you now!"

Max could sense calmness flowing from Minerva to Rudy, who finally lifted her hands from his shoulders and stood up. Straightening, he walked carefully toward Jenn, who looked gratefully up at him. He knelt, lifted Katie gently onto one shoulder, and stood up. Putting out his free hand, he pulled Jenn to her feet. He put his arm around her and they walked slowly back toward his truck, Jenn leaning against him. Rudy held the passenger door open for Jenn to climb in, then placed Katie's limp body on her lap.

Max looked up at Minerva. "Did she tell you what happened?"

Minerva shook her head. "She doesn't really know. She was in the back yard and thought she heard Katie scream. Before she could get to a place where she could see anything, Glynis screamed, too. By the time she reached them, they were both on the ground and the tractor was driving itself across the field." She sighed. "The only explanation I can see for the injuries she described is that Glynis and Katie both fell off the tractor and the baler ran over Glynis."

Max winced. After a moment, he said, "That doesn't make sense, does it? After all the years she's been helping Rudy bring in the hay, why would she be so careless, especially with Katie there to look out for?"

Minerva nodded. "My feeling, exactly."

"We need to find out what really happened."

She nodded. "Indeed, we do. But we won't get that information from anybody here." She looked at him thoughtfully. "I think we must return to the Entry Processing Center as quickly as possible. There's something strange about this accident, and Glynis is the only one who may be able to help us learn what we need to know." She started back toward the car. "Certainly she is going to need our support after such a traumatic experience."

Minerva held open the back door for him and Max leaped onto the cushion kept on the seat for his convenience. He yawned. "Why don't I just meet you Between? You can put my body to bed when you get back to the house."

Making himself comfortable on the cushion, he closed his eyes. Within seconds, his breathing had slowed and he was deeply asleep.

Chapter 39

Arthur Craddock sat in what looked very much like the waiting room of the office he had occupied when his physical body was alive. He wasn't sure why he was here, but the urge to come had been irresistibly strong. As he gazed curiously around, he was startled to realize that the space was exactly like his old waiting room, right down to the scratch on the leg of the coffee table and the struggling ficus tree in the corner by the window.

A voice called his name. Looking toward the back wall, he was amazed to see his former office girl, Annie Boston, holding open the door that led to the inner offices and examination rooms. Before he could speak, she turned and started off down the narrow hallway. He hurried along behind her and found himself being ushered into what he recognized as his own office. He was so taken aback by this unexpected view of his polished desk, solid wood filing cabinets, and soft leather chairs, that he didn't notice when Annie disappeared.

The high-backed executive chair behind the desk was turned away from him, but now it swivelled around. Its occupant was a well-muscled, intense-looking man with black, gleaming eyes. The planes of his face were strongly molded and a dark blue, perfectly tailored suit emphasized his black hair and olive skin. He radiated a confidence and power that Arthur, even in his most secure moments, had never possessed.

The man pushed back the chair and stood up.

"I am Serizzin."

His deep voice cut through the silence of the room, setting up a vibration within Arthur's body that made him feel his very atoms were trembling. A sudden weakness assailed him and he collapsed into the nearer of the two Italian leather chairs in front of the desk. He wanted to ask this stranger who he was and what he was doing here, but his tongue seemed glued to the roof of his mouth.

The man seated himself again. Placing his elbows on the desk top, he leaned toward Arthur.

"I have invited you here to teach you what is important. And what is important is this: what you want does not matter. Nothing matters but what I want." The intensity of his black eyes instantly dispatched any desire on Arthur's part to protest.

"You have taken far too many liberties, ignoring the guidance I sent you and interfering in affairs that do not belong to you." The dark eyes burned into his and the deep voice sank to a needle-sharp whisper that injected him with icy terror. "You think that your pitiful desire for revenge matters, but it is only what I, Serizzin, want that matters. Do not permit yourself to forget that again."

The man leaned closer, and the room suddenly took on the temperature of a meat locker.

"I do not tolerate insubordination, nor do I make allowances. Mistakes I can forgive, if they are not repeated. Defiance, I punish."

The cold eyes held his and the whisper continued. "Serve me well, and I will give you your heart's desire. Serve me ill, and you will suffer." The voice paused a moment. "Do you understand?"

Arthur struggled to nod his head.

"Good." The terrifying eyes continued to bore into his. "Your first opportunity will take place today. You will transport yourself to the hospital where Stacy Addison's body lies and make use of your recently demonstrated influence over the physical world. A prescription has been written, ordering the removal of the medicine that keeps her body paralyzed. You will find a way to alter the date on that piece of paper, changing it so that the order will begin two days from now, rather than at the time for which it was originally written." The voice paused again. "This will keep her physical form in its comatose state, leaving her spirit here, so that I may use her to accomplish my purpose."

Pushing back the chair, Serizzin stood up again, his eyes still locked on Arthur's. "Be sure you understand that from now on your purpose is to serve my purpose. What you desire must wait. Do as I command, and I will see to it that you receive a just reward. Defy me, and you will regret the fact that you are already dead and cannot die again."

The black eyes released him. Collapsing like a puppet whose strings had been cut, Arthur lay in the chair, his mind seething with fear and rage. Although he had no idea of what was going on, he understood that he was somehow playing in a league so far beyond his own that he could not even comprehend the rules. He had no choice but to follow his instructions to the letter, trusting that whoever Serizzin was, he would keep his word and grant Arthur the revenge he could not bring himself to relinquish, despite threats that practically liquified his bones.

Or did he even have bones any more? He wondered, for the first time, about the body he now inhabited. He hadn't eaten since before the accident; his other bodily functions also seemed to be unnecessary. He stifled a hysterical desire to giggle. Couldn't scare the pee out of him! He didn't have any; not any more.

Remembering the dark eyes boring into his, he looked around apprehensively and saw that his menacing companion had disappeared, as had the office and all its furnishings. Even the chair in which he had been sitting was gone. He was now seated on the ground, his back propped against a tree.

He sucked in a deep breath of relief. At least he could still breathe, although the thought flickered through his mind that perhaps he was able to do that only because he believed he needed to. Then he wrinkled his nose and coughed. Phew!

Scrambling to his feet, he backed away from the tree, which was one of several forming a small circle. Another deep breath resulted in a paroxysm of coughing, and he recognized a familiar stench. Apparently his new boss had a sense of humor—he had been delivered directly to the outskirts of the Harpies' grove.

Shaking his head, he hurried off toward a clump of trees just visible in the distance, hoping it would offer him the quiet he needed to launch his assignment of altering Stacy Addison's prescription. Excitement stirred in him. Once he had regained his internal balance, this might even be fun!

§

"Dr. Kinnard, Dr. David Kinnard, please go immediately to Dr.

Elmore's office."

Surprised, David set Colin Elmore's phenobarbitol order on the ICU medications cart and hurried back toward Neurology. He reached the office just as Elmore, his face grim, was leaving it.

"Come with me." The older man pointed toward the hall leading away from the nurses' station.

Passing a group of new interns following a teaching resident, David accompanied him to an alcove where they could have some temporary privacy.

"What is it? What's going on?"

Elmore frowned. "I wanted to catch you before anyone else did. There's more bad news."

David's heart skipped a beat. "Stacy?"

"No." The older man looked at him intently. "Didn't you mention that your wife had a best friend?"

"Sure. Glynis Steele. Stace was supposed to spend the night of the accident at her place."

Elmore sighed. "That's who I was afraid it was."

David stared at him. "What do you mean?"

"Glynis Steele was brought in a few minutes ago by the EMTs."

Cold fingers of apprehension plucked at David's spine. "And?"

"She's dead. Farm accident."

David continued to stare at him, stunned. Glynis dead? How could that be? What the hell was going on, anyway? His knees threatened to buckle and he looked around for a place to sit down.

Elmore took his arm. "Come on." He steered David toward an empty waiting room. "Sit here and put your head between your knees."

David sank into one of the chairs and put his head in his hands. "I'm OK." He took a deep breath. "It's nuts! I didn't do this when I learned about Stacy."

He felt Elmore squeeze his shoulder. "Don't worry about it. You're already on overload; this is probably the final straw."

"God, I hope it's the final one!" He thought of the last time he had seen Glynis, only two days ago, playing with Katie at Jenn's Memorial Day picnic. Sadness swept over him. How was he going to tell Katie about it? First, her mother, then all that stuff about being kidnaped, and now this! The weight of the past ten days pressed down, exhausting him.

Finally, he raised his head. "OK if I take a look?"

"Are you sure you want to? The machinery really did a job on her."

He nodded. "She's the closest thing I've got to a sister. I owe it to her."

Heaving himself to his feet, he started toward the elevators, forcing his legs to move, pushing one in front of the other. His brain felt wrapped in wet flannel, and a stabbing pain behind his left temple warned him a tension headache was revving up for attack.

Enough! he thought. He wasn't sure whether he was directing the command toward himself, or toward God, Fate, or whatever else might be responsible for all this senseless havoc. A bell pinged and the doors of the down elevator opened. David stepped in, relieved to be its only occupant, and pushed the button for the basement, where the morgue was located.

§

Arthur Craddock watched the changing of the guard at the nurses' station. Intensive Care was no different from any other specialty, as far as the staff was concerned. Nurses everywhere, regardless of where they had taken their training, followed certain patterns. One of those was to have everything laid out neatly before beginning any procedure, whether it was entering information into charts or checking on patients. Or dispensing medications.

He watched as the second-shift meds nurse, a heavy-set woman with frizzy blond hair, set her list beside the dispensing cart. Near the list lay two prescription sheets; the first, authorizing medication for a recent brain tumor surgery; the second, an order to cancel the phenobarbitol which had been keeping Stacy Addison in her medically induced coma.

Arthur felt a quiver of nervousness. What if the ability this Serizzin character attributed to him wasn't as good as he thought it was? What if he failed? He had succeeded in influencing what happened to Stacy's daughter and the young woman on the tractor, but that had been easy—just an insertion of his own energy into the electrical field of the tractor's wiring system. This was different. He gritted his teeth, remembering the icy terror that his interview with Serizzin had inspired. He had to make this work!

🐾 🐾 🐾 Between 🐾 🐾 🐾

Concentrating on the two prescriptions, he willed the top one, the order for the brain surgery patient's medications, to fall off the counter top. When the small sheet of paper did not respond, he amplified the intensity of his focus, but it continued to lie exactly where the nurse had placed it.

You're trying too hard, his inner voice informed him.

About time you got here, he thought sourly. *Where were you when I needed you back in that duplicate of my office?*

He did not expect a reply, nor did he receive one. He did, however, ease the pushing quality of his attention and simply envisioned the top sheet of paper moving unobtrusively off the one beneath it. A fraction of a second later, the top script shivered slightly, as if touched by a breeze, then slid away from the one detailing the new order for Stacy Addison. Drifting to the floor, it landed near the feet of the blond nurse, who, unaware, was counting out little fluted paper cups and lining them up in rows on the top shelf of the cart.

Bending over the remaining slip of paper, Arthur Craddock concentrated on the date scribbled at the top. He needed to do this quickly, before the nurse noticed the new prescriptions, but not so quickly that he attacked it with excessive intensity. Calming himself, he focused on the day part of the date. He had to change the number two into a four. Holding this image clearly in his mind, he closed his eyes and visualized that shift taking place. Again. And again. Finally, he opened his eyes.

Excitement surged through him. To the right of the two, a vertical line was slowly moving downward from the top until it intersected, then crossed, the horizontal line that formed the bottom of the number. As this section completed itself, the curved top of the two, on the left, faded and disappeared, leaving only the slightly curved downward stroke, which now ended at what had become the crossbar of a perfect number four.

Delighted, Arthur stepped away from the piece of paper, just as the meds nurse bent over, with a small exclamation of distress, and picked up the prescription that had fallen on the floor. He watched as she read it and added the medication to her list, then waited impatiently as she examined the script he had altered, the order to begin weaning Stacy Addison off her barbiturate. Relief washed over him as she shrugged and clipped the paper behind her daily list.

Reaching for a syringe and a vial of phenobarbitol, the nurse drew up the regularly indicated dose for Addison and set the syringe on the cart. Then, seizing the handles, she steered away from the desk and set off on her afternoon round of the ICU.

Chapter 40

Max gazed around the vast interior of the Entry Processing Center, scanning the lines slowly filing past the Greeters' desks.

"She isn't there." Herm, who periodically indulged his sense of fun by taking the shape of a coyote, watched him from beside an empty desk, pink tongue lolling. "Injuries severe as hers require specialized care."

Max nodded. "That fits, judging from what Jenn told Minerva."

The coyote grinned. "I guess that makes me one up on you, for a change."

"Looks that way."

"Want to visit her? She's in the temporary ward, until she recovers enough to be processed. She's actually been assigned a room across from your protégée."

Trotting off down a side aisle, Herm headed toward the door through which he and Max had introduced Stacy to the Entry Processing Center shortly after her arrival.

Max padded after him. "Does Stacy know Glynis is here?"

"Not yet. The Greeter in charge of trauma cases felt it would be better if some healing could take place first. The young woman has suffered a severe shock. She's conscious, but incoherent. Keeps babbling about a man watching while the machinery ran over her."

Max considered this statement. "As far as I know, there was no one else there, except Katie, and she was unconscious." He looked at Herm. "I think we need to find out what she's talking about; I have a strong feeling it's important." As they veered around a long line of soldiers waiting to be processed, he added, "Does she realize her physical body is no longer available to her?"

"Not sure. She's so confused right now that it's impossible to tell what she understands."

They reached the door leading to the temporary ward and Herm stepped through, without bothering to open it. Max followed him. As they entered Glynis's room, they could see her lying on the bed. Minerva sat beside her, stroking her hand. Max winced at the sight of Glynis's mangled body, even though he knew that what appeared to be terrible damage was, in reality, just a memory imprint of the body she had left behind.

Eyes closed, Glynis was twisting her head from side to side on the pillow. "Storm's coming," she muttered. "Gotta get the hay in!"

Suddenly her eyes flew open and her voice rose. "How did that man get there? He's watching me. He shouldn't be there!" Closing her eyes again, she broke down into choking sobs, but her ravings always returned to the watching man.

As if drawing comfort from Minerva's touch, she grew gradually quieter, her outbursts more and more spasmodic, until they trailed away into silence. Finally, she lay still. An unmeasured time later, her eyes opened again.

"Minerva?" Her hand tightened around the older woman's.

"I'm right here, my dear."

"Something ... awful ... happened."

Minerva tightened her grip slightly. "That's right."

"Hurt bad."

Minerva patted her hand. "Actually, you're fine. It just seems that you're not."

Glynis frowned slightly. "Don't ... understand."

"Don't try to understand right now. Just rest."

Glynis smiled slightly. Her eyes closed again and she drifted off to sleep.

Gently extracting her hand from Glynis's grip, Minerva looked over at Max and Herm.

"I'm glad you two have come. I need to break the news to Stacy that Glynis is here, and I'd appreciate it if you would stay and keep an eye on her while I'm gone."

Max instantly leaped onto the bed and settled himself at Glynis's feet. The coyote grinned. "Your wish is my command, Minerva, dear."

Patting Herm lightly on the head as she left the room, Minerva crossed the hall and knocked on Stacy's door.

Stacy opened it almost immediately. She looked rested and glowing, the coppery halo of her curls shining as if lighted from within. "'Nerva! Wait till I tell you where Max took me!"

The older woman smiled. "May I come in?"

Stacy opened the door wider and stepped back. "Of course."

As soon as she was inside, Minerva took Stacy's hand. "I'm afraid I have some distressing news."

Stacy frowned. "What is it, 'Nerva? What's wrong?"

Still holding her hand, Minerva told her about Glynis. The brightness faded from Stacy's face and her eyes filled with tears.

"How could such a thing happen?" Her voice was anguished. "It just doesn't make any sense."

Pulling her hand free, she began to pace the room. "I can sort of understand why I'm here; it was raining, I was anxious to get home, I got careless. But Glinda! She's such a good person! She was just trying to help Rudy, like she always does."

Minerva shook her head. "From what I can piece together, she went far beyond just helping Rudy this time. Apparently she jumped from the tractor, in order to save Katie from being run over by the baler; unfortunately, she wasn't able to get out of its way herself. We'll have to wait until she is recovered enough to be coherent, but, given where she and Katie were lying, that seems to be what happened."

"Oh, my God!" Stacy stopped pacing. "Is Katie all right?"

"She was unconscious, but breathing normally, when Max and I arrived. Jenn and Rudy took her to David"

"That's good. David will know what to do for her."

Minerva nodded. "It's also good that she was probably unconscious during Glynis's death, and will not have that traumatic memory to deal with."

Stacy chewed her lower lip. "I don't understand. How can God allow something like this to happen?"

Minerva pointed to the bed. "Sit down for a moment, my dear. Please." She waited until Stacy had propped up stiffly against the pillows, then she seated herself on the chair opposite.

"Listen to me, Stacy. God doesn't allow or not allow what happens to us. *We* are in charge of what goes on in our lives, even though some of our decisions are made at a very deep inner level. Sometimes we even make those choices before we're born. We plan certain types of learning before we ever enter our physical bodies and become who we are on Earth."

Stacy shook her head. "I don't understand."

"You do understand that you're more than what you see in the mirror, don't you?"

"Sometimes." Stacy twisted a long, copper curl around one finger. "Once in awhile, I feel like I understand what's going on, but most of the time I'm not even sure who I am."

Minerva smiled. "You are yourself, my dear, a totally unique representation of God, expressing as Stacy Addison."

"Whatever that means."

Minerva gave her the look she had often bestowed on a much younger, even more rebellious Stacy. "It means, among other things, that everything that happens—everything—is useful. No matter what it is, no matter how it seems, it is useful for helping you to grow and expand your understanding and your ability to love."

She gently touched Stacy's cheek. "Have you forgotten your experience with the ivy so quickly?"

Stacy stared. "Did Max tell you about that?"

"He did. And I trust you will remember what you learned."

Stacy thought a moment, then nodded. "I will. I'll remember the crystal people, too."

"Who?"

"The people who were learning about healing. I think of them as made of crystal, because I could see right inside them. They helped me understand how healing really works."

"Ah." Minerva stood up. "Would you like to put some of that knowledge to use?"

"Me? I just watched. I'm not sure I know how to actually do what they did!"

Taking her hand, Minerva pulled her gently off the bed. "I think you're being far too modest. Anyway, this is a strange place and a frightening situation for Glynis. I feel certain that seeing you would make her feel far more secure and less alone."

Looking stricken again, Stacy nodded. "OK. I'll come. But not because I know what to do. I'm coming because Glinda needs me."

"That's enough for now, my dear." Minerva smiled. "That's certainly enough for now."

§

"Jenn!" David looked up, surprised to find her standing in the doorway of the doctors' lounge. "Did you come to see Stacy?"

Shaking her head, Jenn stepped aside, so that Rudy could edge past her. Katie was in his arms, wrapped in a worn blanket. Her face was streaked with dirt and she seemed to be asleep.

"What on earth ...!"

Before either Jenn or Rudy could answer him, Katie stirred and opened her eyes. Seeing David, she practically leaped into his arms. Clutching him with a grip too strong for her years, she buried her face in his neck.

David held her close, stroking her hair. "Hey, hey there, kitten." He looked a question over her head at Jenn.

Jenn moved her eyes toward the sofa. "I think she should lie down and finish her nap."

A chill crept up his spine. First Glynis, downstairs in the morgue; now Katie, obviously in acute distress. He wanted to ask if the two were somehow linked, but first he needed to take care of his daughter.

"Come on, kitten." He carried her across the lounge to the sofa, murmuring, "It's OK, honey, it's OK."

After a moment's resistance, she allowed him to detach her arms from his neck and curled up with her face toward the sofa's back. David tucked the blanket Rudy had wrapped her in more closely around her, and saw that she had already slipped back into sleep. Kneeling beside the sofa, he felt her face, checked her pulse, and listened to her breathing with his stethoscope. Satisfied that she seemed all right, at least physically, he stood up.

Jenn and Rudy had moved back out into the hall. He joined them, leaving the door ajar so he could hear if Katie needed him.

"What the hell is going on?"

When neither of them replied, he looked at them closely for the first time. What he saw in their eyes shocked him. A glance over his shoulder assured him that Katie was sleeping soundly, so he motioned them back into the doctors' lounge. The three of them sat down at a table as far from the sofa as possible, and David looked from Jenn to

Rudy.

"This is connected to Glynis, isn't it?"

Rudy nodded. "You know about that?"

"I just saw her downstairs. I'm really sorry." The intensity of the pain in Rudy's eyes made him look away.

Jenn shook her head. "I just can't believe this is really happening." Her face crumpled. "It was already too late when I got there. It was just too late!" A sob escaped and she wiped her tear-filled eyes with the back of her hand. "There was nothing I could do!"

Reaching across the table, David patted her arm, then looked back at Rudy. "You OK?"

Rudy shook his head. "Don't know what I'm goin' to do without her." He stood up with a quick, angry movement, almost knocking over his chair. "It shouldn't have happened. If I'd been there, it wouldn't have happened!"

He turned and headed for the door. Jumping to her feet, Jenn ran after him and David could hear them whispering in the hall. By the time he reached them, Rudy was striding rapidly away, with Jenn hurrying in his wake.

Shaking his head, David looked back at his sleeping daughter. She might eventually be able to help him make sense out of what had taken place this afternoon, but in the meantime, he'd better see if someone could take his evening rounds, so he could get her home to bed.

Chapter 41

Jenn stood at the kitchen sink, splashing cool water on her face. Except for her shaking hands, her body felt heavy, almost numb. Her mind, on the other hand, seemed to be wheeling in circles, playing the afternoon's events over and over again.

She had been in the back yard when Katie's scream, then Glynis's, sent her racing through the gap in the hedge and across the field of unbaled hay. She thought her heart would stop when she caught sight of the little girl lying face down on the rough ground, next to a heap of what looked like torn, red-streaked rags. Reaching Katie, she realized with horror that what she had assumed was a pile of shredded clothing was Glynis, almost unrecognizable from so many bloody wounds that Jenn could not count them.

She leaned her head against the cupboard door and, putting her hands over her face, shook with harsh, racking sobs. How could such a terrible thing have happened? No one should have to suffer that kind of death, especially not someone as gentle and caring as Glynis! Tears streamed down her face, as if they would never stop. Finally, after what seemed a very long time, she blotted her eyes with a paper towel, rinsed her cheeks again, and patted her face dry with the dish towel.

Hard as this was for her, it had to be infinitely more painful for Rudy. He was blaming himself for not being there to prevent the accident, and beneath the feelings of guilt, she knew that grief was flowing like a strong, underground river. Given his melancholic nature, she feared he might sink into a depression so deep he would never emerge from it.

The storm had finally arrived in full force, so she grabbed her hooded raincoat and opened the back door. Then she stopped. Rudy was such a private person! After helping her deliver Katie to St. Mark's, he had ignored her attempt to convince him to stay and share his feelings with her and David. He had, instead, practically run to the parking area, not even looking to see if she was following. She had finally caught up with him at the truck, and Rudy had driven them home in silence, dropping her off at the foot of her driveway. His response to her thanks for his help had been a curt nod.

Jenn felt torn in half. If she interfered now, she might lose his friendship—this was the threat that always loomed, the sticking point that always stopped her from reaching out to him. But what if he wanted her comfort? What if something she might do or say could ease his pain, divert him from the dark path toward which she feared he was heading?

I'll just have to take the chance, she told herself. Before she could change her mind, she closed the door behind her and, flipping her hood up against the driving rain, ran down the steps and pushed through the opening that Rudy had cut in the hedge long ago. She hurried through the Steele back yard to the kitchen door, hesitated, then knocked firmly against the worn panels. She waited, then knocked again, louder. She was about to leave when Rudy opened the door. He stared at her with red-rimmed eyes. "May I come in?" She took a small step forward.

Rudy neither spoke nor moved aside. Finally, he dropped his eyes and shook his head.

"Oh." She cleared her throat. "Well, I just wanted to tell you how terribly sorry I am about what happened this afternoon."

He nodded, eyes still on the floor.

"If– if there's anything I can do, I hope you'll let me know."

He nodded again and began to close the door, forcing her to step back. Still without a word, he shut the door completely and snapped the lock into place.

Jenn stood unmoving for a moment, stunned; then she turned and stumbled down the steps. What a fool she had been! He didn't need or want her. It was obvious that he considered her nothing but a nuisance.

She fled back through the rain-drenched hedge, driven by the pressure building in her head and chest. Bursting through her back door, she tore off her dripping coat and dropped it on the kitchen floor, then raced down the hallway to the bedroom and threw herself on the bed, releasing another flood of tears. After a time she rolled over, and clutching her pillow, rocked back and forth, sobbing and moaning. Once she bit the pillow and screamed aloud.

She had no way of sorting out how much of her anguish stemmed from Glynis's death and her mounting fear of losing Stacy, and how much was due to what she perceived as her loss of Rudy. She only knew that life suddenly seemed unbearable.

She hovered on the edge of this void long after the storm outside had passed and dusk had melted into darkness. Finally, dry-eyed and exhausted, she turned on her side and slept.

§

Rudy stood behind the closed door, listening to Jenn's footsteps retreating across the porch and down the stairs. She was mad, and he didn't blame her; he'd been downright rude. But better to seem rude, than get close enough for her to smell the drink on him. Closing his eyes, he leaned his head against the door. What did it matter, anyway? It had always been hopeless!

Everything was hopeless. Jenn had always been beyond his touch, and now Glynis was gone because he wasn't where he should have been! Tears squeezed between his closed eyelids and ran down his cheeks. He angrily brushed them away. A stupid, worthless drunk, that's what he was. But at least, he told himself, not a crying drunk!

§

"It was the nasty bird-ladies. They hurt Aunt Glinda; I know it!"

Katie had awakened after a six-hour nap and David, hearing her call, had raced up the stairs and found her sitting up in bed, her face flushed with anger.

"It was the bird-ladies' fault!" she repeated.

"Shhhh!" he soothed. "The bird-ladies aren't here, Katie; it's OK."

She struck the quilt with her fists. "No, Daddy, it is not OK! Those horrid things shouldn't be allowed to get away with it. That isn't right!"

David touched her cheek. "Of course, they shouldn't."

"I'll get even with those nasty things. You just wait— they're going to be sorry for what they did!"

Although he was tempted to smile, uneasiness stirred in him. The bird-women probably didn't exist, but if they did, could she put herself in danger by pursuing them? Too many strange things were happening lately! First, Stacy's accident, now Glynis's death; and, woven through this dark fabric of events, malicious bird-women who kidnaped little girls, Minerva's talking cat, and—the only bright note in this chaos— two incredible nights with Stacy, which might or might not be only his imagination. The world he knew and understood suddenly seemed to be shifting on its foundations, threatening to slide off into an abyss he hadn't even realized was there!

"We'll make them sorry, won't we?" Katie persisted, staring up at him.

David turned back the covers. "Why don't we discuss that later?" He lifted her out of bed and set her on her feet. "Right now, let's go downstairs and I'll fix you some pancakes."

Katie's eyes brightened. "Pancakes in the night time? Can I have maple syrup, too?" She shoved her feet into fuzzy blue slippers and, taking his hand, pulled him out into the hall, toward the stairs. "Hurry, Daddy! Let's have our pancakes, and then we'll decide how to punish those bird-ladies."

Following her down the hall, David shook his head; Katie was more like her mother than she knew. *Two hard-headed women*, he thought. *I don't stand a chance!*

Chapter 42

Max sat curled in a corner of Glynis's room in the temporary facility. He was thinking about the hidden energy he had sensed in the hospital room at St. Mark's, during Stacy's failed attempt to return to her physical body. That same energy had also been present in Katie's bedroom the night that he, Stacy, and Minerva had taken the little girl to the Children's Garden. And once or twice since then, he had become aware of the identical vibrational pattern. It always seemed focused on Stacy with what felt like malicious intent, and always withdrew the moment he turned his attention toward it. His need to make sense of these occurrences had grown particularly urgent since Glynis's arrival Between.

He looked up as Minerva stepped into the room, followed by Stacy. Herm, still in his coyote guise, stood up, shook himself, and trotted quietly past them into the hall.

"Oh, my God! Glinda!" Running across the room, Stacy knelt and took one of Glynis's hands in hers.

Glynis stirred and opened her eyes. "Stacy?" Her hoarse voice was incredulous.

"Yes, it's me; it's really me."

"How?" Glynis whispered. "You're . . . in a coma."

Stacy looked down at Max. *What should I do?* Her silent request was tinged with panic.

Tell her the truth.

Can't you, or Minerva, tell her?

Max stared at her, unblinking. *It will come better from you. Perhaps if you begin with your own arrival here, she may find her experience easier to accept.*

With a reluctant nod, Stacy sat down on the side of the bed. Hesitantly at first, she began to tell Glynis about waking in the room across the hall, following the Thunderbird's encounter with the train. Her voice strengthened as she detailed her subsequent experiences, including her abortive attempt to return to her body, her adventure in the Children's Garden, her visit with Katie, and Katie's kidnaping and rescue from the Harpies. When she finished describing the healing lesson she had recently witnessed, she stopped speaking.

"What?" Glynis whispered.

Stacy smiled at her. "I think I understand what we need to do." She took Glynis's hand, and Max could sense her shifting out of her own uncertainties into that familiar energy state her mind had always labeled "healing mode."

She smiled again. "Glinda, dear, I want you to tell me what you think has happened to you."

Glynis frowned. "The rain was coming. Uncle Rudy couldn't afford to lose that field. But the tractor wouldn't start. So, I– I hot-wired it." Her eyes filled with tears. "It shocked me, so hard my legs jumped. And I knocked Katie off. I knocked her off the tractor!" A sob escaped her. "She just lay there and the baler kept coming. I had to get her out of the way! I jumped down—" Breaking off, she looked up at Stacy. "She was so hard to move! Did I– did I make it? Is she OK?"

Stacy smiled at her tenderly. "Katie's fine. You saved her, Glinda." She could feel some of Glynis's tension relax. "What else do you remember?"

Glynis frowned. "There was a man. He was . . . standing on the tractor, watching. And then . . . oh, my God!" Her voice rose higher. "Oh, my God, the baler! It wouldn't stop!" Tears trickled down her cheeks. "It hurt so much, it hurt so much!" She twisted her head from side to side. "It hurts, it hurts!"

"Glinda!" Stacy grasped her hand firmly and Glynis stopped twisting long enough to turn pain-filled eyes toward her. "Listen to me. You were hurt, terribly hurt, but you aren't hurt any more."

Frowning, Glynis shook her head.

"Listen to me!" Stacy's voice was steady. "It's impossible for you to hurt any more because . . ." she glanced at Max, who nodded encouragingly, "because you aren't in your physical body now."

Glynis stared at Stacy, frowning. Then her eyes widened and a look of terror crossed her face. "You're saying . . . you're saying I'm dead, aren't you?" Her voice became a wail. "You're saying I'm dead!"

She struggled to pull her hand away, but Stacy continued to hold it tightly.

"Listen to me, Glinda. Listen to me carefully. It's true that your physical body is dead, but *you* aren't dead." She spoke slowly and firmly. "You are not in your physical body any more. You're here, talking to me, safe and sound in your spirit body. You're OK."

Glynis became very still. Finally, she said, "If I'm OK, why do I look like this?" She held up a punctured, blood-smeared arm.

Max nudged Stacy's knee. *Remember the 'monster' in the Children's Garden*, he silently reminded her. *What you believe is what you receive.*

Stacy nodded. "You look this way," she told Glynis, "because your mind understands what being run over by a baler would do to your body. And since you realized, at the moment it happened, that the baler was running over you, your mind assumes you still have to look like that happened. So, it's actually your belief that's making your spirit body look this way."

She glanced down at Max, who eyed her approvingly. *Keep going, Stacy. Now is the perfect time to apply the understanding you gained in the Zero Point Field class.*

He could sense his reminder increasing the power already flowing strongly through her. She smiled down at Glynis. "Just do one thing for me, Glinda. Be willing, for a little while, to believe that the way you look and feel can change. Will you do that?"

"I– I guess so."

"Good. Now close your eyes and think of yourself as you were the last time you looked in the mirror." She paused. "Are you doing that?"

Glynis nodded.

"OK. The only thing you need to do is be willing to believe that you look like that right now. At least pretend that you believe it, even if you can't really believe it."

Stacy glanced down again at Max. *Help me!* Her mental plea flew toward him. *I'm not sure I can do this much alone.*

Nodding, Max linked his awareness with hers, and together they sent Glynis an image of herself as she had always looked, strong and healthy. He became aware of Stacy's electrical field expanding, then coalescing into a stream of energy that reached out from her midriff toward the weaker field surrounding Glynis. He focused on the two fields, sensing with satisfaction the almost audible click that signaled their connection.

Sparkling ripples were now undulating both vertically and horizontally across Glynis's body, forming a glowing grid of energy. Within this grid, her torn flesh began to close. The blood retreated into the puncture wounds and the skin regained its smooth perfection. Even her shredded shorts and tank top looked like she had just put them on fresh from the laundry.

The ripples radiated even more strongly, transmuting the grid into a gentle, steady glow, and the stream of energy moved back into Stacy's midriff. Releasing Glynis's hands, she stepped back.

Glynis raised her arms in front of her, turning them so that she could see them completely. Throwing back the covers, she examined the rest of her body.

"I don't believe it!" She shook her head.

"Don't even think that!" Max jumped lightly onto the bed and sat down beside her. "You might cancel the whole process and we'd have to start over."

"Max?" Glynis looked at Stacy. "Is that really Max? And did he say something to me?"

Stacy nodded. "Yes, on both counts." Taking Glynis's hand, she helped her step out onto the floor, smiling at her puzzled expression. "I promise I'll explain later. Right now, the important thing is that you're fine."

Holding her arms away from her body, Glynis examined herself again.

"I don't know how you did it," she said, "but you're right; I'm fine!" She smiled at Stacy. "And we're together again; that alone's enough to make me feel great!"

Stacy shook her head. "You're certainly handling this whole thing a lot better than I did in the beginning."

Glynis grinned at her. "I have you to help me." Looking across the room, she noticed Minerva leaning against the wall. "My goodness, I didn't expect to see you here! Although," she added, "I guess if Max is here, it figures you would be, too."

Minerva smiled. "It's good to know you're feeling so much better, my dear."

"Oh, I do feel better, I do, I do!" Glynis twirled around, laughing.

"And I want to make the most of this crazy dream while it lasts."

Max looked up to see Stacy preparing to speak.

Let it go for now, he told her silently. *There will be plenty of time later to help her adjust to the fact that what's happened is real.* Stacy nodded. Taking Glynis's arm, she pulled her toward the door. "Come on, Glinda, let Minerva and me show you around. It isn't exactly Oz, but it's definitely not Kansas." Arm in arm, they went out the door sideways, Minerva in their wake.

§

Max sat on the bed, mentally replaying Stacy's recitation to Glynis of the events she had experienced since her arrival Between. She had once again mentioned a stranger who helped her free Katie from the Harpies' grove. Although Max had attempted to check out this piece of information at the time of Katie's rescue, his examination had turned up very little; the stench emanating from the grove had effectively disturbed any other energies that might previously have been in the area.

Stacy had said that her Good Samaritan was a man with brown hair and a narrow face. Glynis, in her ravings to Minerva, had described the man standing on the tractor in similar terms. Max understood that coincidence did not exist; there had to be a connection between the two. It was his job to find out what that was.

Sauntering through the door, he looked for Herm, who had left the room to avoid further confusing Glynis by his presence. He eventually found him, coyote tongue lolling, beside one of the empty desks in the Entry Processing Center.

"Come on," Max told him.

Herm stood up and stretched. "Where are we going?"

"For a helicopter ride. I need to check something around a previous bend of that river of time you described to Katie.

"What's the destination?"

Max's tail twitched. "The recent past. In fact, the very recent past, as in yesterday afternoon."

"Glynis's accident." Herm eyed him with interest. "Why then?"

"Because there's something going on, something important, and I'm hoping that what we see will show me what it is. I have an uncomfortable feeling that if we don't uncover the answer, we're going to wish we had."

"That crucial, eh?"

Max nodded. "I've thought all along that the threat I keep sensing is directed toward Stacy, but I'm beginning to think that there's more involved than just her safety—much more, as a matter of fact."

The coyote's mouth split into a grin. "A mystery! All right, old friend; let's go detecting."

Lights sparkled and whirled around them and they faded and disappeared, only to return shortly afterward.

"Get what you were after?" Herm shook the last sparkles from his rough coat.

Max looked thoughtful. "I think I may have done just that."

"You're referring to the intruder who was present during the entire incident with the tractor." It was a statement, not a question.

Max nodded. "He can't belong on the Earth level. Humans almost never know how to move themselves from one location to another simply by the power of thought, and they're always visible to each other. One minute this fellow was on the ground; the next, he was between Glynis and Katie on the tractor, and neither of them noticed him. Glynis only saw him at the very end because she was already leaving the physical world and moving Between, which has to be where he belongs."

Herm nodded.

"And," Max continued, "I feel certain he was responsible for Glynis's accident. It can't be coincidence that just as he reached under the dash, the wires she was touching together gave off a spark so strong that she knocked Katie off the tractor. I don't know much about the electrical systems of tractors, but I do know that Glynis wouldn't have tried to connect those wires with Katie beside her, if there was a chance of that happening."

A low growl vibrated the coyote's throat. "I'm looking forward to meeting this fellow in person. Think he's the same man who helped Stacy rescue Katie?"

"He must be. It would be far too great a stretch to believe there's a second human male with brown hair and a narrow face involved in this." Max paused. "He has to be an inhabitant of Between; it should just be a matter of locating him."

🐾 🐾 🐾 Between 🐾 🐾 🐾

The coyote lifted his muzzle from his front paws. "So how do we go about that?"

"For now, we keep our eyes and ears open, and we monitor both Stacy and Glynis at all times. If they separate, you go with one, I'll stay with the other. It's important that we don't leave either of them unprotected. If we sense his energy, we'll do our best to home in on it. One way or another, we're going to track him down."

The coyote wavered and shifted into the familiar dark haired, tunic-clad boy. Bringing his sandaled heels smartly together, he saluted Max. "I have my orders, sir, and shall obey them."

Before Max could do more than raise one furry eyebrow, the boy dissolved into laughter; then literally dissolving into sparkles of light, he disappeared.

Chapter 43

Glynis sat on her bed in the temporary facility, tears flowing unchecked down her cheeks.

A horrible nightmare of being run over by the baler had, at first, shifted into a delightful dream in which Stacy had held her hand and healed her injuries. Minerva was there, too, as well as Max, who now could talk. It was a dream she had been prepared to enjoy to the fullest. Then Stacy had taken her to the Entry Processing Center.

At first she had been fascinated, but as she saw line after line of new arrivals being processed, she began to feel disturbed. Her distress increased as she watched people with serious injuries being gently carried through the door to the temporary ward, to be cared for until their wounds could be healed.

Glynis had an active imagination, but she didn't think it was strong enough to invent the intricacies of what she was witnessing. The row after row of desks; the long lines of people of every age, size, sex, and color; the huge staff of workers, either constantly moving through the crowds or sitting at computer-like machines; the massive double doors at the back of the vast space, through which most of those being processed were finally escorted—all of these were so far outside her experience that she found it impossible to believe she had simply created them out of her own mind.

She began to have a terrible suspicion that, although she wanted to believe it was a dream from which she would soon awaken, everything here was very real. It was a concept both overwhelming and terrifying. Ignoring the desire to simply curl up and go to sleep, she wiped her tears with a tissue from the box on her bedside table and worked her way through to the conclusion that what Stacy had told her was true—the tractor accident had really happened, and she had been badly injured. No, not just badly injured. She was dead.

Dead. Dead. Dead. The word echoed through her mind.

Fighting down rising panic, she looked around the room. Minerva was sitting in the comfortable chair near the bed; Stacy was perched on its arm. Max, as well as Herm, to whom she had recently been introduced, were both just outside in the hall, where they had stationed themselves protectively. A sensation of warmth flooded her, driving back the fear. If this place was real, then so were they. They were her friends and they loved her. Maybe things weren't as bad as they seemed, after all.

She noticed that Stacy and Minerva were both watching her with concern. Wiping her tears again, she produced a faint smile. "I'm OK. Really, I am. It's just going to take some getting used to."

Rising from the arm of the chair, Stacy moved to the bed and sat down beside her. "I understand, Glinda. I sometimes still have a hard time with it, and I've been here for awhile."

Glynis sighed. "But you have a chance of going back; I don't."

Stacy looked stricken, then shook her head. "You're right. I really don't know what to say to that."

Glynis shrugged. "There isn't anything to say. It is what it is; I'll just have to learn to live with it." Her lips twisted in a humorless smile. "That's funny, isn't it—*live* with it!"

Minerva smiled at her. "Funny, perhaps, but true. You *are* alive, you know, and will continue to be so; you are just in a different kind of body. Once you adjust to that, you'll be surprised at how good it feels."

Glynis nodded. "I guess so." She shrugged again. "I don't have much choice, do I?"

Minerva nodded. "That's also true; but you do have a choice as to how you handle the information."

"I suppose you're right. But I feel so sad that I'm never going to see Uncle Rudy, or Jenn, or my parents and sisters again. Or open up the store, or put away books with pages where somebody spilled coffee…" She sighed again. "I'd even be happy to count up the money—twice a day, if I had to."

Minerva rose from the chair where she had been sitting and took Glynis's hand. "You will see your uncle and your other loved ones again, my dear. If you wish, you can come back here and help them adjust, when it's their time to go through the Processing Center."

Glynis's eyes brightened. "I can?"

"Absolutely." Minerva smiled and gently squeezed her hand. "Now I think that Stacy and I should go and let you get some rest. You have not yet fully recuperated from your transition experience."

"I have to admit I do feel a bit overwhelmed." Glynis looked over at Stacy, who was sitting on the side of her bed. "But if you want to stay and talk awhile, I wouldn't mind."

Stacy stood hurriedly. "I think Minerva's right; you need to rest." She bent and gave Glynis a quick kiss on the cheek.

Swallowing her disappointment, Glynis nodded. "Maybe you're right. If you're both leaving, I guess I will take another nap." Her eyes followed them across the room, which suddenly seemed smaller and more confining than it previously had. "Leave the door open, would you? I don't want to feel so completely alone in here."

"Of course, my dear."

Stepping out into the hall, Minerva almost tripped over Max, who was parked in the doorway. Glynis smiled slightly. She could see Herm, in his coyote form, curled up in front of Stacy's room. He rose, as Max fell into step behind the two women, grinned at her, and took up guard duty at her open door.

§

"How much longer is this going to take, kitten?"

David peered through the gloom of Glynis's café, toward the stacks of books where Katie had disappeared at least five minutes ago. He had resisted bringing her here; but when she continued to insist, he had located Stacy's key and, against his better judgment, let her into the store. He was amazed at her resilience. Last evening's nap and a good night's sleep seemed to have completely restored her.

He glanced at his watch. "Katie!"

"I'm coming." There was a muffled thump and an exclamation. A moment later Katie emerged from one of the aisles clutching a large, obviously old volume that looked far too heavy for her eight-year-old arms.

"I found it!"

"Let me have that." Relieving her of the book, David dropped it onto the nearest table.

"Be careful, Daddy; that's very important!"

David looked at her more closely, noticing her bright eyes and flushed cheeks. "Are you OK?"

Katie nodded. "I'm fine. I just had to find something I needed."

David pulled out a chair and sat down, putting himself at eye level with his daughter. "Any chance you're going to tell me why this beat-up book is so important, and what's in it that you need?"

Katie stared at him. "Do you promise it'll be a secret just between us?"

David considered for a moment. "OK," he said. "I promise."

Katie opened the book. Carefully turning the yellowed pages, she stopped about a third of the way through.

"Here it is." She pointed to a section on the page boxed apart by heavy, black lines. PETRO VODUN, the heading read.

David frowned. "What language is that?"

Katie shrugged. "I don't know. The rest is in English."

David's eyes widened as he skimmed the information in the box and his sense of uneasiness increased. He stared at her. "Why on earth do you want something like this?"

A mulish look settled itself on her freckled face.

David closed the book with a snap. "Promise me you won't mess around with this, Katie. It's just a bunch of nonsense, but it's nasty nonsense."

"Nasty nonsense for nasty bird-ladies," muttered Katie, staring at the floor.

"What?"

"Nothing."

"It's not nothing, Katie. The whole thing makes me feel uncomfortable. Let's just put the book back where you found it."

The intensity in his daughter's voice startled him.

"Please, Daddy, please! I need it. I have to learn something from it that's very important!" Her forehead was wrinkled, her cheeks flushed.

Ah, what the hell! he thought. *The stuff in here is way above her head. It'll give her something to think about besides what's happened to her mother and Glynis.*

"OK," he told her, "you can take the book home, but promise me you'll just look through it. Don't try any of the stuff in there."

Katie laid her hand on his arm. "Don't worry, Daddy." Her voice was solemn. " I'll be very careful."

Looking into her eyes, David caught a glimpse of the self-possessed woman she would become. He wondered if he should protest further, but Katie hefted the book off the table and walked away toward the door. Shrugging, he followed. He switched off the lights and locked the door behind them, then gazed back through the glass into the darkened store. *Ah, Stace,* he thought, *why did all this have to happen?*

Turning, he followed Katie down the sidewalk to the car.

§

"Dollar for your thoughts." Max leaped onto the desk in the Entry Processing Center where Stacy was sitting, chin propped on her hands.

She looked up. "What?"

"You look like whatever you're considering is too involved for just a penny."

She sighed. "Oh, Max, I've lost everything—Mother and Daddy, and David and Katie, and the TV pilot. And now Glynis!" She stared at him, her lower lip trembling. "And I was mean to her just now. I could tell she wanted me to stay, and I left. I left because I couldn't stand her pain any longer."

She looked past him, frowning, as an unaccustomed thought crept into her mind. She examined it cautiously, gently prodding it around the edges, as if a direct approach might cause it to detonate.

"Max," she finally whispered, "do you think, maybe, that my parents were always leaving because . . . because they couldn't stand *my* pain?"

His yellow eyes watched her, unblinking. "Stranger things have happened, Stacy. They were human, just as you are, and some humans do not tolerate pain very well, especially when they don't feel capable of relieving it."

"They could have relieved it if they'd stayed home with me."

"Perhaps. But I think that presented an insoluble dilemma for them. After all, they had spent many years training to do what they did, and they loved doing it."

Stacy's eyes filled with tears. "Do you think I mattered to them at all?"

"Yes. As much as anything outside their work could have mattered." He leaned over and rubbed his head against her arm. "Keep in mind that they were very self-absorbed."

Moving closer, he butted his head against her chest and began to purr. Stacy was suddenly aware of energy moving between them, different from that which had flowed from her into Glynis, but with the same sense of connection. She picked him up and, holding his furry warmth against her heart, closed her eyes and rocked back and forth in her chair.

Cats, Max might have told her, do not like to be clutched, squeezed, or rocked, no matter the motivation for this behavior. He did not, however, share this information. Instead, they sat nourishing each other, oblivious to the continuous flow of the Entry Processing Center as it swirled and eddied around them.

Chapter 44

Katie and her father sat parked outside Uncle Rudy's back door. Talking him into bringing her to the farm on their way home from the bookstore had been a little like trying to slide across the gym floor in her tennis shoes. He had at first refused, saying that he didn't think they should bother Rudy.

"He's grieving, kitten. Glynis's death has really hit him hard."

"I'm sad, too, Daddy." For a moment, she'd been afraid that she was going to cry. "Maybe I can be sad with him for a little while and make him feel better."

Her father had looked at her for a moment, then sighed. "Maybe you can. But I still don't think it's a good idea. Besides, you have homework."

She had finally convinced him by promising that she would slide the voodoo book under her bed and leave it there, spending the evening on her reading and math instead. She had no intention of telling him that, after she had finished her homework, she was going to crawl under the bed with a flashlight and copy out the information she needed.

"I'll stay in the car," her father told her. "One of us is more than enough for Rudy right now."

Katie nodded. "I'll just stay a little while, Daddy."

She knocked on the back door for what seemed like a long time. When there was no response, she marched back past the car to the barn, noticing that her father had closed his eyes and seemed to be napping. Pushing open the big, weathered door, she slipped inside and crossed the wide-planked floor, breathing in the familiar, comforting scents of horses, pine shavings and saddle soap.

Rudy was in the tack room, bent over something on the work table.

Stepping through the door, Katie saw that the object of his attention was a brown bottle, like the one from which her daddy sometimes poured a glass of what he called his evening relaxation.

Rudy slowly lifted his head. For a moment he seemed uncertain, then he set the bottle on the floor beside his feet. "Katie! What are you doing here?"

"Hi, Uncle Rudy." She smiled. "I thought maybe you'd make something for me."

"Naw, honey, I don't think this is a good time for that."

Stepping into the room, she dragged a stool out of the corner and sat down opposite him. "It's really important. I can't tell you how important it is."

He frowned, and she could feel the intensity of his wishing that she'd go away. He wasn't going to do it; not unless she made him.

Pushing aside her awareness of his grief, she straightened her shoulders. She was sad, too. If she let herself, she would start crying and maybe never stop. But crying wouldn't help, and being sad wouldn't bring Aunt Glinda back. More importantly, being sad wouldn't punish the ones who had caused her death.

Grieving would have to wait; getting even came first.

She leaned across the table. "Please, Uncle Rudy. It's really, really important!"

He shook his head and waved her away.

She was going to have to make him do it. Taking a deep breath, she said, "Glynis would want you to help me."

She almost winced at the look on his face, but she held firm. He stared at her for what seemed like forever, and she stared back at him, trying to look certain. Finally, he sighed.

"OK. What is it you want?"

She scrabbled in her pocket, pulled out a rough drawing, and set it on the table in front of him. Picking it up, he studied it carefully.

"What the heck is this?" He frowned at the sketch.

"It's a bird-lady."

"A what?"

"A bird with the face of an ugly lady."

Rudy bent over the drawing. "She's ugly, all right."

Katie nodded. "I need you to carve two of them for me. Right now, if you would, please. They don't need to be very big or fancy."

"That's it?"

"That's it."

Rudy laid the picture on the table. Choosing two small pieces of cherry wood approximately the same size, he picked up his knife, then looked at Katie and shook his head. "I can't imagine what you want these for, but I'm not goin' to ask you. I don't even want to know."

Katie looked steadily back at him. "That's good, 'cause I don't want to tell you."

Hoping her father was soundly asleep in the car by now, she propped her elbows on the table and prepared to instruct Rudy in the details of Harpy carving.

§

Rudy sat staring at the wood scraps left from Katie's bird-ladies. What on earth could that child want with such crazy carvings? Shaking his head, he let his thoughts return to Glynis and shivered a little. *We never know when we'll have to go. We think we'll be here forever, but we won't.* He pushed the scraps of cherry wood around with the blunt tip of one finger.

What if it had been Jenn? What if something happened to her tomorrow or, God forbid, tonight! He would spend the rest of whatever time he had left wishing he'd told her what she meant to him, kicking himself for not letting her know. The thought was unbearable. Even if he was the one to go first, he'd still be mad at himself, given that there was some kind of afterlife, because he hadn't said his piece.

He sat staring at the table without seeing it. Finally, he picked up the half-empty bourbon bottle, set it on the shelf, and hitched up his jeans. Too many years were already gone and couldn't be gotten back. If he didn't take his chance now, he might never get it again.

Without even stopping to put on his Stetson, he strode from the barn, across the yard and through the cut in the hedge. When he reached Jenn's back porch, he hesitated for a moment. Then, clenching his jaw, he raised his fist and pounded on the door.

After a long minute, the kitchen light came on and Jenn opened the door, staring at him in surprise.

"Rudy! What are you doing here? I thought—"

"You thought I was rude and unneighborly last night, that's what you probably thought."

"No. Yes. I mean—" She stopped and, holding the door open, moved aside so he could enter.

He stepped into the kitchen before he could change his mind, then turned to face her where she stood, her hand still on the knob of the open door. A moth, attracted by the ceiling light, whirred into the kitchen and began throwing itself against the brightness of the bulb.

"You see that?" Rudy pointed to the moth. "That's me."

Jenn stared at him. "Excuse me?"

"Spendin' my life beatin' myself up to no purpose."

Taking her hands, Rudy led her over to the kitchen table and pulled out a chair. Jenn lowered herself into it without taking her eyes off his face.

"Rudy, are you OK?"

"I'm fine. At least, I hope I am." Still holding her hands, he looked into her eyes. "I know you probably think I've gone loco, but I want you to listen to what I need to say without interruptin'. If you don't, I may lose my nerve."

He cleared his throat. "I've been thinkin' about Glynis tonight."

Jenn opened her mouth to speak and he squeezed her hands. "No interruptions, remember?"

She nodded, and he continued. "It hurt, but it made me realize how short human life can be and how dumb I've been all these years, wastin' precious time feelin' sorry for myself, time we might have been able to spend bein' happy together."

He saw incredulity, followed by a blaze of hope, in her eyes and knew he had made the right decision.

"Rudy!" Her voice was husky. "Are you proposing to me?"

It was his turn to feel a shock of surprise. "I guess I am."

He knelt in front of her, still clasping her hands, and said in a firm, resonant voice, "Goddamn it, there's no guessin' about it! I *am* askin' you to marry me, Jennifer Sinclair."

Raising her hands to his lips, he kissed each one in turn. "Do you think you could take on a stupid fool who's spent his life lovin' you and just now found the courage to let you know?"

She made a sound, half laugh, half sob. "Oh, Rudy, you're not the only one who's been stupid. Why do you think I never remarried?" She did laugh, then. "I was so afraid I'd lose your friendship, that I never let you know how much I cared."

Rudy suddenly felt he was bursting with joy. Laughing, he pulled Jenn to her feet and into his arms. She came without resistance, hugging him tightly. Suddenly, he stopped and held her away from him.

Her forehead wrinkled. "What is it?"

He would have thought the look of concern on her face comical, had he not been so filled with apprehension about what he was going to say next.

"I– I don't . . . ."

"Rudy Steele!" Jenn's eyes narrowed. "You'd better not tell me you've suddenly changed your mind."

"No, no! It's not that. It's just that . . . ." He cleared his throat again. "Hell! You're goin' to think I'm so stupid, you'll change your mind!"

She smiled. "I seriously doubt that. However, if you don't finish your sentence, I might just think you have another woman stashed away somewhere."

He shot her an agonized look. "That's just it." He paused again. "All right, then, here it is! I've never even kissed a woman before, much less had one." He waited anxiously for her reaction, but she just stood there, staring at him.

Then she smiled. "Oh, my darling," she said softly. "Do you think I care?" She chuckled. "All these years, when I'd fantasize about loving you, I knew I'd probably have to teach you what little experience I'd gained with James." Sliding her arms around his neck, she whispered, "The rest, we'll learn together."

"Oh, Jenn, Jenn!" He buried his face in her neck, breathing in her scent, feeling the softness of her hair against his face.

After a moment, she pulled away, her face serious. "I have just one question, and I want you to consider carefully before you answer it."

He nodded, feeling anxiety tighten his chest again.

"Are you sure that this isn't just a sort of rebound reaction because of Glynis's death? You know, a way of trying to forget your sadness, or deny your grief?"

He expelled the breath he hadn't realized he'd been holding. "I don't have to consider my answer to that. If you don't think it sounds too awful, I can promise you it's *because* of Glynis that I'm here. What's happened brought home to me how short life really is, how quickly we can lose our chances." Slipping his arms around her again, he held her close. "I know it sounds crazy," he murmured, "but I've just found out that you can be sad, and so darn happy you think you'll bust, both at the same time."

Jenn stroked his cheek with tender fingers. "I know," she whispered. "I know."

Taking his hand, she led him out of the brightness of the kitchen, into the dim hallway. "Do you think Glynis would mind if we have our first lesson tonight?"

He chuckled softly. "Given the fact that she's spent the past ten years tryin' to hint me into sayin' something to you, I suspect that, if she could somehow know about it, she'd be more than pleased."

Pushing aside his sadness that, because he had waited so long, Glynis was no longer here to share his joy, he slipped his arm around Jenn's waist. "You show me the room, my darlin' girl, and I'll carry you over the threshold," he told her. "We'll count it as practice for our wedding day."

Chapter 45

Katie tiptoed to the bedroom door and listened. Good! Not a sound from her father's room; he must be asleep by now. Closing the door as quietly as she could, she switched on the overhead light, took the jar with the Harpy feathers out of the dresser drawer, and set it on the small table tucked into the alcove across from her bed.

Reaching under the bed, she extracted a yellow legal pad. She tore off the top sheet, which was covered with writing, and slid the pad back where it had come from.

"Now," she said aloud, "we'll just see who's going to be sorry!"

Reading over the directions she had spent the past hour copying by flashlight from the heavy volume stored beneath the bed, she checked the materials laid out on the table top: Rudy's two carvings of the bird-women; a bottle of glue, complete with applicator; the jar containing the Harpy feathers; a large red T-shirt belonging to her father; a small play drum she had once received as a Christmas gift; and her father's tack hammer. In the place of honor at the center of the table, carefully positioned on a flowered scarf she had taken from her mother's dresser, sat her piggy bank.

Satisfied, she stationed herself in front of this collection. Taking a deep breath, she slowly lifted the red T-shirt from the table and slipped it on over her nightgown. It reached halfway to her ankles, making a respectable ceremonial dress. Next, she picked up the drum. The sound of her hand against the plastic-coated parchment covering the metal frame was barely audible in the quiet room, but she felt sure that the Petro Loa would be able to hear it, while her father would not. Beating the drum rhythmically, she began to dance around the bed, gradually accelerating until she was transported to a place where nothing existed but the sound and movement.

🐾 🐾 🐾 Between 🐾 🐾 🐾

After a time, her frenzy slowed. Flushed, she stopped in front of the table, placed the drum back where she had picked it up, and slowly raised her hands above her head. Reading from the piece of yellow legal paper, she chanted, "Petro Loa, Petro Loa, gods of power, gods of dark. I call upon you for revenge. Send your power into these carvings," here she opened her eyes and touched the effigies of the Harpies, "that they may help me punish the nasty bird-ladies for which they stand. In return, I offer you this sacrifice."

Lowering her hands, she picked up the hammer and brought it smartly down on the back of the piggy bank. Coins, mixed with shards of pink china, flew across the flower-patterned scarf, as the sacrificial pig collapsed. After listening for a few seconds to be sure the noise had not roused her father, Katie folded the scarf corners over the debris, then opened the bottle of glue and applied a generous amount to each of the carvings in turn. Next, holding her breath against the stink, she removed the two Harpy feathers from their jar, pulled them apart, and stuck the pieces onto the sides of the small figures.

Stepping back, she surveyed her work with satisfaction. She raised her hands again. "Thank you Petro Loa. Thank you for placing your power to punish in these pieces of wood. To you I give this sacrifice, to be yours forever." Pulling an empty shoe box from under the table, she gathered up the scarf, with its burden of shards and coins, and set it inside. Replacing the lid, she slid the box back under the table. Tomorrow she would bury it in the back yard.

Now she needed something in which to keep her power objects. Dropping on her knees beside the bed, she reached past the book on voodoo, feeling around in the darkness until her hand touched what it was searching for. With an exclamation of satisfaction, she extracted a small, oblong wooden box that fitted smoothly inside an outer cover. She had bought it with her allowance in an antique shop last summer, certain that she would find a use for it. Sliding out the inner part, she laid the Harpy carvings carefully in it, side by side. The cover slipped back over them with just enough clearance to leave their feather coatings undisturbed. Satisfied, she slid the box back under the bed.

Returning to the desk, she dropped the glue and the empty jar that had held the Harpy feathers into a drawer. The drum went into the toy chest in her closet. Then she lifted the red T-shirt over her head and, folding it neatly, set it on the desk, with the tack hammer on top of it.

These she would return to their proper locations tomorrow, while her father was at the hospital.

Finally, she went into her little bathroom and washed her hands thoroughly. Looking around the room one last time, she checked to be sure the nightlight was on, turned back her quilt and climbed into bed. As she switched off the bedside lamp, she wondered if she would see her mother again tonight. Even if that should happen, she felt strongly that it would be a mistake to mention the ceremony she had just completed. Not yet, anyway.

Scrunching down under the covers, she thought about the two feather-coated figures safely tucked away under the bed. An image of the monstrous creatures they represented rose in her mind and she smiled grimly.

"Just you wait, you nasty things, just you wait," she whispered.

Closing her eyes, she fell peacefully asleep.

§

David stared at the printout Colin Elmore had handed him. "This doesn't make any sense."

He looked up to see Elmore watching him with concerned eyes. "It does, David, if her brain is damaged."

David tossed the paper onto the desk. "Not possible! There's nothing wrong with Stacy's brain. The swelling's down, all the signs are good. Either the machine is faulty, or this is someone else's test."

Pushing back his chair, Elmore came around the desk, moved a stack of papers aside and sat down on the edge, facing David.

"The EEG was checked out just last week, and I ran the test myself—twice. This is the readout." His voice was gentle. "It isn't what I expected, either, and I know how hard it must be to accept, but it looks like Stacy is brain dead."

David jumped to his feet, bumping his chair so hard that it toppled over backwards. "She can't be! There's something wrong, something else. You've got to run the test again."

Elmore raised his hands. "All right. I'm certain it won't make any difference, but we'll do it now. You can monitor."

Following his chief of staff down the hall, David felt like his stomach had turned upside down. It wasn't possible, he told himself. He'd just spent two incredible nights with Stace; she was fine. She was better than fine.

But, a small voice in his mind intruded, *she was out of her body then. What we're dealing with here is her physical body. Besides, how can you be sure those weren't just unbelievably vivid dreams?*

Because I can, he told the voice. *I was with her—twice. They were the most intensely real experiences I've ever had. Not only that, Katie said that she had spent time with her. Either we're both nuts, or it happened.* An image popped into his mind of Minerva's black and white cat informing him that Stacy was in danger from an as yet unidentified source. Of course, that was nuts, too, but what the hell; if he was going to swallow the idea that he had actually spent time with Stace, he might as well buy the whole package!

He imagined himself telling Elmore that he believed Stacy's test had somehow been skewed with malicious intent by a person or persons unknown, because his neighbor's cat had warned him during the second of two incredible nights he had spent with his wife, while they were both out of their physical bodies.

Sure, he thought; I'd share that with him right now, except I couldn't do Stace much good from the psych ward!

He was so deep in thought that he almost missed the turn into Stacy's room. Even as he helped Elmore gently fasten the electrodes in place on her unresisting head, he kept turning the dilemma over in his mind. There had to be some way he could discover what was going on, some way to prove what his gut knew was true!

§

"I don't know what to do."

David looked anxiously at Minerva over the glass-topped table, where he had poured out coffee for himself and hot water for her ginger tea. He rarely came home for lunch when Katie was in school, but he wanted the older woman's opinion on what was happening.

She immersed a tea bag in her cup. "Let me be sure I understand. You're telling me that the electroencephalograph readings indicate that Stacy's brain is no longer functional; is that right?"

He nodded. "I helped administer the last test. Elmore even used a different machine, just to be sure."

"But you feel certain that the information is not correct."

He nodded again.

"Because . . . ?"

"Because I've just spent two nights with Stacy. Her brain is fine."

Minerva lifted out the tea bag, squeezed it against her spoon, and set it on the side of her saucer. "You have to realize, David, that you have spent time with her in her spirit body. The spirit body is always perfect. However, the fact that someone's spirit body is whole and healthy doesn't always mean that the same holds true for their physical body."

"Wait a minute! You're not saying that the machine is right, are you?"

Minerva shook her head. "No, that's not what I'm saying. Nonetheless, you do need to understand that the physical body can be damaged, even while the spirit body remains whole, a good example being children who are born mentally challenged." She sipped her tea. "No, I agree with you that there is almost certainly something else involved. Max has told me he's convinced that someone has been stalking Stacy, with intent to harm her. I think it very likely that this person, whoever he or she might be, may have in some way influenced the machine's response."

"But Elmore had the first machine checked out and the other one is practically brand new."

"Then there may be some other way her brain has been made to seem no longer functional. What else might create that impression?"

David frowned. "If there's nothing wrong with the machinery, the only thing I can think of is medication. But the order to take her off the phenobarbitol was sent down over two days ago; her system should be mostly clear by now."

"Have you tested to be sure the drug is not still in her body?"

"No. It never occurred to me." He jumped up, excited. "I'll get back over there and draw blood right away!"

The wall phone behind him shrilled. For an instant, he considered ignoring it, then picked it up. "Kinnard here." He was surprised to hear Colin Elmore's voice on the other end of the line.

"You'd better cut lunch short and get back here right away."

"What's wrong?"

"It's Stacy. The monitor's registering an accelerated tachycardia.

Her liver must have been more damaged than we thought."

David felt like he'd been punched in the stomach. "Damn! I'll be right there. We've got to get her to the OR, stat!"

"No point in that, David. We've already talked about this. No brain activity, no surgery. Just be here with her; that's all you can do."

David ground his teeth. "The hell it is!"

Slamming the receiver back onto its cradle, he grabbed his keys from the marble-topped hall table. "Can you stay, Minerva? Katie will be home in a couple of hours, and I've got to get back."

"I'll stay. What is it?"

"The bleeding from Stacy's liver has substantially increased. Elmore doesn't want to operate, because he thinks she's brain dead; but if he doesn't, she'll die. I've got to get that blood test done!"

Yanking open the front door, he looked back at her. "It had better do the trick!" The door slammed behind him.

As he roared out of the driveway, Minerva sat back down in the kitchen and focused on Between and Max. A moment later, he appeared.

"You called?" His yellow eyes regarded her with interest.

"I did. Stacy's liver is failing, but Dr. Elmore refuses to operate, because her brain still isn't functioning normally. David has gone to run a blood test, to see if the medication that should be out of her system is still present and causing the problem. I'm convinced that her lack of response is due to some kind of interference in the medical process and thought you might be able to track down what that is."

Max nodded. "I'll do what I can. See you shortly." He disappeared.

§

He located David in Colin Elmore's office.

"There's no point in opening her up," the older doctor was saying. "Even if we did, and she survived the surgery, she'd just exist the rest of her life in a vegetative state. She left a Living Will because she didn't want that to happen."

David brought his fist down on the desk. "I know she has a Living Will, goddamn it; I'm the one who insisted on it. But I'm positive there's something else involved, and if we don't operate, she won't be around for us to find out what it is. We have to give her that chance!"

🐾 🐾 🐾 **Between** 🐾 🐾 🐾

Elmore ran a hand through his shock of white hair. "David, I understand your distress; she's your wife, for God's sake! But that doesn't alter the fact that she isn't there any more. And now her body is telling us it's no longer able to function."

"Her body is telling us it needs to have its liver repaired, so there'll be something for her to come back to!"

Elmore leaned back in his chair. "I don't want to argue any more. Unless you can show me evidence that says otherwise, I'm going to have to deny your request."

David stood up. "All right, Colin. If you won't operate, I will." He turned to leave the room.

"Like hell you will! You can't override my authority."

"You don't give me any choice. It's your authority, or Stacy's life. Under the circumstances, which would you choose?"

Colin Elmore closed his eyes briefly. "You can't operate; she's family. Even if I turn a blind eye, word will reach the board and you'll end up facing reprimand or dismissal. You'll be flushing your chances for promotion down the toilet, David. You could even lose your license."

David scrubbed the top of his head "Do you think I care about that?" he shouted. "What's a promotion, if I buy it with Stacy's blood?"

Elmore raised an eyebrow. "A bit dramatic, but I get your point." He stood up. "All right; give me one piece of evidence, even a small one, that there's a chance she'll come out of the coma, if the rest of her body supports that. Give me even the tiniest bit of proof, and I'll do the surgery myself."

"Phlebotomy!" David exclaimed. Turning, he flung open the door and raced down the hall, followed by Colin Elmore.

Stretching, Max stood up from his vantage point in the corner and trotted after them.

Chapter 46

Arthur Craddock was arguing with his inner voice. Not that it really was his inner voice, he reminded himself. He had realized, after the disturbing interview in the duplicate of his former office, that there was a definite connection between the urgings of this intrusion into his mind and the demands of the dark man who called himself Serizzin. It had been an "aha!" moment which gave him no pleasure whatsoever.

Now he was resisting the voice's insistence that he continue to play the part of benefactor to Stacy Addison. He felt particularly resistant, because the voice was pressuring him to help her achieve her desire to reanimate her comatose body. He didn't care, he told himself, that this command was actually coming from Serizzin. The very idea of Stacy, beautiful and successful, continuing to foist herself on the unsuspecting public as a healer made him want to puke.

But she isn't beautiful any more, the voice reminded him, and Arthur smiled, remembering the dressings he had seen around her head and on her face. *Under those bandages, the damage is extensive*, the voice continued. *It will be many years, perhaps never, before she looks as she did prior to her accident. And*, it reminded him, *her appearance is more important to her than anything else.*

Arthur's mood was improving with every word he heard. *Serves her right*, he thought. *Let her suffer, like I have.* For a moment the phrase, "and like Charlotte has," flitted through his mind followed by a fleeting twinge of sorrow, but he quickly squashed it, as he would a competitor who might block his path to achieving what he wanted.

Invite her to return to the hospital room with you, the voice suggested. *Tell her you have discovered a way to help her reanimate her body. This is what she wants more than anything else.* When he didn't agree, the voice continued, *The doctor is going to have the bandages changed before he takes her into surgery. If you escort her there immediately, you may have the pleasure of watching her expression when she sees her damaged face for the first time.*

Yes! Arthur thought. The prospect of watching Stacy Addison view the wreckage of her beauty was undeniably entrancing. If he hurried, he might convince her to accompany him back to Earth before that blasted cat interrupted again. Smiling, he focused on transporting himself to the outskirts of wherever she presently was. A moment later, he was gone.

§

"I knew it! I knew something was screwy!"

Max, from his observation post by the door of the doctor's lounge, watched David pound his fist enthusiastically on one of the tables.

The older doctor, Elmore, shook his head. "I can't understand it." He looked at the piece of paper he was holding in his hand. "I dated this script for the second. How can it say the fourth?"

"Doesn't matter." David's voice was exultant. "That's why she isn't showing any signs of activity—she's still full of phenobarbitol!" David pounded the table again, then smiled apologetically at a young woman two tables over, who looked up with a frown from the book she was studying.

"Come on," he told Elmore. "We've got to line up an OR!"

David headed out the door and Elmore followed. Max trotted behind them, turning into the Intensive Care Unit, while the other two hurried on down the hall. Passing through a closed door, he entered Stacy's room, where he carefully scrutinized every corner, paying special attention to the section of the wall opposite the bed where he had originally sensed the suspicious energy pattern.

Satisfied that he had checked everything, he stared briefly at Stacy's motionless body; then he focused on Minerva and disappeared.

§

"No go," Max informed her. "Whoever is stalking Stacy wasn't in the hospital, although I checked her room as I was leaving and could still detect a trace amount of the negative energy I first sensed there. It definitely matches that of the energy that I've sensed hanging around Stacy, as well as that of the man Herm and I observed watching Glynis from the tractor. By the way, Herm and I traveled back into that now where Glynis saw him. Not only did he watch her die, but his earlier behavior indicated that he was responsible for her so-called accident."

"That certainly is disturbing!" Minerva stared at him. "What about Stacy's liver?"

"A blood test did show that Stacy still has the medicine in her body that's been keeping her in the coma. David and the older doctor, Elmore, are going to operate as soon as they arrange for a place to do it."

Minerva sighed. "Thank goodness!"

"Exactly." He frowned. "I'd better get back Between and keep a close watch on Stacy, since she seems to be the focus of the man producing this elusive energy field. I asked Herm to keep an eye on her, but he's got Glynis to look after, too." He yawned. "I'm afraid my visit to the hospital didn't accomplish much, except give you information about what's going on, although rechecking Stacy's room did confirm that the energy I first sensed there definitely belongs to the man we're tracking."

Minerva smiled at him. "I appreciate your efforts and I'm glad your trip wasn't completely wasted." Her eyes dropped to her lap. "Oh, no, not again!" Holding up the afghan on her lap, she stared at it in frustration, then began ripping out stitches.

"'Nerva?" Katie's voice floated down the stairwell. "Where's Max?"

"Right here beside me on the sofa; at least for a few more minutes."

"Oh, good!" Holding her nightgown up, so she wouldn't trip, Katie galloped down the stairs, bedroom slippers flapping.

Minerva smiled at her as she entered the living room. "Isn't it a little early to be going to bed?"

Katie nodded. "But I want to be ready, because tonight might be important." Plopping down beside Max, she eyed him critically. "You look funny."

"That's because you're seeing me in my spirit body."

Katie stared at him with interest. "Where's your other body?"

"Asleep at Minerva's house."

She thought a moment. "How come I can see you, if this isn't your real body?"

Max's yellow eyes grew rounder. "This *is* my real body. It's the one that goes inside my physical body when that body is awake and makes it possible for it to see and hear and move. And you can see me, because you know who I truly am, regardless of how I present myself."

"Can I touch you?" Katie stretched out her hand. When Max nodded, she ran the hand down his back and giggled when it sank into him. "Wow! Look, 'Nerva! My hand's inside him! What a weird feeling!" She wiggled her fingers. "Does that tickle?"

"Somewhat." Max rolled his eyes up at her. "Please remove your hand now, Katie. I'm beginning to feel like a cookie jar."

Withdrawing her hand, Katie examined it carefully. "It's all tingly!"

Minerva finished unraveling the most recent row of threads and set her afghan aside. "That's because you're still reacting to Max's internal energy field." She looked closely at the little girl. "Now, please tell me what you think might be important about tonight, Katie."

Katie kicked her heels against the front of the sofa, then looked up at her. "Remember the stinky feathers I brought back?"

"I do."

With the air of a magician producing a rabbit from a hat, Katie pulled an oblong box from under the edge of her nightgown, where she had been almost sitting on it. "You'd better hold your nose," she warned. Sliding open the top, she held the container up for Minerva to examine. Inside were two roughly carved figures plastered with feather pieces.

"Mmhm." Minerva nodded. "You may close that up again."

Katie followed her suggestion, then laid the box beside her on the sofa.

"Just what are you planning to do with those?"

Katie shrugged. "Something. I'm not sure."

"Yes, you are." Max sniffed at the container. "You're planning to do something with them you almost certainly shouldn't do." He looked over at Minerva. "Those things are absolutely reeking with more than just Harpy stink; they're loaded with some kind of negative energy."

Katie frowned. "It isn't negative. It's power—Petro Loa power."

"Voodoo!" Minerva raised her eyebrows. "Is that what was in that big book you were carting around?"

Katie nodded.

"I didn't even know Glynis had such a thing in the bookstore. And I can't understand why your father allowed you to bring it home."

Katie put her hand on Minerva's arm. "Don't blame Daddy. He didn't want me to. I sort of promised him I'd leave it under the bed until we took it back today."

"Obviously, you didn't keep your word."

"Yes, I did!" Jumping off the sofa, she clutched the box to her chest. "I got all the information I needed using my flashlight."

She could see a smile twitching the corners of Minerva's mouth.

Max was staring at her. "Enterprising, aren't you? I suppose you think you're going to march up to those unpleasant creatures, wave your carvings at them, and they'll disappear in a poof of smoke."

Katie frowned. "I'm not sure what I'm going to do; I just know that I'm going to do something. But I need your help to get back to where they are. Tonight. Tonight feels right; tonight feels important."

Max continued to stare at her. "I'm not sure that's a good idea," he said finally. "I think you may be right about something important happening tonight, but that's exactly the reason why you shouldn't be there. It might be dangerous."

"Bah!" Katie kicked her slippered foot against the sofa. "I have these," she waved the box holding the effigies at him, "and I'll have you to look after me. I'll be fine."

Max cocked his head toward Minerva. "Help me out here, will you?"

Minerva shrugged. "I'm not sure I can. I know it doesn't make much sense, but it seems to me that Katie may be right. It could be important for her to be present if something does take place tonight."

"You're sure about that?"

Minerva nodded.

"All right," he told Katie. "I give up. I have to go find your mother right now, but I'll come back for you later this evening."

"You promise?"

"I promise. And," he eyed her sternly, "I keep my promises."

He turned to Minerva. "You probably need to be on call, so to speak. If there really is a blowup, we'll need your help, too."

Minerva nodded. "I'll be ready. If David comes home before we get back, he'll just assume I've fallen asleep with Katie. And Max, be careful, will you?"

"I always am." Max turned around twice and disappeared.

Katie smiled at Minerva. "He's a good guy, isn't he?"

Minerva smiled back. "Yes, he is. One of the best."

"You're a good guy, too. But most of all," she leaned over and hugged Minerva hard, "you're my 'Nerva!"

Chapter 47

Stacy gazed around the intensive care room. Not much had changed since her first visit, almost two weeks ago. Certainly her body, silent and motionless under the covers, appeared to have made no progress at all toward returning to consciousness.

She looked over at the man who had accompanied her here. He was not quite a stranger, having assisted in Katie's rescue from the monstrous creatures who had carried her off, but she knew very little about him, except that he seemed, for some unexplained reason, to be interested in helping her.

He had approached her this evening on one of her rare trips outside the Entry Processing Center. She was sitting on a carved wooden bench beneath one of the large trees dotting the park-like expanse of grass surrounding the vast complex, trying to work out some means of returning to her body in time to film the television pilot.

David had warned her that she would need a long recuperation period, but he always did tend to be overly cautious. She was young, strong, and healthy. There should be no reason why she could not quickly get herself into good enough condition to stand in front of a camera for an hour, demonstrating her work.

Gradually an uncomfortable feeling seeped into her. There had been no one in sight when she sat down on the bench, but now a man stood a short distance away, staring at her. A chill of apprehension shivered through her; then she recognized the watcher as the unexpected ally who had helped her rescue Katie from the Harpies' grove.

"Hello!" She smiled and put out her hand. "I'm Stacy Addison. I didn't have an opportunity to thank you for you helping me save my daughter from those monsters."

Stepping forward, the man took her hand and held it tightly for a moment. Resisting an inexplicable urge to pull away, she squeezed his fingers in return. His cool, blue eyes gazed into hers and, as she had at their meeting on the prairie, she glimpsed in them an unreadable emotion that almost instantly shifted into a smile.

"I'm glad to meet you, Stacy Addison." His voice was low and pleasant. "How is your daughter?"

"Katie's fine, in great part thanks to you."

He made a deprecating gesture. "My pleasure." He looked at the bench. "May I join you?"

"Oh, sure." She moved over to make room for him. "You know, I don't even know your name."

"It's . . . Charles. My name is Charles." He smiled.

"Well, thanks again, Charles, for all your help." For reasons she didn't understand, his attention made her uncomfortable. She stood up. "I guess I'd better be getting back."

Charles also stood up. "You know, I've learned that you're having some other problems," he said.

Stacy frowned. "What problems?"

"You're only here temporarily, but you're having a hard time getting back into your body. Isn't that so?"

The tiny chill of apprehension rippled through her again and she took a step back. "It might be; but I don't understand how you could know that."

"A mutual friend." He smiled again. "I'm here because I've recently acquired other information that may be helpful to you in changing that situation."

A surge of hope overrode the apprehension. "Really?"

"Most definitely. With this new data, I see no reason why we can't reunite you with your body—right now, in fact, if you'd like to do that."

Magic words. As she heard them, she made an instantaneous decision, pushing aside her qualms about leaving the Entry Processing area without telling Max, or anyone else, where she was going. She would accompany Charles back to Earth and give him a chance to prove that what he was promising was true. If it he couldn't help her, she would return Between immediately. He put out his hand and, shivering now with expectation, she took it.

And here they were, back in the intensive care room with her body, which seemed to be in no better condition than it had been the last time she saw it.

She turned to her companion. "I don't think there's been any progress. Just what did you find out that might help me get back in?" She stared at the bed. "My husband's already told me that the doctor in charge has been prescribing phenobarbitol, so that my body can't wake up. That doesn't seem to have changed."

Charles moved closer to her. "I have it on good authority that a prescription was written two days ago, authorizing the removal of that medication. By this time your body should be ready for your return; waiting for it, as a matter of fact."

Excitement rippled through Stacy at the thought of opening her eyes and seeing again, of moving her arms and legs, of getting out of bed and calling Evan Chastain to tell him that she would, after all, be available to film the television pilot.

The door opened. A nurse pushing a stainless steel cart entered, followed by a second nurse. Carefully maneuvering through the maze of cords and machinery, they positioned the cart beside the bed. One of the nurses, a fresh-faced young girl with curling brown hair, leaned over and began working with the dressings that swathed the head and face of the woman in the bed.

That's how Stacy labeled her—the woman in the bed. It was almost impossible to think of the motionless body as herself, although somewhere deep inside she understood this *was* her body, no matter how intensely she wanted to deny that. She watched, fascinated, as the two nurses carefully unwound the bandages covering the woman's head— her head—and gasped as they revealed a shaven skull, splotched with patches of short, copper hair and dark, scabbed stitches.

Unable to look away, she stared in growing horror as the brown-haired young nurse now delicately peeled away the dressing from the right side of the woman's face. A network of angry red lines, displaying what looked like thousands of fine stitches, extended from nose to ear, criss-crossing the cheek and dipping down toward a reddened crater beneath the bruised eye, where the bones had obviously been crushed, but not yet repaired.

"Looking good." The brown-haired nurse handed the bandages to her companion, who placed them in a red plastic container.

"Not bad," the other agreed. "But she's still got a long way to go—if she comes out of it at all. Sure glad I don't have all those surgeries ahead of me!"

They proceeded to clean the damaged areas and cover them with fresh dressings. Then they straightened the covers around the woman's unconscious body and wheeled their cart back out of the room.

Stacy barely noticed their departure. She had been frantic when she first discovered that she was out of her body and, for the time being at least, unable to get back into it. But that had been a problem she believed she would eventually solve. And once she was back in her body, she would then move forward with her life and her career, perhaps even improve both areas with information gathered during her time Between.

But this! How would she ever be able to resume her existence on Earth with a face like this! Who would even begin to trust that she could heal them, when her own body had become such a total disaster? No one would want to get near her, not even David or Katie! She was ugly. No, not ugly—she was hideous!

She collapsed on the floor, doubling over with an agony that permeated every atom of her being. She wanted to scream until she shattered into a million shrieking pieces, but could not squeeze out even a moan. Suddenly she felt a touch on her shoulder. Looking up, she saw Charles bending over her. She gaped helplessly at him as he picked her up, then closed her eyes against the vertigo that carried them away.

§

Katie lay staring at the shadows thrown on the wall by her nightlight. She had changed back into the T-shirt, jeans, and tennis shoes she had worn earlier in the day, deciding that her day clothes were more suitable than her nightgown for whatever might happen Between. Excitement, combined with a touch of nervousness, threatened to keep her awake, but she resolutely closed her eyes and began to practice the deep breathing she had once seen demonstrated on a television yoga program.

Eventually she drifted into sleep, the box containing the Harpy carvings clutched in one hand. Inside, next to the little figures, nestled a small, sharp needle she had borrowed from Minerva's knitting bag.

Chapter 48

It was the end of the world. From the height of a life filled with promise, Stacy had plummeted into what must surely be hell. Everything she lived for—her rising career, her chance at fame, David's love, Katie's devotion—all had been destroyed in the single, terrible moment when she had seen her face. That image seemed painted on the insides of her eyelids; even without a mirror, she would never escape it. A hundred, a thousand, surgeries would never be able to disguise the vermillion road map carved into her ruined cheek!

Evan Chastain would find some other healer to host his program. She, if she recovered from her coma, would end up as nothing but a housewife and mother, a doctor's wife, whose importance was measured by her husband's accomplishments, rather than her own. And perhaps not even that. Why would a rising young physician like David want a woman so repulsively ugly at his side? She would only hold him back. Even if she could tolerate the many surgeries it would take to restore even a semblance of normality, her appearance would never be more than passable.

The pain was unbearable. There was no relief. There would never be any relief again.

"Stacy!"

She became aware that someone was calling her name, had perhaps been calling it for some time, repeating it over and over. Opening her eyes, she realized that Charles was still holding her in his arms. It was his voice she was hearing. She began to struggle weakly and he set her down on the same bench outside the Entry Processing Center where he had found her sitting, what seemed like eons ago.

Looking up into his eyes, she saw what seemed to be elation, and frowned. "Why . . . are you happy?" Her voice welled up slowly, like rusty water that had been stagnating in an ancient pipe.

The elation flickered, receded, then returned. "I'm happy," he said, "because I understand your pain and I know there's a cure for it."

"A cure?"

"Yes."

"That's impossible!"

Charles shook his head. "No. I know someone who has the power to change what has happened to you."

She stared at him, unbelieving.

"Let me take you to him, Stacy."

She shook her head. "No one can help me."

"Serizzin can. He's very powerful."

Her eyes filled with tears. "He'd have to be the most powerful person in existence, to do me any good."

Charles smiled again, but this time the smile didn't reach his eyes. "Perhaps he is," he said softly. "I think perhaps he is."

He took her unresisting hand. "Let's see what he can do for you. You may have to promise something in return, but I'm sure he'll make the bargain worthwhile."

She could feel his insistence pressing into her. Under other circumstances, it might have been disturbing, but at this point she didn't care. If there was help to be found anywhere in the universe, she was willing to take it, regardless of the cost.

Charles caught her up in his arms again and, closing her eyes, she relinquished herself to the vertigo and her only chance to salvage what was left of her life.

§

Herm, still in his coyote shape, slipped from behind the bush where he had been crouching. After Glynis had fallen asleep in her room, he had gone looking for Stacy and found, to his surprise, that she was not in the Entry Processing Center. Uneasy, he had moved his search outside, exiting the building just in time to see her materialize in the arms of the very man for whom he and Max had been searching.

Flattening himself at the base of the nearest bush, he watched as her companion set her on a bench and spoke to her. Although Stacy appeared to be listening to him, she also seemed distressed and dazed.

🐾 🐾 🐾 Between 🐾 🐾 🐾

Before he could reveal himself and demand an explanation, the man swept her into his arms again and disappeared.

Herm was amazed and disturbed to find her involved with the very person whose behavior he and Max found highly suspicious. And although he had not been able to hear everything the man said to her, he had caught the name of Serizzin, which fully alarmed him. If Serizzin was involved, it was not only Stacy who was in danger; all of them, perhaps even the whole human world, would be affected.

It had been some years, Earth time, since the massive power bearing that name had found a tool through which it could expand its negative influence. But the Earth level of experience continually moved in cycles, and everything had to be kept in balance. Light balanced dark, good balanced evil; one could not exist without the other. It was quite easy, given Earth's present tendency toward negativity, to suspect that Serizzin was planning another attempt to gain greater control there.

Herm could not yet see how the Lord of Darkness might use Stacy, a relatively unknown young woman, to help him rise to fuller power once again, but certainly her simultaneous existence in both the physical and non-physical worlds gave her an unusual status, as did her ability to heal. It was not impossible that he might see in her a useful tool. What strategy he could use to manipulate her was, as yet, unclear; but the fact that she had apparently gone to visit him indicated that there almost certainly was a strategy, one that would produce good results for no one but Serizzin.

Herm needed to find Max, and he needed to do it now! Shaking himself, the coyote transformed once more into Hermes, messenger of the gods. His lips a grim line, he focused on his destination and disappeared in a flash of light.

§

Max watched with amusement as the two Harpies, feathers flying in all directions, hopped up and down in distress. Backed up against the smallest tree in their grove, they were cringing before Katie, who stood brandishing the box containing Rudy's cherry wood images of them.

"You see these?" Katie shouted, sliding back the cover. "These are you. And," she waved one of the effigies in front of them. "those are your feathers covering them. That means I have part of your spirits trapped in there, you nasty, ugly things!" Picking up Minerva's needle, she jabbed it into one of the little figures. Squawking, Urania flinched and tried to hide behind her larger sister. Smiling, Katie stabbed the other carving and watched with satisfaction as Klio jumped, her wings madly flapping.

Max rubbed against her knee. "Aren't you being a little bloodthirsty?"

"No! They deserve worse than this." Katie, arm outstretched, continued to hold the pair at bay.

"I'll teach you to carry me off and hurt my Mommy and my Aunt Glinda!"

"No!" Klio screeched, hopping frantically around the tree. "Your accusations are false. We do not even know your mother or your aunt. We have never heard of them, much less injured them."

"Never!" echoed Urania, anxiously peering around Klio's wing.

Katie narrowed her eyes. "You're lying!"

"No, not lying. We have never seen or hurt them."

"You know, I think they might be telling the truth." Max eyed the huge creatures speculatively. "You don't deny that you carried off this child, do you?"

"Of course we do not deny it." Klio drew herself up as straight as she could. "We were balancing a debt of honor."

"Honor," squawked Urania.

Max looked at them with interest. "Is that so? To whom, may I ask, did you owe this debt?"

"To Arthurcraddock." Their screech was simultaneous.

Klio bobbed her head. "He honored us by believing. But then he did a strange thing."

"Very strange." Urania fluttered her wings.

"After he had us bring you here," Klio told Katie, "he returned and helped to free you. He had a woman with him. He helped her take you from our grove. We did not understand such behavior, but he later said it was necessary and thanked us for helping him. But still, we found it upsetting and strange."

"Strange!" Urania began to hop on one foot and then the other. Klio, caught up in the rhythm, enthusiastically joined her and they began to circle, chanting, "Found it strange, very strange, very strange, indeed."

Max butted Katie's leg. "Come on," he said. "I need some fresh air to clear my head, so I can think this through."

Leaving the Harpies caught up in their dance, they backed out of the grove into the tall grass surrounding it, where Max rolled over and over, trying to rub the stench out of his fur. Finally, he sat up, shook himself and looked at Katie.

"I think we've just learned something very important," he told her.

"What?"

"We now know the name of the person responsible for your kidnaping. And unless my powers of deduction are failing, he's also the man responsible for your Aunt Glynis's accident."

"But who is he? Who is Arthurcraddock? What an odd name!"

"I suspect it's two names—Arthur Craddock." He enunciated each word separately. "And I think we need to find out what his motivation is as soon as possible. The puzzle pieces are finally starting to fit together, and I don't like the picture they're making."

Turning back toward the grove, he said, "Come on. Let's see if we can persuade those two to tell us where this Craddock person is."

He had barely finished speaking when the tall grass in front of him trembled and Herm, dressed in his tunic and winged cap, appeared.

Max looked at him in surprise. "I thought you were taking care of things at the Entry Processing Center."

"I was, but—" Herm caught sight of the little girl.

"Katie! What are you doing here?"

"Hi, Herm!" She hugged him. "Max and I came to punish the nasty bird-ladies."

"Why don't you leave that to me?"

"Because it's me they kidnaped."

Herm chuckled. "I can't argue with that. Nevertheless, I think my claim is at least as good as yours. What do you say we punish them together?"

Katie nodded. "OK. You can help, if you want to. But I've already scared them with this." She held out the little wooden box containing the Harpy images.

Herm touched it and drew back his hand. "What do you have in there, Katie?" The laughter had disappeared from his voice.

"It's a secret."

Kneeling in the tall grass in front of her, Herm took her chin in his hand and looked into her eyes. "Listen to me, little one. The secret in that container is not a good one for you to be carrying around."

Closing her fingers around the box, Katie twisted her head away and stuck out her lower lip. "It's mine. It belongs to me."

"That's as it may be; however, it is exposing you to forces far beyond your ability to master." He held out his hand. "Give it to me. I will take good care of it."

"No!" Katie tightened her grip on the box. "It's mine."

Herm looked over Katie's head at Max. "Are you aware of the negative energy stored in there?"

"I am. It has, however, served the purpose of frightening those two feathered nightmares into giving us some important information."

Herm frowned at him. "That, in itself, should have warned you of its danger."

Max lifted a furry eyebrow. "I was following the principle of free will. It was her choice to bring it Between with her."

Herm looked thoughtful. "You're right, of course. But she's only a child, with a child's lack of experience. I think that warrants stepping over the line of proper protocol, at least enough to give her the choice of whether or not she will harm herself—and perhaps others."

He turned back to Katie. "Do you understand the difference between Light and Darkness, little one?"

"Of course! Light lets you see things, and darkness hides them."

Herm nodded. "That's right. And that is true not only of the light of daytime and the darkness of night. It is also true of the purposes that human beings, as well as other creatures, hold inside their minds and hearts. The thoughts and beliefs you have in here," he tapped Katie's forehead lightly with one finger, "determine the things you do outwardly. If those thoughts and beliefs are filled with Light, they will cause you to behave in loving ways that honor other people and yourself. But if your mind and heart are filled with Darkness, you will bring sorrow and misery to everyone around you, as well as to yourself."

Katie stared at him without speaking and he touched the box again. "What you have in here does not belong to the Light, little one. If you keep it, Darkness will seep out of it and poison you." He looked at her closely. "I think perhaps its hatred and cruelty has already touched you."

Katie caught her lower lip between her teeth. Max, sensing her inner struggle, pressed himself against her, weaving in and out between her legs. Finally she sighed and laid the box in Herm's hand.

"OK. You win."

"No, Katie, you are the one who wins." He slipped the box inside his tunic and looked solemnly at her. "You have just made a very important decision. And since you have been willing to give up something of great meaning to you, I would like to gift you with something to take its place, something important to me." Reaching inside his tunic again, he pulled out a small, opalescent globe strung on a leather thong. Lifting this over his head, he offered it to Katie.

"What a pretty pearl!" Her mulish expression melted into one of delight. "Are you really giving it to me?"

"I really am." He smiled. "But this isn't a just a pearl." He laid it gently in the palm of her hand.

Leaning closer, the little girl stared at the sphere and her eyes widened. "It's glowing, like there's a light bulb inside it!"

"That's right. It is filled with Light." He placed the leather thong over her head and let the gleaming globe slip down inside her shirt. "Always keep it as close to you as possible. As long as you wear it, you will be reminded that you can always call upon the power of the Light." Giving her shoulder a little squeeze, he stood up.

Katie laid her fingertips on the front of her shirt, where the sphere now lay concealed. "Thanks, Herm." She gave him a half smile. "I guess I don't mind you having my bird-lady box—not much, anyway." She wrinkled her nose. "Those feathers really are stinky."

Max looked up at Herm. "Now that you've taken care of that little matter, would you care to share what brought you here?"

"I came to get you. We need to find Stacy as quickly as we can."

"I didn't realize she was missing."

Herm's face became grim. "Well, she is. Worse yet, I'm afraid she's somewhere we don't want her to be. I believe our friend from the tractor has taken her to Serizzin."

Max frowned. "How did Serizzin get into this? And how did our mystery man get near Stacy?"

"I have no idea how he managed it. After you left, I found her outside the Entry Processing Center, talking with him. They disappeared almost immediately, but not before I heard the man mention Serizzin's name." He shook his head. "As for Serizzin's part in this, your guess is as good as mine. Whatever the answer, we need to reach Stacy before she gets sucked into one of his schemes."

Katie tugged at Herm's tunic, her face anxious. "Is Mommy OK?"

"That's what we're going to make certain of," he told her.

Max looked toward the Harpies' grove. "I think that disgusting pair in there know how to locate the man we're looking for. From what you're telling me, if we find him, we should find Stacy."

"Good!" Herm nodded at Max. "And as soon as we finish here, I think you should go collect Minerva and Glynis. I have a strong feeling that we all need to be present when we confront Serizzin."

Katie tugged at his tunic. "Me, too, right?"

Herm smiled at her. "You, too, little one. I do not know what part you may play, but even though there may be danger, I think it is important for you to be there."

Taking her hand, he looked down at Max. "In the meantime, let's go interview some Harpies."

He strode off toward the trees, Katie trotting beside him. Max followed, bounding through the tall grass in their wake.

Chapter 49

The uniformed guard behind the black marble entry counter looked up. "Name and business, please."

"Arthur Craddock and Stacy Addison. We're here to see Mr. Serizzin."

They waited while the guard picked up a telephone and dialed a single digit. "Mr. Craddock and Ms. Addison to see you, sir."

He listened, then nodded to them. "Mr. Serizzin will see you right away." Reaching under the counter, he pressed a concealed button. A polished wooden door in the wall to their right clicked open.

Stacy let Arthur Craddock take her arm and guide her through the door. She found herself in a large, windowless room softly illuminated by concealed lights. Thick pile carpet in shades of gray and green covered the floor, and deep-cushioned sofas, spaced around the walls, carried out the same color theme. Plush armchairs surrounded a long table whose top matched the black marble of the counter in the vestibule, while paintings from the old masters, including Stacy's favorite, Van Gogh, graced three sides of the room. The entire far wall was occupied by a blank white screen that would have easily fitted into a small movie theater.

Stacy stared dully around this unusual space, wondering vaguely why Charles had brought her here. She had expected a doctor's office; this was obviously someone's very expensive private viewing room. Perhaps this Serizzin was some kind of TV or movie producer.

"Welcome."

She turned toward the thin, whistling voice and saw what appeared to be a shadow emerging from a door in the left-hand wall. As it approached, it solidified into a small, thin man with sparse gray hair and a sharply pointed nose. He was carrying a silver tray on which rested a crystal goblet half filled with pale golden liquid.

"Please be seated, Ms. Addison. I have brought you some refreshment." Setting the tray on the black marble table, the small man pulled out the plush armchair directly in front of it. Bemused, Stacy allowed herself to be seated on the cushioned softness, barely noticing Charles moving around the table to her right, where he positioned himself so that he could see her face.

"Please help yourself to champagne," the small man told her. "Mr. Serizzin is presently occupied elsewhere, but he will join you momentarily."

Stacy, struggling to pull her tattered thoughts together, turned to thank him, but he seemed to have melted into the air. Forcing her attention toward the tray, she carefully picked up the goblet. The intricately twisted strands of blown glass that formed its stem felt warm and almost fluid, as if they were subtly twining and shifting even as she held them, adapting themselves to fit perfectly into the curve of her hand. The urge to taste its golden contents was irresistible.

She lifted the glass and sipped. A tingling warmth immediately spread through her, and the dulling sense of misery lifted. She sipped again.

A voice spoke from somewhere behind her, softer and deeper than the cushions of the gray-green sofas.

"Good evening, Stacy. I am Serizzin. I trust that Iblis has taken good care of you."

Turning in her chair, she saw a tall, strongly-built man in a suit and tie. She had thought Charles good looking, but Serizzin's features were so handsome that she found her eyes devouring his face, then moving down across his body, noticing the sculpted muscles barely concealed by his suit's exquisite tailoring. Despite the shock and hopelessness that had settled over her at the sight of her damaged face, a little tingle ran through her and she suddenly found herself imagining his long fingers touching her skin, his powerful arms moving around her, pulling her close to him.

Power emanated from his very pores, surrounding him with an aura of strength and self-assurance unlike anything she had ever experienced. This was a man who could conquer the world! He was what she had wanted to be, before she had seen— The memory of why she had come here cut through her rising excitement, and depression

🐾 🐾 🐾 Between 🐾 🐾 🐾

wrapped itself around her again like a heavy, gray blanket.

Serizzin's soft, deep voice interrupted her misery. "Come, now, Stacy. We can't have you feeling so distressed, can we?"

Stepping to her side, he took her hand. His touch was warm and strong, and his energy rushed up her arm, discharging itself throughout her body in tiny electrical explosions. For a fleeting moment, she was reminded of the two nights she had recently spent with David. Then the understanding flooded through her that what had seemed an incredible experience then had been only a foreshadowing of what she could have with Serizzin. David was her husband, but this man could become her world!

Serizzin nodded toward Charles. "Our mutual friend here has told me about the problem you are experiencing with your physical body." His smiled. "It is a problem I would like to help you solve."

"You can do that?" Her voice was hoarse.

Serizzin nodded, his smile now intimate and full of promise. "I can, indeed." Still holding her hand, he pointed toward the screen on the far wall. "Relax, my dear. Let me show you what I plan for you."

Stacy leaned back in the comfortable chair. The recessed lighting along the ceiling dimmed, as Serizzin seated himself next to her.

He handed her a remote control. "Press the 'play' button and watch the screen."

Hand trembling, she followed his direction. An image of herself immediately appeared on the screen, the right side of her face looking like it had when she last saw it, scarred and hideous. Tears sprang into her eyes. Then, incredibly, the wounds began to heal. The red seams faded and disappeared; the bones beneath the flesh knitted themselves back into their normal configuration. The delicate arch of her eyebrow reappeared and her lip regained its tender curve. The crater beneath her eye began to fill in, restoring the lovely, high line of her cheekbone, and from her ravaged head vibrant curls began to spring, soft and thick, until their coppery cloud framed her now perfect face.

Tears poured down her cheeks as she watched this transformation. But before she could speak, Serizzin's voice commanded, "Watch!" The screen exploded with a rush of people, hands waving, voices cheering, all focused on the figure standing in the center of an outdoor platform—a slender woman with a cloud of copper hair, laying her hands on those who, one by one, made their way across the stage to be healed. And healed they were, unending lines of sufferers made whole, their pain and despair transformed into joy and gratitude.

The scene shifted to a newsreel, where a reporter was interviewing a sampling of those who had experienced her healing touch, all of them relating ecstatic accounts of their experiences. The reporter, himself, attested with tears in his eyes that Stacy Addison had saved his own two-year old daughter from the deadly grip of leukemia. Doctors were interviewed, expressing their amazement. Even an archbishop stated that, if she were Roman Catholic, she would have to be considered for sainthood.

A short segment followed, focusing on David, as he acknowledged to the press that he had not, in the beginning, understood the incredible importance of his wife's work, but had come to realize that her abilities far outshone any he might develop as a result of medical training. There was also a close-up of Katie watching her mother work, a look of adoration on her face.

Other images followed—Stacy in Africa, in Russia, in China; Stacy receiving an audience with the Pope and being honored by the Queen of England. Finally, the display was over. The lights came up and she sat back in her chair, overwhelmed.

Looking at Serizzin, she whispered, "Is it possible?"

He gazed into her eyes. "Not only is it possible, it is a certainty. The one thing needed to set it all in motion is for you to accept me as your agent. I will then accomplish your healing, make the connections, set up the meetings, prepare all the information for the media. You will be left free to do what you do best—provide healing for all who come to you. Together, we cannot fail."

Together. It sounded solid and comforting; and, if she was honest with herself, exciting. Serizzin opened a folder and extracted a single sheet of paper.

"Here is the contract. Just sign on the line above your name." He handed her a fountain pen.

As she set the nib on the line, she heard Minerva's voice speaking clearly in her mind: "Remember, my dear; there is no free lunch." It was an admonition she had received more than once over the years. Paying attention to it had several times saved her from making a serious mistake.

Laying the pen on the table, she looked up at Serizzin. "If you don't mind my asking, what will you get out of this?"

He smiled. "I shall receive the great pleasure of nurturing the growth of the most remarkable healing talent that has emerged on Earth in the past several centuries. And," his voice softened as he touched her cheek briefly, "I will have the opportunity to be near you on a daily basis."

The electric shiver ran through her again. Minerva's warning faded into the background of her awareness, banished by a vision of herself, arms raised in triumph, surrounded by cheering crowds. At her side, exuding pride and delight, stood Serizzin. Stacy picked up the pen again and began to write.

As she did so, the door through which she had entered, what seemed a lifetime ago, buzzed and clicked open.

Chapter 50

The black-and-white cat glared over his shoulder at the Harpies. "How many times do I have to tell you two to stay downwind of us?" he hissed.

Backing away, Klio hunched a huge wing. She should have known better than to expect manners from the creature; cats were notorious for their rudeness. She nudged Urania.

"We shall return to our grove as soon as we have kept our bargain with the god." She muted her usual screech as much as she could manage.

"Yes, yes! I do not like this strange place." Urania made an effort to imitate her sister's whisper. "I still do not understand why we are here."

"We are here because the god demanded it," Klio bobbed her head. "It is not safe to deny the wishes of a god."

Urania nodded again. "Not safe," she echoed, as they lurched along behind the travelers ahead of them.

It was a strangely assorted group. The god leading them was known to her from times long gone. She had also seen the cat before, and the fierce little girl, who had once been their captive. But the old woman and the brown-haired younger woman were complete strangers who seemed to have no reason to be a part of whatever was happening. Bringing her thoughts back into the moment, Urania hopped over a large stone in the path. "But why did the god demand that we come?"

"Because he wishes to find Arthurcraddock. I think he is angry with him."

"Ah. We are angry with Arthurcraddock, too." When Klio did not immediately reply, Urania looked up anxiously. "We *are* angry, are we not?"

Klio bobbed her head. "Yes, we are angry." She stopped, letting the group ahead momentarily move on without them. "Arthurcraddock only pretended to be our friend. Not only did he lie to the god about us, but he behaved in a manner both strange and rude, acting as if he did not know us, and helping the woman who invaded our grove to steal back the child."

Urania nodded. "He only pretended to be our friend."

"We will revenge ourselves by leading the god to where he is."

Urania hopped up and down excitedly. "We will revenge ourselves!" She stopped and looked at Klio. "But why can the god not find Arthurcraddock by himself? Why must we go, too?"

"Because the god says we are connected to him. Our connection draws us to him along a line that they," she gestured with her head toward the group now steadily moving away from them, "can follow."

"But *we* are following *them*," Urania protested. "How can we be leading them anywhere?"

Klio shrugged, raining a shower of feathers on a cluster of yellow flowers blooming near her clawed feet. The blossoms withered and dropped onto the grass. Looking up, she saw that the little girl was running back toward them.

"Herm said to tell you to hurry up." She glared at them. "So hurry up!"

Klio looked at Urania. "Not only does she have her own power, but she is also a messenger of the god! I think, sister, that she is worthy of our allegiance."

"Worthy, worthy!" echoed Urania.

Turning to the child, Klio bobbed her head. "We regret that we have caused you distress, young mistress. You are far more worthy, more powerful than Arthurcraddock." She looked at her sister, who nodded, then back at the child. "We have determined that we will serve you, in the same way that we serve the god."

Narrowing her eyes, the little girl stared at them until they both felt uneasy. Finally, she nodded her head. "OK. I don't trust you, but I guess you can serve me, if you want to. But remember—I'm keeping an eye on you."

She started back toward the rest of the group and the Harpies lurched along at her heels, careful to leave plenty of space, so she would not become angered by their nearness.

🐾 🐾 🐾 Between 🐾 🐾 🐾

The journey continued, until at last a huge, stone box appeared in the distance. Picking up their pace, the group hurried toward it, stopping next to one of its tall sides. Klio edged forward as unobtrusively as possible, in time to hear the cat rudely address the god. "You're sure this is the place?"

"Yes," the god replied. "The trail connecting the Harpies to the man they call Arthurcraddock ends here. He is definitely in this building. So is Stacy. Serizzin must have constructed this place to conceal whatever energies are inside it, but now that we're this close, I can sense their presence."

"Then we need to be careful." The cat began sniffing the side of the box. "Let me go first and check things out. I'm not as noticeable as you are."

Klio watched with surprise as he walked straight into the side of the box and disappeared. He returned almost immediately. "There's a guard at an entry desk," he told the god. "His eyes are open, but he's either asleep, or he's some sort of thought form. I actually jumped up on the counter in front of him and he never even blinked."

"Good." The god turned to the others. "Everyone, follow me as quietly as you can." He looked back at the Harpies. "That includes you two. Just stay behind us and make as little noise as possible, at least until we discover what's taking place in there."

Heads bobbing, Klio and Urania trailed after the little group, saying nothing. It was frightening to think of going inside a block of stone, no matter how large it might be, but they must trust the god to take care of them. All they needed to do otherwise was remember that, no matter what happened, they should not so much as flutter a wing.

§

"He's a simple level thought form." Herm bent over the desk to examine the guard, who was staring blankly into the distance. "That's why you didn't get any response."

Straightening, he waved his hand. The guard rippled, dissolved, and disappeared.

Glynis was shocked. "What did you do to him?"

"I just dissipated the energy that was used to temporarily create him." He grinned. "Don't worry. He wasn't real to begin with."

"Oh." She wondered how long it was going to take her to get used to how things worked here.

Herm had already moved to a door set in the far wall. Running his fingers along its edges, he stood back and closed his eyes. He looked like he was listening.

Eyes still fixed on the wall, he said, "Arthur Craddock is in there and, unfortunately, Serizzin. Stacy is there, too, in greater danger than I suspected." He turned back toward the others. "We need to reach her soon, but first I think you all need to know what's taking place in there. Once you have some idea of what's going on, you can better assist me in helping her."

He turned back to the door and closed his eyes. This time he raised his arms, and Glynis began to hear sounds of cheering, growing steadily louder as the door, and the wall it was set in, thinned and transmuted into what appeared to be clear glass. Through this window Glynis could see Stacy seated at a table, face rapt, her eyes riveted on a screen set in the wall across from her. On the screen, multitudes of excited followers thronged her healing meetings and testimonials dropped like ripe fruits from every side. Several close-up shots showed her face, exquisitely perfect, smiling at the waving, cheering crowds. Sitting beside her at the table, his arm almost touching hers, was the most handsome man Glynis had ever seen. There was a sheen between him and Stacy, as if some sort of electricity connected them.

"Who is that?" Glynis turned to Herm. "He certainly is good looking!"

"The name he prefers is Serizzin."

She looked back, fascinated The man smiled and leaned closer to Stacy. The sheen between them darkened, then shimmered and lightened again. A little shiver ran through Glynis. "He's handsome," she said slowly, " but something about him feels, well, sort of wrong."

"A very apt description."

She was finding it difficult to pull her gaze away from the man at the table. "But I can see why Stacy's listening to him. He's not only extremely good-looking, he seems so . . . so appealing."

"Not really." Max had moved up beside her.

She frowned. "What do you mean?"

"What you see is not his true appearance, which bears no resemblance to a human being. Serizzin is an extremely complex thought form that has, over the millennia, taken on a life of its own. Although he still draws his nourishment from the human beliefs and emotions that have created him, every negative word and act also strengthens his influence at the Earth level. Periodically he convinces some unsuspecting human being to give the power they possess over their lives to him. Of course, they don't understand until later that they are agreeing to let him control them—they only hear his promises to give them what they think they want."

Glynis shivered again. Max's words had broken the spell that seemed to have been settling over her. She looked again at the handsome man beside Stacy. A shadow seemed to flit across his elegant face, briefly transforming his dark eyes into gleaming black pools and his smile into an expression of gloating triumph.

She turned back to the display of Stacy's successes, still being projected onto the screen. "How can we be seeing all those things? Nothing like that has ever happened."

Minerva, who had said very little during their journey, stepped to Glynis's other side. "Serizzin is demonstrating to Stacy what it would be like to live out her heart's desire." She looked at Herm. "Isn't that correct?"

He nodded. "He's also showing her what could happen, if he can get her to do what he wants. This entire display is leading up to his trying to persuade her to participate in something important to him. I don't know yet what it is, but I do know Serizzin. He won't lie to her, at least, not directly; but he won't show her the full picture, either. He isn't giving any indication that, if she lets him convince her, he'll be able to use her to create tremendous havoc—both for her and for a lot of other people."

Glynis tore her gaze away from the tableau in the other room. "Then why are we standing out here? Let's go in there and tell her that! If this Serizzin guy can show her what could happen if she listens to him, you can surely show her what really will happen if she lets him con her into doing what he wants."

Herm shook his head. "I regret to say that I'm only permitted to encourage her to consider carefully before she makes her decision. As a servant of the Light, I am not permitted to show her the specifics of what may result from her choice; she must decide on her own, guided by her free will. Free will is always the determining factor; it's the one thing by which all of us are bound, no matter which side we serve, the one law none of us can set aside. Once she has made her decision, even Serizzin will be forced to honor it."

"But Serizzin is messing around with her free will by showing her what he wants her to see!"

Herm frowned. "Unfortunately, Serizzin is not bound by the ethics of the Light. The Dark Lord never plays by the rules, unless it suits him to do so. However, he must allow her to make her own final choice, which he is then obligated to accept."

Glynis ground her teeth in frustration. "But if he's lying to her, he's skewing her choice! Can't you see that?"

Herm regarded her solemnly. "Everything you say is true. But there is a greater truth that those of us who serve the Light are obligated to honor. Regardless of the behavior of the servants of the Dark or of any immediate outcome, we are not permitted to tamper with human free will. We are allowed to persuade, but in a general, not a specific way." He shrugged apologetically. "It is a primary premise of the Light."

"It's a stupid premise! How can you—"

Glynis stopped, suddenly realizing that the room they were watching had fallen silent. Looking over, she saw that the scenes playing on the screen had disappeared and Serizzin was bending over Stacy, offering her a piece of paper and a pen. Stacy accepted both, then set the pen aside; she seemed to be asking Serizzin a question. Then she picked up the pen again.

"Zero hour," Max announced. "We have to try to keep her from signing that!"

Herm strode back to the marble-topped counter. "I'll open the door. Just remember that we can't order Stacy to not sign the paper, or persuade her by unfair means." Reaching under the counter, he pressed the concealed button.

A buzzer sounded and the door to the room where Stacy was sitting clicked open.

Chapter 51

"She came through beautifully." Colin Elmore stood with David just outside the open door of Stacy's recovery room. "If she continues to respond well, she should be out of the woods before long."

"Thank you, Colin." David smiled at him. "I'm very grateful for your support."

Elmore shook his head. "No thanks necessary. In fact, I should apologize. If you hadn't insisted on that blood test . . . ." He shook his head again. "A lesson to me to consider every possible angle before I make a judgment."

He glanced through the open door at Stacy. "You staying with her?"

David nodded. "As long as I can."

"Stay as long as you like. I'll take your rounds for you." Turning, Elmore sauntered off toward the elevators.

David entered the cubicle and pulled a rolling stool over to the bed. God, she looked terrible! But really no worse, he reminded himself, than any other post-surgery patient. Straddling the stool, he gently stroked her undamaged cheek. The phenobarbitol ought to be out of her system before long; in a few hours, she'd be returning to consciousness.

He imagined Stacy opening her eyes, smiling at him, speaking to him. No, probably not speaking; at least, not right away. Her throat would need time to recover from the irritation caused by the ventilator. Then the long process of repairing her shattered cheekbone would have to be discussed. Even though the surface cuts were healing nicely, that conversation was going to be an ordeal. His mind pushed further, picturing Stacy's dismay when she saw her face without the bandages. No, not dismay, he admitted; dismay wouldn't begin to touch what she was going to feel the first time she looked into a mirror. He felt sick as he remembered the damage the windshield had inflicted.

It had been her exquisite face, surrounded by that ethereal cloud of copper hair, that had first attracted him. An overworked first-year student at the OSU College of Medicine, he was taking a beer break at Kilkenny's. The moment he entered the pub, his gaze was drawn to the table where she sat, talking with Glynis.

She looked up, her luminous eyes meeting his, and he stopped, transfixed. Finally, the friend he had come with shoved him from behind and he stumbled on into the room. When he recovered his balance, Stacy's dark eyes were dancing, and she smiled—at him, not at his clumsiness—a warm, understanding smile. In that instant, he knew with a certainty he could not explain that she was the only woman he would ever want. Even after he began to realize that her angelic facade concealed a soul of steel and grit, even after differences and arguments became commonplace, he found it impossible to think of life without her.

An intense yearning assailed him to see her again as she had been, to hold her close, smell the perfume of her hair, feel the silky perfection of her cheek against his. The knowledge that this could never happen again in the same way filled him with almost unbearable sadness. How could thirty seconds have changed their lives so radically? Thirty seconds—that's all it had taken for the train to drag her into that ravine.

He closed his eyes against the pricking of tears. His hunched shoulders ached, and he felt exhausted and helpless. No matter how much he wanted to, he could never make this right. It was his fault it had happened. If only he had listened, heard what she was really saying, thought of her needs, instead of just his own, she would not be lying here like a smashed doll, her lovely face ruined!

Come on! he told himself. *This is Stace you're talking about. She's not a doll; she's a strong, courageous woman. She'll be able to handle this. She may never look the same, but she'll still be herself, she'll still be the woman you fell in love with.*

But will she? a voice whispered in his mind. *Will she be able to handle the destruction of the beauty that's always been so important to her? And if she can't handle it, will she still be the person you know and love? And if she isn't, what then?*

For a moment, panic tingled through him. Then it dissolved into an unexpected sense of peace, a deep, grounded calmness that seemed to soak into his cells, saturating the very atoms of which he was constructed.

If Stacy couldn't be who she had been, then he would learn to love who she became. Everyone changed; no one could grow without changing. Whoever Stacy grew into as a result of this trauma, he would grow with her, no matter how difficult that might be. His soul was entwined with hers—he had known that instinctively from the moment she smiled at him in Kilkenny's. This single truth was the wellspring of what really mattered.

He would inevitably get caught up again in the drama that was everyday life, but he knew that the peace now filling him would always be available, whenever he was willing to tap into it. Through it, he would be able to handle whatever problems the future might bring. And, he trusted, he would be able to help Stacy do the same.

Lifting her unresisting hand, he held it against his cheek. She was out there, somewhere, between this world and the next. He had seen her, touched her, and the two of them had merged into a oneness he had never considered possible. He refused to believe that those experiences had been nothing more than dreams. They were real when they happened; they would be real again. Kissing the palm of her hand, he gently placed her arm back under the blanket.

"Come back soon," he told her softly. "I'm here, waiting for you."

§

Arthur Craddock was furious. He had finally separated Stacy Addison from her protectors, but instead of bringing about her destruction, he was being forced to watch a bullying, smooth-talking meddler offer her international fame and the restoration of her beauty! The video of her taking the world by storm had made him want to puke. It took every ounce of self-restraint he could generate, prompted by the memory of his own intimidating meeting with Serizzin, to sit silently at the table without interrupting.

As Stacy picked up the pen to sign Serizzin's agreement, Arthur felt his control slipping away; in another second he was liable to do something he might regret. Suddenly the door clicked open. He looked up, startled, to see the dark-haired young man he had observed in Stacy's intensive care room step through it, along with that damn, interfering cat. Behind them crowded an old woman in purple, and the young woman who had jumped from the tractor to save Stacy's daughter.

To his amazement, those two were followed by the child herself. Before Arthur could decide whether the little girl was actually dead, or just out of her body again, he caught the whiff of a familiar stench. It wasn't possible, of course, but it smelled like this ill-assorted group had brought the Harpies with them! The stink intensified and his eyes widened as Klio and Urania, heads bobbing, pushed into the room behind the others.

The little gray man stepped forward. "You have no right to enter this room uninvited!" Raising a bony arm, he pointed at the door through which they had just entered. "Please leave immediately."

The dark-haired young man glanced at him briefly, then raised his own arm. The gray man quivered, and an expression of surprise rippled across his face. His spindly frame seemed to harden, as if it had been flash frozen, and he stood unmoving, arm extended and finger pointing. *Good!* Arthur thought, suddenly recognizing the reedy voice as that of his former mental advisor. *Serves you right!*

Dragging his attention back to Stacy, he saw confusion on her face. Instead of completing her signature and binding herself to Serizzin, she laid the pen on the table and stared at the interlopers. As she did so, Serizzin stepped forward.

"You and your ragtag retinue do not belong here," he informed the young man. "Please leave immediately." Arthur could hear annoyance in his smooth voice. He looked even more annoyed when the little girl pulled away from the old woman and ran toward Stacy, shouting, "Mommy, Mommy!"

Jumping up from the chair, Stacy caught the child in her arms and hugged her tightly. Looking over the little girl's head at the others, she said, "What's going on? Why are you all here? Especially," she nodded toward the Harpies, frowning, "those creatures?"

The young man stepped forward. Although almost a head shorter than Serizzin, he appeared to be equal in self-assurance and presence. Certainly he seemed far less agitated.

"Universal law grants us equal right of persuasion," he told Serizzin, whose black eyes were filled with a rage Arthur could easily see from his position several feet away. "We may be prohibited from using the more direct methods you have at your disposal, and from dispensing half truths and incomplete information, but we have as much right to be here as you do." He grinned, looking for a moment like a mischievous little boy. "Surely you aren't going to tell me you've forgotten?"

Serizzin glared, as the young man turned to Stacy.

"We came here to find you, Stacy. Serizzin constructed this place," he looked around the room, "to conceal your energy, but the Harpies helped us find you, anyway." He smiled reassuringly at her. "We've come to suggest that you might want to think twice before you agree to anything that he," he nodded toward Serizzin, "wants you to do."

Stacy looked toward Serizzin and back at the young man. Arthur could read confusion in her expression. "But he's trying to help me. He says he can make my face the way it used to be; maybe even better." She paused. "You don't know how horrible I look, how awful it would be to go back into my body with my face the way it is now! And," her gaze included the rest of the little gathering, "he's shown me that, with my face healed, I'll have even greater power to heal others. I'll be known around the world!"

She looked down at the child standing in the circle of her arms. "Don't you want Mommy to be a famous healer?"

The child shook her head. "I just want you to come home."

The young woman whose death Arthur had caused stepped out in front of the others.

"Stacy!" Her voice sounded loud in the quiet room. "How can you bear to be anywhere near that terrible person!" She pointed accusingly at Arthur.

Stacy's eyes followed her pointing finger. "You mean Charles? Glinda, he's the one who helped me free Katie from those monstrosities you brought with you."

Arthur's smile of what he hoped looked like modest acknowledgment seemed to inflame the young woman even further.

"All I know is that he's the one who was on the tractor platform, watching the baler run over me!" Her tone grew even more intense. "He may have even made the whole thing happen. How can you consider having anything to do with him?"

Stacy looked from her to Arthur. "Is that true? Were you there, Charles?"

The situation was falling apart. Arthur began considering the possibility of escaping the room before things became any more unpleasant, but the only door was blocked by the great bulks of the Harpies, hovering in the background.

As if they had heard his thoughts, the monstrous bird-women began jumping up and down, releasing a cloud of noxious feathers. The rest of the group, coughing and gagging, moved farther into the room to escape the smell, while the larger Harpy, wings flapping, screeched, "That is not Charles, but Arthurcraddock. He had us carry off the child. Arthurcraddock, Arthurcraddock! Never Charles, but Arthurcraddock." The chant was immediately picked up by the smaller one, and the two of them began to circle, hopping, bobbing, and shedding feathers in every direction.

Stacy, still holding her daughter tightly, turned toward Arthur, her expression incredulous. "Charles! What are they talking about?"

Serizzin's voiced boomed across the room. "STOP! Be silent, all of you!

The Harpies halted in mid-hop and cringed back against the door, while the others stared at him, speechless.

"Listen to me." Serizzin's voice was cold and angry. "This human," he gestured toward Stacy, "has business to complete with me. Once that is done, you may continue your conversations and accusations, whatever pleases you. But for now, be still!"

Turning to Stacy, his voice softened. "Why don't you finish signing the contract? Then we can heal your injuries and begin our work together."

Watching Stacy's face, Arthur could see Serizzin's mesmerizing influence at work again. After a brief hesitation, she seated her protesting daughter in the chair next to hers, picked up the pen, and once again positioned the contract so that she could sign her name.

The young woman from the tractor pushed her way out of the group by the door. "Crap on this 'we can't interfere with her free will' business!" she told the dark-haired young man. "You may be bound by that, but I'm not going to stand by and watch my best friend do something we'll all regret!" Darting across the room, she grabbed the pen from Stacy's hand and threw it against the wall. "I've always followed you before," she said, "but this is different."

Serizzin, face twisted with rage, raised his arm, and the interfering young woman and Stacy Addison both froze in mid-movement. Raising his own arm, the young man moved toward Serizzin, seeming to grow larger and taller as he approached. For a moment, they stared at each other, then Serizzin made a growling noise in his throat and let his arm fall to his side, releasing the two women from their immobility.

Arthur swelled with excitement—the seemingly all-powerful Serizzin was not invincible! And now Stacy would most likely refuse to sign herself into his power, which meant he should soon lose interest in her. This was the perfect moment for Arthur to reveal the enormity of Stacy's crime against him and Charlotte. Once he had done that, her would-be rescuers would want no more to do with her, either, and she would finally be his, to punish as he chose! Elation surged through him and, ignoring a qualm he could not completely repress at the thought of focusing attention on himself with the glowering Serizzin still in the room, Arthur took a step toward her.

She looked up at him, a puzzled frown on her face. "Charles?"

"Not Charles," he said. "Those stinking freaks were right. My name is Arthur Craddock." She stared at him blankly. "The husband of Charlotte Craddock." Still seeing no recognition in her eyes, he continued. "You supposedly healed my wife of epilepsy a couple of years ago; at least, you convinced her she was healed. Because of you, she quit taking her medication."

Placing his hands on the table, he leaned over, thrusting his face near hers. "We were on our way to the best job I'd ever had. We were almost there. We were starting a new life. And because of you, she had a seizure. She had a grand mal seizure on the expressway! Do you understand what that meant?" He was barely able to control his voice.

"The car went into the ditch. We were killed! We died because she believed your fake little act." He was practically snarling. "And now I'm stuck in this goddamned, crazy place where nothing makes any sense, and it's your fault, you stupid, irresponsible charlatan! It's all your fault!"

This time understanding dawned in her eyes. Then horror replaced it, draining the color from her cheeks. "Oh, my God!" Putting shaking hands to her face, she shrank away from him. "What have I done?" she whispered. "What have I done?"

"You've wrecked my life, that's what you've done, you goddamned bitch!" He leaned over her, oblivious of Serizzin and the others watching him. "You deserve to rot in hell."

She looked up at him. "I– I'm sorry. I'm so sorry."

"I'm dead and you're sorry! Do you think that evens things out?" With difficulty, Arthur resisted the urge to grab her by the throat and throttle her.

As the thought entered his mind, he felt his own neck gripped from behind. He was lifted from the floor, like a kitten being picked up by a mother cat, except that the hand holding him was neither gentle nor loving. It released him and he dropped to the floor. Looking up, he saw the face of Serizzin, dark with fury.

"Enough, Craddock!" Serizzin's voice was softly menacing. "She is mine. Your time with her may come, but for now, she belongs to me."

Chapter 52

Leaving Arthur Craddock to recover from the paralyzing intensity of his grip, Serizzin extracted a second pen from the inside pocket of his coat. Placing it in Stacy Addison's unresisting hand, he closed her fingers around it.

"Sign!" he commanded.

It required tremendous effort to contain his fury, to hold this human form he had taken in order to appear unthreatening to her. Stacy Addison's cooperation was essential, her circumstances offering him a far broader scope than any he had previously taken advantage of over the millennia. He was not about to let this chance escape him; not now, with success so close he could already feel its vibrations trembling into manifestation!

He glanced toward the mismatched group of intruders milling about in front of the doorway and stifled another surge of rage. How dare that young upstart who called himself a god interfere!

He, Serizzin, had been in existence long before northern raiders had overrun the dark-skinned inhabitants of the Hellenic peninsula, eventually blending with them to create the brilliant, volatile people that human history knew as the ancient Greeks. He had outlasted most of their gods, as well as the divinities of myriad other cultures, who had come and gone over the long span of human habitation of the Earth. And he would continue to exist, as long as the souls who entered the Earth sphere of life nurtured him with their negative feelings and beliefs.

He had responded to many names: Ba'al, Oni, Asmodeus, Satanas, as well as a host of others. And always, he had been forced to depend for his existence on the unreliable whims of those puny mortal beings whose emotions had created and still sustained him. But once this human known as Stacy Addison had placed herself fully in his power, he would finally have the opportunity to control and feed on a consistent supply of negative energy. Through her, he would attain a pinnacle of power unmatched by the combined deities of humankind!

He would intensify her ability to heal to a level of perfection formerly achieved only by direct representatives of the Light. She would become the bearer of a gift that no human would be able to refuse. And each time she shared this gift, she would, unaware, insert a splinter of his darkness into every individual she touched. That person, in turn, would pass it on to everyone with whom he or she came in contact; and each fragment would be connected to Serizzin.

Her desire for importance, her hunger for fame, had already opened her to his power. The last remaining step was his acquisition of her signature, symbol and seal of the agreement that even now was binding her to him. With that in his possession, the human world would at last be his to control.

"Sign!" he repeated, turning the contract toward her.

She had been staring at the wall, obviously shaken by Craddock's violent verbal attack. Now she slowly transferred her dazed focus to the piece of paper. Briefly raising anguished eyes to his face, she let them fall and began, once again, to write.

§

"Stacy, stop! Don't do it!"

Glynis's shout pierced the fog of misery that had descended on Stacy as she listened to Arthur Craddock's terrible, damning words. It yanked her back into the present moment where she teetered, caught between Serizzin's determination and Glynis's resolve. Raising her eyes, she was startled to see her friend once again sprinting toward her, face set in lines of grim determination.

"Give me that!" Reaching her, Glynis snatched the pen from her hand. "I can't believe I've had to do this twice! How can you let him," she gestured with her head toward Serizzin, "sucker you in again?"

Stacy stared blankly at her, seeing, not Glynis, but the joyful face of the epileptic woman weeping before the crowd, claiming her healing. Charles's wife. No, not Charles. Arthur something.

Arthur and his wife, now both dead because of her, because she hadn't spoken out. She had known, deep inside, that something wasn't right, but she hadn't owned up, afraid that it would destroy her credibility. She had saved her credibility; but in doing so, she had destroyed two people, one of whom had trusted her.

Her vision slowly cleared. Glynis's anxious face replaced that of Arthur's wife, and an excruciating pain shot through Stacy. She had destroyed not two people, but three. Her beloved Glinda was dead too, and not by accident, if the story Charles—Arthur, whoever—told was true. She was dead because her supposed best friend, Stacy Addison, the want-to-be-famous healer, had been too wrapped up in her own desires to be honest. She was dead as the result of a fatal chain of events set in action by Stacy's selfish decision to hope a healing had been completed, rather than letting the client know that she wasn't sure.

"Here." Lobbing the pen toward the far side of the table, Glynis picked up the remote control and thrust it into her hand. "Minerva just told me you should focus hard on what will really happen if you sign that paper. Concentrate on that, then press the 'play' button again."

Stacy stared at the remote, then set it back on the table.

"Oh, Glinda," Her voice was hoarse with unshed tears, "it's my fault. It's all my fault. His death, his wife's, even yours! My fault."

She felt Glynis's fingers close around hers insistently. "We'll talk about that later, Stacy, dear. Right now, we need to be sure that you don't do something you'll regret even more. Here!" She picked up the remote control again and placed it back in Stacy's hand. "Do what Minerva said. Concentrate on seeing what will happen if you sign that contract for what's-his-name with the ice-cube eyes. It's important!"

"I can't," Stacy wailed. Her thoughts seemed like mice racing around a revolving cage. "I can't concentrate. My mind's too full of stuff."

"Well, clear it out!"

Making a tremendous effort, Stacy pulled the fragments of her attention together. Staring at the remote control, she focused on the idea of a different version of Serizzin's video, one showing what would actually happen if she signed the contract he was offering her. She had barely begun to concentrate, when the overwhelming intensity of Serizzin's presence began to press against her mind, coaxing it back toward the visions of cheering crowds and her own flawless face smiling down on them. Closing her eyes, she smiled dreamily.

🐾 🐾 🐾 Between 🐾 🐾 🐾

Her eyes snapped open with a jolt as Glynis slapped her. "Stop that! Stop thinking about anything except what Minerva said."

Shock and anger spurted through her, but her mind cleared and steadied. Looking up at Glynis, who was watching her with tear-filled eyes, she nodded. Closing her eyes again, she imagined a wall forming between her and Serizzin. Behind its safety, she focused once more on knowing the truth of what would result, should she sign the contract. Finally, she pressed the "play" button, and opened her eyes.

Once again, a newsreel appeared on the screen. For a moment, she thought that it was simply the same tape, replaying her incredible successes. But as she watched closely, she saw, with growing horror, that each time she laid her hands on one of the multitude of sufferers passing before her, a fragment of darkness slipped from her into that person, where it was absorbed.

This time the scene continued beyond the healing services, following those who had received treatment, as they went on with their lives. Stacy watched as each one, like a spiritual Typhoid Mary, passed on a piece of the darkness received from her to every person with whom he or she came in contact.

The scene flickered, then steadied. Superimposed on it was a huge, semi-transparent figure of Serizzin, the countless splinters of darkness connected to him by a maze of hollow attachments, like straws, through which he was sucking part of the life force of each person into himself. In return, he was sending back a mixture of hatred and despair, which was instantly accepted and absorbed by its human recipient. As Stacy watched, the darkness within each person grew, fed and strengthened by this exchange. Then the image flashed and disappeared; the video was over.

Revulsion rose like vomit in her throat, and she reached for the contract with a hand shaking so violently that she had to steady it with the other one. She finally managed to pick up the piece of paper and was tearing it in half, when she felt an iron grip on her wrist. Looking up, she saw Serizzin, his face rigid, bending over her.

"You've already made your bargain." His voice was still soft, but no longer caressing. "You passed the point of no return the moment your desire accepted my offer." His hand tightened on her wrist, and she winced with pain. She tried to pull her arm away, but Serizzin jerked her back, forcing her to her knees. His black eyes bored down into hers.

"You've seen more than you were ever meant to, Stacy. You've learned far more than you ever needed to know. But the machinery has already been set in motion; the changes have already begun."

His lips drew back in a triumphant smile. "It's too late for you to back out now."

Chapter 53

His neck still throbbing from the pain of Serizzin's crushing grip, Arthur Craddock pulled himself to his feet and staggered toward Stacy, who was kneeling in front of Serizzin, trying to free her wrist from his hand. If what the bastard had just said was true, any chance for his own revenge was long gone. Serizzin had simply been using Arthur to do all the work, so that he could reap the benefits himself.

Suddenly, the rage that had sustained Arthur in his desolate prison exploded, its intensity almost blinding him. *That's not how it's going to be!* he muttered through gritted teeth. *I don't care who or what you are—you're not going to cheat me out of what's rightfully mine!*

Grabbing Stacy's other arm, he yanked her to her feet. Serizzin, face suffused with rage, dragged her back toward him. Tightening his grip, Arthur pulled harder.

"Stop it!" Stacy leaned back, resisting. "Let me go!"

Swinging her arm hard, she threw Arthur off balance. He fell against one of the chairs, but regained his footing and began to pull harder. Stacy kicked at him and he jumped back, barely dodging the blow.

Above the noise of the struggle he heard the little girl's clear voice. "Do something!" she was screaming. "Make them stop hurting my mother!"

Glancing in her direction, Arthur realized that she was shouting at the Harpies. To his dismay, the huge bird-women began flapping across the room toward him.

"You lied," the larger Harpy shrieked. "You made the god angry with us." She and the smaller one began beating him with their wings, releasing a foul-smelling rain of feathers.

Arthur ducked his head, trying to avoid the onslaught. Their stench gagged him, but he couldn't use his arms to protect himself or cover his nose. If he let go of Stacy, even with one hand, Serizzin's strength would pull her away from him.

He grunted with surprise as the child barreled into him. She ducked under the Harpies' flailing wings and grabbed his arm, sinking her teeth into his wrist, and an agonizing pain shot all the way up to his shoulder. Cursing, he released Stacy and struck out wildly with his free hand in an attempt to dislodge the little girl. She flinched as his fist glanced off the side of her face, but dug her fingernails in and hung on, her teeth firmly imbedded in his arm.

"You leave her alone!"

Arthur looked up as Stacy frantically yanked her wrist out of Serizzin's grasp. Running to the table, she snatched up the video recorder and hefted it into the air. Arthur tried to dodge, but the weight of the child clinging to his arm made escape impossible. Stacy swung the heavy box down against his skull and he sank to his knees, vaguely aware that the little girl had finally released him. His wrist burned and he could barely raise his arm to protect himself from the Harpies, who continued to dart in and out, battering him with their wings.

Without warning the bird-women backed away. Tears streaming down his face, Arthur saw Stacy running toward the cat and the old woman, pulling the child behind her, the Harpies flapping along in their wake. Behind this procession strode Serizzin.

Despite his throbbing arm and aching head, Arthur's rage rose again, almost choking him. Scrambling to his feet, he lunged at Serizzin, catching him around the knees in a tackle that should have brought him to the floor. To Arthur's surprise, the legs he was embracing felt like rock hewed from the depths of a frozen mountain. Serizzin's hand reached down, plucked Arthur away, and tossed him aside, as if he had been a burr picked up in passing. Crashing into the table, Arthur lay on the floor, dazed, as Serizzin continued his pursuit of Stacy and her daughter.

§

Relief washed through Stacy as she reached the little group gathered by the door. She and Katie were finally free and safe! They could stay here with Glynis and Minerva, while Herm and Max took care of getting them out of this place. Kneeling to see if Katie had been injured, she saw with dismay that the little girl was staring at something behind her, eyes wide with fear.

Turning, Stacy felt her stomach clench; Serizzin stood no more than three steps away. Looking up at his handsome features, she saw what seemed to be movement beneath the flawless skin, as if something was crawling there. She shuddered. How could she ever have thought he was someone she could love?

Serizzin stared icily at Herm, who had moved between him and Stacy. "Step aside, you who consider yourself a god. Stacy Addison made her choice before you and your pitiful little entourage ever stepped into this room. She has used her free will to accept my offer, even though the finalization of our contract has twice been interrupted."

Herm frowned. "You tricked her. You told her only part of the truth, the part that suits your needs."

"What if I did? I merely followed what those on the Earth level would call the principles of good business. Of course," Serizzin's smile twisted into a sneer, "I realize that you are prohibited from such useful activities. One of the disadvantages of following the rules, isn't it?"

Holding out his hand toward Stacy, he fixed her with an implacable gaze. "Come!" he commanded. "You belong to me."

She stared at him. Her mind felt frozen and her tongue refused to form words. Serizzin's eyes locked themselves into hers; she could not pull free. Perhaps, given all the misery she had caused, she did not even deserve to be free. Slowly turning toward Minerva and Glynis, she placed Katie between them.

As she turned back to Serizzin, Max leaped into her arms. Clutching his furry warmth, she held him against her. His voice dropped into her mind: *Remember that what you believe is what you receive!*

She focused on him, frowning; then nodded slightly and set him at her feet. Ignoring Serizzin's outstretched hand, she crossed her arms as if she were hugging herself and stood unmoving, eyes closed. An expression of peace settled over her features and her body relaxed. When she opened her eyes again, Serizzin was glaring at her, a look of baffled fury on his face.

His voice, barely above a whisper, cut through the silence of the room. "You think you have beaten me, little human, but you have had assistance. I promise you a time will come when that help will not be available." The chilling whisper continued. "Patience is perhaps my only virtue, Stacy Addison. I am patient; I will wait."

The look in his eyes made her want to run screaming from the room, but she forced herself to stand still. As she watched, his handsome features melted and his business-suited body dissolved, expanding into a huge, whirling column of black smoke. Tongues of flame licked hungrily through its coils toward her, and she backed away. Laughter boomed and the column spun toward the still-frozen form of the little gray man. With a roar, it drew him in, then revolved back toward the table, where it hovered in front of Arthur Craddock.

§

Icy terror flooding him, Arthur backed frantically away from the flaming column. It moved closer, and he retreated again, and yet again. The column followed, never lessening the distance between them. With a shock that almost dissolved his knees, he struck something solid behind him. Pushing frantically against it, he realized that he had backed into a wall; there was no place left to go.

He watched in horror as a sooty, hand-like appendage extended itself from the center of the column. Arthur flattened his back against the hard surface. He tried to remember how to let his atoms flow into the wall, but his thought processes felt frozen. Slowly, an almost teasing finger reached out and touched his chest. Arthur screamed.

The hand reached up and caressed his face; then, seizing his skull in a crushing grip, it began to pull. Frantic, he felt himself sliding into the column's flaming coils. Distorted faces whirled past, their screams rising and falling as the column revolved. With a last, futile effort to hold himself together, he felt his atoms separate. The fiery vortex sucked the strands of his being into itself, and Arthur Craddock was propelled into the tormented frenzy of Serizzin's dance.

§

Katie watched, wide-eyed, as the man who had been trying to hurt her mother disappeared into the huge, flaming column. She wasn't sure whether she should feel frightened by what had happened, or pleased that the man had gotten what was due to him. She decided she would be pleased now, and let herself feel scared afterwards.

The fiery funnel turned, as if it had heard her thought, and began to revolve in her direction. Terrible noises poured out of it, like a pack of dogs fighting with a bunch of cats. Catching her lower lip between her teeth, Katie stepped behind her mother. The column spun closer, the crackling of its flames almost drowning out the awful shrieks and screams.

The blazing thing was so near its hotness touched her face. It made her think of the sudden scorching blast she felt when she opened Minerva's oven door to take out a batch of cookies. Blinking, she was distressed to see that the top of the column was bending down, leaning closer and closer to her mother. In a moment, it might touch her, like it had touched the man! Despite the intensity of its heat, Katie felt cold.

Except for the center of her chest. She suddenly realized there was a spot of warmth there, encouraging and comforting, and her hand crept up to cover it. Beneath her fingers, the smooth roundness of Herm's gift vibrated strongly, as if the Light inside it was strengthening and expanding.

She flinched as a tongue of flame rolled out of the column toward her mother. Pulling the pearl from inside her T-shirt, she clutched it tightly and stepped forward. A clear, high-pitched note was now issuing from the globe. Its singing filled her mind with wordless urgency.

Pulling the leather thong over her head, Katie shook the sphere at the whirling column. "You leave my mother alone!" The column paused and drew back, as if in surprise. Then it slowly leaned in her direction. Clenching her teeth, Katie swung back her arm and threw the pulsating orb as hard as she could into the center of the column. There was a moment of complete silence. The screaming and screeching stopped; even the flames flickered and fell silent.

The column almost stopped whirling; then it began to spin again, faster and faster. It reeled crazily across the room, bumping into the table and bouncing off the walls, leaving a trail of burning draperies and upholstery. A furious shriek, like a freight train braking, rose from its center, growing louder and shriller until Katie and everyone in the room, except Max and the Harpies, clapped their hands over their ears.

With a final screech, the fiery funnel exploded. Katie was thrown backward, hitting the wall with a force that knocked her to her knees. Arrows of fire shot in all directions; even Herm ducked as one whistled over his head. Rooted to the floor in shock, Katie watched as a burning nugget flew in her direction. Out of the corner of her eye, she could see her mother running toward her, screaming, "Duck, Katie, duck!"

Before she could get her brain to follow orders, something big and smelly knocked her flat and she heard a loud screech of pain. The object rolled away, and she saw that it was the larger Harpy, whose left wing was now on fire. Shrieking, the bird-woman flapped frantically around the room, spreading the flames to her other wing. The smaller Harpy hopped along in pursuit, finally catching up and beating out the fire with her own wings, leaving the room full of the stench of smoke and singed feathers. Finally, the bedraggled pair hobbled slowly back toward the group gathered by the door.

Minerva and Glynis ran to Katie and helped her to her feet. She smiled shakily at them, then pulled away and ran back to the point of Serizzin's spectacular departure. Dropping to her knees, she began to run her hands over the scorched remnants of the rug. After a brief search, she raised her closed fist above her head and shouted, "I found it! It's still here!"

Opening her hand, she showed the group that had gathered around her a small, smoke-streaked sphere. "It's all nasty and dirty, though." She looked anxiously up at Herm. "Is it dead?" He reached out and gently wiped off one of the smudges with his fingertips, and Katie felt like crying with relief. Deep within her pearl, the Light still glowed. Searching out a clean corner of her T-shirt, she carefully polished the remaining ash smears away.

"The Light cannot die," Herm told her. "It can only be temporarily dimmed." He smiled. "Would you like me to carry your pearl awhile, until you find something new from which to hang it? I fear the leather thong did not survive Serizzin's fire."

"That won't be necessary." Minerva stepped forward. "Katie can use this for as long as she likes." She pulled a strong-linked gold chain from beneath her blouse and, removing the front door key to the Addison house that hung from it, offered the necklace to the little girl.

"Thanks, 'Nerva." Katie strung the orb on the chain and slipped it over her head, then turned to her mother. "The bird-lady kept me from getting burned, didn't she?"

Her mother nodded. "Yes, Katie. I have to admit she did."

"She said she wanted to serve me, and she did serve me." Katie looked up into her mother's tear-filled eyes. "I guess we have to forgive her for carrying me off, don't we?"

Her mother hugged her hard. "I guess we do."

Squirming loose, Katie ran to Herm. "The bird-ladies' wings are all burned. Can you do something to help them?"

Herm knelt in front of her and gently touched her cheek. "I'm sure I can, if you want me to."

Katie nodded.

He smiled. "Good leaders always take care of the needs of those who serve them well."

Getting to his feet, he turned to the larger Harpy and raised his hand. The scorched feathers of her wings trembled, then dropped to the floor, revealing a growth of new, glossy plumage. He repeated the process with the smaller bird-woman. Both Harpies flapped their refurbished wings gently, as if testing them. Then the big one looked back at Herm.

"We are grateful, Lord Hermes." Her screech was almost soft. "We are nourished by your kindness." Turning, she hopped a few steps toward Katie, who held her ground, despite a flash of fear. The Harpy stopped at a respectful distance.

"I am Klio, young mistress. And this," she bobbed her head toward the smaller Harpy, who had moved up beside her, "is my sister, Urania. We both are willing servants of the god; but," Klio's harsh voice softened even further, "if you permit us, we shall be honored to also continue serving you."

"Continue serving you," Urania echoed.

The expressions on their hideous faces now seemed to Katie hopeful, rather than threatening.

She looked at Herm, who nodded. Turning back to the Harpies, she drew herself up regally. "All right then, I give you permission to continue serving me. And," she smiled tentatively at Klio, "thanks for keeping that fire ball from hitting me."

🐾 🐾 🐾 Between 🐾 🐾 🐾

§

Chuckling at the alliance between Katie and her former enemies, Herm looked around him, making sure that everyone else was all right. Minerva and Glynis were talking quietly on the only sofa left untouched by Serizzin's flames, while Stacy sat on the floor, eyes closed, her back slumped against the wall. Katie was leaning against her, gently stroking Max, who had curled himself on her lap. The Harpies were huddled together near the door, whispering in muted screeches.

Herm surveyed the wreck of the once elegant room, then knelt beside Stacy and gently touched her shoulder. "I apologize for interrupting your well-earned relaxation, but I have to ask what you finally did that proved so effective in breaking your obligation to Serizzin."

Stacy slowly opened her eyes; in them he saw a mixture of remembered horror and profound sadness. He watched her struggle through these emotions, until she reached a place where she could respond to his question.

She looked up at him. "I couldn't have done it without Max. He reminded me that what I believed, I would receive."

"And that was . . . ?"

She smiled faintly. "I believed that I had the right to change my mind."

Chapter 54

The Entry Processing Center hummed with activity. Long lines of souls being processed filed past the Greeters, and assistants-on-call, their bodies peacefully asleep on Earth, labored side by side with regular workers.

One corner of the vast space was furnished like the lobby of an upscale hotel, complete with soothing greenery and comfortable furniture. Here Minerva was relaxing in a pillowy chair. Max sat at her feet, one hind leg in the air, engaged in the serious task of grooming that hard-to-reach spot where the leg joined his body.

Across from them, Stacy sat at one end of a soft, blue sofa, Katie curled against her. At the other end, Glynis had propped herself against one of the overstuffed arms. Minerva smiled at Glynis. "You're quite a hero, my dear. If it hadn't been for you, Stacy might have had a much more difficult time resisting Serizzin's power."

Glynis shook her head. "She'd have come through in the end. I just speeded the process up a bit."

"Don't be so modest, Glinda." Stacy looked at her over Katie's head. "If it hadn't been for you, we probably wouldn't be sitting here now, talking about it." She frowned. "I'm not sure it's over yet. Serizzin may be gone for now, but he didn't strike me as the type to give up easily." A shudder rippled down her spine. "That's something I don't like to think about!"

Max looked up at her. "It's probably best if you don't think about it—at least, not directly. Serizzin feeds on negativity, so just go about your business and keep releasing whatever fears come up. If he should reappear, we'll deal with him then."

Stacy shivered again. "You know, I can't get Arthur Craddock out of my mind. What Serizzin did to him was horrible! I know he was mean, and he did some terrible things, but maybe my mistake with his wife made him worse than he might have been."

Katie uncurled her legs and sat up straight. "He deserved everything he got, Mommy. He was a very bad man!"

Stacy hugged her. "I know, but now he doesn't have the chance to stop being bad, if he should ever want to do that."

"That's not exactly true." Max finished grooming his leg and settled himself more comfortably. "It might be difficult under Craddock's present circumstances, but it's possible to make almost any kind of change, if you truly want to do it, even such a big change as deciding you no longer want to be bad."

"Hmf!" Katie crossed her arms. "He'd never want to stop being bad. Not in a million years!"

Max eyed her sternly. "Be careful how you judge people, Katie. Keep in mind that what you send out, returns to you multiplied."

Katie frowned. "That doesn't make sense."

"It makes very good sense. If you send out angry thoughts and feelings toward someone, even someone who has hurt you, you're going to attract unpleasant circumstances into your life. On the other hand, when you forgive, you attract pleasant experiences."

"Oh, pooh. I don't want to forgive him. He doesn't deserve it."

Max's yellow eyes held hers. "Forgiveness is not about deserving. It's about letting go of your anger, so it doesn't control your life." He turned toward Stacy. "We all make mistakes and we all need forgiveness at times. Sometimes we even need to forgive ourselves." Jumping to his feet, he gave himself a spine-rippling shake and winked at Katie. "And that's enough of that sermon—for now, at least."

Katie giggled. "You're funny!" Slipping off the sofa, she ran to him and began to scratch behind his ears, giggling again as his tail twitched with pleasure.

Minerva looked at Glynis. "Have you decided to allow yourself to be processed, my dear, now that the excitement has settled down?"

Glynis hugged her knees and stared thoughtfully into the distance; finally she turned her gaze toward Minerva. "I suppose I don't really have much choice, do I?"

"Oh, yes, my dear. You definitely have a choice. You are free to remain here in the Center for as long as you wish. But," the older woman smiled gently, "I think it may become very boring after awhile. You won't, as a rule, be able to acquaint yourself very well with anyone, because the Greeters are usually busy, and almost all of the new arrivals are either processed straight through, or are too stunned to be able to communicate with you."

Sighing, Glynis nodded. "That figures." She sighed again, even more deeply. "Can I at least wait until Stacy goes back into her body? I'd like to stay with her until she does."

Max, still enjoying Katie's attentions, looked up. "I'm sure no one would object to that." He transferred his yellow gaze to Stacy. "You'll be happy to know that there's no longer anything standing in your way. Your system is clear of medication and your surgery was successful; you should be able to return any time you choose."

Katie stopped stroking Max and smiled at her mother. "Mommy's coming back right now, so she'll be there when I wake up, aren't you, Mommy?" When her mother did not reply, she repeated, "Mommy?"

Stacy slipped off the sofa and knelt in front of her. Resting her hands on Katie's shoulders, she looked into the little girl's eyes. "I don't know, honeybunch. I'm not sure I can do that."

Katie wrinkled her forehead. "Then when *are* you coming back?"

Stacy took Katie's hands in hers. "Listen to me, Katie." She shifted her position, as if she could not find a comfortable spot on the thick carpet. "I know I told you I'd be back just as soon as I could, but things have . . . ," she expelled her breath in a sigh, "things have changed."

"What things?"

"Well, things about my physical body that I didn't know when I made that promise. You see," she stroked the little girl's sandy hair, "I've found out that my face was really badly hurt in the accident." She blinked back a sudden ambush of tears.

Katie touched her cheek. "Don't cry, Mommy. Daddy and I will take care of you until you're well."

Stacy smiled tenderly at her. "I know you would. The problem is, I don't think I'll ever be able to get completely well; and even if I could, it would take a whole lot of operations to make that happen." She gnawed at her lower lip. "Please try to understand, Katie. I just don't think I can do it."

Katie stared at her. "Yes, you can, Mommy. You can do anything! You can heal yourself." Her eyes widened with excitement. "You can! Just hold your face and tell it to get well, like you do with all those people who come to your meetings."

"Oh, Katie, sweetheart, I can't. My face is hurt too badly for me to make it well." Tears leaked down her cheeks and she swiped at them angrily with the back of her hand.

"But Mommy, Max says that what you believe, you receive. Just believe you can do it—"

"No! My healing works on other people, not on me." She squeezed Katie's hands. "Try to understand, baby. I'm going to look like a freak. I'll probably never be able to do healing work again, because no one will want me to touch them." She sighed, adding almost under her breath, "Given the disasters I've caused, I probably shouldn't try, anyway." She looked at Katie pleadingly, "Even you and Daddy might not want to look at me."

"Daddy and I will always want to look at you. We don't care what your face is like."

Stacy shook her head. "Please Katie; please try to understand!"

Katie twisted free and scrambled to her feet. "I do understand." Her fists were clenched and her lower lip trembled. "You don't want to come back because you don't care about me or Daddy. You've never cared about us. All you care about is how you look and what those stupid other people will think! You promised you'd come back, but you don't love us enough to even try!" A storm of tears shook her and she ran to Minerva, burying her head in the older woman's lap.

Getting to her feet, Stacy followed. She knelt beside Katie and began to stroke her hair, but the little girl jerked her head away. "Leave me alone! Don't touch me!" Her voice was muffled in Minerva's purple skirt.

Stacy closed her eyes and forced herself to be calm. Then she opened her eyes and said softly, "Katie, I do love you and Daddy, but it's just too hard. I can't come back, knowing how it will be. Please understand. But," her voice lifted hopefully, "we can spend time together when you go dreaming. Not every night, because that won't be good for your body, but some of the time."

Katie slowly raised her tear-stained face. "No." Her voice was expressionless. "I don't want to spend time with somebody who doesn't care about me. Anyhow," her face hardened, "you lied to me. You promised to come back, and now you're going back on your word, because you're scared. You're a coward and a liar!" Jumping to her feet, she climbed into Minerva's lap and deliberately turned her back on her mother.

A sharp pain stabbed Stacy's chest. For a brief moment she thought she was having a heart attack; then she remembered that her physical heart was back in her body in the hospital bed at St. Mark's. Suddenly she frowned. She recognized this pain; it was how she had felt each time her parents left on an expedition—abandoned, bereft, her heart breaking.

Turning back toward the sofa, she saw the reflection of her distress in Glynis's face. "Help me, Glinda! She'll understand if you explain it."

Unfolding her legs, Glynis stood up and placed her hands on Stacy's shoulders. "I'm not allowed to interfere this time," she said softly. "Somehow I know that. You're the only one who can make things right between you and Katie."

Hopelessness welled up inside Stacy. "I don't know how! I only know how to do what I've always done, and that's not good enough now." She looked into Glynis's eyes. "It's never been good enough, has it? I just keep doing what doesn't work, because I don't know how to do anything else."

Putting her arms around Glynis, she laid her head on her friend's shoulder, blinking hard against the insistent pressure behind her eyes. For a moment, she berated herself for turning down Serizzin's offer; then sanity reasserted itself and she knew she had made the only decision her soul would allow. But how could she return to her body, knowing what lay ahead of her? And how could she not return, knowing that if she didn't, she would lose Katie and David? It was an impossible choice. The pressure behind her eyes grew more intense, and she clenched her jaw, refusing to give in to it.

Tears were useless; she had understood that by the time she was four. Certainly tears had never influenced her parents' decisions to abandon her to the care of others, while they went traipsing off into the wilds. Even if she had flooded Tulsa with weeping, they would have simply rented canoes and paddled away to Peru. From the moment of that realization, she had not permitted herself to cry, except in anger.

Yet in this moment of imminent loss and almost unbearable pain, something inside her shifted. Holding Glynis tightly, like a drowning

🐾 🐾 🐾 Between 🐾 🐾 🐾

sailor clinging to a life preserver, Stacy finally allowed the protective shell she had constructed around herself to dissolve in tears of anguish.

Eventually, her sobbing subsided, and Glynis gently led her back to the blue sofa. Sinking onto the seat, she fell back exhausted against the cushions. She heard Katie ask Minerva to take her home and made an effort to protest, but her tongue could not form the words.

Raising her head with difficulty, she watched them leave. Katie marched along staring straight ahead, clutching Minerva's hand. Minerva glanced back once, compassion in her eyes, and Max, tail swaying, padded along behind them.

Chapter 55

Colin Elmore shook his head. "I can't understand why she isn't coming out of it. Her system's clear of the meds and her brain waves look normal; she should be waking up."

"Give her a little more time." David did his best to sound confident. He had gone to sleep last night, hoping he might find Stacy waiting for him, but she had not appeared. He was beginning to fear that he had, after all, simply dreamed the two nights that he had spent with her, and had been mistaken in assuming she would return to her body as soon as it was free of the phenobarbitol.

But, he reminded himself, Katie and Minerva believed in the reality of that other world. And while Katie might be indulging in a flight of fancy, Minerva had never struck him as what his mother would refer to as 'flaky'. She was definitely unconventional in both her behavior and her beliefs, as far as he was aware of them, but she had always been solid and reliable.

No, he decided, it was not just his imagination. Stacy really was alive and well in that place she called Between; she had not yet returned to her body because something must be going on there, something of which he was unaware. Unfortunately, he had no idea how to find out what it was.

But that was not necessarily true. He could talk to Minerva; it was quite possible that she would know. He waited until Elmore had left the room to make his afternoon rounds, then picked up the phone on Stacy's night stand and dialed nine for an outside line. As the tone sounded, the door opened and Jenn peered around it.

"David? May we come in?"

He set the receiver back on its cradle. "Sure," he said. "Come on in." Minerva must be with Jenn; he could take her aside and find out what he needed to know.

Jenn opened the door wider and stepped into the room. To David's surprise, she was followed by Rudy, dressed in fresh jeans and a new shirt, his hand outstretched in greeting. David looked from him to Jenn, who colored slightly and smiled. Rudy put his arm around her shoulders and David, stunned, opened his eyes wide. "Are you two…?" he pointed from one to the other.

They nodded simultaneously. "We're going to be married next month," Jenn said.

"I want you to be my best man," Rudy added, smiling. Then the smile faded. "Glynis always wanted this; just wish she could be here to enjoy it."

"Stacy, too." Jenn's eyes moved to the bed. "We're hoping she'll come back to us in time to be part of the celebration."

David nodded. "I hope so, too." He took a deep breath and smiled. "Well, this is great news! Congratulations to both of you!" Shaking Rudy's hand again, he gave Jenn a hug; then he looked toward the door. "Did Minerva come with you?"

"Not this time." Jenn set her purse on the windowsill. "She dropped Katie off at my house; then she and Max went home for what she said was a much-needed nap."

David swallowed his disappointment; then he looked toward the door. "Katie's here? Where is she?"

"In the waiting room. She didn't seem to want to come in with us, for some reason."

David frowned; that didn't sound like Katie, who was always anxious to visit her mother whenever she could. He strode to the door. "I'll go get her."

He found her ensconced on an uncomfortable-looking sofa in a corner of the waiting room, staring straight ahead.

"Hey, you!" He forced his voice to sound cheerful.

Katie continued her observation of the wall. David sat down beside her. "How's it going, kitten?"

Dropping her head, she crossed her arms and pushed herself more firmly against the hard plastic back of the sofa. David bent forward, so that he could see her face. It was set in the mulish expression that only showed itself when she was upset.

"What is it, Katie?"

"Nothing." He could barely hear the word.

"Don't you want to come and say hello to Mommy?"

The little girl shook her head.

"Why not?"

"Because she doesn't love me." She looked up at him, her eyes hard. "She doesn't love you, either."

He slipped off the sofa and knelt in front of her. "I know you miss her, but it's not her fault she hasn't waked up. That doesn't mean she doesn't love us."

"Yes, it does! That's exactly what it means." Her face was so pale that the dusting of freckles across her nose stood out in relief.

"Katie, that doesn't make any sense." Standing up, David took her hand and pulled her, resisting, off the sofa. "I want you to come with me now. Rudy and Nana Jenn are already in Mommy's room and I want you to be there, too. Maybe if all of us concentrate, Mommy will be able to feel us and it will help her wake up."

"A lot you know!" she muttered. Pulling her arm out of his grip, she stalked off down the hall ahead of him.

Like a shepherd herding a single, unwilling lamb, David followed.

§

"Why am I doing this?" Stacy stared with distaste at her pale, unmoving body in the hospital bed. At least, she thought with relief, the bandages hiding her face were still in place.

"Call it closure." Herm, still in his handsome young man form, stood beside her. "Surely you don't want to move on from this level without at least saying goodbye in some manner."

She frowned. "I suppose not."

Looking over at Colin Elmore and David, who were quietly discussing her condition, she sensed David's uneasiness at her lack of response, his fear that perhaps she wasn't coming back. She squinted against a sudden onslaught of tears. It was so unfair! She couldn't even explain to him the impossible choice that had been forced on her. Not that he'd probably understand, anyway. Certainly Katie hadn't!

Elmore left and David remained standing beside her bed, his gaze unfocused, as if his mind had wandered off somewhere else. Stacy studied his face, noticing his bloodshot eyes and the deep lines scoring his forehead. Scrutinizing him more closely than she had ever done when they were sharing their lives on the physical level, she recognized exhaustion and discouragement in the droop of his shoulders. Had he looked this way before her accident? Maybe he had, and she had been too taken up with her own interests to notice.

She sighed. Perhaps it really was better that she wasn't going to return; she hadn't done him much good, except to give him Katie. A sharp pang of loss cut through her as she thought about the two of them going on without her. Probably they would find someone new to share their lives; someone, she told herself, who might make them happier than she ever had.

The sound of the door opening distracted her from these unpleasant future projections, and when Jenn entered the room, closely followed by Rudy, Stacy felt a rush of warmth and gratitude toward this woman who had devoted much effort and many years to making her childhood less lonely, first as a loving aunt, then as a surrogate mother. She realized that she had never told Jenn how much she appreciated that kindness and caring. Now those words would have to remain unspoken.

She felt a momentary burst of joy when Jenn and Rudy announced their impending marriage, and the thought of Glynis's excitement at the news helped to temper the sadness of knowing that neither she nor Glynis would be with them to share their happiness. But even that small measure of comfort disappeared when she learned that, although Katie was in the hospital, she had refused to enter the room.

When the little girl finally appeared in the doorway, Stacy could tell that her daughter had not yet forgiven her. Practically pushed into the room by her father, Katie stopped just inside the door and stubbornly refused to go any farther. David did his best to coax her, but finally gave up and left her backed against the dresser, her shoulders almost brushing the crowd of cards and flowers sent by Stacy's clients.

Stacy looked at Herm and sighed. "I certainly have made a mess of things, haven't I?"

He shrugged. "No more so than many human beings." He smiled slightly. "You really should cut yourself a little slack. Remember that you came to the Earth level to be human, which means having the ability, even the need, to make mistakes. In fact," the smile broadened a little, "to be human and to be perfect is a contradiction in terms."

"I didn't say I needed to be perfect!"

His smile slid into the impish grin of the little boy she had first met in the Entry Processing Center. "It isn't necessary to mention the obvious."

She gave him a grudging smile. "Are you always so obnoxiously right?"

"Invariably." He shrugged. "It's one of the perks of being a god."

Stacy looked away from him as David moved to the bed and took her hand in his. My body's hand, she reminded herself, briefly wishing Max were here to approve her terminology. As she watched, David turned to Jenn and Rudy.

"It's my fault this happened," he told them, his face haggard. "I knew how important that TV thing was to her, and all I could think of was that it might ruin my chance to move up. I called her work a side show." He shook his head. "If I'd listened, if I'd been less concerned with me, she wouldn't be here! But, no, I had to be a selfish asshole. And now," he shot an agonized look toward the bed, "I may lose her!"

"That's not true!" Breaking her silence, Katie ran to David and threw her arms around his waist. "It's not your fault she isn't coming back; Daddy, it's hers. She could come back, if she wanted to, but she cares more about looking pretty than she does about us."

Holding her a little away from him, David knelt in front of her. "Now that, Katie, is definitely not true. You know Mommy would come back to us if she could."

"It is, too, true! She doesn't want to come back. She promised she would, but she's a liar and a coward!"

Darting back to the dresser, the little girl snatched up a large vase filled with roses and smashed it against the floor. Water and shards of glass sprayed everywhere, leaving the roses a limp heap of red against the gray tiles.

"There!" Katie screamed at the bed. "That's what I think of you. I hate you, Mommy, I hate you! I don't even want you to come back!" Sobbing frantically, she stood frozen in the middle of this florist's nightmare, one leg bleeding slightly, where a flying sliver of glass had nicked it.

David ran to her and, scooping her rigid body up in his arms, gently stroked her hair. "It's OK, kitten," he murmured, "it's OK." Katie collapsed against him, crying so hard that Stacy could hear her gasping for breath. Jenn and Rudy gently patted her back, murmuring reassurances.

Stacy watched helplessly as Katie's sobbing gradually subsided into hiccoughs. Finally, David pulled a tissue from the box on the bedside table and blotted her eyes. Taking it, she blew her nose.

He smiled. "Better now?"

She nodded. "You can put me down. I'm OK."

He set her on her feet. "You got pretty upset, there."

She nodded again, looking up at him with red, swollen eyes. "You know what, Daddy?"

"What?"

"If I had a little girl and I didn't have any money and someone said they would give me a million dollars if I'd leave her, I would never, ever do it." She sniffled. "Not even for a million dollars."

David put his arms around her and held her tightly. "I know you wouldn't. You're my true blue girl."

Stacy looked at Herm and sighed deeply. "It's another damn lesson, isn't it?"

The corners of his mouth twitched. "You could say that."

"I did say it, much as I didn't want to." She looked back at David and Katie. "If I stay Between, I'll be doing to her what my parents did to me, won't I?" She sighed again. "Why does everything have to be so difficult? All I want is to be happy. Is that asking too much?"

"Do you want me to answer that?"

She made a face. "Probably not. At least, not if you're going to give me a lecture."

Herm eyed her sternly. "I never lecture. I leave that to Max; he's much better at it than I am. However," the stern look softened, "I will tell you that staying focused on the truly important things, such as love and loyalty, does make a difference in the ease with which you are able to live your life." He nodded toward Rudy and Jenn. "Put your focus where it needs to be, and happiness will follow."

Stacy shook her head. "For someone who never lectures, you do a mean imitation."

Herm smiled and shrugged.

David was now talking quietly with Rudy and Jenn, one arm still around Katie's shoulders. Watching them, Stacy sighed again. "I'm not going back with you, am I?"

Herm shrugged. "That's entirely up to you."

Stacy chewed her lower lip. "I don't know if I'm responsible enough to be in my body again. I came close to making a second terrible mistake with that offer from Serizzin. I almost couldn't turn it down. I could have wrecked a lot of people's lives."

"But you didn't, did you?"

"No, but if it hadn't been for Glinda and the rest of you, I might have. I was so caught up in my own stuff, I couldn't see anything else."

"Oh, I don't know," said a familiar voice. "You probably would have figured it out."

Stacy whirled to see Glynis, with Max and Minerva on either side of her.

The rush of joy she felt at the sight of them almost immediately shifted into sadness. They had brought Glynis to tell her goodbye; she could feel it in the energy surrounding them. Stepping forward, she put her arms around her friend, ignoring the tears that crept down her cheeks.

"Oh, Glinda," she whispered. "How am I going to manage without you? There won't be a day that I don't miss you and wonder where you are and what you're doing."

Glynis held her close and Stacy could feel her shaking with sobs. "You won't miss me any more than I'll miss you, dearest Dorothy."

Stacy hugged her hard. "I'll never find a truer friend than you! You always love me, even when I'm being stupid."

When they finally stepped apart, Stacy took Minerva's hands in hers. "I can't tell you how glad I am that you'll be there when I get back. I'm going to need all the help you can give me."

Minerva gently squeezed her hands and smiled. "You know I will support you any way that I can, my dear."

Stacy looked down at Max, who was sitting like an Egyptian statue, tail curled around his feet. "I'll be needing your help, too, but I guess I won't actually get to see you until I finally come home. I don't think this hospital is going to allow you visiting privileges."

Max sniffed. "A further proof of the lack of good taste demonstrated by the majority of humans. By the way," he unwound his tail and stood up, "you might like to know that David risked his position here at St. Mark's on your behalf."

"What?"

🐾 🐾 🐾 Between 🐾 🐾 🐾

"The older doctor, Elmore, at first refused to do your surgery, because Craddock's tampering had made it appear that your brain was no longer functional. David said that he himself would operate, if necessary. He told Elmore that losing his job and his license would be nothing compared to the risk of losing you."

Stacy looked over at David. Katie was leaning against him and he was gently massaging the back of her neck with one hand, as he talked to Jenn and Rudy. Warmth spread through her as she thought of him challenging Colin Elmore, risking his promotion—maybe even his livelihood— to see she received what she needed. Before the accident, she had begun to wonder if he still loved her; apparently, he did. She felt a tiny prick of excitement at the thought of sharing with him what this meant to her.

She transferred her gaze back to Herm. "Thanks for all your help. I don't know what I'd have done without you." Standing on tiptoe, she kissed his cheek. "Tell that kid in the dress I'll buy him a pair of long pants next time I see him, OK?"

Smiling, Herm nodded.

Jenn's voice caught Stacy's attention. "Goodby, my sweet girl," she was saying. She gave Katie a hug and joined Rudy, who was waiting for her by the door. As they left the room, Stacy turned back to Herm. "I guess I'd better go, too, before I lose my nerve. You and Max help think me in, OK?"

She closed her eyes, then immediately popped them open again. "God, I'm scared! What if getting back into my body still doesn't work? What if it does work and I make another mess of things? What if I can't stand the pain, or being ugly, or—"

Stop!" Max interrupted. "Stop trying to second-guess your life." His yellow eyes held hers. "Didn't you learn from your experience with Serizzin that your choices create what you think of as the future? If you choose based on fear, you'll make the worst possible choice every time." His voice softened. "You've been given a second chance, Stacy, something most humans don't receive; don't waste it by worrying."

Stacy stared at him, then turned to Herm. "Well, I got the lecture, after all; two, counting yours, and they both sound pretty much the same."

She could hear David calling a nurse to have someone pick up the shattered vase and its contents. Looking one last time around the circle of her companions, she did her best to smile; then she closed her eyes.

"OK." Her voice shook slightly. "Here I go!"

§

The room was tidy once again. As he and Katie prepared to leave, David turned in the doorway for one last look. He frowned. Had something changed?

"Wait here," he told Katie. Moving back toward the bed, he stopped and stared, his heartbeat accelerating. Stacy's right hand was no longer under the covers. It lay, instead on the bedspread, the fingers slightly spread. Covering the distance in two strides, he carefully picked up the hand. It was warm! The fingers fluttered against his in a small, convulsive twitch.

"Oh, my God," he whispered. Glancing back at the doorway, he saw Katie watching, a puzzled expression on her tear-stained face.

"Katie," he called. "Katie, look!"

The little girl ran back to the bed. "Daddy, she's waking up!" Her voice rose and she began to bounce excitedly on her heels. "She's coming back!"

David put a hand on her shoulder. "I think we need to be quieter, kitten; she's still pretty sick."

"I know, Daddy, but she changed her mind. She does love us, after all!"

David nodded. "I guess she does." Tears of relief streaming down his cheeks, he knelt beside the bed and held Stacy's warm, twitching hand against his wet cheek.

A long moment passed. Then, turning her head a little to one side, she shifted her legs under the covers. David and Katie watched, mesmerized.

With a small intake of breath that sounded like a sob, Stacy Addison opened her eyes.

Epilogue

Herm and Max gazed down into the fragrant meadow at the heart of the Children's Garden. Max was lying motionless between two gnarled roots of a massive oak tree, front legs folded under him, his long, ringed tail curled closely around his body. Herm was propped comfortably against a large root that stretched out, smooth and broad, into the lush, green grass. Below them a laughing group of boys and girls were playing a circle game.

Herm picked up a perfectly formed acorn and bounced it in the palm of his hand. "I wasn't sure Stacy had it in her." He looked over at Max. "I have to admit she showed real courage."

Max nodded. "She did, didn't she?" Easing himself to his feet, he stretched elaborately. "I felt almost positive she'd come through; but, of course, you never know with humans." He gave himself a shake. "I think I'll take a walk before returning to Earth. Care to join me?"

Brushing off his snowy tunic, Herm dropped the acorn and accompanied Max down the broad, grassy path leading toward the woods. "Do you think she'll stick it out?"

Max looked up at him. "I expect she will, although that remains to be seen. Humans, except for Minerva, are notoriously unreliable. Cats, on the other hand . . . ."

A breeze swept by, chuckling to itself as they disappeared into the trees.

The End

Author's Note

A fuller coverage of Max's teachings is available in the inspirational non-fiction book, *What You Believe Is What You Receive*, due to be released by the spring of 2006.

What You Believe Is What You Receive

Are you unhappy or dissatisfied with your life? Do you have problems you can't solve? Are there questions which seem to have no answers? Are you hurt, angry, unable to forgive? Are you caught in a "focus lock"?

What You Believe Is What You Receive helps you deal with these and other issues by showing you how to shift your focus and change your life for the better. Practice this Seven-Step Method and transform your daily experience into one of greater happiness and fulfillment!

For more information about *What You Believe Is What You Receive*, or to make comments or ask questions about Between, please go to www.shelbybeckett.com.

Or write to: Shelby Beckett, c/o BookMasters, Inc., P.O. Box 2139 Mansfield, OH 44905